The Lost Girls Of Paris

Pam Jenoff

WITHDRAWN FROM STOCK

ONE PLACE. MANY STORIES

This novel is entirely a work of fiction. The names, characters and incidents portrayed in it are the work of the author's imagination. Any resemblance to actual persons, living or dead, events or localities is entirely coincidental.

HQ
An imprint of HarperCollins*Publishers* Ltd
1 London Bridge Street
London SE1 9GF

This edition 2019

1
First published in Great Britain by
HQ, an imprint of HarperCollins*Publishers* Ltd 2019

Copyright © Pam Jenoff 2019

Pam Jenoff asserts the moral right to be identified as the author of this work.
A catalogue record for this book is available from the British Library.

ISBN: 978-1-84845-742-3

MIX
Paper from responsible sources
FSC™ C007454

This book is produced from independently certified FSC™ paper to ensure responsible forest management.

For more information visit: www.harpercollins.co.uk/green

Printed and bound by CPI Group (UK) Ltd, Croydon CR0 4YY

All rights reserved. No part of this publication may be reproduced, stored in a retrieval system, or transmitted, in any form or by any means, electronic, mechanical, photocopying, recording or otherwise, without the prior permission of the publishers.

This book is sold subject to the condition that it shall not, by way of trade or otherwise, be lent, re-sold, hired out or otherwise circulated without the publisher's prior consent in any form of binding or cover other than that in which it is published and without a similar condition including this condition being imposed on the subsequent purchaser.

For my family

Also by Pam Jenoff

Kommandant's Girl
The Diplomat's Wife
The Ambassador's Daughter
The Winter Guest
The Last Embrace
The Orphan's Tale

The Lost Girls Of Paris

'In wartime, truth is so precious that she should always be attended by a bodyguard of lies.'

Winston Churchill

CHAPTER ONE

GRACE

New York, 1946

If not for the second-worst mistake of Grace Healey's life, she never would have found the suitcase.

At nine twenty on a Tuesday morning, Grace should have been headed south on the first of two buses she took to get downtown, commuting from the rooming house in Hell's Kitchen to the Lower East Side office where she worked. And she *was* on her way to work. But she was nowhere near the neighborhood she had come to call home. Instead, she was racing south on Madison Avenue, corralling her corkscrew hair into a low knot. She quickly removed her coat, despite the chill, so she could take off her mint green cardigan. She didn't want Frankie to notice it was the exact same one she had been wearing at work the previous day and question the unthinkable: whether she had gone home at all.

Grace paused to study herself in the window of a five-and-dime. She wished the store was open so she could buy some powder to hide the marks on her neck and sample a bit of perfume to conceal the stench of day-old brandy mixed with that delicious-but-wrong smell of Mark's aftershave, which made her dizzy and ashamed with every inhale. A wino sat on the corner, moaning to himself in sleep. Looking at his gray, lifeless pallor, Grace felt a certain solidarity. From the adjacent alley came the banging on a trash can, a sound marching in time with the thudding in her own head. The whole city of New York seemed green and hungover. Or perhaps she was confusing it for herself.

Sharp gusts of February wind cut across Madison, causing the flags that hung from the skyscrapers above to whip furiously. An old crumpled newspaper danced along the gutter. Hearing the bells of Saint Agnes's toll half past nine, Grace pressed on, her skin growing moist under her collar as she neared a run. Grand Central Terminal loomed hulking ahead. Just a bit farther and she could turn left on Forty-Second Street and catch an express bus downtown on Lexington.

But as she neared the intersection at Forty-Third, the street ahead was blocked. Police cars sat three across, cordoning off Madison and preventing anyone from going farther south. A car accident, Grace suspected at first, noting the black Studebaker, which sat jackknifed across the street, steam billowing from the hood. More cars clogged the Midtown streets than ever these days, jockeying for space with the buses and taxis and trucks making deliveries. There did not appear to be another vehicle involved, though. A lone ambulance sat at the corner. The medics did not rush about urgently, but stood leaning against the vehicle, smoking.

Grace started toward a policeman, whose paunchy face pushed up from the high collar of his uniform, navy with gold buttons. "Excuse me. Will the street be closed for long? I'm late for work."

He looked out at her disdainfully from under the brim of his hat, as if despite all of the women who had worked dutifully in the factories to take the place of the men who had enlisted and gone overseas during the war, the notion of a woman holding a job was still laughable. "You can't go this way," he replied officiously. "And you won't be able to anytime soon."

"What happened?" she asked, but the policeman turned away. Grace took a step forward, craning to see.

"A woman was hit by a car and died," a man in a flat wool cap beside her said.

Taking in the shattered windshield of the Studebaker, Grace suddenly felt sick. "Such a shame," she managed finally.

"I didn't see it," the man replied. "But someone said she was killed instantly. At least she didn't suffer."

At least. That was the phrase Grace heard too often after Tom had died. At least she was still young. At least there had not been children—as if that made it somehow easier to bear. (Children, she sometimes thought, would not have been a burden, but a bit of him left behind forever.)

"You just never know where it will all end," mused the flat-capped man beside her. Grace did not answer. Tom's death had been unexpected, too, an overturned jeep on the way from the army base to the train station in Georgia, headed to New York to see her before he'd deployed. They called him a casualty of war, but in fact it had been just another accident that might have happened anywhere.

A flashbulb from a reporter's camera popped, causing her to blink. Grace shielded her eyes then backed away blindly through the crowd that had formed, seeking air amid the cigarette smoke and sweat and perfume.

Away from the police barricade now, Grace looked over her shoulder. Forty-Third Street was blocked to the west as well, preventing her from cutting across. To go back up Madison and around the other side of the station would take at least another half an hour, making her even later for work than she already was. Again, she cursed the night before. If it weren't for Mark, she wouldn't be standing here, faced with no other choice than to cut through Grand Central—the one place she had sworn to never go again.

Grace turned to face it. Grand Central loomed before her, its massive shadow darkening the pavement below. Commuters streamed endlessly through its doors. She imagined the inside of the station, the concourse where the light slatted in through the stained glass windows, the big clock where friends and lovers met. It was not the place she couldn't bear to see, but the people. The girls with their fresh red lipstick, pressing tongues against teeth to make sure the color hadn't bled through, clutching purses expectantly. Freshly washed children looking just a bit nervous at seeing a father who they could not remember because he had left when they were scarcely toddlers. The soldiers in uniforms rumpled from travel bounding onto the platform with wilted daisies in hand. The reunion that would never be hers.

She should just give up and go home. Grace longed for a nice bath, perhaps a nap. But she had to get to work. Frankie had interviews with a French family at ten and needed her to take dictation. And after that the Rosenbergs were coming, seeking papers for housing. Normally this was what she loved about the work, losing herself in other peoples' problems. But today the responsibility weighed down heavy upon her.

No, she had to go forward and there was only one choice. Squaring her shoulders, Grace started toward Grand Central.

She walked through the station door. It was the first time she had been here since that afternoon she'd arrived from Connecticut in her best shirred dress, hair perfectly coiffed in victory rolls and topped with her pillbox hat. Tom hadn't arrived on the three from Philadelphia, where he should have changed trains, as expected and she assumed he had missed his connection. When he didn't get off the next train either, she became a bit uneasy. She checked the message board beside the information booth at the center of the station, where people pinned notes in case Tom had come early or she had somehow missed him. She had no way to reach him or check and there was nothing to do but wait. She ate a hot dog that smudged her lipstick and turned sour in her mouth, read the newspaper headlines at the kiosk a second, then a third time. Trains came and emptied, spilling onto the platform soldiers who might have been Tom but weren't. By the time the last train of the night arrived at eight thirty, she was frantic with worry. Tom never would have left her standing like this. What had happened? Finally, an auburn-haired lieutenant she'd recognized from Tom's induction ceremony came toward her with an expression of dread and she'd known. She could still feel his unfamiliar hands catching her as her knees buckled.

The station looked the same now as it had that night, a businesslike, never-ending stream of commuters and travelers, undisturbed by the role it had played so large in her mind these many months. *Just get across*, she told herself, the wide exit at the far side of the station calling to her like a beacon. She didn't have to stop and remember.

Something pulled at her leg strangely, like the tearing of a small child's fingers. Grace stopped and looked behind her. It was only a run in her nylons. Had Mark's hands made it? The tear was growing larger with every step now, an almost gash across her calf. She was seized with the need to get them off.

Grace raced for the stairs to the public washroom on the lower level. As she passed a bench, she stumbled, nearly falling. Her foot twisted, causing a wave of pain to shoot through her ankle. She limped to the bench and lifted her foot, assuming that the heel that she had not had fixed properly had come off again. But the shoe was still intact. No, there was something jutting out from beneath the bench she had just passed that had caused her to trip. A brown suitcase, shoved haphazardly beneath. She looked around with annoyance, wondering who could have been so irresponsible as to leave it like that, but there was no one close and the other people passed by without taking notice. Perhaps whoever owned it had gone to the restroom or to buy a newspaper. She pushed it farther underneath the bench so that no one else would trip on it and kept walking.

Outside the door to the ladies' room, Grace noticed a man sitting on the ground in a tattered uniform. For a fleeting second, she was glad Tom had not lived to fight and return destroyed from what he had seen. She would always have the golden image of him, perfect and strong. He would not come home scarred like so many she saw now, struggling to put a brave face over the brokenness. Grace reached in her pocket for the last of her coins, trying not to think about the coffee she so dearly wanted that she would now have to do without. She pressed the money into the man's cracked palm. She simply couldn't look away.

Grace continued into the ladies' room, locking herself in a stall to remove her nylons. Then she walked to the mirror to smooth her ink-black hair and reapply her Coty lipstick, tasting in its waxiness all that had happened the night before. At the next sink, a woman younger than herself smoothed her coat over her rounded belly. Pregnancies were everywhere now, it seemed, the fruits of so many joyous reunions with the boys who came home from the war. Grace could feel the woman looking at her disheveled appearance. *Knowing.*

Mindful that she was even later now for work, Grace hurried from the restroom. As she started across the station once more, she noticed the suitcase she had nearly tripped over moments earlier. It was still sitting under the bench. Slowing, she walked to the suitcase, looking around for someone coming to claim it.

When no one did, Grace knelt to examine the suitcase. There was nothing terribly extraordinary about it, rounded like a thousand other valises that travelers carried through the station every day, with a worn mother-of-pearl handle that was nicer than most. Only this one wasn't passing through; it was sitting under a bench unattended. *Abandoned.* Had someone lost it? She stopped with a moment's caution, remembering a story from during the war about a bag that was actually a bomb. But that was all over, the danger of invasion or other attack that had once seemed to lurk around every corner now faded.

Grace studied the case for some sign of ownership. There was a name chalked onto the side. She recalled uneasily some of Frankie's clients, survivors whom the Germans had forced to write their names on their suitcases in a false promise that they would be reunited with their belongings. This one bore a single word: *Trigg.*

Grace considered her options: tell a porter, or simply walk away. She was late for work. But curiosity nagged at her. Perhaps there was a tag inside. She toyed with the clasp. It popped open in her fingers seemingly of its own accord. She found herself lifting the lid a few inches. She glanced over her shoulder, feeling as though at any minute she might get caught. Then she looked inside the suitcase. It was neatly packed, with a silver-backed hairbrush and an unwrapped bar of Yardley's lavender soap tucked in a top corner, women's clothes folded with perfect creases. There was a pair of baby shoes tucked in the rear of the case, but no other sign of children's clothing.

Suddenly, being in the suitcase felt like an unforgivable invasion of privacy (which, of course, it was). Grace pulled back her hand quickly. As she did, something sliced into her index finger. "Ouch!" she cried aloud, in spite of herself. A line of blood an inch or more long, already widening with red bubbles, appeared. She put her finger to her mouth, sucking on the wound to stop the bleeding. Then she reached for the case with her good hand, needing to know what had cut her, a razor or knife. Below the clothes was an envelope, maybe a quarter inch thick. The sharp edge of the paper had cut her hand. *Leave it*, a voice inside her seemed to say. But unable to stop herself, she opened the envelope.

Inside lay a pack of photographs, wrapped carefully in a piece of lace. Grace pulled them out, and as she did a drop of blood seeped from her finger onto the lace, irreparably staining it. There were about a dozen photos in all, each a portrait of a single young woman. They looked too different to be related to one another. Some wore military uniforms, others crisply pressed blouses or blazers. Not one among them could have been older than twenty-five.

Holding the photos of these strangers felt too intimate, wrong. Grace wanted to put them away, forget what she had seen. But the eyes of the girl in the top photo were dark and beckoning. Who was she?

Just then there were sirens outside the station and it felt as though they might be meant for her, the police coming to arrest her for opening someone else's bag. Hurriedly, Grace struggled to rewrap the photos in the lace and put the whole thing back into the suitcase. But the lace bunched and she could not get the packet back into the envelope. The sirens were getting louder now. There was no time. Furtively, she tucked the photos into her own satchel and she pushed the suitcase back under the bench with her foot, well out of sight.

Then she started for the exit, the wound on her finger throbbing. "I should have known," she muttered to herself, "that no good could ever come from going into the station."

CHAPTER TWO

ELEANOR

London, 1943

The Director was furious.

He slammed his paw-like hand down on the long conference table so hard the teacups rattled and tea sloshed over the rims all the way at the far end. The normal banter and chatter of the morning meeting went silent. His face reddened.

"Another two agents captured," he bellowed, not bothering to lower his voice. One of the typists passing in the corridor stopped, taking in the scene with wide eyes before scurrying on. Eleanor stood hurriedly to close the door, swatting at the cloud of cigarette smoke that had formed above them.

"Yes, sir," Captain Michaels, the Royal Air Force attaché, stammered. "The agents dropped near Marseille were arrested, just hours after arrival. There's been no word and we're presuming they've been killed."

"Which ones?" the Director demanded. Gregory Winslow, Director of Special Operations Executive, was a former army colonel, highly decorated in the Great War. Though close to sixty, he remained an imposing figure, known only as "the Director" to everyone at headquarters.

Captain Michaels looked flummoxed by the question. To the men who ran the operation from afar, the agents in the field were nameless chess pieces.

But not to Eleanor, who was seated beside him. "James, Harry. Canadian by birth and a graduate of Magdalen College, Oxford. Peterson, Ewan, former Royal Air Force." She knew the details of every man they'd dropped into the field by heart.

"That makes the second set of arrests this month." The Director chewed on the end of his pipe without bothering to light it.

"The third," Eleanor corrected softly, not wanting to enrage him further but unwilling to lie. It had been almost three years since Churchill had authorized the creation of Special Operations Executive, or SOE, and charged it with the order to "set Europe ablaze" through sabotage and subversion. Since then, they had deployed close to three hundred agents into Europe to disrupt munitions factories and rail lines. The majority had gone into France as part of the unit called "F Section" to weaken the infrastructure and arm the French partisans ahead of the long-rumored cross-Channel Allied invasion.

But beyond the walls of its Baker Street headquarters, SOE was hardly regarded as a shining success. MI6 and some of the other traditional government agencies resented SOE's sabotage, which they saw as amateurish and damaging to their own, more clandestine, operations. The success of SOE efforts were also hard to quantify, either because they were classified or because their effect would not be fully felt until the invasion. And lately things had started to go wrong, their agents arrested in increasing number. Was it the size of the operations that was the problem, making them victims of their own success? Or was it something else entirely?

The Director turned to Eleanor, newfound prey that had suddenly caught the lion's attention. "What the hell is happening, Trigg? Are they ill prepared? Making mistakes?"

Eleanor was surprised. She had come to SOE as a secretary shortly after the organization was created. Getting hired had been an uphill battle: she was not just a woman, but a Polish national—and a Jew. Few thought she belonged here. Oftentimes she wondered herself how she'd come from her small village near Pinsk to the halls of power in London. But she'd persuaded the Director to give her a chance, and through her skill and knowledge, meticulous attention to detail and encyclopedic memory, she had gained his trust. Even though her title and pay had remained the same, she was now much more of an advisor. The Director insisted that she sit not with the other secretaries along the periphery, but at the conference table immediately to his right. (He did this in part, she suspected, to compensate for his deafness in his ear on that side, which he admitted to no one else. She always debriefed him in private just after the meeting to make certain he had not missed anything.)

This was the first time, though, that the Director had asked for her opinion in front of the others. "Respectfully, sir, it isn't the training, or the execution." Eleanor was suddenly aware of every eye on her. She prided herself on lying low in the agency, drawing as little attention as possible. But now her cover, so to speak, had been blown, and the men were watching her with an unmasked skepticism.

"Then what is it?" the Director asked, his usual lack of patience worn even thinner.

"It's that they are men." Eleanor chose her words carefully, not letting him rush her, wanting to make him understand in a way that would not cause offense. "Most of the young Frenchmen are gone from the cities or towns. Conscripted to the LVF, off fighting for the Vichy collaborationist militia or imprisoned for refusing to do so. It's impossible for our agents to fit in now."

"So what then? Should we send them all to ground?"

Eleanor shook her head. The agents could not go into hiding. They needed to be able to interact with the locals in order to get information. It was the waitress in Lautrec overhearing the officers chatter after too much wine, the farmer's wife noticing changes in the trains that passed by the fields, the observations of everyday citizens that yielded the real information. And the agents needed to be making contacts with the *reseau*, the local networks of resistance, in order to fortify their efforts to subvert the Germans. No, the agents of the F Section could not operate by hiding in the cellars and caves.

"Then what?" the Director pressed.

"There's another option…" She faltered and he looked at her impatiently. Eleanor was not one to be at a loss for words, but what she was about to say was so audacious she hardly dared. She took a deep breath. "Send women."

"Women? I don't understand."

The idea had come to her weeks earlier as she watched one of the girls in the radio room decode a message that had come through from a field agent in France with a swift and sure hand. Her talents were wasted, Eleanor thought. The girl should be transmitting from the field. The idea had been so foreign that it had taken time to crystalize in Eleanor's own mind. She had not meant to bring it up now, or maybe ever, but it had come out nonetheless, a half-formed thing.

"Yes." Eleanor had heard stories of women agents, rogue operatives working on their own in the east, carrying messages and helping POWs to escape. Such things had happened in the First World War as well, probably to a greater extent than most people imagined. But to create a formal program to actually train and deploy women was something altogether different.

"But what would they *do*?" the Director asked.

"The same work as the men," Eleanor replied, suddenly annoyed at having to explain what should have been obvious. "Courier messages. Transmit by radio. Arm the partisans, blow up bridges." Women had risen up to take on all sorts of roles on the home front, not just nursing and local guard. They manned antiaircraft guns and flew planes. Why was the notion that they could do this, too, so hard to understand?

"A women's sector?" Michaels interjected, barely containing his skepticism.

Ignoring him, Eleanor turned to face the Director squarely. "Think about it, sir," she said, gaining steam as the idea firmed in her mind. "Young men are scarce in France, but women are everywhere. They blend in on the street and in the shops and cafés."

"As for the other women who work here already..." She hesitated, considering the wireless radio operators who labored tirelessly for SOE. On some level they were perfect: skilled, knowledgeable, wholly committed to the cause. But the same assets that made them ideal also rendered them useless for the field. They were simply too entrenched to train as operatives, and they had seen and knew too much to be deployed. "They won't do either. The women would need to be freshly recruited."

"But where would we find them?" the Director asked, seeming to warm to the idea.

"The same places we do the men." It was true they didn't have the corps of officers from which to recruit. "From the WACs or the FANYs, the universities and trade schools, or in the factories or on the street." There was not a single résumé that made an ideal agent, no special degree. It was more of a sense that one could do the work. "The same types of people—smart, adaptable, proficient in French," she added.

"They would have to be trained," Michaels pointed out, making it sound like an insurmountable obstacle.

"Just like the men," Eleanor countered. "No one is born knowing how to do this."

"And then?" the Director asked.

"And then we deploy them."

"Sir," Michaels interjected. "The Geneva Convention expressly prohibits women combatants." The men around the table nodded their heads, seeming to seize on the point.

"The convention prohibits a lot of things," Eleanor shot back. She knew all of the dark corners of SOE, the ways in which the agency and others cut corners and skirted the law in the desperation of war. "We can make them part of the FANY as a cover."

"We'd be risking the lives of wives, daughters and mothers," Michaels pointed out.

"I don't like it," said one of the other uniformed men from the far end of the table. Nervousness tugged at Eleanor's stomach. The Director was not the most strong-willed of leaders. If the others all lined up behind Michaels, he might back away from the idea.

"Do you like losing a half-dozen men every fortnight to the Germans?" Eleanor shot back, scarcely believing her own nerve.

"We'll try it," the Director said with unusual decisiveness, foreclosing any further debate. He turned to Eleanor. "Set up an office down the street at Norgeby House and let me know what you need."

"Me?" she asked, surprised.

"You thought of it, Trigg. And you're going to run the bloody thing." Recalling the casualties they had discussed just minutes earlier, Eleanor cringed at the Director's choice of words.

"Sir," Michaels interjected. "I hardly think that Miss Trigg is qualified. Meaning no offense," he added, tilting his head in her direction. The men looked at her dubiously.

"None taken." Eleanor had long ago hardened herself to the dismissiveness of the men around her.

"Sir," the army officer at the far end of the table interjected. "I, too, find Miss Trigg a most unlikely choice. With her background..." Heads nodded around the table, their skeptical looks accompanied by a few murmurs. Eleanor could feel them studying her, wondering about her loyalties. *Not one of us,* the men's expressions seemed to say, *and not to be trusted.* For all that she did for SOE, they still regarded her as an enemy. Alien, foreign. It was not for lack of trying. She had worked to fit in, to mute all traces of her accent. And she had applied for British citizenship. Her naturalization application had been denied once, on grounds that even the Director, for all of his power and clearances, had not been able to ascertain. She had resubmitted it a second time a few months earlier with a note of recommendation from him, hoping this might make the difference. Thus far, she had not received a response.

Eleanor cleared her throat, prepared to withdraw from consideration. But the Director spoke first. "Eleanor, set up your office," he ordered. "Begin recruiting and training the girls with all due haste." He raised his hand, foreclosing further discussion.

"Yes, sir." She kept her head up, unwilling to look away from the eyes now trained upon her.

After the meeting, Eleanor waited until the others had left before approaching the Director. "Sir, I hardly think…"

"Nonsense, Trigg. We all know you are the man for the job, if you'll pardon the expression. Even the military chaps, though they may not want to admit it or quite understand why."

"But, sir, even if that is true, I'm an outsider. I don't have the clout."

"You're an outsider, and that is just one of the things that makes you perfect for the position." He lowered his voice. "I'm tired of it all getting mired by politics. You won't let personal loyalties or other concerns affect your judgment." She nodded, knowing that was true. She had no husband or children, no outside distractions. The mission was the only thing that mattered—and always had been.

"Are you sure I can't go?" she asked, already knowing the answer. Though flattered that he wanted her to run the women's operation, it would still be a distant second-best to actually deploying as one of the agents in the field.

"Without the paperwork, you couldn't possibly." He was right, of course. In London, she might be able to hide her background. But to get papers to send her over, especially now, while her citizenship application was pending, was another matter entirely. "Anyway, this is much more important. You're the head of a department now. We need you to recruit the girls. Train them. It has to be someone they trust."

"Me?" Eleanor knew the other women who worked at SOE saw her as cold and distant, not the type they would invite to lunch or tea, much less confide in.

"Eleanor," the Director continued, his voice low and stern, eyes piercing. "Few of us are finding ourselves where we expected at the start of the war."

That, she reflected, was more true than he possibly could have known. She thought about what he was asking. A chance to take the helm, to try to fix all of the mistakes that she'd been forced to watch from the sidelines these many months, powerless to do anything. Though one step short of actual deployment, this would be an opportunity to do so much more.

"We need you to figure out where the girls belong and get them there," the Director continued on, as though it had all been settled and she'd said yes. Inwardly, Eleanor felt conflicted. The prospect of taking this on was appealing. At the same time, she saw the enormity of the task splayed before her on the table like a deck of cards. The men already faced so much, and while in her heart she knew that the women were the answer, getting them ready would be Herculean. It was too much, the kind of involvement—and exposure—that she could hardly afford.

Then she looked up at the photos on the wall of fallen SOE agents, young men who had given everything for the war. She imagined the German security intelligence, the Sicherheitsdienst, at their French headquarters on the Avenue Foch in Paris. The SD was headed by the infamous Sturmbannführer Hans Kriegler, a former concentration camp commandant who Eleanor knew from the files to be as cunning as he was cruel. There were reports of his using the children of locals to coerce confessions, of hanging prisoners alive from meat hooks to withdraw information before leaving them there to die. He was undoubtedly planning the downfall of more agents even as they spoke.

Eleanor knew then that she had no choice but to take on the task. "Fine. I'll need complete control," she added. It was always important to go first when setting the terms.

"You shall have it."

"And I report only to you." Special sectors would, in other circumstances, report through one of the Director's deputies. Eleanor peered out of the corner of her eye at Michaels, who lingered in the hallway. He and the other men would not be happy about her having the Director's ear, even more so than she already had. "To you," she repeated for emphasis, letting her words sink in.

"No bureaucratic meddling," the Director promised. "You report only to me." She could hear then the desperation in his voice, how very much he needed her to make this work.

CHAPTER THREE

MARIE

London, 1944

The last place Marie would have expected to be recruited as a secret agent (if indeed she could have anticipated it at all) was in the loo.

An hour earlier, Marie sat at a table by the window in the Town House, a quiet café on York Street she had come to frequent, savoring a few minutes of quiet after a day of endless clacking at the dingy War Office annex where she had taken a position as a typist. She thought of the coming weekend, just two days off, and smiled, imagining five-year-old Tess and the crooked tooth that surely would have come in a bit more by now. That was the thing about only seeing her daughter on the weekend—Marie seemed to miss years in the days in between. She wanted to be out in the country with Tess, playing by the brook and digging for stones. But someone had to stay here and make a few pounds in order to keep their aging row home in Maida Vale from falling into foreclosure or disrepair, assuming the bombs didn't take it all first.

There was a booming noise in the distance, causing the dishes on the table to rattle. Marie started, reaching instinctively for the gas mask that no one carried anymore since the Blitz had ended. She lifted her gaze to the plate glass window of the café. Outside the rain-soaked street, a boy of no more than eight or nine was trying to scrape up bits of coal from the pavement. Her stomach ached. Where was his mother?

She remembered the day more than two years ago that she'd decided to send Tess away. At first, the notion of being separated from her daughter was almost unthinkable. Then a bomb had hit the flats across the street, killing seven children. But for the grace of God, that might have been Tess. The next morning, Marie began making arrangements.

At least Tess was with Aunt Hazel. The woman was more of a cousin and a bit dour to be sure, but was nevertheless fond of the little girl. And Tess loved the old vicarage in East Anglia, with its endless cupboards and musty crawl spaces. She could run wild across the fens when the weather permitted, and help Hazel with her work at the post office when it did not. Marie couldn't imagine putting her girl on a train to be sent off to the countryside to a cold convent or God-knows-where-else, into the arms of strangers. She had seen it at King's Cross almost every Friday last year as she made her way north to visit Tess—mothers battling back tears as they adjusted coats and scarves on the little ones, younger siblings clinging to older, children with too-large suitcases crying openly, trying to escape through the carriage windows. It made the two-hour journey until she could reach Tess and wrap her arms around her almost unbearable. She stayed each Sunday until Hazel reminded her that she had best take the last train or miss curfew. Her daughter was safe and well and with family. But that didn't make the fact that it was only Wednesday any more bearable.

Should she have brought Tess back already? That was the question that had dogged Marie these past few months as she had seen the trickle of children coming back to the city. The Blitz was long over and there was a kind of normalcy that had resumed now that they weren't sleeping in the Tube stations at night. But the war was far from won, and Marie sensed that something far worse was yet to come.

Pushing her doubts aside, Marie pulled a book from her bag. It was poetry by Baudelaire, which she loved because his elegant verse took her back to happier times as a child summering on the coast in Brittany with her mother.

"Excuse me," a man said a moment later. She looked up, annoyed by the interruption. He was fortyish, thin and unremarkable in a tweedy sport coat and glasses. A scone sat untouched on the plate at the table next to her from which he had risen. "I was curious about what you are reading." She wondered if he were trying to make advances. The intrusions were everywhere now with all of the American GIs in the city, spilling from the pubs at midday and walking three abreast in the streets, their jarring laughter breaking the stillness.

But the man's accent was British and his mild expression contained no hint of impropriety. Marie held up the book so that he could see. "Would you mind reading me a bit?" he asked. "I'm afraid I don't speak French."

"Really, I don't think..." she began to demur, surprised by the odd request.

"Please," he said, cutting her off, his tone almost imploring. "You'd be doing me a kindness." She wondered why it meant so much to him. Perhaps he had lost someone French or was a veteran who had fought over there.

"All right," she relented. A few lines couldn't hurt. She began to read from the poem, "N'importe où hors du monde (Anywhere Out of the World)." Her voice was self-conscious at first, but she felt herself slowly gain confidence.

After a few sentences, Marie stopped. "How was that?" She expected him to ask her to read further.

He did not. "You've studied French?"

She shook her head. "No, but I speak it. My mother was French and we spent summers there when I was a child." In truth, the summers had been an escape from her father, an angry drunk unable to find work or hold down a job, resentful of her mother's breeding and family money and disappointed that Marie wasn't a boy. That was the reason Marie and her mother summered far away in France. And it was the reason Marie had run away from the Herefordshire manor where she'd been raised to London when she was eighteen, and then took her mother's surname. She knew if she stayed in the house she had dreaded all her childhood with her father's worsening temper, she wouldn't make it out alive.

"Your accent is extraordinary," the man said. "Nearly perfect." How could he know that if he didn't speak French? she wondered. "Are you working?" he asked.

"Yes," she blurted. The transition in subject was abrupt, the question too personal. She stood hurriedly, fumbling in her purse for coins. "I'm sorry, but I really must go."

The man reached up and when she looked back she saw he was holding a business card. "I didn't mean to be rude. But I was wondering if you would like a job." She took the card. *Number 64 Baker Street*, was all it said. No person or office named. "Ask for Eleanor Trigg."

"Why should I?" she asked, perplexed. "I have a job."

He shook his head slightly. "This is different. It's important work and you'd be well suited—and well compensated. I'm afraid I can't say any more."

"When should I go there?" she asked, though certain that she never would.

"Now." She'd expected an appointment. "So you'll go?"

Marie left a few coins on the table and left the café without answering, eager to be away from the man and his intrusiveness. Outside, she opened her umbrella and adjusted her burgundy print scarf to protect against the chill. She rounded the corner, then stopped, peering over her shoulder to make sure he had not followed her. She looked down at the card, simple black and white. *Official.*

She could have told the man no, Marie realized. Even now, she could throw out the card and walk away. But she was curious; what kind of work, and for whom? Perhaps it was something more interesting than endless typing. The man had said it paid well, too, something she dearly needed.

Ten minutes later, Marie found herself standing at the end of Baker Street. She paused by a red post box at the corner. The storied home of Sherlock Holmes was meant to be on Baker Street, she recalled. She had always imagined it as mysterious, shrouded in fog. But the block was like any other, drab office buildings with ground floor shops. Farther down the row there were brick town houses that had been converted for business use. She walked to Number 64, then hesitated. Inter-Services Research Bureau, the sign by the door read. What on earth was this all about?

Before she could knock the door flew open and a hand that did not seem attached to anybody pointed left. "Orchard Court, Portman Square. Around the corner and down the street."

"Excuse me," Marie said, holding up the card though there seemed to be no one to see it. "My name is Marie Roux. I was told to come here and ask for Eleanor Trigg." The door closed.

"Curiouser and curiouser," she muttered, thinking of Tess's favorite book, the illustrated version of *Alice in Wonderland* Marie read aloud to her when she visited. Around the corner there were more row houses. She continued down the street to Portman Square and found the building marked "Orchard Court." Marie knocked. There was no answer. The whole thing was starting to feel like a very odd prank. She turned, ready to go home and forget this folly.

Behind her, the door opened with a creak. She spun back to

face a white-haired butler. "Yes?" He stared at her coldly, like she was a door-to-door salesman peddling something unwanted. Too nervous to speak, she held out the card.

He waved her inside. "Come." His tone was impatient now, as though she was expected and late. He led her through a foyer, its high ceiling and chandelier giving the impression that it had once been the entranceway to a grand home. He opened a door on his right, then closed it again quickly. "Wait here," he instructed.

Marie stood awkwardly in the foyer, feeling entirely as though she did not belong. She heard footsteps on the floor above and turned to see a handsome young man with a shock of blond hair descending a curved staircase. Noticing her, he stopped. "So, you're part of the Racket?" he asked.

"I have no idea what you're talking about."

He smiled. "Just wandered in then?" He did not wait for an answer. "The Racket—that's what we call all of this." He gestured around the foyer.

The butler reappeared, clearing his throat. His stern expression gave Marie the undeniable sense that they were not supposed to be speaking with one another. Without another word, the blond man disappeared around the corner into another of what seemed to be an endless number of doors.

The butler led her down the hallway and opened the door to an onyx-and-white-tiled bathroom. She turned back, puzzled; she hadn't asked for the loo. "Wait in here."

Before Marie could protest, the butler closed the door, leaving her alone. She stood awkwardly, inhaling the smell of mildew lingering beneath cleaners. Asked to wait in a toilet! She needed to leave but was not quite sure how to manage it. She perched on the edge of a claw-footed bathtub, ankles neatly crossed. Five minutes passed, then ten.

At last the door opened with a click and a woman walked in. She was older than Marie by at least a decade, maybe two. Her face was grave. At first her dark hair appeared to be short, but closer Marie saw that it was pulled tightly in a bun at the nape of her neck. She wore no makeup or jewelry, and her starched white shirt was perfectly pressed, almost military.

"I'm Eleanor Trigg, Chief Recruitment Officer. I'm sorry for the accommodations," she said, her voice clipped. "We are short on space." The explanation seemed odd, given the size of the house, the number of doors Marie had seen. But then she remembered the man whom the butler seemed to chastise for speaking with her. Perhaps the people who came here weren't meant to see one another at all.

Eleanor appraised Marie as one might a vase or piece of jewelry, her gaze steely and unrelenting. "So you've decided then?" she said, making it sound as if they were at the end of a long conversation and had not met thirty seconds earlier.

"Decided?" Marie repeated, puzzled.

"Yes. You have to decide if you want to risk your life, and I have to decide if I can let you."

Marie's mind whirled. "I'm sorry… I'm afraid I don't understand."

"You don't know who we are, do you?" Marie shook her head. "Then what are you doing here?"

"A man in a café gave me a card and…" Marie faltered, hearing the ridiculousness of the situation in her own voice. She had not even learned his name. "I should just go." She stood.

The woman pressed a firm hand on her shoulder. "Not necessarily. Just because you don't know why you've come, doesn't mean you shouldn't be here. We often find purpose where we least expect it—or not." Her style was brusque, unfeminine and unquestionably stern. "Don't blame the man who sent you. He wasn't authorized to say more. Our work is highly classified. Many who work at the most senior levels of Whitehall itself have no idea what it is that we do."

"Which is what, exactly?" Marie ventured to ask.

"We're a branch of Special Operations Executive."

"Oh," Marie said, though the answer really didn't clarify matters for her.

"Covert operations."

"Like the codebreakers at Bletchley?" She'd known a girl who had left the typing pool to do that once.

"Something like that. Our work is a bit more physical, though. On the ground."

"In Europe?" Eleanor nodded. Marie understood then: they meant to send her over, into the war. "You want me to be a spy?"

"We don't ask questions here," Eleanor snapped. Then it was not, Marie reflected, the place for her. She had always been curious, too curious, her mother would say, with never-ending questions that only made her father's temper worsen as Marie progressed through her teen years. "We aren't spies," Eleanor added, as though the suggestion was offensive. "Espionage is the business of MI6. Rather, here at SOE, our mission is sabotage, or destroying things like railroad tracks, telegraph lines, factory equipment and such, in order to hinder the Germans. We also help the local partisans arm and resist."

"I've never heard of such things."

"Exactly." Eleanor sounded almost pleased.

"But what makes you think I could have any part in something like this? I'm hardly qualified."

"Nonsense. You're smart, capable." How could this woman, who had only just met her, possibly know that? It was perhaps the first time in her life that anyone had described her that way. Her father made sure she felt the very opposite. And Richard, her now-gone husband, had treated her as if she was special for a fleeting moment, and look where all that had led. Marie had never thought of herself as any of those things, but now she found herself sitting a bit taller. "You speak the language. You're exactly who we're looking for. Have you ever played a musical instrument?" Eleanor asked.

Though it seemed nothing should surprise her anymore, Marie found the question strange. “Piano when I was very young. Harp in school.”

“That could be useful. Open your mouth,” Eleanor ordered, her voice suddenly terse. Marie was certain that she had misheard. But Eleanor’s face was serious. “Your mouth” came the command again, insistent and impatient. Reluctantly, Marie complied. Eleanor stared into her mouth like a dentist. Marie bristled, resenting the intrusion by a woman she had only just met. “That back filling will have to go,” Eleanor said decisively, stepping back.

“Go?” Marie’s voice rose with alarm. “But that’s a perfectly good filling—just a year old and was quite expensive.”

“Exactly. Too expensive. It will mark you as English right away. We’ll have it replaced with porcelain—that’s what the French use.”

It all came together in Marie’s mind then: the man’s interest in her language skills, Eleanor’s concern over whether a tooth filling was too English. “You want me to impersonate a Frenchwoman.”

“Among other things, yes. You’ll receive training in operations skills before you are deployed—if you make it through training.” Eleanor spoke as though Marie had already agreed to go. “That’s all I can say about it for now. Secrecy is of the utmost importance to our operations.”

Deployed. Operations. Marie’s head swam. It seemed surreal that in this elegant town house just steps from the shops and bustle of Oxford Street, covert war against Germany was planned and waged.

“The car will be here for you in one hour to take you to training school,” Eleanor said, as though it were all settled.

“Now? But that’s so soon! I would have to sort out my affairs and pack.”

“It is always the way,” Eleanor replied. Perhaps, Marie reflected, they didn't want to give people a chance to go home and have second thoughts. "We'll provide everything you need and give notice to the War Office for you." Marie stared at Eleanor with surprise. She hadn't said where she worked. She realized then that these people, whoever they were, knew too much about her. The meeting in the café had not been by chance.

"How long would I have to be gone?" Marie asked.

"That depends on the mission and a variety of other circumstances. You can resign at any time."

Leave, a voice not her own seemed to say. Marie was into something much bigger and deeper than she had imagined. But her feet remained planted, curiosity piqued. "I have a daughter up near Ely with my aunt. She's five."

"And your husband?"

"Killed in action," she lied. In fact, Tess's father, Richard, had been an unemployed actor who had gotten by on parts as extras in West End shows and disappeared shortly after Tess was born. Marie had come to London when she was eighteen, fleeing her father's home, and had promptly fallen for the first bad apple that dropped at her feet. "He went missing at Dunkirk." The explanation, a morbid lie, was preferable to the likely truth: that he was in Buenos Aires, spending what was left of her mother's inheritance, which Marie had naively moved to a joint account to cover their household expenses when they had first married.

"Your daughter is well cared for?" Marie nodded. "Good. You would not be able to concentrate on training if you were worried about that."

She would never stop worrying about Tess, Marie thought. She knew in that instant that Eleanor did not have children.

Marie thought about Tess up in the countryside, the weekend visits that wouldn't happen if she accepted Eleanor's proposal. What kind of mother would do such a thing? The responsible choice would be to stay here in London, to thank Eleanor and go back to whatever ordinary life was left during the war. She was the only parent Tess had. If she failed to come back, Tess would have no one but aging Aunt Hazel, who surely couldn't look after her much longer.

"The work pays ten pounds per week," Eleanor added.

That was five times what Marie made typing. She'd found the best work she could in London, but it hadn't been enough. Even combined with a second job, the kind that would have kept her from getting up to see Tess at the weekends, she would not have made what Eleanor was offering. She did the calculations. She would have enough to keep up the house even after sending money to Hazel each week to cover Tess's care and expenses, something that simply was not possible now. She imagined a new dress for her daughter, perhaps even a few toys at Christmas. Tess was unspoiled and never complained, but Marie often wished to give her more of the things she had taken for granted in her own childhood. It wasn't like she could be with Tess now while she was stuck working in London anyway. And, in truth, Marie was curious about the mysterious adventure Eleanor was dangling in front of her. She felt so useless sitting here in London, typing endlessly. Might as well do some good, make a real difference in the war effort—if, as Eleanor had said, she in fact had what it took.

"All right then. I'm ready. But I have to phone and let my daughter's caretaker know that I won't be coming up."

Eleanor shook her head firmly. "Impossible. No one can know where you are going—or even that you are going. We'll send a telegram informing your family that you've been called away for work."

"I can't simply leave without saying anything."

"That is exactly what you must do." Eleanor stared at her evenly. Though her expression did not change, Marie saw a flicker of doubt behind her eyes. "If you aren't prepared to do this, you can just leave."

"I have to speak to my daughter. I won't go unless I can hear her voice."

"Fine," Eleanor relented finally. "But you cannot tell her that you are going. There's a phone in the next room you can use. Keep it brief. No more than five minutes." Eleanor spoke as though she was in charge of Marie now, owned her. Marie wondered if accepting had been a mistake. "Say nothing of your departure," Eleanor reiterated. Marie sensed it was some sort of test—perhaps the first of many.

Eleanor started for the door, indicating that Marie should follow. "Wait," Marie said. "There's one thing." Eleanor turned back, the start of annoyance creeping onto her face. "I should tell you that my father's family is German." Marie watched Eleanor's face, half hoping the information might cause Eleanor to change her mind about accepting Marie for whatever she was proposing.

But Eleanor simply nodded in confirmation. "I know."

"But how?"

"You've sat in that same café every day, haven't you?" Marie nodded. "You should stop that, by the way. Terrible habit. Varying one's routine is key. In any event, you sit there and read books in French and one of our people noticed and thought you might be a good recruit. We followed you back to work, learned who you are. We ran you through the cards, found you qualified, at least for initial consideration." Marie was stunned; all of this had been going on and she'd had no idea. "We have finders, recruiters looking for girls who might be the right sort all over Britain. But in the end I decide if they are the right sort to go. Every single one of the girls passes through me." There was a note of protectiveness in her voice.

"And you think I do?"

"You might," Eleanor said carefully. "You've got the proper credentials. But in training you'll be tested to see if you can actually put them into use. Skills on paper are useless if you don't have the grit to see it all through. Do you have any political allegiances of your own?"

"None. My mother didn't believe in…"

"Enough," Eleanor snapped. "Don't answer a question with any more than you have to." Another test. "You must never talk about yourself or your past. You'll be given a new identity in training." And until then, Marie thought, it would be as if she simply didn't exist.

Eleanor held open the door to the toilet. Marie walked through into a study with high bookshelves. A black phone sat on a mahogany desk. "You can call here." Eleanor remained in the doorway, not even pretending to give her privacy. Marie dialed the operator and asked to be connected to the post office where Hazel worked each day, hoping she had not yet gone home. She asked for Hazel from the woman who answered.

Then a warbling voice came across the line. "Marie! Is something wrong?"

"Everything's fine," Marie reassured quickly, so desperately wanting to tell her the truth about why she had called. "Just checking on Tess."

"I'll fetch her." One minute passed then another. Quickly, Marie thought, wondering if Eleanor would snatch the phone from her hand the moment five minutes had passed.

"Allo!" Tess's voice squeaked, flooding Marie's heart.

"Darling, how are you?"

"Mummy, I'm helping Aunt Hazel sort the mail."

Marie smiled, imagining her playing around the pigeonholes. "Good girl."

"And just two more days until I see you." Tess, who even as a young child had an acute sense of time, knew her mother always came on Friday. Only now she wouldn't be. Marie's heart wrenched.

"Let me speak to your auntie. And, Tess, I love you," she added.

But Tess was already gone. Hazel came back on the line. "She's well?" Marie asked.

"She's brilliant. Counting to a hundred and doing sums. So bright. Why, just the other day, she…" Hazel stopped, seeming to sense that sharing what Marie had missed would only make things worse. Marie couldn't help but feel a tiny bit jealous. When Richard abandoned her and left her alone with a newborn, Marie had been terrified. But in those long nights of comforting and nursing an infant, she and Tess had become one. Then she'd been forced to send Tess away. She was missing so much of Tess's childhood as this bloody war dragged on. "You'll see for yourself at the weekend," Hazel added kindly.

Marie's stomach ached as though she had been punched. "I have to go."

"See you soon," Hazel replied.

Fearful she would say more, Marie hung up the phone.

CHAPTER FOUR

GRACE

New York, 1946

Forty-five minutes after she had started away from Grand Central, Grace stepped off the downtown bus at Delancey Street. The photographs she'd taken from the suitcase seemed to burn hot against her skin through her bag. She'd half expected the police or someone else to follow her and order her to return them.

But now as she made her way through the bustling Lower East Side neighborhood where she'd worked these past several months, the morning seemed almost normal. At the corner, Mortie the hot dog vendor waved as she passed. The window cleaners alternated between shouting to one another about their weekends and catcalling at the women below. The smell of something savory and delicious wafted from Reb Sussel's delicatessen, tickling her nose.

Grace soon neared the row house turned office on Orchard Street and began the climb that always left her breathless. Bleeker &

Sons, a law practice for immigrants, was located in a fourth-floor walk-up above a milliner and two stories of accountants. The name, etched into the glass door at the top of the landing, was a misnomer because it was just Frankie, and always had been as far as she could tell. A line of refugees fifteen deep snaked down the stairs, hollow cheekbones above heavy coats and too many layers of clothing, as though they were afraid to take off their belongings. Their faces were careworn and drawn and they did not make eye contact. Grace noticed the unwashed smell coming from them as she passed, and then was immediately ashamed at herself for doing so.

"Excuse me," Grace said, stepping delicately around a woman sitting on the ground with a baby sleeping on her lap. She slid into the office. Across the single room, Frankie perched on the edge of his worn desk, phone receiver cradled between his ear and shoulder. He grinned widely and waved her over.

"I'm sorry I'm late," she said as soon as he hung up the phone. "There was an accident by Grand Central and I had to go around."

"I moved the Metz family to eleven," he said. There was no recrimination in his voice.

Closer she could see the imprint of papers creasing his cheek. "You were here all night again, weren't you?" she accused. "You're wearing the same suit, so don't try to deny it." She immediately regretted the observation. Hopefully, he would not realize the same about her.

He raised his hands in admission, touching the spot near his temples where his dark hair was flecked with gray. "Guilty. I had to be. The Weissmans needed papers filed for their residency and housing." Frankie was tireless when helping people, as though his own well-being did not matter at all.

"It's done now." She tried not to think about what she had been doing while he had been working all night. "You should get some sleep."

"Don't lecture me, miss," he chided, his Brooklyn accent seeming to deepen.

"You need rest. Go home," she pressed.

"And tell them what?" He gestured with his head toward the line of people waiting in the hallway.

Grace looked back over her shoulder at the never-ending stream of need that filled the stairwell. Sometimes she was overwhelmed by all of it. Frankie's practice consisted mainly of helping the European Jews who had come to live with relatives in the already teeming Lower East Side tenements; it sometimes felt more like social work than law. He took all of their cases, trying to find their relatives or their assets or get them citizenship papers, often for little more than a promise of payment. He had never missed her salary, but she sometimes wondered how he kept up the lights and rent.

And his own health. His white shirt was yellowed at the neck and he was covered as always in a fine layer of perspiration that made him seem to glow. A lifelong bachelor ("Who would have me?" he'd joked more than once) approaching fifty, he was a dilapidated sort, five-o'clock shadow even at ten in the morning and hair seldom combed. But there was a warmth to his brown eyes that made it impossible to scold and his quick smile always brought out her own.

"You need to at least eat breakfast," she said. "I can run and get you a bagel."

He waved away the suggestion. "Can you just find me the number for social services in Queens?" he asked. "I want to freshen up before our first meeting."

"You'll do our clients no good if you make yourself sick," she scolded.

But Frankie just smiled as he started out the door for the washroom. He ruffled the hair of a young boy who sat on the landing as he passed. "Just a minute, okay, Sammy?" he said.

Grace picked up the ashtray from the corner of his desk and

emptied it, then wiped the top of the table to clear away the dust left behind. She and Frankie had, in a sense, found each other. After she had taken the narrow room with a shared bath off Fifty-Fourth Street close to the West River, she'd quickly run through what little money she had and started to look for a job, armed with no more than a high school typing class. When she'd gone to answer an ad for a secretary for one of the accountants in the building, she had walked into his law office by mistake. Frankie said he'd been looking for someone (whether or not that was the case, she would never actually know) and she'd started the next day.

He didn't really need her to work there, she quickly came to realize. The office was tiny, almost too small for the both of them. Though his papers were seemingly tossed in haphazard piles, he could put his fingers on a single page he needed within seconds. The work was hectic, but he could do it all by himself; in fact, he had been doing it all for years. No, he hadn't needed her. But he sensed that she needed the job and so he had made a place. She loved him for it.

Frankie walked back into the office. "Are you ready?" he asked. She nodded, though she still wanted to go home for a bath and a nap, or at least find coffee. But Frankie was headed purposefully toward his desk with the young boy from the landing in tow. "Sammy, this is my friend Grace. Grace, I'd like to introduce Sam Altshuler."

Grace looked behind the boy toward the door for the others. She had been expecting a whole family, or at least an adult, to accompany him. "Mother? Father?" she mouthed silently over the boy's head so he could not see.

Frankie shook his head gravely. "Sit down, son," he said gently to the boy, who could not be older than ten. "How can we help?"

Sammy looked up uncertainly through long eyelashes, not sure whether to trust them. Grace noticed then a small notebook in his right hand. "You like to write?" she asked.

"Draw," Sammy replied with a heavy East European accent. He held up the pad to reveal a small sketch of the queue of people waiting on the stairs.

"It's wonderful," she said. The details and expressions on the people's faces were stunningly good.

"How can we help you?" Frankie asked.

"I need sumvere to live." He spoke the broken but functional English of a smart kid who had taught himself.

"Do you have any family here in New York?" Frankie asked.

"My cousin, he shares an apartment vith some fellas in the Bronx. But it costs two dollars a veek to stay vith them."

Grace wondered where Sammy had been living until now. "What about your parents?" she couldn't help asking.

"I vas separated from my father at Vesterbork." Westerbork was a transit camp in Holland, Grace recalled from a family they had helped weeks earlier. "My mother hid me vith her for as long as she could in the vomen's..." He paused, fumbling for a word. "In the barracks, but then she was taken, too. I never saw them again."

Grace shuddered inwardly, trying to imagine a child trying to survive alone under such circumstances. "It's possible that they survived," she offered. Frankie's eyes flashed above the boy's head, a silent warning.

Sammy's expression remained unchanged. "They vere taken east," he said, his voice matter-of-fact. "People don't come back from there." What was it like, Grace wondered, to be a child with no hope?

Grace forced herself to focus on the practicalities of the situation. "You know, there are places in New York for children to live."

"No boys' home," Sammy replied, sounding panicked. "No orphanage."

"Grace, can I speak with you for a moment?" Frankie waved her over to the corner, away from Sammy. "That boy spent two years in Dachau." Grace's stomach twisted, imagining the awful things Sammy's young eyes had seen. Frankie continued, "And then he was in a DP camp for six months before managing to get here by using the papers of another little boy who died. He's not going to go to another institution where people can hurt him again."

"But he needs guardians, an education…" she protested.

"What he needs," Frankie replied gently, "is a safe place to live." The bare minimum to survive, Grace thought sadly. So much less than the loving family a child should have. If she had a real apartment, she might have taken Sammy home with her.

Frankie started back toward the boy. "Sammy, we're going to start the process of having your parents declared deceased so that you can receive payments from social security." Frankie's voice was matter-of-fact. It wasn't that he didn't care, Grace knew. He was helping a client (albeit a young one) get what he needed.

"How long vill that take?" Sammy asked.

Frankie frowned. "It isn't a quick process." He reached in his wallet and pulled out fifty dollars. Grace stifled a gasp. It was a large sum in their meager practice and Frankie could hardly afford it. "This should be enough to live with your cousin for a while. Keep it on you and don't trust anyone with it. Check in with me in two weeks—or sooner if things aren't good with your cousin, okay?"

Sammy looked at the money dubiously. "I don't know ven I can repay you," he said, his voice solemn beyond his years.

"How about that drawing?" Frankie suggested. "That will be payment enough." The boy tore the paper carefully from the notepad and then took the money.

Watching Sammy's back as he retreated through the doorway, Grace's heart tugged. She had read and heard the stories in the news, which came first in a trickle then a deluge, about the killings and other atrocities that had happened in Europe while people here had gone to the cinema and complained about the shortage of nylons. It was not until coming to work for Frankie, though, that she had seen the faces of the suffering and began to truly understand. She tried to keep her distance from the clients. She knew that if she allowed them into her heart even a crack, their pain would break her. But then she met someone like Sammy and just couldn't help it.

Frankie walked up beside her and put his arm on her shoulder. "It's hard, I know."

She turned to him. "How do you do it? Keep going, I mean." He had been helping people rebuild their lives out of the wreckage for years.

"You just have to lose yourself in the work. Speaking of which, the Beckermans are waiting."

The next few hours were a rush of interviews. Some were in English, others she translated using all of the high school French she could muster, and still others Frankie conducted in the fluent German he said he had learned from his grandmother. Grace scribbled furiously the notes Frankie dictated about what needed to be done for each client. But in between meetings, Grace's thoughts returned to the suitcase she had found at the train station that morning. Why would someone simply have abandoned it? She wondered if the woman (Grace assumed it was a woman from the clothing and toiletries inside) had left it inadvertently, or if she knew she wasn't coming back. Perhaps it was meant for someone else to find.

"Why don't we break for lunch?" Frankie asked when it was nearly one o'clock. Grace knew he really meant that she should take lunch, while he would keep working, at most eat whatever she brought back for him. But she didn't argue. She hadn't eaten either today, she recalled as she started down the stairs.

Ten minutes later, Grace stepped out onto the flat rooftop of the building where she liked to eat when the weather permitted. It had a panoramic view of Midtown Manhattan stretching east to the river. The city was beginning to resemble one big construction site, from the giant cranes building glass-and-steel skyscrapers across Midtown to the block apartments going up on the edge of the East Village. She watched a group of girls on their lunch hour step out of Zarin's Fabrics, long-legged and fashionable, despite the years of shortages and rationing. A few even smoked now. Grace didn't want to do that, but she wished she fit in just a bit. They seemed so sure of their place. Whereas she felt like a visitor whose visa was about to expire at any moment.

Grace wiped off a sooty windowsill and perched on it. She thought of the photos in her purse. A few times that morning, she'd wondered if she had imagined them. But when she'd gone into her purse to fish out some coins for lunch, there they sat, neatly wrapped in the lace. She had wanted to bring them with her and have another look over lunch, but the roof tended to be breezy and she didn't want them to blow away.

Grace unwrapped the hot dog she'd bought from the vendor, missing the egg salad sandwich she usually packed. She liked a certain order to her world, took comfort in its mundaneness. Now the whole apple cart seemed toppled. With last night's misadventure, she had moved just one piece out of place (admittedly a very big one, but a single piece nonetheless) and now it seemed that everything was in complete disarray.

Turning her gaze uptown, her eyes locked on the vicinity of a certain high rise on the East River. Though she couldn't see it, the elegant hotel where she had spent the previous night loomed large in her mind. It had all started innocently enough. On her way home from work, Grace had stopped for dinner at Arnold's, a place on Fifty-Third Street that she had passed dozens of times, because she didn't have anything in the shared icebox in the boardinghouse kitchen. She had planned to ask for her meal to go, broiled chicken and a potato. But the mahogany bar, with its soft lighting and low music, beckoned. She didn't want to sit in her cramped room and eat alone again.

"I'll have a menu, please," Grace said. The maître d's eyes rose. Grace made her way to the bar trying to ignore the looks of the men, surprised to see a woman dining alone.

Then she noticed him, a man at the edge of the bar in a smart gray suit, facing away from her. He had broad shoulders and close-cut, curly brown hair tacked into place with pomade. A long-forgotten interest stirred in her. He turned and rose, his face lifting with recognition. "Grace?"

"Mark..." It had taken a second for her to place him so far out of context. Mark Dorff had been Tom's college roommate at Yale.

More than Tom's roommate, she realized as the memories returned. His best friend. Though two years older than Tom, Mark had been a constant presence among the sea of boys in navy wool blazers at events, and at the homecoming dances. He had even been an attendant in her wedding. But this was the first time they had really spoken, just the two of them.

"I didn't realize that you were living in New York," he remarked.

"I'm not. That is, sort of." She fumbled for the right words. "I'm here for a time. And you?"

"I'm living in Washington. I was here for a few days for work, but I'm headed back first thing tomorrow. It's good to see you, Gracie." She had always disliked the nickname her family had given her, that Tom had picked up for his own. It felt diminutive, designed to keep her in her place. But now there was a kind of warmth to hearing it that she realized she had missed during her months alone in the city. "How are you?"

There it was, the question she dreaded most since Tom's death. People always sounded as though they were trying to get the level of sympathy in their voices just right, to ask in a personal-but-not-too-personal way. Mark looked concerned, though, like he really meant it. "That's such a stupid thing to ask," he added when she did not answer. "I'm sorry."

"It's fine," she said quickly. "I'm managing." In truth, it had gotten easier. Being in New York and not seeing the places that would remind her of Tom every day allowed her to put it behind her, at least for a time. That numbness, that kind of forgetting, was part of what had driven her to New York. Yet she felt guilty for having found it.

"I'm sorry I couldn't be at the funeral. I was still overseas." He dipped his chin. His features were not perfect, she noticed then. Hazel eyes a bit too close together, chin sharp. But the way they fit together was handsome.

"It was all a blur," she confessed. "But those flowers..." They had towered over the others. "It was so kind of you."

"It was the least I could do. Losing Tom like that, it was just so goddamned wrong." Grace could see from his face that the loss of his friend had affected him deeply. Mark had been different than the other boys at Yale, she recalled then, and not just because he was Tom's best friend. A bit quieter, but in a confident rather than shy sort of way. "We're going to put together a scholarship fund in his name."

Grace felt a sudden urge to flee as the past seemed to well up all around her. "Well, it was lovely seeing you."

"Wait," he said, touching her arm. "Sit a minute. It would be nice to talk to someone who knew Tom."

Grace didn't think it would be nice at all. But she sat, allowing the bartender to pour a healthy snifter of brandy. At some point Mark moved his bar stool closer without seeming presumptuous or wrong. From there the rest of the night grew fuzzy around the edges and hours faded. Later she would realize how the restaurant was actually much more of a bar. What had she been thinking, going there? She was a widow of just under a year and had no business talking to strange men.

But Mark was not a stranger. He had known Tom, really known him, and she found herself lost in his stories. "So then I discovered Tom on the roof of the dormitory and he had no recollection of how he'd gotten there. But he was only worried about being late for class," Mark finished the story, which was meant to be funny.

But instead, Grace's eyes began to burn. "Oh!" She brought her hand to her mouth as the tears spilled over.

"I'm sorry," he said quickly.

"It's not your fault. It's just that you and I are here to laugh about it..."

"And Tom isn't." Mark understood, in a way no one else had. He reached over to smooth a smear of lipstick from her cheek. His hand lingered.

Mark switched the subject to something else then, she recalled. Music or politics, or maybe both. Only later would she realize that he had said nothing about himself.

Forcing her gaze from the direction of the hotel, Grace pushed the images from her mind. It was all done now. She had slipped from the elegant hotel room while he slept and hailed a taxi. She would never see him again.

Instead, she let herself think of her husband, the memories she usually kept so steadfastly at bay now a welcome distraction. She'd met Tom one high school summer during a family vacation on Cape Cod. He was just the right boy: fair-haired and charming, the son of a Massachusetts state senator and headed for an Ivy League college, larger than life in that captain-of-the-football-team kind of way. It was hard to believe he wanted her. She was the daughter of an accountant, and the youngest of three girls. Her sisters were both married and living within a square mile of where they had grown up in Westport, Connecticut. Tom's attention was a welcome draw away from the small-town life that had always felt so stifling, and the future of interminable bridge games and rotary club meetings that seemed inevitable if she stayed.

She and Tom married after her high school graduation and rented a house in New Haven while he was in college, making plans to move to Boston when he finished. They spoke of a belated honeymoon, a cruise to Europe perhaps upon an ocean liner. But then the Japanese had bombed Pearl Harbor and Tom had insisted on signing up for officers' school after he graduated. He'd been training down at Fort Benning and about to deploy.

"I've gotten weekend leave," he said that last night on the phone, arranging things as he always had. "It isn't long enough for me to come up to Connecticut, but meet me in Manhattan and we'll have a weekend. You'll see me off at New York Harbor."

That was the last she'd heard from him. The jeep carrying him had crashed, going too quickly around a curve on the way to the rail station, a stupid accident that might have been prevented. Grace often looked wistfully at the yellow ribbons, the flowers that the other women wore. Not just the trappings of war widowhood but the pride and the purpose—the sense that all of the loss and pain had been for something.

Grace had gone back to Westport briefly after Tom's funeral. Marcia, a childhood friend who wanted to help Grace, had kindly offered to host Grace for a visit at her family's place in the Hamptons. Grace had felt such immense relief at being away from her family's sympathetic gazes and the too-close town of her youth. She had found the silence of the coast out of season deafening, though, and so she had left for Manhattan. But she had told her family she was going to stay with Marcia and recover for an extended time, knowing they would never agree to her living alone in the city. Marcia had gone along with the scheme, forwarding any letters from her family that came. That was nearly a year ago and Grace still hadn't gone back.

Grace finished eating and returned to the office. The ragtag queue of clients had dispersed now that morning-intake hours were over. Frankie was nowhere to be found, but he had left her a pile of correspondence to be typed, letters to various city agencies on behalf of their clients. Grace picked up the first one and studied it, then inserted a sheet of paper in the typewriter, losing herself in the repetitive clack-clack sound.

When it was finished, she reached for the next paper, then stopped. She opened her bag and pulled out the envelope containing the photos, splaying them out in front of her in a fan shape. Twelve girls, each young and beautiful. They might have been part of a sorority. But most wore uniforms and beneath the smiles their jaws were set grimly, eyes solemn. The photos had been wrapped lovingly in the lace. They were still worn from handling, though, cupped like the shape of a palm. Putting her fingers beneath, Grace could almost feel the energy radiating from them.

She turned one over and there was a name scrawled on the back. *Marie. Madeline*, read another, and *Jean* and *Josie.* On and on, sounding like attendees at a garden party. Who were they?

She glanced up. Frankie had returned and was on the phone across the room, gesturing animatedly to whomever was on the other end of the line, verging on angry. She could show the photos to him, ask his advice. He might know what to do. But how could she explain having reached in the suitcase and looked, much less taken something that was not hers?

Grace ran her finger lightly over the first photo she had seen, of the young, dark-haired beauty called Josie. *Look away*, a voice inside her seemed to say. Studying the photographs, Grace was suddenly overcome by an uneasy feeling. Who was she anyway, stealing photos and sleeping with strange men? This wasn't her business. She needed to return them to the suitcase.

Frankie started across the office toward her and she scooped up the photos hurriedly, tucking them back into her bag. Had he seen? She held her breath, waiting for him to ask about them, but he did not. "I've got papers to file at the courthouse," he said instead.

"I'll take them," she replied quickly.

"Are you sure?"

"It will do me good to stretch my legs," she said. "I'll do it on my way home."

"All right, but be sure to leave early to make sure you're there by four thirty because the fellas in the clerk's office tend to knock off early." She nodded; that had been part of the plan. Leaving early would let her get back to Grand Central so that she could rid herself of the photos more quickly.

Nearly two hours later, Grace emerged from the subway at Grand Central, headed for the place she had sworn never to go again for the second time that day. She rode the escalator up to the main concourse level. The station had changed into its late-day colors now, the commuters moving more slowly now, rumpled and ready for home.

She reached into her bag, pulling the envelope out as she started for the bench. Her heart raced. She would slip the photos into the suitcase quickly, then hurry away before anyone could see her and ask questions. Then the whole mess would be over.

She reached the bench and looked over her shoulder to make sure no one in the hurried crowd was watching. She knelt and peered beneath the bench.

The suitcase in which she had found the photos was gone.

CHAPTER FIVE

MARIE

Scotland, 1944

Marie was dreaming of a morning when she and Tess were making scones, warm and buttery. She put them in a paper-lined basket for Tess to take so they might have a picnic in the garden. Marie reached for a scone and was ready to pop it in her mouth when a sudden bang caused her hand to freeze, suspended in midair.

Pounding on the door shook Marie from sleep. "What is it?" Before she could stand, the door flew open and she was doused with a bucket of icy water. Her skin screamed as the freezing wetness seeped through her nightgown and bedclothes.

Harsh lights switched on. *"En Français!"* a female voice scolded.

Marie sat up, trying to get her bearings. Scotland, she remembered. It had been nearly midnight when the taxi from the rail station had left her in front of the fog-shrouded manor. A sentry at the desk had led her to a room with several beds and left her without further instructions.

She swung her feet to the floor. A woman in a gray dress loomed over her, glowering. "You must answer in French, even when asleep. It is not enough to know the language. You must think in French, dream in it. You are to be out front and dressed for the run in five minutes." She turned and walked through the door, leaving Marie cold and shaking.

As Marie scampered to her feet, she looked at the empty bed next to hers. There were six beds in all, arranged in two dormitory-style rows flush against the bare, beige walls. Except for her own, they were neatly made. There had been other girls. She recalled hearing their breathing in the darkness as she had tried to change into the nightdress she'd been issued without waking them. But the rest of the girls were gone, up and out already, as they were meant to be. Why had no one woken her?

Hurriedly, Marie hung the wet nightdress on the hissing radiator. In the trunk at the foot of the bed, there were two identical sets of clothing, olive cotton trousers and shirts and a pair of black rubber-soled boots. She changed into one and put on the similarly drab coat she'd been issued, then stepped from the dorm room into the musty corridor of Arisaig House, the gray stone manor turned Special Operations Executive training facility. Though it was not yet dawn, the hallway was bustling with agents, mostly men as well as a smattering of women, presumably going to various classes and assignments.

Outside, the predawn February air of the western Scottish Highlands was biting, and despite her dry clothes, Marie shivered from the earlier dampness. She dearly wished for the muffler that had been confiscated upon arrival, deemed by the clerk as "too English." The fog had lifted and she could see now that the manor was situated on a sloping bluff, nestled among bare, ancient woodlands that had not yet awakened from winter. The back of the estate rolled gently down to dark, still waters, set against a cluster of hills on the far banks. On a pleasant day, it might have felt more like a country resort than a covert training center.

Marie looked about uncertainly, then spied a small group of women who had assembled on the front lawn. None of them spoke as she approached.

The ground rumbled suddenly under Marie's feet. She flinched and braced for impact, immediately transported back to the bombing raids in London just a few years earlier that sent them all into the subways and shelters at night. But the earth stilled.

"Just a practice drill," one of the other girls whispered. "Some of the blokes at explosives training." The explanation, meant to be reassuring, was not. They were training with actual explosives, which made the mission ahead seem all the more real.

The cluster of women started on their run without speaking, following a path along the water's edge. At the front of the pack, a slight girl who could not be more than twenty seemed to lead the group, setting the pace with her short, spindly legs. If Marie had ever given thought to what an agent might look like, she would not have fit the bill. But she was surprisingly fast, and as the others followed behind her in a formation that seemed silently agreed upon, Marie struggled to keep up.

The run proceeded along a narrow trail up a tall hill, perhaps a mountain; Marie could not see the top and she was already struggling to control her breath as the incline grew steeper. Taking in the path ahead, the doubts she'd had at signing on for this grew; no one had ever considered her particularly strong or worthy of doing meaningful things, not even Marie herself. What made her think she could do this now?

To distract herself from the effort, she studied the assembly of bobbing heads in front of her. There were five women, all dressed in khaki pants and boots like herself. They ran with an ease that suggested they had been doing it for some time and were considerably more fit.

They reached a rocky plateau. "Rest," the lead girl instructed and they paused, some taking drinks from canteens they'd carried. Marie had seen a metal water bottle alongside the clothing she'd been issued, but in her haste had not thought to bring it along.

"Onward!" the girl at the front cried after less than a minute. The others tucked away their canteens and the pack surged forward, only their footsteps breaking the silence. What seemed like hours later, they reached the summit. The fog had begun to lift and sparrows called morning greetings to one another. Marie took in the pinkening sky above Arisaig House, and the sparkling waters of the loch below. She had never been to the Scottish Highlands before coming here to train. Under other circumstances, it would have been idyllic.

The girls started down the hill without pausing. The run was less physically strenuous, but navigating the twisted, rocky path seemed almost harder in descent. Suddenly, Marie's foot came down unevenly on a stone and her ankle folded inward. She yelped as pain shot through her lower leg. She stumbled, trying not to fall. Her first training activity and already a failure. *Keep going*, she thought. Through gritted teeth she willed herself forward. But the throbbing ache grew worse with every step. She began to lag behind the others even more, the distance growing too great not to notice. She simply could not keep up.

The girl at the front of the pack seemed to sense this. She slowed her pace and dropped to the rear. Marie waited for the younger woman to berate her for being slow and weak. Instead, she put her arm around Marie's shoulder. Though she was not quite as tall as Marie, she somehow lifted her until the toes of her injured foot seemed to scarcely touch the ground.

"Come," she said. "Pretend we're dancing at one of those fancy clubs in London." The notion was so far-fetched and removed from what they were doing that Marie found herself smiling through the pain. With a strength that seemed superhuman, the girls pushed forward, the slight girl nearly carrying Marie as they ran to the front of the pack once more. The uneven terrain jarred her sore ankle harder with each step. Another woman came to Marie's other side and helped to support her. Marie tried to at least make herself light, so as not to be a burden. They sailed as one down the hill.

When they reached the front lawn of Arisaig House, the lead girl let go of Marie so abruptly that she almost fell. The other woman who had been helping her stepped away, too. "Thank you," Marie said, reaching for a low stone wall that ran the perimeter of the property to support herself. "I don't think it's broken," she said, testing out if it would bear her weight and grimacing. She sat on the short fence. "But perhaps some ice… Is there an infirmary?"

The girl shook her head. "No time. The run took longer because we had to help you and we're late for breakfast." She did not bother to hide the annoyance in her voice. "You don't want to miss meals because there's nothing to eat in between. No food allowed in the barracks, so it's either eat now or go hungry." Her accent was northern, Marie decided. Manchester, maybe, or Leeds. "I'm Josephine, by the way. They call me Josie." She had a cap of dark curls that had been cut into a short, crude bob and skin a shade darker than the others, like warm caramel.

"Marie."

Josie lowered her arm to help her to her feet, then gestured toward Marie's still-damp hair. "I see you've had the Poirot shower." Marie cocked her head, not understanding. "She doused you for not getting up." Josie's dark eyes sparkled with amusement. Marie wondered if the other girls had left her sleeping purposefully so she would get soaked, a kind of hazing. "Madame Poirot, she's our instructor in all things French. Somewhere between a headmistress and a drill sergeant."

Marie followed the others into the manor. The dining hall was a massive ballroom that had been converted, with long wooden tables running the length of the room. It had an air of civility that stood in sharp contrast to the dark, cold hike. The tables were set with linen napkins and decent porcelain. Servers poured coffee from silver urns. A smattering of agents, male and female, were already seated. The men sat separately, and Marie wondered if that was by rule or preference.

Marie found an open place at the women's table next to Josie. She took a too-large sip from her water glass, nearly spilling it in her thirst from the run. Then she reached for a piece of baguette. The food was French, but austere—no extras, as if to acclimate them to what they would find in the field.

"How many of us are there?" Marie asked. It almost felt audacious to include herself in their number when she had just arrived. "The women, I mean."

"We don't ask questions," Josie said, her words a rebuke of Eleanor's when she recruited Marie. But then she answered. "About forty, including those who already deployed—and those who've gone missing."

Marie's head snapped around. "Missing?"

"Missing in action, presumed dead."

"What happened to them?"

"No one knows."

"But we're radio operators, for goodness sake. Is it really that dangerous?"

Josie threw back her head and laughed so loudly the men at the next table looked up. "Where do you think you'll be broadcasting from, BBC Studios? You're transmitting in Occupied France and the Germans will do anything to stop you." Then her expression grew serious. "Six weeks."

"Excuse me?"

"That's the average life expectancy of a radio operator in France. Six weeks."

A cold chill ran up Marie's spine. Though she had known on some level that the work she'd accepted was dangerous, she had not grasped how deadly it was. If she'd realized the likelihood that she wouldn't be returning to Tess, she never would have accepted. She needed to leave, now.

A blonde woman about her age seated across from Marie reached over and patted her arm. "I'm Brya. Don't let her worry you, dear."

"In French," Madame Poirot scolded from the doorway. Even among themselves they were to maintain the fiction they would have to portray once deployed. "Good habits start now." Josie mimicked this last phrase, mouthing the words silently.

A whistle, shrill and abrupt, caused Marie to jump. She turned to see a burly colonel in the doorway to the dining hall. "Breakfast canceled—all of you back to barracks for inspection!" There was a nervous murmur among the girls as they started from the table.

Marie swallowed a last mouthful of baguette, then followed the others hurriedly down the corridor and up a flight of stairs to their dormitory-style room. She flung the nightdress she'd hung to dry on the radiator beneath her pillow. The colonel burst in without knocking, followed by his aide-de-camp.

Josie was staring at her oddly. It was the necklace, Marie realized. A tiny locket shaped like a butterfly on a simple gold chain, Hazel had given it to her when Tess was born. Marie had hidden it, a flagrant violation of the order that all personal belongings be surrendered at the start of training. This morning, in the scramble to get dry and dressed, she had forgotten to take it off.

Josie reached around Marie's neck and unclasped the necklace quietly and slipped it into her own pocket. Marie started to protest. If Josie got caught with it, the necklace would be confiscated and she would be in trouble as well.

But the gesture had caught the attention of the colonel. He walked over and flung open the trunk lid and studied Marie's belongings, seizing on her outside clothes, which she had folded neatly in the bottom. The colonel pulled out her dress and reached for the collar, where Marie had darned a small hole. He tore out the thread. "That isn't a French stitch. It would give you away in an instant."

"I wasn't planning to wear it here," Marie blurted out before realizing that answering back was a mistake.

"Having it on you if you were caught would be just as bad," he snapped, seemingly angered by her response. "And these stockings..." The colonel held up the pair she'd worn when she'd arrived the night before.

Marie was puzzled. The stockings were French, with the straight seam up the back. What could possibly be wrong with that? "Those are French!" she cried, unable to restrain herself.

"*Were* French," the colonel corrected with disdain. "No one can get this type in France anymore, or nylons at all for that matter. The girls are painting their legs now with iodine." Anger rose in Marie. She had not been here a day; how could they expect her to know these things?

The aide-de-camp joined in, snatching a pencil from the nightstand beside Marie's bed, which wasn't even hers. "This is an English pencil and the Germans know it. Using this would give you away immediately. You would be arrested and likely killed."

"Where?" Josie burst out suddenly, interrupting. All eyes turned in her direction. "We don't ask questions," she had admonished just a few minutes earlier at breakfast. But she seemed to do it deliberately now to draw the focus from Marie. "Where would it get me killed? We still don't know where we are bloody well going!" Marie admired Josie's nerve.

The colonel walked over to Josie and stood close, glowering down his nose at her. "You may be a princess, but here you're no one. Just another girl who can't do the job." Josie held his gaze, unwavering. Several seconds passed. "Radio training in five minutes, all of you!" he snapped, before turning on his heel and leaving. The aide followed suit.

"Thank you," Marie said to Josie when the others girls had left the room for training.

"Here." Josie handed Marie back her necklace. She went to her own drawer of clothing and rummaged about, then pulled out a pair of woolen tights. "They have this kind in France, so they won't dock you for it. They're my last pair, though. Don't wreck them."

"He called you a princess," Marie remarked as they straightened out the belongings that had been set topsy-turvy during the inspection. "Is it true?" She reminded herself that she should not be asking. They were not supposed to talk about their backgrounds.

"My father was the leader of a Sufi tribe." Marie would not have taken Josie for Indian, but it explained her darker complexion and beautiful, coal-like eyes.

"Then what on earth are you doing fighting for Britain?" Marie asked.

"A lot of our boys are fighting. There's a whole squadron who are spitfire pilots—Sikhs, Hindus—but you don't hear about that. I'm not supposed to be here, really," she confided in a low voice. "But not because of my father. You see, my eighteenth birthday isn't until next month." Josie was even younger than she thought.

"What do your parents think?"

"They're both gone, killed in a fire when I was twelve. It was just me and my twin brother, Arush. We didn't like the orphanage, so we lived on our own." Marie shuddered inwardly; it was the nightmare she feared in leaving Tess, a child left parentless. And Tess would not even be left with a sibling. "Arush has been missing in action since Ardennes. Anyway, I was working in a factory when I heard they were looking for girls, so I turned up and persuaded them to take me. I keep hoping that if I get over there, I can find out what happened to him." Josie's eyes had a determined look and Marie could tell that the young girl who seemed so tough still hoped against the odds to find her brother alive. "And you? What tiara are you wearing when you aren't fighting the Germans?"

"None," Marie replied. "I've got a daughter."

"Married then?"

"Yes..." she began, the lie that she had created after Richard left almost a reflex. Then she stopped. "That is, no. He left me when my daughter was born."

"Bastard." They both chuckled.

"Please don't tell anyone," Marie said.

"I won't." Josie's expression grew somber. "Also, since we are sharing secrets, my mother was Jewish. Not that it is anyone's business."

"The Germans will make it their business if they find out," Brya chimed in, sticking her head in the doorway and overhearing. "Hurry now, we're late for radio training."

"I don't know why I'm here," Marie confessed when it was just the two of them once more. She had signed up largely for the money. But what good was that if it cost her life?

"None of us do," Josie replied, though Marie found that hard to believe. Josie seemed so strong and purposeful. "Every one of us is scared and alone. You've said it aloud once. Now bury it and never mention it again.

"Anyway, your daughter is your reason for being here," Josie added as they started for the doorway. "You're fighting for her and the world she will live in." Marie understood then. It was not just about the money. To create a fairer world for Tess to grow up in; now, that was something. "In your moments of doubt, imagine your daughter as a grown woman. Think then of what you will tell her about the part you played in the war. Or as my mother said, 'Create a story of which you will be proud.'"

Josie was right, Marie realized. She had been made all her life, first by her father and then Richard, to feel as though she, as a girl, had no worth. Her mother, though loving, had done little through her own powerlessness to correct that impression. Now Marie had a chance to create a new story for her daughter. If she could do it. Suddenly Tess, the one thing that had held her back, seemed to propel her forward.

CHAPTER SIX

ELEANOR

Scotland, 1944

Eleanor stood at the entrance to the girls' dormitory, listening to them breathe.

She hadn't been planning to come north to Arisaig House. The trip from London wasn't an easy one: two train transfers before the long overnight that reached the Scottish Highlands that morning at dawn. She hoped the sun might break through and clear the clouds. But the mountains remained shrouded in darkness.

Upon arrival, she slipped into Arisaig House unannounced, but for showing her identification to the clerk at the desk. There was a time to be seen and a time to keep hidden from sight. The latter, she'd decided. She needed to see herself how the training was going with this lot, whether or not the girls would be ready.

It was a cool midmorning in March. The girls had finished radio class and were making their way to weapons and combat. Eleanor watched from behind a tree as a young military officer demonstrated a series of grappling moves designed to escape a choke hold. Hand-to-hand combat training had been one of the harder-fought struggles for Eleanor—the others at Norgeby House had not thought it necessary for the women, arguing that they would not possibly find themselves in a situation where it was needed. But Eleanor had been firm, bypassing the others and going straight to the Director to make her case: the women would be in exactly the same position as the men; they should be able to defend themselves.

She watched now as the instructor pointed out the vulnerable spots (throat, groin, solar plexus). The instructor gave an order, which Eleanor could not hear, and the girls faced each other with empty hands. Josie, the scrappy young Sikh girl they'd recruited from the north, reached up and grabbed Marie in a choke hold. Marie struggled, seeming to feel the limits of her own strength. She delivered a weak jab to the solar plexus. It was not just Marie who struggled; almost all of the girls were ill at ease with the physicality of the drill.

The doubts that had brought Eleanor north to check on the girls redoubled. It had been three months since they had dropped the first of the female recruits into Europe. There were more than two dozen deployed now, scattered throughout northern France and Holland. From first, things had not gone smoothly. One had been arrested on arrival. Another girl had her radio dropped into a stream and she had to wait weeks until a second could be sent to begin transmitting. Still others, despite the months of training, were simply unable to fit in and pass as Frenchwomen or maintain the fiction of their cover stories and had to be recalled.

Eleanor had fought for the girls' unit, put forth the idea and defended it. She had insisted that they receive the very same training, just as rigorous and thorough as the men. Watching them struggle in training now, though, she wondered if perhaps the others had been right. What if they simply didn't have what it took?

A shuffling behind Eleanor interrupted her thoughts. She turned to find Colonel McGinty, the senior military official at Arisaig House, standing behind her. "Miss Trigg," he said. They had met once before when the colonel had come to London for a debriefing. "My aide told me you were here." So much for quiet arrivals. Since taking charge of the women's unit, Eleanor's reputation and profile within SOE had grown in ways that made it difficult to operate discreetly.

"I'd prefer the girls not know, at least not yet. And I'd like to review all of their files when I'm done here."

He nodded. "Of course. I'll make arrangements."

"How are they doing?"

The colonel pursed his lips. "Well enough, I suppose, for women."

Not good enough, Eleanor fought the urge to scream. The women needed to be ready. The work they would be doing, delivering messages and making contact with locals who could provide safe houses for weapons or fleeing agents, was every bit as dangerous as the men's. She was sending them into Occupied France and several of them into the Paris area, a viper's nest controlled by Hans Kriegler and his notorious intelligence agency, the SD, whose primary focus was finding and stopping agents exactly like the girls. They would need every ounce of wit, strength and skill to evade capture and survive.

"Colonel," she said finally. "The Germans will not treat the women any more gently than the men." She spoke slowly, trying to contain her frustration. "They need to be ready." They needed this group of girls on the ground as soon as possible. But sending them before they were ready would be a death sentence.

"Agreed, Miss Trigg."

"Double their training, if necessary."

"We're using every spare minute of the day. But as with the men, there are some who simply aren't suited."

"Then send them home," she said sharply.

"Then, ma'am, there would be none." These last words were a dig, echoing the sentiments of the officers at Norgeby House that the women would never be up to the task. He bowed slightly and walked away.

Was that true? Eleanor wondered, as she followed the girls from the field where they'd practiced grappling to the nearby firing range. Surely they could all not be so unfit for the job.

A new instructor was working with them now, showing them how to reload a Sten gun, the narrow weapon, easily concealed, that some of them might use in the field. The women, as couriers and radio operators, would not be issued guns as a rule. But Eleanor had insisted they know how to use the kinds of weapons they might encounter in the field. Eleanor followed at a distance. Josie's hands were sure and swift as she loaded ammunition into the gun, then showed Marie how to do it. Though younger, she seemed to have taken Marie under her wing. Marie's fingers were clumsy with the weapon and she dropped the ammunition twice before managing to get it in place. Eleanor watched the girl, doubts rising.

Several minutes later, a bell rang eleven thirty. The girls moved in a cluster, leaving the weapons field and starting for a barn on the corner of the property. *Keep the girls busy*, that was the motto during training. No time to worry or think ahead, or to get into trouble.

Eleanor followed them from a distance so they would not notice. The converted barn, which still had bits of hay on the floor and smelled faintly of manure, was an outpost of Churchill's Toyshop, the facility in London where gadgets designed for the agents were made. Here, the girls learned about the makeup compacts that hid compasses and lipstick containers that were actually cameras—things that each would be issued just prior to deployment.

"Don't touch!" Professor Digglesby, who oversaw the toyshop, admonished as one of the girls went too near to a table where the explosives were live. Unlike the other instructors, he was not military, but a retired academic from Magdalen College, Oxford, with white hair and thick glasses. "Today we are going to learn about decoys," he began.

Suddenly a loud shriek cut through the barn. "Aack!" a girl called Annette cried, running for the door. Eleanor stepped back so as not to be seen, then peered through the window to see what had caused the commotion. The girls had scattered, trying to get as far away as possible from one of the tables where a rat perched in the corner, seeming strangely unafraid.

Marie did not run, though. She crept forward carefully, so as not to startle the rat. She grabbed a broom from the corner and raised it above her head, as if to strike a blow. "Wait!" Professor Digglesby said, rushing over. He picked up the rat, but it didn't move.

Marie reached out her hand. "It's dead."

"Not dead," he corrected, holding it up for the others to see. The girls inched closer. "It's a decoy." He passed the fake rat around so the girls could inspect it.

"But it looks so real," Brya exclaimed.

"That's exactly what the Germans will think," Professor Digglesby replied, taking back the decoy and turning it over to reveal a compartment on the underbelly where a small amount of explosives could be placed. "Until they get close." He led them outside, then walked several meters away into the adjacent field and set down the rat. "Stay back," he cautioned as he rejoined the group. He pressed a button on a detonator that he held in his hand and the rat exploded. A murmur of surprise rippled through the girls.

Professor Digglesby walked back into the workshop and returned with what appeared to be feces. "We plant detonators in the least likely of places," he added. The girls squealed with disgust. "Also fake," he muttered good-naturedly.

"Holy shit!" Josie said. A few of the others giggled. Professor Digglesby looked on disapprovingly, but Eleanor could not help but smile.

Then the instructor's expression turned grave. "The decoys may seem funny," he said. "But they are designed to save your life—and to take the enemy's."

As Professor Digglesby herded the girls back inside the barn to learn more about hidden explosives, Eleanor made her way to the manor and asked for the records room and a tray for tea. She spent the rest of the day sitting at a narrow desk beside a file cabinet on the third floor of Arisaig House, reviewing records on the girls.

There was a file on each, meticulous notes dating from her recruitment through each day of training. Eleanor read them all, committing the details to memory. "The girls," they were called, as though they were a collective, though in fact they were so very different. Some had been at Arisaig House for just a few weeks; others were about to graduate on to finishing school at Beaulieu, a manor in Hampshire, which was the last step before deployment. Each had her own reasons for signing up. Brya was the daughter of Russians, driven by a hatred of the Germans for what they had done to her family outside Minsk. Maureen, a working-class girl from Manchester, had left the funeral of her husband and enlisted to take his place.

Josie, though the youngest, was the best of this lot, perhaps the best SOE had ever seen. Her skills came from the need to survive on the street. Her hands, which had surely stolen food, were sure and swift, and she ran and hid with the speed of someone who had fled the police more than once, to avoid arrest, or perhaps being sent to a children's home. She was whip-smart, too, with a kind of instinct that was bred, not taught. There was a tenacity in how she fought that reminded Eleanor of the dark places in her own past.

Eleanor had been just fifteen at the time of the pogrom in

their village outside Pinsk. She had hidden in an outhouse while the Russians savaged their village, raping wives and mothers, and killing children before their parents' eyes. She kept the knife under her pillow after that, sharpened it in the darkness when no one was looking. She'd watched helplessly as her mother whored herself to a Russian officer who lingered behind in the village. She'd done so in order to feed Eleanor and her stunning younger sister, Tatiana, who had skin of alabaster and eyes that were robin's-egg blue. But it wasn't enough for the bastard. So when Eleanor woke up one night to find him standing over her little sister's bed, she didn't hesitate. She had been preparing for that moment and she knew what she had to do.

Later in the village, they would tell the story of the Russian captain who had disappeared. They couldn't imagine that he lay buried just steps from the house, killed by the young girl who had fled with her mother and sister into the night.

But her effort to save Tatiana had come too late; she died shortly after they arrived in England, weakened by the Russian's brutal assault. If Eleanor had only known what was happening and been able to stop it sooner, her little sister might still be here today.

Eleanor and her mother never spoke of Tatiana after that. It was just as well; Eleanor suspected that if her mother did let herself think about the daughter she had lost, she would have blamed Eleanor, who hadn't been half as pretty or as good, for fighting back against the Russian. Everyone handled grief in their own way, Eleanor reflected now. For Eleanor's mother it was escaping the life she had known in the old country, changing their surname to sound more English and eschewing the Jewish neighborhood of Golders Green for the tonier Hampstead address. For Eleanor, who had felt quite literally on the run since the old country, SOE had given her a place. But it was in the women's unit that she had found her life's work.

Eleanor analyzed each file thoroughly now. The records

charted progress in each girl, to be sure, a growing sureness in marksmanship, wireless transmissions and the other skills they would need in the field. But would it be enough? In each case, it fell to Eleanor to make sure the girl had what she needed. Headquarters might deploy them too soon in the name of expediency and getting support into the field. But Eleanor would not send a single girl a moment before she was ready. And if that meant blowing the whole operation, then so be it.

Sometime later, an aide appeared at the door. "Ma'am, it's dinnertime if you'd like to come down."

"Please have a tray sent up."

The next file was Marie's. Her basic skills were competent enough, she noted from the instructor's comments. But they described her as having a lack of focus and resolve. That was something that could not be taught or punished to overcome. She recalled watching Marie struggle earlier with weapons and grappling. Had recruiting her been a mistake? The girl had looked weak, a society girl not able to last the week in these strange circumstances. But she was a single mother raising her child in London, or at least she had been before the war. That took grit. She would test the girl tomorrow, Eleanor decided, and make the call whether to keep her or send her packing once and for all.

It was nearly eleven o'clock, well after the lights-out bell had sounded in the barracks below, when her vision blurred from too much reading and she was forced to stop. She set down the files and crept from the records room to the barracks below.

She listened to the girls' breathing in the darkness, almost in unison. She could just make out Marie and Josie in adjacent beds, their heads tilted toward one another conspiratorially in sleep, as though they were still talking. Each girl had come from a different place, united here into kind of a team. But they would be scattered again just as quickly. They could not find their strength from one another because out in the field they would have to rely on themselves. She wondered how they would take the news tomorrow, how one would fare without the other.

The aide who had brought her food earlier came up behind her. "Ma'am, a phone call from London."

Eleanor walked to the office he indicated and lifted the receiver to her ear. "Trigg here."

The Director's voice crackled across the line. "How are the girls?" he asked without preamble. "Are they ready?" It was not like him to be at headquarters so late and there was an unmistakable urgency to his voice.

Eleanor struggled with how to answer the question. This was her program and if anything was out of sorts, she would be held to blame. She could hear the men back at headquarters, saying that they had known it all along. But more important than her reputation or her pride was the girls. Their actual preparedness was all that would save them and the aims they were trying to achieve.

She pushed aside her doubts. "They will be."

"Good. They must. The bridge mission is a go." Eleanor's stomach did a queer flip. SOE had taken on dozens of risky missions, but blowing up the bridge outside Paris would be by far the most dangerous—and most critical. And one of these girls would be at the center of it. "It's good that you are there to deliver the news in person. You'll let her know tomorrow?"

"Yes." Of course, she would not be telling the girl everything, just that she was going. The rest would come later, when she needed to know.

Then remembering the sleeping girls, she was flooded with doubts anew. "I don't know if she's ready," she confessed.

"She has to be." They couldn't wait any longer.

There was a click on the other end of the line and then Eleanor set the receiver back into the cradle. She tiptoed back to the girls' dorm.

Josie was curled into a ball like a child, her thumb close to her mouth in a habit she had surely broken years ago. A wave of protectiveness broke and crested over Eleanor as she remembered the sister she had lost so many years ago. She could protect these girls in a way she hadn't been able to her own sister. She needed them to do a job that was dangerous, potentially lethal, though, and then she needed them to come home safely. These were the only two things that mattered. Would she be able to manage both?

A faint smile played about Josie's lips and Eleanor wondered what she was dreaming. Just a young girl with a young girl's dreams. Eleanor would let her remain that—at least for a few more hours.

She tiptoed from the room, closing the door softly behind her.

CHAPTER SEVEN

MARIE

Scotland, 1944

Marie still hated running.

She had been at Arisaig House for almost six weeks and every morning it was the same: five miles up and back, partway around the loch and up a dreaded incline only known among the girls as "The Point." Her heels were cracked and bleeding and the blisters on her feet from all of the damp hikes seemed on the constant verge of infection. Just thinking about doing it again made her bones ache.

But, she reflected as she made her way to breakfast after splashing some water on her face to freshen up, she no longer ran at the rear of the pack. Over the weeks she had been here, she had built up speed and stamina she hadn't imagined herself to possess. She liked to keep up with Josie so that they could talk as they ran. Nothing detailed really, just a few words here or there. Josie, who had spent much of her early childhood summers in the mountains of Cumbria, would point out bits of the Scottish landscape or tell stories she'd heard from the war.

Marie had gotten to know Josie well during her weeks at training. Not just through the classes and meals; they spent long sleepless nights talking, Josie sharing stories of her childhood on the streets of Leeds with her brother, fending off scoundrels who wanted to take advantage of defenseless children. Marie shared her own past, too, of how Richard had left her penniless. She felt silly, though, complaining after all Josie had been through at such a young age. Her own childhood, while cruel, had been one of unmistakable privilege, not at all like Josie's street urchin–like experience. The two would not have known each other in different circumstances. Yet here they had become fast friends.

In the dining hall, they took their usual spots at the women's table, Josie at the head, Marie and Brya on either side. Marie unfolded her napkin carefully and placed it in her lap and started eating right away, mindful that Madame Poirot was, as ever, watching. Meals were constantly part of the lesson. The French wipe up their gravy with bread, she'd learned soon after arrival. And never ask for butter—they no longer have any. Even at mealtime, it seemed the girls were being scrutinized. The slightest mistake could trip you up.

Marie recalled a night shortly after she had arrived at Arisaig House when they had been served a really good wine at dinner. "Don't drink it," Josie had whispered. Marie's hand froze above her glass. "It's a trick." For a second she thought Josie meant the drink had been poisoned. Marie lifted the wineglass and held it beneath her nose, sniffing for the hint of sulfur as she had been trained but finding none. She looked around and noticed them plying girls with a second glass, then a third. The girls' cheeks were becoming flushed and they were chatting as if they didn't have a care. Marie understood then that the test was to see if they would become reckless after drinking too much.

"You're in an awful hurry," Josie observed as they ate breakfast. "Hot date?"

"Very funny. I have to retake codes."

Josie nodded, understanding. Marie had already failed the test for the previous unit in radio operator class once. There would not be a third chance. If she couldn't do it today and prove that she could transmit, she would be sent packing.

What would be so bad about that? Marie mused as she ate. She had not asked for this strange, difficult life, and a not-so-small part of her wanted to fail and go home so she could see Tess.

She'd trained intensively from morning until night since coming to Arisaig House. Most of her time was spent in front of a radio set, studying to be a wireless telegraph operator (W/Ts, they were called). But she'd learned other things, too, things she could not have possibly imagined: how to set up dead and live letter drops and the difference between the two (the former being a pre-agreed location where one agent could leave a message for another; the latter an in-person, clandestine meeting), how to identify a suitable rendezvous spot, one where a woman could plausibly be found for other reasons.

But if running had gotten easier, the rest of the training had not. Despite all she learned, it was never enough. She couldn't set an explosives charge without her fingers shaking, was hopeless at grappling and shooting. Perhaps most worryingly, she could not lie and maintain a cover story. If she could not do that under mock interrogation, when the means of coercion were limited, how could she ever hope to do it in the field? Her one strength was French, which had been better than everyone else's before she arrived. On all other fronts, she was failing.

Marie was suddenly homesick. Signing on had been a mistake. She could take off the uniform and turn it in, promise to say nothing and start home to Tess. Such doubts were nothing new; they nagged at her all through the long hours of lecture and at night as she studied and slept. She did not share them again, of course. The other girls didn't have doubts, or if they did they kept them to themselves. They were resolute, focused and purposeful, and she needed to be, too, if she hoped to remain. She could not afford to show fear.

"Headquarters is here," Josie announced abruptly. "Something must be going on."

Marie followed Josie's gaze upward to a balcony overlooking the dining hall where a tall woman stood, looking down on them. *Eleanor.* Marie had not seen the woman who had recruited her since that night more than six weeks earlier. She'd thought of Eleanor often, though, during these long, lonely weeks of training. What had made Eleanor think she could do this blasted job, or that she would want to?

Marie stood and waved in Eleanor's direction, as though seeing an old friend. But Eleanor eyed her coolly, giving no sign of recognition. Did Eleanor remember their meeting in the toilet, or was Marie one of so many faceless girls she had recruited? At first, Marie's cheeks stung as if slapped. But then Marie understood: she was not to acknowledge her past life or anyone in it. Another test failed. She sat back down.

"You've met her?" she asked Josie.

Josie nodded. "When she recruited me. She was up in Leeds, for a conference, she said."

"She found me, too," Brya added. "In a typing pool in Essex." Each, it seemed, had been selected by Eleanor personally.

"Eleanor designed the training for us," Josie said in a low voice. "And she decides where we will go and what our assignment might be."

So much power, Marie thought. Remembering how cold and disdainful Eleanor seemed during their initial meeting in London, Marie wondered if this perhaps did not bode well for her.

"I like her," Marie said. Despite Eleanor's undeniable coldness, she possessed a strength that Marie admired greatly.

"I don't," Brya replied. "She's so cold and she thinks she's so much better than us. Why doesn't she put on a uniform and fly to France herself if she can do better?"

"She tried," Josie said quietly. "She's asked to go a dozen times, or so I've heard." Josie had an endless network of connections and sources. She made friends with everyone from the kitchen staff to the instructors and those relationships provided valuable bits of information. "But the answer is always the same. She has to remain at headquarters because her real value is here getting the lot of us ready."

Watching Eleanor on the balcony, looking out of place and almost ill at ease, Marie wondered if it might be lonely to stand in her place, and whether she sometimes wished she was one of them.

The girls finished their breakfast swiftly. Fifteen minutes later, they slipped into the lecture hall. A dozen desks were lined three by four, a radio set atop each. The instructor had posted the assignment, a complex message to be decoded and sent. Eleanor was in the corner of the room, Marie noticed, watching them intently.

Marie found her seat at the wireless and put on the headset. It was an odd contraption, sort of like a radio on which one might listen to music or the BBC, only laid flat inside a suitcase and with more knobs and dials. There was a small unit at the top of the set for transmitting, another below it for receiving. The socket for the power adapter was to the right side, and there was a spares kit, a pocket with extra parts to the left. The spares pocket also contained four crystals, each of which could be inserted in a slot on the radio to enable transmission on a different frequency.

While the others started working on the message on the board, Marie looked down at the paper the instructor had left for her to take the retest. It was the text of a Shakespeare poem:

From this day to the ending of the world,
But we in it shall be remember'd;

We few, we happy few, we band of brothers;
For he to-day that sheds his blood with me
Shall be my brother; be he ne'er so vile,
This day shall gentle his condition:
And gentlemen in England now a-bed
Shall think themselves accursed that they were not here,
And hold their manhoods cheap whiles any speaks
That fought with us upon Saint Crispin's day.

The message first had to be coded through a cipher. The ciphers were contained in a small satchel, each printed on an individual square of silk, one inch long by one inch wide. Each silk contained what was called a "worked-out key," a printed onetime cipher that would change each letter to another (for example, in this key, *a* became *m* and *o* became *w*) until the whole message made no sense at all to the naked eye. Each cipher was to be used to code the message, then discarded. Marie changed the letters in the message into the code given on the cipher and wrote down the coded message. She lit a match and burned the silk cipher as she'd been taught.

Then she began to tap out the message using the telegraph key. Marie had spent weeks learning to tap out the letters in Morse code and had spent so much time practicing she had even begun to dream in it. But she still struggled to tap swiftly and smoothly and not make mistakes, as she would need to in the field.

Operating the wireless, though, was more than a matter of simple coding and Morse. During her first week of training, the W/T instructor, a young lieutenant who had been seconded to SOE from Bletchley Park, had pulled her aside. "We have to record your fist print and give you your security checks."

"I don't understand."

"You see, radios are interchangeable—if someone has the coils and the crystals to set the frequency, the transmission will work. Anyone who gets his hands on those can use the radio to transmit. The only thing that lets headquarters know it is really you is your security checks and your fist print."

The instructor continued, "First, your fist print. Type a message to me about the weather."

"Uncoded?"

"Yes, just type." Though it seemed an odd request to Marie, she did it without question, writing a line about how the weather changed quickly here, storms blowing through one moment and giving way to sunshine the next. She looked up. "Keep going. It can be about anything really, except your personal background. The message needs to be several lines long for us to understand your fist print."

Puzzled, Marie complied. "There," she said when she had filled the page with nonsense, a story about an unexpected snowstorm the previous spring that had left snow on blooming daffodils.

The transmission printed on the teletype at the front of the room. The instructor retrieved it and held it up. "You see, this is your fist print, heavy on the first part of each word with a long pause between sentences."

"You can tell that from a single transmission?"

"Yes, although we have your other transmissions from training on file to compare." Though it made sense, Marie hadn't considered until that moment that they might have a file on her. "But really, it doesn't change from session to session. You see, your fist print is like your handwriting or signature, a style that identifies your transmission as uniquely you. How hard you strike the transmission key, the time and spacing between letters. Every radio agent has her own fist print. That's one of the ways we know it is you."

"Can I vary my fist print as kind of a signal if something is wrong?"

"No, it is very hard to communicate unlike oneself. Think about it—you don't choose your handwriting consciously. It just flows. If you wanted to write really differently, you might need to switch to your nondominant hand. Same with your fist print—it's subconscious and you can't really change it. Instead, if something is wrong, you must let us know in other ways. That's what the security checks are for."

The instructor had gone on to explain that each agent had a security check, a built-in quirk in her typing that the reader would pick up to know that it was her. For Marie, it was always making a "mistake" and typing *p* as the thirty-fifth letter in the message. There was a second security check, too, substituting *k* where a *c* belonged every other time a *k* appeared in the message. "The first security check is known as the 'bluff check,'" the instructor explained. "The Germans know we have checks, you see, and they will try to get yours out of you. You can give away the bluff check if questioned." Imagining it, Marie shuddered inwardly. "But it's the second check, the true check, that really verifies the message. You must not give it up under any circumstances."

Marie completed the retest now, making sure to include both her bluff and true checks. She looked behind her. Eleanor was still there and she seemed to be watching her specifically. Pushing down her uneasiness, Marie started on the assignment on the board, picking up speed as she worked through the longer message with a new silk cipher. A few minutes later, Marie finished typing the message. She looked up, feeling pleased.

But Eleanor ripped the transmission off the teletype and strode toward her with a scowl. "No, no!" she said, sounding frustrated. Marie was puzzled. She had typed the message correctly. "It isn't enough to simply bang at the wireless like a piano. You must communicate through the radio and 'speak' naturally so that your fist print comes through."

Marie wanted to protest that she had done that, or at least ask what Eleanor meant. But before she had the chance, Eleanor reached over and yanked the telegraph key from the wireless. “What on earth!” Marie cried. Eleanor did not answer but picked up a screwdriver and continued dismantling the set, tearing it apart piece by piece with such force that screws and bolts clattered across the floor, disappearing under the tables. The other girls watched in stunned silence. Even the instructor looked taken aback.

“Oh!” Marie cried, scrambling for the pieces. She realized in that moment she felt a kind of connection to the physical machine, the same one she had worked with since her arrival.

“It isn’t enough just to be able to operate the wireless,” Eleanor said disdainfully. “You have to be able to fix it, build it from the ground up. You have ten minutes to put it together again.” Eleanor walked away. Marie’s anger grew. This was more than payback for her earlier outburst; Eleanor wanted her to fail.

Marie stared at the dismantled pieces of the wireless set. She tried to recall the manual she’d studied at the beginning of W/T training, trying to envision the inside of the wireless set in her mind. But it was impossible.

Josie came to her side then. “Start here,” she said, righting a piece of the machine’s base that had fallen on its side and holding it so that Marie could reattach the baseplate. As she worked, the other girls stood and helped to gather the pieces that had scattered, going on hands and knees for the missing bolts. “Here,” Josie said, handing her a knob that screwed into the transmitter. She managed to tighten a screw Marie was struggling with, her tiny fingers quick and deft. Josie pointed to a place where she had not inserted a bolt just right.

At last the machine was reassembled. But would it transmit? Marie tapped the telegraph key, waited. There was a quiet click, a registering of the code she had entered. The radio worked once more.

Marie looked up from her work, wanting to see Eleanor’s reaction. But Eleanor had already left.

"Why does she hate you so much?" Josie whispered as the others returned to their seats.

Marie didn't answer. Her spine stiffened. Not bothering to ask permission, Marie stormed from the hall, looking into doorways until she found Eleanor in an empty office, reviewing a file. "Why are you so hard on me? Do you hate me?" Marie demanded, repeating Josie's question. "Did you come here just to finish me off?"

Eleanor looked up. "This isn't personal. You either have what it takes or you don't."

"And you think I don't."

"It doesn't matter what I think. I've read your file." Until that moment, Marie had not considered what it might say about her. "You are defeating yourself."

"My French is as good as any of the others, even the men."

"It is simply not enough to be as good as the men. They don't believe we can do this and so we have to be better."

Marie persisted, "My typing is getting quicker by the day, and my codes…"

"This isn't about the technical skills," Eleanor interjected. "It's about the spirit. Your radio, for example. It isn't just a machine, but it is an extension of yourself."

Eleanor reached down for a bag by her feet that Marie had not noticed before and held it out. Inside were Marie's possessions that she had arrived with that first night, her street clothes and even the necklace from Tess. Her belongings, the ones that she had stowed in the locker at the foot of her bed, had been taken out and packed. "It's all there," Eleanor said. "You can change your clothes. There will be a car out front in one hour, ready to take you back to London."

"You're kicking me out?" Marie asked, disbelieving. She felt more disappointed than she might have imagined.

"No, I'm giving you the choice to leave." She could have left anytime, Marie realized; it wasn't as if she'd enlisted. But Eleanor was holding the door open, so to speak. Inviting her to go.

Marie wondered whether it was some sort of test. But Eleanor's face was earnest. She was really giving Marie the chance. Should she take it? She could be back in London tomorrow, be with Tess by the weekend.

But curiosity nagged at her. "May I ask a question?"

Eleanor nodded. "One," she said begrudgingly.

"If I stay, what would I actually be doing over there?" For all of the training, the actual mission in the field was still very difficult to see.

"The short answer is that you are to operate a radio, to send messages to London for the network about operations on the ground, and to receive messages about airdrops of personnel and supplies." Marie nodded; she knew that much from training. "You see, we are trying to make things as difficult as possible for the Germans, slow their munitions production and disrupt the rail lines. Anything we can do to make it easier for our troops when the invasion comes. Your transmissions are critically important in keeping communications open between London and the networks in Europe so they can do that work. But you might be called on in dozens of other ways as well. That is why we must prepare you for anything."

Marie started to reach for the bag, but something stopped her. "I put the radio back together. The other girls helped a good deal, too," she added quickly.

"That's quite good." Eleanor's face seemed to soften a bit. "Well done, too, with the rat during explosives training." Marie hadn't realized Eleanor had been watching. "The others were startled. You weren't."

Marie shrugged. "We've had plenty in our house in London."

Eleanor looked at her evenly. "I would have thought your husband dealt with them."

"He did, that is he does..." Marie faltered. "My husband's gone. He left when our daughter was born."

Eleanor didn't look surprised and Marie wondered if she had learned the truth during the recruitment process and already knew. She didn't think Josie would have told. "I would say I'm sorry, but if that's the kind of scoundrel he is, it sounds like you are better off without him."

The thought had crossed Marie's mind more than once. There were lonely times, nights racked with self-doubt as to what she had done to make him leave, how she would ever survive. But in the quiet moments of the night as she nursed Tess at her breast, there came a quiet confidence, a certainty in knowing she could only rely on herself. "I suppose I am. I'm sorry I didn't say anything sooner."

"Apparently," Eleanor said drily, "you are capable of maintaining a cover story after all. We all have our secrets," she added, "but you should never lie to me. Knowing everything is the only way for me to keep you safe. I suppose, it doesn't matter, though. You're leaving, remember?" She held out the bag containing Marie's clothes. "Go change and turn in your supplies before the car arrives." She turned back to the file she had been reviewing and Marie knew that the conversation was over.

When Marie returned to the barracks, W/T class had ended and the others were on break. Josie was waiting for her, folding clothes on her neatly made bed. "How are you?" she asked with just a hint of sympathy in her voice.

Marie shrugged, not quite sure how to answer. "Eleanor said I can leave if I want."

"What are you going to do?"

Marie dropped to the edge of the bed, her shoulders slumped. "Go, I suppose. I never had any business being here in the first place."

"You never had a good reason to be here," Josie corrected

unsentimentally, still folding clothes. Her words, echoes of what Eleanor had said, stung Marie. "There has to be a *why*. I mean, take me, for instance. I've never really had a place to call home. Being here is just fine for me. It's what they want, you know," Josie added. "For us to quit. Not Eleanor, of course, but the blokes. They want us to prove that they were right—the women don't have what it takes after all."

"Maybe they *are* right," Marie answered. Josie did not speak, but pulled a small valise out from under her bed. "What are you doing?" she asked, suddenly alarmed. Surely Josie, the very best of them, had not been asked to leave SOE school. But Josie was placing her neatly folded clothes in the suitcase.

"They need me to go sooner," Josie said. "No finishing school. I'm headed straight to the field."

Marie was stunned. "No," she said.

"I'm afraid it's true. I'm leaving first thing tomorrow morning. It isn't a bad thing. This is what we came for after all."

Marie nodded. Others had left to deploy to the field. But Josie had been their bedrock. How would they go on without her?

"It isn't as if I'm dying, you know," Josie added with a wry smile.

"It's just so soon." Too soon. Though Josie couldn't say anything about her mission, Marie saw the grave urgency that had brought Eleanor all the way from London to claim her.

Remembering, Marie reached into her footlocker. "Here," she said to Josie. She pulled out the scone she'd bribed one of the cooks to make. "I had it made for your birthday." Josie was turning eighteen in just two days' time. Only now she wouldn't be here for it. "It's cinnamon, just like you said your brother used to get you for your birthday."

Josie didn't speak for several seconds. Her eyes grew moist and a single tear trickled down her cheek. Marie wondered if the gesture had been a mistake. "I didn't think after he was gone that anyone would remember my birthday again." Josie smiled slightly then. "Thank you." She broke the scone into two pieces and handed one back to Marie.

"So you see, you can't leave," Josie said, brushing the crumbs from her mouth. "You'll need to stay to take care of these youngsters." She gestured toward the empty beds. Marie did not answer, but there was a note of truth in Josie's joke. Three of the girls were newer than herself now, having replaced some of the agents who had already deployed.

"There will be a new girl to take my place." The thought was almost unbearable. But Josie was right; whoever came next would need her help to navigate this difficult place as Josie and the others had done when Marie herself first arrived.

"The girls need you now more than ever. It's not just about how long you've been here," Josie added. "You've grown so much since that day you stumbled in here, unable to make it to The Point on a run or to hide your English contraband." They both smiled at the memory. "You can do this," Josie said firmly. "You are stronger than you know. Now, on to detonation. I can't wait to see what piece of crap Professor Digglesby blows up today." Josie started from the barracks. She did not wait or ask if Marie was coming. In that moment, it was as if she was already gone.

Marie sat motionless on her bed, staring out at the dark waters of the loch. Behind the windswept hills, the sky was a sea of gray. She imagined if she did not move, nothing would change. Josie would not deploy and she would not have to face her own terrible choice of whether to leave. They had created kind of a separate world here where, despite the training, it was almost possible to forget about the danger and sorrow outside. Only now that world was ending.

She looked down at her belongings in the bag, relics from another era. She could have her life back, as she'd been dreaming for weeks. But she was part of something bigger now, she realized as she looked across the barracks. The days of training and struggling with the other girls had woven them together in a kind of fabric from which she could not tear herself away.

She pulled her hand back. "Not yet," she whispered. She closed the bag, then went and joined the others.

CHAPTER EIGHT

GRACE

New York, 1946

The suitcase was gone.

Grace stood motionless in the concourse of Grand Central, letting the end-of-day crowds swirl around her as she stared at the space beneath the bench where the suitcase had been that morning. For a moment, she thought she might have imagined it. But the photographs she had removed from the suitcase were there, thick in her hand. No, someone had taken or moved it in the hours while she had been at work.

That the suitcase was no longer under the bench should not have been a surprise. It belonged to someone and hours had passed. It was only natural that someone had come to claim it. But now that it was gone, the mystery of the suitcase and the photographs became all the more intriguing. Grace looked down at the photos in her hand, which she felt bad for having taken in the first place.

"Excuse me," Grace called to a porter as he passed.

He stopped, tipped his red cap in her direction. "Ma'am?"

"I'm looking for a suitcase."

"If it's in the stored luggage, I can get it for you." He held out his hand. "Can I have your ticket?"

"No, you don't understand. It isn't my bag. There was one left under a bench earlier this morning. Over there." She pointed. "I'm trying to find out where it went. Brown, with writing on the side."

The porter looked perplexed. "But if it isn't your bag, why are you looking for it?"

Good question, Grace thought. She considered saying something about the photographs, but decided against it. "I'm trying to find its owner," she said finally.

"I can't help you without a ticket. You might want to ask at the lost and found," he replied.

The lost and found was on the lower level of the station in a quiet, musty corner that seemed worlds away from the bustle above. An older man with white sideburns wearing a brimmed visor and a vest sat behind the counter, reading a newspaper. "I'm looking for a suitcase, brown with chalk writing on it."

The clerk shifted the unlit cigar he was chewing to the corner of his mouth. "When did you lose it?"

"Today," she said, feeling that it was in some sense true.

The man disappeared into a back room and she heard him rummaging through bins. Then he reemerged and shook his head. "Nothing."

"Are you certain?" She peered over his shoulder, craning her neck and trying to see the stacks of bags and other lost belongings on the other side of the wall.

"Yup." He pulled a ledger from beneath the counter and opened it. "Everything that gets turned in is logged here. No suitcases in the past day."

Then why, she wondered, had he bothered checking in the back? "Is it unusual for a person to lose something as big as a suitcase?"

"You'd be surprised the things people leave behind," he replied. "Bags, boxes. A couple of bikes. Even dogs."

"And it all comes here?"

"All except the dogs. Those go to the city pound. You can leave your name and information. If someone turns in your bag, we'll contact you," he added.

"Grace Flemming," she said, using her maiden name as a reflex. She stopped, suddenly ashamed. Was she erasing Tom already, as if their marriage had never happened at all?

Hurriedly, she scribbled down the address of the boardinghouse in the ledger where the clerk indicated. Then she stepped away from the counter and started up the steps. When she reached the main level, she crossed the concourse to the bench and stopped, staring at the spot underneath where the suitcase had been. Perhaps the owner had come back for it after all. Guilt washed over her as she imagined a woman opening the bag and finding the photographs gone.

Grace stood, holding the orphaned photos uncertainly. She could turn them in to the lost and found on their own. They weren't her problem, really. Then she would be done with the whole matter. But they remained weighty in her hand. She was responsible for separating the photos from the suitcase. The owner was probably wondering where her pictures had gone. Perhaps she was even distraught over losing them. No, Grace had taken the photos and it was her responsibility to return them.

But how? The suitcase had disappeared and Grace had no idea as to the owner or who might have claimed it. Or almost no idea, she corrected, remembering the single name that had been chalked on the bag: *Trigg*. She recalled, too, that there was a watermark on the photos. She opened the envelope furtively, as though someone might be watching. The watermark was there: *O'Neill's, London*. The suitcase was from England, or at least the photos were. Perhaps she should take them to the British consulate.

But the clock in the middle of the station showed half past five and the throng of rush hour commuters was beginning to thin. The consulate would be closed now. Grace was suddenly weary.

She wanted to go home to her room at the boardinghouse—which she hadn't seen in nearly two days—and soak in a hot bath and forget all of this.

Grace's stomach rumbled. She started out of the station toward the coffee shop across the street. Ruth's, it was called, though the *th* of the lighted sign above the door had burned out. No fancy steakhouse dinner tonight. Really she needed to stop eating out altogether, get some groceries to make simple meals in the rooming house kitchen and save a bit of money. Frugality was not something she'd grown up with, but a skill that she had honed these past months living in the city and stretching what little she had left.

She took a seat at the nearly empty counter. "A grilled cheese sandwich and a Pepsi, please," she said to the yellow-haired waitress after counting the change in her purse mentally and deciding that she had enough.

As the waitress pulled her drink from the soda fountain, Grace's eyes traveled to the television above the counter. An image of Grand Central flashed across the screen. They were talking about the woman who had been hit by a car and killed in front of the station that morning.

"Turn it up," she said suddenly, forgetting in her urgency to be polite.

The newscaster continued, "The accident took place at 9:10 a.m…" That was just a few minutes before she walked by.

Then a woman's image flashed across the screen, dark hair drawn back, face somber. "The victim," said the newscaster, "has been identified as British citizen Eleanor Trigg."

Remembering the name that had been chalked on the suitcase, Grace froze. The woman whose photographs Grace had taken was the very one who had been killed in the accident.

CHAPTER NINE

MARIE

England, 1944

Marie sat in her room in the barracks at Tangmere Airfield, trying not to sweat through the wool of her travel suit because she would surely be wearing it for days. As she waited, alone, she rechecked her papers: identification and ration cards, travel and work permits. Each was false—and each had to be perfect.

It was not the first time Marie had prepared to go. Three nights earlier, as she waited, she had watched the fog roll in, low and menacing. She knew there would be no flying that night. Still she'd gone through the motions, picking up her bag and walking dutifully outside to the car. She had made it to the side of the plane before the mission was called off.

Now Marie waited in her room once more, hoping that the rain she felt coming in the night air was not enough to stop the flight. It was nearly a month since that day at Arisaig House when Eleanor had given her the option of giving up and going home. Often she wondered if she had made the right choice. Each night before she went to bed, she told herself she might ask the next day if the offer to leave still stood. But there was something about the crispness of those mornings in the Scottish Highlands, the mist rising above the hills as the girls marched stiff-backed around the loch, that had gotten into her soul. This was where she was meant to be, and there was no turning away.

It was more than just the beauty of the Scottish countryside, which she would inevitably leave behind, that held her. And it wasn't just about the money anymore either. After Josie had deployed, something within Marie had changed. She became engrossed in the training. She strained to learn her radio codes quicker and faster. "You might have to transmit from inside a toilet so quickly no one suspects anything more than a trip to the loo," the instructor had once explained. She'd completed a three-day mission outside without food, forced to trap or scavenge from the brush whatever she needed to eat. She could feel the other girls watching and following her lead. It was as if she had risen up to take Josie's place. She became so focused on her role and succeeding at the job that she forgot to be afraid.

Then a week earlier, she'd been called to the office at Arisaig House before the morning run and told to pack her things. Her departure was so abrupt she had not even had time to say goodbye to any of the others. There was no explanation, just a black sedan with a driver who hadn't spoken. As the rugged coast faded behind her, she wondered if she were being sent home. But instead, they had brought her down to the military airfield in rural West Sussex to take care of the last-minute items. There was endless paperwork to be completed, which seemed odd for a job and a mission that wasn't meant to exist at all.

The morning after she arrived at the air base there was a knock on her door. "Eleanor." Marie had not seen her since her visit to Arisaig House. Eleanor, she had come to realize, was much more than just the recruitment officer she professed to be at their first meeting. In fact, she ran everything at SOE having to do with the women.

Eleanor had summoned her to follow and led Marie to a private office in a building not far from the barracks at the airfield where Marie had been staying. She produced a bottle of wine. It seemed strange that they would serve alcohol in the middle of the day.

But Eleanor didn't mean for them to drink the wine this time; instead, she unwrapped the newspaper that covered the bottle and pored over the first page. "Ah, the ration cards are changing in Lyon!" It was the news, not the drink inside it, which interested Eleanor.

Eleanor continued, "You must stay current on affairs. Outdated intelligence is worse than no intelligence at all and will give you away twice as quickly.

"And you must never neglect the importance of open-source intelligence," Eleanor continued. Marie cocked her head. "Information you can learn that is publicly available, from the newspapers, the locals. The flotsam method of intelligence gathering, it's called. Little pieces of information gathered from the most mundane sources. Things that you can observe with your own eyes, like movements of trains and soldiers. Like when you see a bunch of Jerrys cashing in their francs, you know they are about to deploy."

Eleanor looked up from the newspaper. "You are Renee Demare, a shopgirl from Épernay, a town south of Reims," she began without introduction.

Marie understood then that she was being given her cover. Her heart surged with excitement and fear. "So you're sending me after all?"

"It was always the plan. I just had to be sure," Eleanor said simply.

"About me?" Eleanor nodded. Marie wanted to ask if she was sure, but even now feared the answer.

"So your cover..." Eleanor said. Marie's excitement at going was quickly replaced by nervousness. Cover was the last step before deployment. When she had learned this during training, Marie had been surprised. It seemed to her that it would have made more sense to have the story well in advance and begin to wear it like a second skin. They didn't want the agents talking about their cover during training at SOE school, though, knowing details about one another that they should not. "You are to say that your family was killed during an early air raid," Eleanor explained. "And that you've come to live in an apartment owned by your late aunt."

"But if they check the records in Épernay..."

"Impossible. The *mairie* has been destroyed by fire." The location had been chosen deliberately for the lack of records available from the town hall. So much detail and thought. "If you are captured, you must maintain this identity. If impossible, you may reveal only your name and rank, nothing more. You hold out for forty-eight hours. That will give the others time to recover from the damage."

"And then?"

"And then they will break you. The region you are going to is controlled in part by a high-ranking German officer called Hans Kriegler, who heads up the Sicherheitsdienst, or SD, German intelligence. They are ruthless and absolutely committed to hunting down every last one of our agents. Do not expect to be treated any differently because you are a woman. If you are caught, they will torture you, and once they have learned all that they think you know, you will likely be killed. You should kill yourself first if it comes to that." Eleanor stared at her levelly, not blinking. Marie struggled not to show emotion on her face. Though she had been warned of the danger before, it never got easier to hear. Eleanor continued, "You'll be landed by Lysander."

"What about parachute training?" Marie asked. She had heard that this was how some of the girls had been sent.

Eleanor shook her head. "There's no time. You are needed on the ground sooner." Josie had gone in a rush, too, Marie recalled. What had given rise to the sudden need? "You will be deploying as a radio operator with the Vesper network. Vesper is one of our most important circuits because it covers Paris, as well as so much of the ground the Allies will need to cross after the invasion. The network is engaged in a very aggressive campaign of sabotage and their need for radio communication is frequent. At the same time, it is one of the most heavily occupied regions in France. You will have to avoid detection by both the SD and the police." Eleanor's voice was sharp with intensity and her pupils narrowed as she focused. "Do you understand?"

Marie nodded, taking it all in. But her stomach had a queer feeling. This was the most she had learned about her mission. In some ways, it had been easier not knowing. "You'll be working for Vesper himself," Eleanor said. "He fought in Marseille, survived many battles. He's an excellent commander. He'll expect the best from you."

"Like someone else," Marie said, realizing her mistake too late. She had never joked with Eleanor before and she waited for her to bristle at the familiarity.

But the older woman smiled. "I suppose I should take that as a compliment." Marie saw then that Eleanor was neither rude nor mean. She had been hard on the girls because they could not afford an accident that might cause themselves or others their lives.

There came a knocking at the door, drawing Marie from her memories of her conversation with Eleanor days earlier. "Yes?" She rose, but before she could reach the door, it opened a crack.

"Hearse is here," a man's voice called. Marie cringed at the reference to the car that would take her to the plane. He reached in the room and picked up the case containing her wireless radio, which had been brought from Scotland along with her.

Eleanor waited in front of the barracks in the darkness. Marie was surprised to see the tip of a cigarette gleaming just above her hand. Eleanor did not speak, but started toward the black Vauxhall. Marie followed, handing her bags to the driver. She and Eleanor climbed into the back of the car. "The curfew in Paris has been changed to nine thirty," Eleanor said as they drove through the military base in the darkness.

The night air tickled Marie's nose and she sneezed. She reached into a pocket. Her hand closed around something unfamiliar. She pulled out a tailor ticket and a cinema stub, both printed in French. Little things designed to create authenticity.

"Here." Eleanor passed Marie a purse. It contained a compact, lipstick and wallet. Marie realized these were not simple toiletries, but devices like those she had seen in Professor Digglesby's workshop at Arisaig House during training, tools she might need to survive once deployed.

They passed an RAF sentry holding a lantern and stopped at the edge of the aerodrome. Marie stepped from the car and walked to the boot where the driver was unloading bags. She picked up the case containing her radio, but Eleanor reached out and stopped her. "I don't understand..."

"The radio is too heavy for the Lysander. It will be dropped separately."

"But..." Marie was dismayed. She had grown used to the radio being by her side these past few months, felt attached to it. It was like a kind of armor and without it she would be exposed. She let go of the radio reluctantly, then looked up toward the tarmac at the tiny Lysander. How could a plane be unable to manage her thirty-pound wireless set but transport her safely to France?

"It will be dropped from a separate flight," Eleanor promised.

"How will I find it?" Marie asked, dubious.

"They will get it to you," Eleanor reassured her. "Don't worry. They're very good."

Whoever "they" were, Marie thought. All she had heard was one code name: Vesper. She knew no one.

They stood on the edge of the airfield, the dampness of the grass soaking through Marie's nylons at the ankle. The sickly sweet smell of early dogwood roses wafted moist across the field. Eleanor checked Marie's cuffs to see that they were folded just so. She was calm as ever, nonemotional. But her hand trembled slightly as she fixed Marie's collar and there was faint perspiration on her upper lip—little signs of nervousness Marie wished she had not seen because they scared her more than anything else had.

At last Eleanor led her toward the plane. The words *batting order* were chalked on the side of the plane, followed by names she didn't recognize. "What's that?" Marie asked.

"The priority of persons to be extracted if they are at the landing site. We can only fit three and the plane can't wait more than a minute." Inwardly, Marie blanched. Even as she was going over, there were countless others trying to escape. She wondered when she would be on the return flight home to Tess. She had to believe it would happen in the end, or she wouldn't be going at all.

"Here." Eleanor passed her a neat stack of francs, wrapped with a rubber band. "Half your pay comes in cash when you are in the field to use for things that you need. The rest will be paid for you in pounds sterling when you return.

"And one other thing," Eleanor said. She held out her hand, palm opened and upturned. Marie knew she was asking for the butterfly necklace, the reminder of Tess that she secretly wore.

Reluctantly, Marie took it from her neck. Then she hesitated. It was the one bit of her old life Marie had held on to these lonely months of training. Now it was being stripped from her. But she knew she had no choice; it was time to let go.

"I'll keep it safe for you," Eleanor said, her voice sounding as though she was talking about something much larger. Marie let her take the necklace from her fingers. "You'll want this instead." Eleanor produced a necklace with a silver bird charm and held it out. Marie was surprised. But it was not a gift; Eleanor twisted the necklace and it unscrewed to reveal a cyanide capsule. "The final friend," Eleanor declared. "You have to chew it quickly because the Germans know the smell and will try to make you spit it out." Marie shuddered. She had trained for it, of course. If she found herself captured and unable to hold out from talking, she was to end her life. But she could not imagine actually doing it.

Marie took a last look at Eleanor. "Thank you."

Eleanor stiffened, a slight dip of her chin the only response. "Thank me by getting the job done." She took Marie's hand and pressed it a second too long. Then she turned and walked off across the field.

Marie approached the plane warily. She had never flown before and even this small plane, a metal contraption with a glass dome top, seemed strange and intimidating.

A man sat in the cockpit. He gestured to her impatiently to come aboard. She had expected a military pilot but the man's hair was longish, curling against the neck of his American-style brown bomber jacket. His face was stubbled with whiskers. Was this the man who was to fly her to France? As she squeezed through the narrow door of the plane, Marie looked back over her shoulder for Eleanor. But she had already disappeared across the airfield.

Marie took the narrow seat behind the pilot and felt for a seat belt but found none. She had scarcely sat down before the ground crew closed the door from the outside. "Change of plans," the pilot announced without introduction, his accent Irish.

Her skin prickled. "What is it?"

"You'll be landing blind." He turned to the controls, dozens of unfamiliar dials and gauges. Through the front windshield, Marie saw the propeller on the nose of the plane begin to turn.

The plane rolled forward, jostling her as it rolled over the uneven earth.

"Blind?" she repeated before the meaning caught up to her. That meant she would be on her own, without the customary reception committee to meet her and help her rendezvous with her circuit. "But I was supposed to be met."

The pilot shrugged. "Nothing goes as planned in the field. Something must have happened and it isn't safe for them to come." Then how, she wondered, could it possibly be safe for her to arrive? For a minute, she wanted to ask to turn back and cancel. But the plane was picking up speed, the engine growing to a deafening roar. She fought the urge to cry out as the ground seemed to slip from beneath her. Feeling the strange sensation for the first time, she almost forgot to be afraid. She looked out the window, hoping to catch sight of Eleanor. But she and the Vauxhall had already gone. The separation between Marie and England grew greater by the second. There was no turning back now.

As the plane shot up at a steep angle, Marie's stomach dropped, and it occurred to her for the first time that she might be one to get airsick. Taking shallow breaths as they had been instructed in training, she looked down at the houses below, muted by the blackout. She imagined if she gazed far enough north she might see the old vicarage in East Anglia, Tess asleep beneath a thick plaid duvet in the attic room with the sloping rafters.

Neither Marie nor the pilot spoke further, for there was no chance of being heard over the incessant rattling of the engine that caused Marie's teeth to chatter painfully. The air inside the plane grew colder, almost frigid. Below the earth was a sheet of perfect black. A silver ribbon broke through like a beacon, the Channel waters illuminated in the moonlight with a brilliance that no rules or blackout could dim.

The plane dropped suddenly, then listed sharply to the left. Marie grasped the seat hard to avoid being sent sprawling by the unexpected jolt. She had not imagined flying to be this rough. She tried to conceal her nerves, but a cool sweat broke out on her skin. "Is anything wrong?" Marie called. She tried to see the pilot's face, searching for some sign of panic.

He shook his head, not looking up from the controls. "You feel every bump in this baby. That's the thing about the Lysander—it's small and slow and a German could shoot it with a slingshot." He patted the control panel. "But I can put it down on a mosquito's ass or in five hundred yards of shit." Marie cringed at his crudeness, but he did not bother to apologize.

As they neared the French coast, the pilot eased forward on the throttle. The plane lowered and a thick fog seemed to encircle it. The pilot looked out the window, trying to get a better view of the ground below. Surely, Marie thought, there had to be a better way to navigate. "We may have to turn back," he said.

"Can we wait until it clears?" Marie asked, relieved and disappointed at the same time.

He shook his head. "We've got to make sure we're back in Allied space before daylight. If we're spotted over France, there's no way to fly high or fast enough to escape enemy fire." Marie's skin prickled with fear. She might actually die before landing. The pilot wrinkled his brow as he studied the earth below. "I think we're in the right spot, though, or close enough. I'm going to make a go at it."

"That hardly inspires confidence," she replied, before thinking better of it.

He turned to give her a wry look. "You'll want to hold on tight."

The plane dropped, then shot downward nose first at a sharp angle, so unexpected and steep Marie thought they might be crashing. The earth raced at them with alarming speed. She clung to the seat, closing her eyes and preparing for the worst.

Marie braced herself for a hard jolt as she had been trained as they neared the ground. But the pilot leveled the plane at the last minute and set it down gently, gliding over the uneven field with deft hands so that if she hadn't looked out and seen the earth she might not have believed they had landed at all.

The brakes screeched loudly as the plane ground to a halt. Surely someone would hear the landing, which was meant to be covert. But the air outside was still. The pilot opened the door and peered out into the darkness. "No one for the return." Remembering Eleanor's explanation of the names chalked on the side of the plane, Marie wondered if that was a bad sign. He continued, "You'll want to head east for the train station. Keep low, move quickly and stay in the cover of the trees. There should be a blue bicycle chained behind the station, a shopper. You'll find further instructions inside the handlebars."

"Should?" Marie repeated, wondering how he could know this. "And if it isn't there, then what?"

"This is Vesper's circuit," he replied firmly. "Everything will be in order."

If that were true, Marie wanted to say, then someone would have been here to meet her. But she didn't, sensing it would go too far.

Marie hesitated, fearful of the prospect of making her way across the strange countryside alone. The pilot was watching her expectantly, though, and she had no choice but to get out of the plane.

"I'd come with you if I could," he said apologetically as she stood. "But the Lysander…"

"I understand." Every minute the plane sat on the exposed field risked greater detection.

"Good luck…" He trailed off. They did not know one another's names. It was the first rule she had learned, never to reveal her identity lest they compromise one another. Was this some sort of test?

"Renee," she said finally, trying on the new name Eleanor had given her.

The pilot blinked twice, as if not convinced. Her first attempt at subterfuge had been a failure. "I'm William. They call me Will," he said, and she sensed from the sincerity in his voice that it was his real name. Perhaps there were different rules for pilots—or he simply had less to lose. He gestured toward the trees with his head. "You had best go now."

"Yes, of course." She climbed from the plane and as she started away, she could feel him watching her. When she turned back again, the door to the plane was already closed. The Lysander engine revved and it rolled forward, picking up speed. It had been on the ground all of three minutes.

Marie started across the field in pitch darkness, feeling for the cover of the trees. The sweet smell of daffodils rose from the damp earth to meet her, and for a moment it was as if she had stepped into her childhood, playing in the French countryside as a girl. But she had to move quickly, the pilot had said. She looked in all directions, trying to remember the exact direction he had pointed when he'd told her to head east. She reached for her torch. Then recalling their training, thought better of it. Instead, she pulled out the makeup compact equipped with a compass at the bottom and lifted it out, trying to see by the light of the moon. But it was impossible. She reached into her purse and found the lighter and flicked it on, holding it above the compass just long enough to see the *north* marking on it.

Orienting herself east, Marie started through the trees. She stumbled over a rock, and the pain in her ankle carried her back to the early morning run at Arisaig House when she had fallen. If only Josie were here to help her now as she had been that day. Marie righted herself and started walking once more.

"Halt!" a voice ordered in French. Marie froze, certain she was to be arrested. There was no way to know if it was the Germans or the French police, who were sympathetic to the Germans. Equally bad either way. Should she reach for her cyanide capsule? she wondered. She had not imagined needing it so soon.

She turned and a tall, imposing man emerged from the shadows. She froze, seeing his gun leveled at her. "Fool!" he said in English, his voice a growl. "You never should have done as I said. Run or fight, but for God's sake, don't obey."

Before she could reply, he grabbed her elbow and began to lead her roughly through the woods. Instinctively, she pulled back, unable to stand the stranger's touch. "Come!" he commanded, as though ordering a stubborn horse. "Or you can stay here to be found by the *milice*." For a moment, she hesitated. She had been given no information about anyone she was to meet. In fact, the pilot had said no one was meeting her at all. Was this man really one of them, or was it some sort of a trap?

But the man urged her on and it seemed Marie had no choice but to follow. They padded through the moonlit forest not speaking, his silhouette cutting the sky above.

They reached a clearing on what seemed to be the edge of a farm. There was a small, windowless gardener's shed. "This is yours," he said. Marie looked at him, not understanding. "You are to stay here tonight."

"But I was instructed to go to the train station and find a bike. And where is Vesper? I was told I would be working with him."

"Quiet!" the man ordered, anger flaring. He had a heavy brow and deep-set blue eyes. "Never say that name—or anyone else's—aloud."

Heedless, Marie continued, "I need to speak with him. And I need to find my wireless."

"You're to follow orders and stay here." He raised his hand, warding off further questions. "Someone will come for you in the morning."

He fiddled with the lock on the door, then let her in. There was no light and the thick, warm air was stifling. As she stepped inside, the heavy smell of manure assaulted her nostrils. There was no bed and no toilet.

Not speaking further, the man walked from the shed and closed the door. On the far side, she heard a key turn in a lock, trapping her inside. "You're locking me in?" she called through the door, not quite believing what was happening. She realized then that she did not know his name. He could be anyone. To place her life in the hands of strangers—how could she have been so naive? "If you think I'm going to be locked up by some courier, you are sorely mistaken. I demand to speak with Vesper immediately!" she insisted, ignoring his warning not to use names.

"It's for your own good, in case someone should come along. Stay low and out of sight. And for God's sake, be quiet!" She heard his footsteps growing softer on the other side and then there was only silence.

As Marie turned away from the door, something scurried nearby in the darkness. A mouse or a rat? she wondered, thinking of the decoy she'd almost destroyed in training weeks earlier, how she and Josie had laughed about it afterward. If only Josie were here now. She sank down to the floor, never in her life so alone.

CHAPTER TEN

GRACE

New York, 1946

Grace awoke, and for a second it was just like any other day. Bright sunlight streamed through the lone window of the tiny, fourth-floor walk-up, casting shadows on the sloped ceiling. The rooming house was just on the edge of Hell's Kitchen, a block too close to the Hudson River for a respectable woman, but not dangerous. Grace had gotten the place on the cheap because of the old man who had vacated the unit by dying in it the previous week. She'd scrubbed the flat before she moved in, trying without success to remove the lingering pipe smoke odor that clung to the walls and the sense that someone else quite nearly still lived here. And beyond that she hadn't done anything to make it more like home, because that would mean acknowledging she might stay for good—and the hard truth that she didn't want to go back.

Grace rolled over and saw the envelope containing the photos on the nightstand by the narrow bed, beside the lone photo of

Tom in his dress uniform at graduation from basic training. The night before came crashing back: the news story about the woman (Eleanor Trigg; she now had a name) who had been killed in the car accident, and the realization that the suitcase Grace found had been hers. Grace wondered if the series of bizarre events might have been a dream. But the photographs sat neatly on her nightstand like an expectant child, reminding her that it was not.

After hearing the news on the television in the coffee shop the previous evening, Grace had been so surprised that she had left without waiting for her grilled cheese. She hailed a cab, too surprised to think about the cost. As the taxi had woven perilously through crosstown traffic, she had tried to make sense of it all. How could it be that the very woman whose bag she'd rummaged through was the same one who had died in the accident on the street?

It shouldn't have been such a surprise, really, Grace thought now. The fact that Eleanor Trigg had died explained why no one had come back for the suitcase and it was standing there abandoned in the first place. But why had she left it in the middle of Grand Central? That the woman was English just seemed to add to the mystery.

More puzzling was the fact that the bag had then disappeared. It was possible, of course, that someone had simply stolen the bag, having seen that it was sitting unattended for a long time and decided to claim it for his own. But something told Grace that there was more to it than simple theft—and that whoever had come and taken the suitcase knew something about Eleanor Trigg and the girls in her photos.

Enough, Grace could almost hear her mother's voice say. Grace had always had an overactive imagination, fueled by Nancy Drew and the other mysteries she liked to read as a girl. Her father, a science fiction buff, found Grace's wild stories amusing. But he would have said here that the simplest explanation was the most likely: Eleanor Trigg might well have been traveling with a relative or other companion, who retrieved her bag after the accident.

Grace sat up. The photographs lay on the nightstand, seeming to call to her. She had taken the pictures from the suitcase, and now she needed to do something with them. She washed and dressed, then started down the stairs of the rooming house. In the foyer, there was a phone on the wall, which Harriet the landlady didn't mind the tenants using every so often. On impulse, Grace picked up the phone and asked the operator for the police station closest to Grand Central. If Eleanor had been traveling with someone, perhaps the police could put Grace in touch so she could return the photos.

The line was silent for several seconds and a man's voice crackled across the line. "Precinct," he said, sounding as though he was chewing something.

"I wanted to speak with someone about the woman who was hit by a car near Grand Central yesterday." Grace spoke softly, so that her landlady, who lived in the room just off the foyer, wouldn't hear.

"MacDougal's handling that," the policeman replied. "MacDougal!" he bellowed into the phone so loudly Grace drew the phone away from her ear.

"Whaddya want?" A different voice, with a heavy Brooklyn accent, filled the line.

"The woman who was hit outside the station, Eleanor Trigg. Was she traveling with anyone?"

"Nah, we're still looking for next of kin," MacDougal replied. "Are you family?"

Grace ignored his question, pressing forward with her own. "Did anyone recover her belongings, like a suitcase?"

"She didn't have any bags. Say, who is this? This is an open investigation and if you're going to be asking questions, I'm really gonna need your name..." Grace set the receiver back into the cradle, hanging up. The police didn't have Eleanor's bag, or a relative to whom Grace could return the photos. The British consulate, which she'd considered the previous evening, was the better option. A stop at the consulate would take extra time on her way to work, though, and she'd have to hurry not to risk being late again.

An hour later, Grace neared the British consulate, a bustling office building on Third Avenue uncomfortably close to the hotel she'd found herself in with Mark two nights earlier. At the corner, a boy in worn trousers and a cap was selling newspapers. He reminded Grace of Sammy, who she hoped was managing all right at his cousin's. She took a copy of *The Post* and paid the boy. The headline read, "Truman Warns of Soviet Menace in the East." Not a year ago, everyone still feared Hitler. But now Stalin was spreading communism in countries still too weak from the war to resist and dividing Europe in a whole new way.

Grace flipped through the paper. On page nine, a picture of Eleanor Trigg, the same one that had been on the news the previous evening, was displayed on the bottom half. There was a second photo, a grainy, nondescript image of the street, not the grisly scene itself, thankfully. Grace scanned the article but it contained nothing more than she already knew.

It was not, Grace reminded herself, her problem. She smoothed her skirt and then marched into the consulate, eager to be rid of the photos and on her way to work.

The lobby of the British consulate was unremarkable, with just a few hard-backed chairs and a low table holding a plant that had died weeks ago. A lone man in a suit and derby hat sat in one of the chairs, looking as though he would rather be anywhere else. The receptionist, an older woman with her gray hair swept up in a knot and reading glasses perched on the end of her nose, clacked at a Remington.

"Yes?" the woman asked. She did not look up from the typewriter as Grace approached.

Grace saw how it must look—an unknown woman, arriving unannounced. She was nobody here.

But Grace had learned much from her months of working with Frankie to help the immigrants about wheedling her way through government bureaucracy, getting what she wanted from tired civil servants. Steeling herself, she held up the envelope. "I found these photos and I believe they belong to a British citizen." *Belonged*, she corrected herself silently.

"And you want us to do what with them, exactly?" The woman, her English accent cold and clipped, did not wait for an answer or bother to mask her impatience. "Thousands of British citizens come to New York every day. Very few of them ever check in with the consulate."

"Well, this one won't be checking in with the consulate at all," Grace replied, more snappishly than she intended. She held up the newspaper. "The photographs were owned by Eleanor Trigg, the woman who was hit by a car outside Grand Central yesterday. She was British. I was thinking if there was a family member or next of kin, they might want these photographs."

"I can't comment on the personal matters of British citizens," the receptionist said officiously. "If you would like to leave them here, we can hold them and see if someone claims them." The receptionist held out her hand impatiently.

Grace hesitated. This was her moment and she could just leave the photos and be done with them. But she felt a connection to the photos now, a sense of ownership. She couldn't just abandon them to someone who so clearly couldn't care less. She pulled back her hand. "I'd rather speak with someone. Perhaps the consul."

"Sir Meacham isn't here." *And wouldn't see you even if he was*, the receptionist's tone seemed to say.

"Then can I make an appointment?" Even before Grace finished, she knew she would be turned away.

"The consul is a very busy man. He doesn't get involved

in these types of matters. If you would prefer not to leave the photos, you can leave your contact information in case anyone inquires about them." Grace took the pencil the receptionist offered and jotted down the address and phone number of the boardinghouse. She could practically hear the paper falling into the wastebasket as she reached the exit.

Well, that hadn't worked out, Grace thought as she started out the door of the consulate. She lifted the envelope of photographs to study it for further clues. Then she glanced up at the clock on the building across the street. Nine thirty. She was late for work again. Maybe if she told Frankie what had happened, he might have some idea what she should do next.

As she started down the steps of the consulate, an older man with a waxed moustache wearing a pinstripe suit passed her in the other direction, entering the building. "Excuse me?" Grace called out impulsively. "Are you Sir Meacham?"

Confusion crossed the man's face, as though he were not quite sure himself. "I am," he said. His expression changed to one of annoyance. "What is it that you want?"

"If you have a moment, I just need to ask you a few questions."

"I'm sorry, but I really don't have the time. I'm late for a meeting. If you make an appointment at the front desk, I'm sure the vice consul will..."

She did not wait for him to finish. "It's about Eleanor Trigg."

He cleared his throat, an almost cough. Clearly, he had heard. "I suppose you saw the news story. Very sad. Were you a friend of hers?"

"Not exactly. But I have something that belonged to her."

The consul waved her hurriedly back inside the building. "I have two minutes," he said, leading her across the lobby. Seeing Grace with the consul, the receptionist's eyes widened with surprise.

The consul led her to a room off the main lobby that was well-appointed, with brown leather chairs scattered around dark oak tables and heavy red velvet curtains held back by gold rope. A bar or club of some sort, presently closed. "How can I help?" Sir Meacham asked, not bothering to hide the annoyance in his voice.

"Eleanor Trigg was a British citizen, wasn't she?"

"Indeed. We received a call last night from the police. They knew from her passport that she was British. We're trying to locate family to claim her body."

Grace hated the cold, impersonal way that sounded. "Did you know her?"

"Not personally, no. I knew of her. I happened to be detailed to Whitehall during the war. She worked for our government, did something clerical for one of the sections of SOE, that is, Special Operations Executive."

Grace had never even heard of Special Operations Executive and wanted to ask the consul about it. But he was looking at the grandfather clock in the corner impatiently. She was running out of time.

"I found some photos," Grace said, being purposefully vague as to how. She took them out of the envelope and spread them before the consul like a hand of cards. "I brought them to the consulate this morning because I believe they belonged to Miss Trigg. Do you know who these women are?"

The consul pulled out his reading glasses to study the photographs. Then he shifted his gaze away. "I've never seen them before. Any of them. Perhaps they were friends of hers, or even relatives."

"But some of them are in uniform," she pointed out.

The consul waved his hands dismissively. "Probably just FANYs, members of the women's nursing auxiliary." Grace shook her head. Something about the girls' grimly set jaws, their serious expressions, suggested more. The consul looked up. "What exactly is it that you want from me?"

Grace faltered. She had come here just to return the photos.

But now she found she wanted answers. "I'm curious who these girls are—and what their connection was to Eleanor Trigg."

"I have no idea," Sir Meacham replied firmly.

"You could make some inquiries in London and try to find out," Grace challenged.

"Actually, I couldn't," the consul replied coldly. "When SOE was shut down, its records were shipped to your War Department in Washington. Where," he added, "I'm quite certain they're sealed." He stood up. "I'm afraid I really must be going."

Grace rose. "What was she doing in New York?" she persisted.

"I have absolutely no idea," Sir Meacham replied. "As I said, Miss Trigg was no longer affiliated with the British government. Her whereabouts were her own business. This is a private matter. I'm not sure that it is any of your concern."

"What if they can't find anyone?" Grace asked. "To claim Eleanor, I mean."

"I suppose the city will put her in a pauper's grave. The consulate has no funds for such things." *A woman who served your country—even as a secretary—deserved better,* Grace wanted to say. She gathered up the photos and put them in the envelope. The consul held out his hands. "Now, if you would like to give me her photos, I'm sure we can reunite them with her personal effects," the consul said.

Grace started to give them over, compliance almost a reflex. Then she pulled back. "How?"

Sir Meacham's eyebrows raised, white above his glasses. "Pardon me?"

"If there is no next of kin, how can you reunite them?"

The consul huffed, unaccustomed to being challenged. "We'll hold on to them, make inquiries." Grace knew from his tone that nothing of the sort would happen. "They aren't your concern." He reached for the photos.

Grace hesitated. Part of her wanted to be done with the photos, hand them over and walk away. But she couldn't abandon them.

She had to do more. "On second thought," she said evenly. "I'll just hang on to them." She stood to leave.

"But I really don't think..." the consul fumbled. "You were so eager to return them. That is why you came to the consulate, wasn't it? I wouldn't want them to be a burden."

"Really, it's no trouble." Grace managed a smile through gritted teeth. "I found them. They're mine."

"Actually," the consul replied, his voice steely. "They're Eleanor's." They stared at one another for several seconds, neither wavering. Then Grace turned and walked from the consulate.

Outside, Grace paused to consider the photos once more. She hadn't left them after all, and she still had no idea what to do with them. But she could figure that out later; right now, it was time to get to work.

Still clutching the photos in her hand, she stepped onto the sidewalk, merging with the current of commuters that surged along Third Avenue. "Grace," a male voice called. She stopped, certain she was mistaken. No one knew her here. For a second, she wondered if it was Sir Meacham coming after her to insist she leave the photos. But the accent was American, not English. It came again, following and more insistent. "Grace, wait!"

She turned toward the voice and as she did, a passing businessman bumped into her, sending the photos scattering. She knelt to retrieve them.

"I didn't mean to startle you." The male voice was familiar. "Here, let me help."

Grace looked up, stunned by the sight of the man she'd been sure she would never see again. "Mark."

Memories cascaded through her: a crush of crisp white hotel sheets tangled between her limbs, the sensation of floating in midair above the bed. A man's hands on her that were not Tom's.

Yet here he was. Mark helped her to her feet, the sleeve of his gray wool overcoat scratchy against her arm. Grace stared at him. He seemed to smile with the whole of his face, hazel eyes dancing. A single lock of his dark curly hair peeked out from beneath the wide brim of his fedora. He kissed her on the cheek like they were old friends, and the scent of his cologne hurled her back to the night before last and all the places she never should have been.

Remembering the photographs, Grace scurried to collect them from the pavement. "Let me help you," Mark offered again. Did he feel awkward, too, she wondered, about having slept with his dead best friend's wife?

She waved him off. "I can manage." She didn't want him to see the girls and start asking questions. But he raced toward the curb, deftly plucking up one of the photographs before it slipped into the gutter.

When Grace had collected all of the pictures, she straightened. "What are you doing here?" she blurted, feeling her cheeks flush. The other night he had said that it was his last in town. Yet here he was.

"I was delayed on business." He did not elaborate.

They stood awkwardly for several seconds and her eyes seemed to catch where the collar of his tweed overcoat brushed against the freshly shaved skin of his neck. There wasn't any more to say. "I have to go." She took a step away from him, the movement more difficult than she might have imagined.

"Wait." He reached for her arm, the light touch reminding her all too much of the night they had shared. "I was hoping we could make plans to meet up again. Only when I woke up…"

"Shush!" she scolded, looking over her shoulder. That it had happened was bad enough; she certainly didn't want anyone else to hear about it.

"Sorry. Anyway, now that we've run into one another, I was hoping that I could see you again?" His voice ended on an upward note, making it into a question.

For what, Grace wondered, another night? There could hardly be anything more between them. "I couldn't possibly…"

"At least let me buy you breakfast," he pressed.

"I need to get to work." She tucked the envelope back in her bag.

"You work?" Hearing the surprise in his voice, her irritation rose. Why wouldn't she have a job? It wasn't that uncommon, although with men returning from Europe, many women had stopped working, either by choice or because they had been forced from their jobs. But it wasn't that he underestimated her, she realized. Rather, it was just that they had spoken so little about themselves the night they spent together. That was the comfort of it; they had talked about the war, about Tom. But her actual self and the realities of her world had remained safely out of sight. Mark really didn't know her at all.

And she would like to keep it that way. "I do work," she said. "And I'm late. But thank you for your offer."

"Coffee then?" he persisted.

"I really can't." She tried to leave again.

"Gracie," he called.

She turned. "Didn't you hear me when I said no?"

But it was just a paper he was holding out, one of the photographs she had missed on the ground. "You dropped this. Pretty girl," he commented at the photo.

"I'm sorry. That was rude of me," Grace said, softening. She took the photo and tucked it away.

"It was," he agreed, and they both chuckled. "You really don't have time for coffee?" he asked, his expression pleading.

She could use a cup of coffee, Grace realized. And Mark had been nothing but kind. But seeing the consul had made her late. She considered how mad Frankie would be, then decided she could stretch it just once more. "I've got fifteen minutes," she said.

Mark smiled broadly. "I'll take what I can get."

She followed him to the Woolworths on the next block. They found two spots at the end of the Formica counter. "There, we don't even have to sit in a proper booth," he chided. Ignoring him, she climbed onto one of the stools. On the wall behind the counter, bright posters exhorted them to try Coca-Cola and Chesterfield cigarettes.

"Two coffees, please," Mark said to the waitress. He turned to Grace. "Something to eat?" She shook her head. Though she could have used breakfast, she didn't want to stay that long. "How long have you been in New York?" he asked, when the steaming mugs had been set on the counter in front of them.

"Almost a year." She could feel the anniversary coming around, the sameness of the weather as it had been that day.

"Since Tom died," he noted.

She tried to take a sip of coffee, but the too-hot liquid scalded her lips so she set it down once more. "More or less. I was here to meet him for a weekend when I got the news."

"And you stayed."

She nodded. "Sort of." Technically, it wasn't true; she had gone back to Boston for the funeral, then to her family's house in Westport. But the overly concerned looks had been stifling and the murmurs of sympathy made her want to scream. She left for Marcia's place in the Hamptons less than a week later.

"You said you were delayed in New York for work?" she asked, purposefully changing the subject.

"Yes, I'm a lawyer. The hearing that we started was continued so I extended my stay at The James." She blushed, remembering his well-appointed suite.

"So those photographs," he continued, before she could ask about the type of law and what it was that he actually did. He nodded toward her bag, where she'd tucked the envelope safely away once more. "Do they have to do with your job?"

Grace hesitated. She dearly wanted to speak with someone about the photos, to have help figuring out what to do. And there was something in Mark's hazel eyes, the inquisitiveness and concern as he studied her face, that made her feel as though she could trust him. She took a breath. "You heard about the woman who was hit by a car near Grand Central?" she asked in a low voice.

He nodded. "I just read about it in the paper."

"Well, I saw it."

"You saw her get hit?"

"Not exactly. But I was there after, with the police and an ambulance."

"That must have been awful."

"It was. And there's more." Grace found herself telling Mark how she had been detoured through Grand Central and found a suitcase. He rested his elbow on the counter and his chin in his hand, listening intently. "When I was looking inside for some identification, I found these," she added, trying to make her nosiness sound purposeful. She pulled out the photos and showed him. "I tried to put them back, but the suitcase was gone. Then I found out that it belonged to the woman who was killed. She was English. At first I just wanted to find a way to return the photos to their owner. That's why I went to the British consulate."

"But you didn't leave the photos at the consulate, though. Why not?"

Grace faltered. "I don't know. I wanted to make sure they were getting into the right hands. I did speak to the consul, though. He didn't know who the girls were, but he said Eleanor worked for the British government during the war. Something called Special Operations Executive."

"I've heard of it, actually. SOE, I think it's called."

"That's what he said."

"It was a British agency that sent agents into Europe during the war to do secret missions, sabotage and such. What did Eleanor do for SOE?"

"Something clerical, the consul said. He really didn't know

more about it, except that the agency records were sent to the War Department in Washington after the war. That still doesn't tell me who the girls were—or get me any closer to returning her photos."

"So what are you going to do now?" Mark asked.

"I'm not sure," Grace confessed. "Place an ad in the *Times*, maybe." As if she had the money. She had seen Frankie do it when one of his clients was looking for her husband, from whom she'd been separated during the war. "Right now, I need to get to work. I'm so very late. Surely you have things to do as well."

"I'm expected back in Washington this afternoon," he admitted, leaving some coins on the counter and following her to the door of the coffee shop. "My case settled."

"Oh," she said, with an unexpected feeling of disappointment.

Outside, they both stood for several seconds without speaking, neither of them seeming ready to part. "Say, the consul said there are files at the War Department," Mark said suddenly. "I might have a contact there. I could do some checking for you, if you'd like."

"No," she said abruptly. "I mean, thank you. That's very kind of you. But this is my problem and I've taken enough of your time already."

"Or," he continued with a smile, "you could come and do the checking yourself."

"Me?" Grace stared at him, surprised. New York alone after losing Tom had been an adventure. But going all the way to Washington sounded preposterous. "I couldn't possibly."

"Why not?" he challenged. "You've hit a dead end with the consulate. There's nothing more to be learned here. Otherwise, you're stuck with the photos. Why not take a chance and see what we can learn?"

We. Grace squirmed. "Why are you doing this?" she asked.

"Maybe I'm curious, too. Or maybe I'm just not ready to say

goodbye to you," he blurted. Grace was surprised. She had liked Mark enough the few times she'd met him previously, mostly because Tom liked him and that was enough for her. That, along with her loneliness and a healthy amount of liquor was what had driven her to sleep with him the other night. But now he was suggesting that for him it had been something more than she had intended.

She pulled her hand away. "You don't know me that well."

"That," he said, "is something I would like to rectify. Come on, one day in Washington. Do you want to know about Eleanor and the girls or not?"

"Yes, of course." Grace wasn't supposed to be hopping on a train to Washington on some wild quest, but figuring out her life here, whether to stay in New York or go home and what to do next.

"So are you in?" His eyes locked with hers, deep and cajoling.

Grace wanted to walk away from him, from the girls, from all of it. But even more than that, she wanted to know. "When?"

"Today."

"I have work."

"Tomorrow then. Take a day off, if you have one, or call in sick. It's only a day. What's that in exchange for all of the answers you want?" Not waiting for an answer, he continued, "Tell you what—you get things sorted out here and let your boss know. I have to head back on the two o'clock today, but there's a train first thing tomorrow at seven. Take that one. I'll be waiting on the platform at Union Station and I hope you'll be there." He tipped his hat. "See you then." He spoke as though she had acquiesced, her meeting him already a foregone conclusion.

Watching him stride away, Grace's doubts swelled. She should not mind him leaving so much. She should be glad he was gone so she could put the mistake of the other night behind her and get back to sorting out her life here. Seeing him again would be a mistake, and meeting him in Washington an even worse one.

Which was exactly why she had to say yes.

CHAPTER ELEVEN

MARIE

France, 1944

In the predawn stillness there was a scratching sound outside the shed. Marie sat up, terrified and exhausted. She had spent the night half sitting, half lying against a rough wooden wall. Her bones ached from the cold, hard ground, and there was a wet spot on the seat of her dress where the dampness of the earth had soaked through.

The noise came again, like the rustling of deer that poked at the garden each summer she and her mother had spent outside Concarneau when she was a girl. This was not a deer, though; the footsteps were heavier, crushing twigs beneath them. Marie leaped to her feet, imagining a German on the other side of the door. She tried to remember from her training what to do. Her skin prickled.

But then a key turned in the lock and the door opened. It was the tall, angry man who had brought her the previous night. Marie smoothed her skirt, embarrassed at how the shed reeked now from the spot in the corner where she had tried discreetly to use the ground as a toilet. She hadn't wanted to, but with the door locked and no facilities, there really hadn't been a choice.

The man did not speak, but gestured for her to follow. She obeyed, working her dishwater-blond hair into a low knot as she stepped from the shed. Her mouth was sour and her stomach gnarled with hunger. Outside the sky was pink at the horizon, the air damp. Since he had brought her to the shed in the middle of the night, she couldn't have been there for more than a few hours. But the time waiting and worrying about when he would come back and what she would do if he did not had seemed like much longer.

She could see that the shed was sunk in a ravine behind a row of poplar trees. "You managed all right?" the man asked in English as they climbed up the hill, his voice so low she could barely hear it.

"Yes. No thanks to you," she added, too loudly, her annoyance at how she'd been treated bursting forth.

He turned back. "Quiet!" he commanded in a low, gravelly voice, grabbing her wrist so hard that it hurt.

"Don't touch me!" Marie tried to pull back, but his iron-like grip held her fast.

His eyes blazed. "I'm not going to get arrested because you can't keep your mouth shut." They stared at each other for several seconds, not speaking.

The man started onward once more, leading her through the forest in a direction that seemed different than the way he'd brought her the previous night, though she could not tell for certain. As they walked, she studied him out of the corner of her eye. His hair was close-cropped and his jaw square. Though he wore the trousers and shirt of a French peasant, his too-straight posture and gait suggested he was military, or once had been.

The trees broke to a clearing and on the far side sat a small, unmarked rail station scarcely bigger than the hut where she had been forced to sleep the night before. The man looked in both directions expertly, like one who had spent much time ensuring that he had not been detected or tracked. Then he grasped her arm once more. Marie pulled away. "Don't touch me again." The unwanted hands of strange men always transported her back to her childhood, where her father's painful grip was always followed by a slap or strike.

She waited now for the courier's rebuke. Instead, he nodded, a slight assent. "Then stay close." He started across the clearing and walked behind the station, where a lone bike sat. "Get on," he said, gesturing to the crossbar. She hesitated. The early morning sun was well above the trees now. Riding openly across the French countryside seemed foolish and sure to attract attention. To refuse would mean angering this man further, though, and she knew nothing in this country but him and that miserable shed. He steadied the bike as she climbed on the crossbar and then he mounted the bike, encircling her with his long, broad forearms to reach the handlebars. She shifted, uncomfortable at being so close to a man she didn't know. He began to pedal over the uneven ground down a narrow path.

They reached the edge of the clearing and the path gave way to a country road, flanked on either side by a low wall of crumbling stones. A valley unfurled below them, the quilt of lush green and neatly tilled fields, dotted with red-roofed cottages and the occasional château. The rich scent of damp *chevrefeuille* wafted upward. They were in the Île-de-France region, she guessed from the gently rolling hills and the route the Lysander had taken the previous evening, somewhere northwest of Paris and deep in the heart of Nazi-occupied territory.

They passed a farmhouse, where a young woman was hanging clothes in the yard to dry. Marie seized with fear. Until this point, she had been shrouded in darkness. Now they were out in plain sight. Surely something would give her away. But the woman simply smiled, taking them for a couple out for a morning bike ride.

A few minutes later the man turned the bike off the main road so abruptly that Marie nearly fell. She grabbed for the handlebars as he pulled up in front of a château. "What are we doing here?" she ventured to ask.

"One of our safe houses," he explained. Looking up at the stately home with its steeply pitched roof and dormer windows, Marie was surprised; she had expected caves and woods, or at most a shed like the one where she'd spent the night. "The house is abandoned. And the Germans would have taken it except for this." He gestured toward something lodged between two of the paving stones in front of her. Ordnance, she recognized from training. A bomb that had been dropped by the Germans ahead of the occupation, but had not detonated. "There are another half dozen in the garden."

Inside, the mansion appeared untouched, fine linens and china intact, furniture not covered. In the dining room to the left, Marie could see a table set, as though company was expected anytime. Whoever had lived here had gone without notice, she thought, recalling *l'exode*, the flight of millions of citizens of northern France four years earlier ahead of the advancing German army. A thin coat of dust on everything was the only sign that the house was vacant.

There came a scratching from above, the faint titter of laughter. The man took the wide stairs two at a time without waiting for her and she hurried to follow. He opened a door to reveal what had once been a study. A handful of men, all about her own age, were gathered around a broad oak desk that had been pressed into service as a dining table. The heavy curtains were drawn and several candles flickered on the table. Overflowing bookshelves climbed to the ceiling.

In an armchair by the window sat Will, the pilot who had flown her here the previous night. Marie was surprised to see him and wondered what had kept him from flying out of France after the Lysander had taken off from the field. He was the only familiar face in the room and she started toward him. But closer she could see that he was dozing, eyes closed.

Marie stood uncertainly on the edge of the room. The group had presumably assembled on the upper floor of the abandoned villa to stay out of sight. Yet they laughed and joked as easily as though they were in a Paris café. The air was warm with the delicious smells of coffee and eggs. Remembering the cold, dark shed where she had spent the past several hours, Marie was suddenly angry. She glared in the direction of the courier, who was now standing across the room by the window. He might have brought her here the night before. But he had not. Perhaps it had been some sort of a test.

One of the men seemed to notice her then. "Come, come," he said with an accent she recognized as Welsh. He had a wide moustache, ill-suited to fitting in among the French. "Don't wait for an invitation. Have some bacon before it's all gone." Marie was certain that she heard him wrong. There hadn't been bacon back home since before the war. But here it was, thick and crispy on a nearly empty plate, calling to her. The man held out the plate. "Go on. We don't eat like this every day. One of the lads was able to buy a rasher off the black market near Chartres and it all has to go. We've got nowhere to store it and we can't risk taking it along." She moved closer. The table bore an odd assortment of food that might have not gone together in other circumstances: a bit of baked beans (*far too English*, she could hear Eleanor criticize) and some bread, cheese and fruit.

Marie's stomach rumbled, reminding her that she had not eaten since yesterday. She reached for the bacon the man held out. Searching for a fork and finding none, she popped the piece in her mouth as neatly as she could.

The man with the moustache poured her coffee. "I'm Albert,"

he said, holding out his hand. She reached to shake it, mindful of her newly greasy fingers.

But Albert took Marie's hand and kissed it. Her cheeks flushed. "Bonjour," she offered back, wondering he if was flirting with her and not entirely sure how to respond. *"Enchanté."*

His eyebrows raised and she wondered if she had done something wrong. "Your accent is perfect. Are you French?"

"Half, on my mother's side," Marie replied. "I was raised in England, but spent summers in Brittany when I was younger."

"That'll be useful. Most of us speak French abysmally."

"Speak for yourself," retorted the ginger-haired boy next to Albert, who had not introduced himself.

"You'll be a courier then?" Albert asked, ignoring him.

"Non!" she blurted out, alarmed. The idea of messengering all over the French countryside, constantly risking arrest, alarmed her. "Radio operator."

"Ah, a pianist." The term sounded strange. But she remembered someone referring to the wireless set as a piano once during training. "With your language skills, keeping you inside seems a waste," he lamented. "But I suppose Vesper knows what he is doing."

"Speaking of Vesper, I was wondering if you could point me in his direction," Marie said. Albert's eyebrows raised. "I'd like to speak to him about the courier who met me last night and brought me here this morning." She spoke in a low voice so that the courier himself would not hear.

"Courier?" Albert threw back his head and chortled so loudly that the conversation around the table ceased. "Courier?" He tilted his head in the direction of the man by the window. "Oh, love, that *is* Vesper!"

The others joined, laughing with him at her mistake. The man who had left her in the shed and brought her here wasn't merely some courier after all, but Vesper, the legendary circuit leader Eleanor had spoken about. She looked in the direction of the courier whom she now knew was Vesper, certain he had heard the exchange. Embarrassed by the gaffe, Marie felt her cheeks burn. But how was she to have known when he hadn't told her?

"Shh!" Vesper hissed suddenly, raising a hand. Their merriment ceased and Marie heard a high-pitched keening noise coming from outside the château. Sirens. The agents looked at one another, their hardened expressions suddenly clouded with concern.

Only Albert looked unworried, waving his hand dismissively. "When Kriegler and his louts come for us," he said calmly, "they won't announce themselves with sirens." A few of the men laughed uneasily.

The sirens rose to a pitch as they neared. One second passed then another. At last, they began to fade as the police car raced by the château, chasing other prey. "I heard there was an arrest in Picardy," one of the men offered when the sirens had faded into the distance. "Two agents, picked up at their safe house." Marie shuddered. Picardy, the region just to the north, was not far from here. She wondered if the arrest had taken place at a too-nice safe house like this, and whether the agents had been laughing and enjoying one another's company just before it had happened.

Albert waved his hand. "Don't speak of such things." As though the bad luck was contagious—and might rub off on them.

But the other man persisted. "They must have been careless." Heads nodded in agreement, wanting to differentiate and distance themselves from those whom ill fate had befallen.

"Don't be too certain." Vesper spoke sharply. Marie hoped he would dispel the rumor of the arrest, but he did not. His heavy brow was furrowed, expression grave. "Those were some of the best agents we had." She could tell from his voice that the loss had been personal and hard for him. "It can happen to anyone, at any time. Don't ever let your guard down." Vesper turned away and the others sat around the table, now quiet and somber. One of the men lit a cigarette and its ominous burning filled the air.

Suddenly there was a clattering at the door. Albert leaped to his feet and across the room Vesper's hand dropped instinctively toward his waist, as though reaching for a gun. Marie froze, remembering his warning seconds earlier that arrest could come anytime.

The door flung open and a woman entered the room, smartly dressed with a Sten gun tucked neatly under one arm like a purse. It was Josie.

At the sight of her friend, Mare's heart leaped. She had not expected to see Josie again, maybe ever, and certainly not so soon. Marie stood, nearly calling out, before remembering that she should not.

"Bloody hell, you gave us a scare!" Albert exclaimed. "We weren't expecting you back for another two days."

"We received word that the Maquis training grounds in the forest were compromised," Josie said. "It was no longer safe. We had to disperse."

Marie hurried to Josie, who had begun dismantling her gun on a low table by the door. There was a faint smell of burning powder and Marie wondered why the gun had been fired. "Josie."

"Hello." Josie looked up and smiled warmly. She kissed Marie on the cheek. "I'm glad you arrived safely," Josie said. Her nose wrinkled. "There's a toilet if you want to freshen up." Embarrassment rose in Marie, followed by defensiveness: of course she was a mess—how could she be otherwise when she had spent the night in that awful shed? But Josie had been in the field weeks longer and her hair was well coiffed, dress freshly pressed. Her shoes were slingbacks, and bore no trace of dirt or wear. Even her nails were perfect pale pink ovals. "You'll want to look proper before you head out," Josie added. Where, Marie wondered, would she be going?

In the water closet, Marie smoothed her hair as well as she could and washed her face, noting with dissatisfaction that the strong camphor soap had turned her cheeks bright red. The travel and night in the hut had left her skin sallow, with dark circles under her eyes.

When Marie returned from the bathroom, Josie had finished disassembling the gun and was cleaning the pieces expertly with a soft white cloth. Marie studied her friend. "You're well?"

"Never better." Josie looked invigorated. There was a healthy blush to her cheeks and her eyes were bright. "I've been traveling the countryside, arming the partisans and teaching them how to use our weapons."

"You aren't on the radio then?" Josie had been so good at transmitting in class at Arisaig House; it would be a waste not to have her working with one. Of course, she had been good at everything else, too. Marie saw then what an asset her friend must be to the circuit, and felt her own inadequacies grow by comparison.

"At times I am," Josie replied. "But everything is more fluid in the field. We must do what is needed." Josie sounded years older than when Marie had seen her last, more confident than ever. The work here clearly suited her. Marie was not at all sure she would feel the same.

"You're Tuesday-Thursday on the skeds," Josie said. That meant the days Marie would broadcast and send her messages back to London.

Marie pictured Eleanor waiting to receive and hoped her typing would be good and clear enough. She wondered what she would be asked to transmit. "Do I broadcast from here?"

Josie shook her head. "From wherever you'll be staying. You'll have to ask Vesper." Marie's eyes traveled across the room to where Vesper stood, studying him closely. He was a few years older than the rest of them, she guessed, with high cheekbones and cerulean-blue eyes. Some might call him good-looking, including herself, if she hadn't disliked him from the start. "He controls everything for the operation in Paris and the northern part of France, dozens and dozens of agents and maybe a hundred local contacts."

Marie was puzzled. They had learned in training that the work in France consisted of small groups of agents, usually working in threes, a circuit leader, a radio operator and a courier. They were separated because if one was compromised, it wouldn't taint the rest. But here Vesper was in charge of it all. Was it really safe to have one man know so much?

Across the room, voices rose. At the table, Vesper stood huddled over a map with Albert and Will, who had awoken during the earlier commotion of Josie's arrival. A disagreement had erupted among the men, their voices rising so all could hear.

"Cousins," Josie said, tilting her head in the direction of Vesper and Will. Marie was surprised they looked and acted so different. Will's devil-may-care style and gentle demeanor seemed in sharp contrast to his cousin's sternness. "You wouldn't have guessed it, I know. Keep an eye out for that one," she added, nodding toward Will. "Not hard on the eyes and a total ladies' man to be sure. He's got girls everywhere, they say, including at a cathouse in Paris."

"Josie!" Marie brought her hand to her mouth, surprised.

Her friend shrugged. "These are long, lonely months out here and things happen. Just keep your head about you and don't get distracted."

"I thought Will returned to England."

Josie shook her head. "He had mechanical troubles after taking off. So he had to land at another one of our fields. We towed the plane to one of our safe sites for repair." Marie shuddered, grateful that they had landed safely before the plane broke.

The men at the table grew louder. "We need to find another safe house near Mantes-la-Jolie," Vesper said.

Will shook his head. "It's too much, too soon. After the other arrests, we can't ask the locals to chance it. We need to tighten our ranks and lay low for a while."

"Impossible!" Vesper flared. "We've got orders to take the bridge within the month. We need to be ready."

"Then at least warn the locals what is to come, so they can get their families to safety," Will pressed.

"And risk leaking word of the operation?" Vesper countered.

Marie turned to Josie. "What are they fighting about?"

Josie shrugged. "Those two are always like that. Best not to get involved."

But Marie moved closer, too curious to help herself. "What is it?" she asked, surprised at her own audacity.

Vesper looked in her direction, clearly annoyed. "No questions. The less you know, the better for you—and for all of us."

But Will answered. "Right now we're constructing a network of safe houses and drop boxes between here and Mantes-la-Jolie. We have a dangerous operation coming up, and the agents who will undertake it need places to hide so that they can flee after. But the locals have grown wary of helping us. In another village, Neuilly-sur-Seine, there were mass reprisals for helping the partisans. Under orders of the chief of the German SD Kriegler, the men were shot and the women and children locked in a church that was set afire." Marie stifled a gasp. "The whole town was killed."

"That's why I'm headed out myself to find new locations," Vesper explained. "We have the best shot of the locals listening to me."

"But your French," Albert said, clucking his tongue. "You can't possibly go alone."

"I can go with you," Marie ventured, instantly regretting it.

Vesper looked as surprised as she at the offer. Then he scowled. "Impossible!" he snapped. "You've only just arrived. You have zero actual experience. It's too dangerous."

"Her French is brilliant—and yours nonexistent," Albert

added chidingly. Marie wondered how it was possible for the leader of the circuit to operate in France without speaking the language.

Vesper did not answer but stared at her, considering. Did he prefer to travel alone or simply not want her? Either way, he was going to say no, she thought with a mix of disappointment and relief.

"Only as far as Mantes-la-Jolie," he conceded finally, and she could see the surprise on the faces around her that he agreed at all. "Come."

As Vesper started through the door, Marie looked back over her shoulder at Josie. They had been reunited for such a short time, and who knew when they would see each other again? She wanted to run to Josie, to say goodbye and see if she had any words of wisdom or advice. But Josie simply raised her hand to say farewell, and Marie knew she had no choice but to go.

She raced down the stairs and out the front door of the villa to catch Vesper, slowing only as she passed the unexploded ordnance in the garden. Vesper did not take the bike they had ridden earlier, but instead set out on foot across the field opposite the house. Neither spoke. His strides were long and she had to nearly run to keep up. Her skin was unpleasantly damp beneath her dress.

They walked on for some time, neither speaking. In the distance, church bells pealed ten. "You're slow," he said accusingly a moment later as the field ended at a country road.

"What do you expect?" she spat, all of the anger and fear of the past few days flaring up in her. "You left me in a shed alone and freezing overnight without food or water. I'm exhausted."

"I haven't slept a full night in two weeks," he replied. "It's the nature of the work, always on the move. But you'll have rest and food as soon as we have you settled with your wireless. I'm surprised you'd want to come along to help a simple courier," he added, changing the subject.

Marie flushed. "I had no idea I'd been met by the famous Vesper," she replied, trying to make light of her earlier gaffe. "What an honor."

He looked surprised, as if no one had ever joked with him. "You could sound as if you meant it," he replied stiffly. "I'm also called Julian, by the way."

"How do you manage without speaking French?" she asked, before hearing Eleanor's admonishment for asking too many questions.

"As circuit leader, I seldom interact with the locals. It would be too dangerous if I was caught. So I stay low, operate through the other men."

"And women," she pointed out. "Or do you think we shouldn't be here?"

"I think women can be just what the operation needs, if they are good enough—and committed to the task." This last part sounded pointed—and directed at her. A question seemed to linger under his words, echoing her own doubts.

She decided to ignore it. "You said that we are headed to Mantes-la-Jolie?"

"To a nearby village, actually, Rosny-sur-Seine. Presently we have no safe house in the region, other than the villa, which is too big and visible to hide an agent on the run. We're trying to establish one, but we can't simply walk into town and ask who is willing to risk their lives by hiding fleeing agents. So we start smaller and find a local who will act as a drop box for our messages, before asking if they will hide people."

Before she could reply, there came a rumbling sound from around the corner. A large brown military truck appeared, traveling toward them. Marie tensed and started toward the trees once more. Julian grabbed her arm, and this time she was too terrified to protest. "Easy," he said in a low voice. "We are just a French couple, out for a morning walk." She forced herself to continue walking normally, eyes down. A moment later, when the truck had disappeared around the corner, he dropped her arm roughly. "You do know that your cover is that of a Frenchwoman?"

"Yes, of course."

"Then act like one."

She lowered her head. "I'm sorry. If you'd like me to go back to the villa, you can take someone else. Perhaps Josie…"

"It's too late," he said, as they neared a village with a tangle of limestone houses and a canal winding along one side. "We're here." Marie was surprised that their destination was so close to the villa; they could not have walked more than a few miles. He paused before a stone bridge that ran low over the canal. "This region is one where we haven't had many local contacts. The village is new to us but we've been told that there may be townsfolk sympathetic to the resistance and willing to help. We need to find a house or a café where we can leave messages—and where one of our agents can eventually hide for a night if need be."

"Not a café," Marie replied. Her eyes traveled down the main road into the town, a twisting cobblestone thoroughfare ending at a small square. "A bookshop," she added slowly, the notion forming as she spoke. Messages could be exchanged while perusing the books or perhaps even left in a particular volume. "If they have one."

"A bookshop," Julian repeated, turning the idea over in his head. "It's brilliant!" He was looking at her with approval now. She felt her cheeks flush. "There is one, just off the square. The Germans would never go there because they hate books." Then his smile faded. "You have to do it—persuade the shopkeeper."

"Me alone?" Marie asked. She had been on the ground less than twelve hours.

"Yes. A man walking into the shops at midday raises too many questions."

Marie nodded. People would wonder why he was not off

fighting. "But I came with you only to translate. You saw how poorly I did back there acting calmly when the army truck passed us."

"Are you here to do the job or not?" he snapped.

Her job, Marie wanted to retort, was to operate the radio from somewhere hidden away. Yet somehow in her first twenty-four hours on the ground, she'd become first translator, and now operative. She recalled then how Eleanor said the agents must be well trained in all aspects of the job because they might be called upon to do anything at any time, as well as Josie's comment that they must do the work that was needed. This *was* her mission, or part of it, at least.

"I know you're nervous," Julian said, his voice softening. "Fear is always the first instinct—and rightly so. It's what keeps us on our guard—and alive. But you must train it, harness it. Now go. Ask the owner if he has *The Odyssey* by Homer in the original."

"How will that signal anything?"

"There's a well worked-out series of questions we use to test whether someone is sympathetic to the resistance. We might ask a fishmonger if haddock is in season or the flower shop clerk about tulips. It is usually something out of season or hard to get." He exhaled impatiently. "I really don't have time to explain further. If he has helped before, he will understand the message."

Marie started into the village, past an *école* with children playing in the yard at recess. The bookstore was just north of the square, a quiet storefront beneath a balconied home with a window box of withered poppies between open cornflower blue shutters. *Librairie des Marne*, read the faded yellow paint on the sign outside. Inside, the tiny shop was quiet, save for a boy browsing a rack of comic books. The air was thick with the smell of old paper.

Marie waited until the boy had paid and gone, then approached the bookseller behind the counter in the rear. He was a wizened man with a ring of white hair and spectacles that seemed to rest directly on his bushy moustache with nothing in between. She noticed then a decoration of the First World War on the wall. The bookseller was a veteran—and perhaps something of a patriot. "Bonjour. I am looking for a book."

"Oh?" The shopkeeper sounded surprised. "So few people read today. Most just want my books for kindling."

The bookseller looked so pleased at the prospect of actual business that Marie felt reluctant to disappoint him. "A volume of *The Iliad* in the original." He turned toward the shelf behind him and started to rifle though the books. "I mean, *The Odyssey*," she corrected hastily.

The bookseller turned back slowly. "You don't actually want the book, do you?"

"No."

His eyes widened. Clearly he knew the signal. "You can accept a package?" she asked.

He shook his head vehemently. *"Non."* His eyes traveled across the narrow cobblestone street to a café. Seated behind the plate glass window were several SS, eating breakfast. "I have new neighbors. I'm sorry."

Marie's heartbeat quickened. Surely the Germans had seen her walk into the bookshop.

Pushing down her fear, she tried again. "Monsieur, it would be low profile. Just a letter box in one of the books. You wouldn't even notice." She did not mention the prospect of agents needing to hide in his shop, knowing it would be too much.

"Mademoiselle, my daughter lives upstairs with her son, who is not yet one year old. For myself and even my wife, I would not care at all. But I have to think of my grandchild."

Marie thought of Tess back home in East Anglia. Leaving a child behind was one thing, but to have her right in the middle of the danger would be unbearable. She had no right to ask this of the poor man. She started for the door. Then she saw Vesper in her mind, waiting on the edge of the town expectantly. She could not fail.

"Monsieur, your assistance is dearly needed." A note of desperation crept into her voice.

The bookseller shook his head, then walked from behind the counter to the front of the store and turned the sign in the window to Closed. "Adieu, mademoiselle." He disappeared through a door at the back of the shop.

Marie paused, debating whether she should go after him. But she would not convince him, and drawing attention to herself might make things worse. She started out on the street, dejected. She had failed.

Marie walked from the shop, retracing her steps out of the village and across the low bridge. When she reached the place where she had left Julian, she did not see him. Had he abandoned her? For a moment, she was almost relieved; she would not have to tell him about her failure. But without him, she would have nowhere to go.

She spied Julian then, half-hidden among the trees. She made her way up the embankment to him. "How did it go?"

Marie shook her head. "He wouldn't agree."

She waited for Vesper to berate her. "I'm not surprised," he replied instead. "There have been many reprisals in the region. Everyone is scared to help now."

"Perhaps another shop in the town," she suggested.

"We can't afford to ask anyone else today. We've already stirred up matters with the bookseller and if we ask too many questions around town, people will start to talk."

"What now?"

"I'll take you to the place where you'll be staying. I would have had another agent bring you to the flat, but since we are here I'll take you myself. We can regroup and come up with a new plan." Marie felt a tug of disappointment. She had hoped that they might go back to the safe house and see Josie again. "Come."

Marie had expected him to start back into the forest. She watched with surprise as he instead started toward the town from which she'd just come. "I thought you said you couldn't be seen here," she said, not following him.

He turned back. "Do you always ask so many questions?" The frustration in his voice was unmistakable. "I said I *shouldn't* be seen here. And if you follow me quietly, I won't be." He led her into the village once more, taking one back street and then another, just skirting the square. "The flat from which you'll transmit is in this village as well," he whispered. "In staying here, you should be able to get a sense as to who else we might be able to approach about a safe house."

"And the flat itself can't be used as a safe house?"

Julian shook his head. "Too visible. It wouldn't be safe to hide agents on the run there." Then how, Marie wondered, could it possibly be safe enough for her? "There are different types of safe houses for different purposes," he explained. "Messages, radio operators, agents on the run. Each designated for a specific purpose and separate than the rest."

He led her through an alley and stopped before the rear of one of the houses. "Here." He produced a skeleton key and unlocked a door, then started up a set of steep stairs.

When they could not climb any farther, he opened a door so low he had to duck to get through it. The room was a garret, with a sloping roof. There was a bed and a washstand and not much else. Still, it was much better than the shed where she'd spent the previous night.

"I suppose that's yours." He tilted his head toward the corner, where a familiar case sat.

"My radio!" Marie crossed the room eagerly. She reached for the radio case and opened it, running her hands over the machine. She was relieved to see that it had not been badly damaged in the landing. The coil of the antennae was a bit bent, but she was able to straighten it with her finger. And the telegraph key was loose. It had not been quite right since Eleanor had dismantled the machine, and it seemed to have worsened in transit. She could fix that, though. "Do you have any glue?" she asked.

"No, but I'll have some sent over." Marie made a note in her head to find some pine sap or tar if the glue didn't arrive. She understood then that Eleanor's tearing apart the radio at Arisaig House had prepared her exactly for a moment like this.

"You'll need to hang your wire out the window to transmit," he said. She looked out the window, where he indicated a poplar tree, its buds just beginning to bloom. Then she noticed something familiar across the street. The bookstore. Her stomach did a queer turn. Her flat was just over the café where she had seen the SS.

"But the SS..." she began. "How can this possibly be safe?"

"Because they would never expect you to be here."

"And if they find out?"

"They won't—if you are discreet. Are you hungry?" he asked.

"I am," she admitted. The bit of breakfast she had enjoyed with Albert and the others was a distant memory. Julian went to the cupboard and pulled out half a loaf of bread and some cheese wrapped in paper. Marie wondered whether he had stocked the larder or someone else had a key.

He brought the food to the table and went back for two glasses of water. His hand trembled as he passed one of them, sloshing the water. "Are you all right?" she asked.

"Just exhaustion," he said, trying to smile. "Sleeping in a different place every night, being alone for weeks on end... It wears on you."

But hands didn't tremble just because one was tired. "How long has it been like that?"

His smile faded. "I've had it for years, nerve damage from some shrapnel earlier in the war. It's only been the past few months that it's worsened. Please don't say anything. If the others knew..."

"I swear it."

"Thank you."

They ate in silence. The air grew chilly. "Is it all right if I make a fire in the grate?" she asked, fearing that she would be expected to stay in the cold and dark as she had been in the shed.

He nodded. "Yes. It's no secret that the apartment is occupied." As she tended to the fire, he sat back and stretched his legs out, crossing his black boots. It was the most relaxed she had seen him since they had met.

"So what happens now?" she asked.

"You'll stay here and you'll receive messages to transmit. They'll be brought by couriers or Will, the pilot who flew you in." Julian didn't mention that Will was his cousin, and Marie wondered if the omission was intentional or whether, in his focused world, he considered the information irrelevant. "He's the air movements officer, but he helps coordinate the transmissions as well as the flights. It likely won't be me," he added. "My men—and women," he added, this time correcting himself, "are spread across two hundred miles of northern France. I'm constantly traveling between them to make sure they are doing what is needed." She saw then the responsibility he carried on his shoulders.

"One other thing—be careful when you are transmitting. The SD have become more aware of what we're doing and they're on the lookout for transmissions." Eleanor had said the same, Marie recalled, right before her departure. "Don't transmit for too long and keep an eye out for the direction-finding wagons or other signs that anyone is onto you." Marie nodded. She had heard of the vans that prowled the streets, containing special equipment to detect the source of radio signals. It was hard to imagine the police had such things in this sleepy little town. "You can't stop transmitting, though," Julian continued sternly. "You have to get the messages through. The information we send to London is critical. They need to know that we are making everything as hard as possible for the Germans to respond when the invasion comes."

"When will that be?" It was the ultimate question, and asking it felt audacious even for her.

"I don't know," he admitted, frustration creeping into his voice. "But it's supposed to be that way. Need to know, remember? Safer for everyone. The invasion is coming. That much is certain. And we are here to make sure it is a success." His tone was not boastful but clear and unwavering, one of ownership. Marie saw then that his intensity came not from being arrogant or mean, but from having the weight of the entire operation on his shoulders. She saw him in a new light then, admired his strength. She wondered again if it was wise to have so much go through one person. "That's all you—or anyone else—needs to know."

They were risking their lives, Marie thought. It seemed they had a right to know more.

He rose from his chair. "I have to go. You're to stay here, act normally and transmit the messages the couriers bring you on schedule."

Marie stood. "Wait." She didn't particularly like Julian; she found him prickly and ill-mannered and too intense. But he was one of the few people she knew here and she was not eager to be left alone in this strange apartment, surrounded by Germans.

There was nothing to be done about it, though; going was his work and staying hers. "Goodbye, Marie," he said, and walked out the door, leaving her alone again.

CHAPTER TWELVE

GRACE

Washington, 1946

The next morning, Grace found herself on a train headed south for Washington.

After leaving Mark the previous day, she'd gone straight to work, still thinking about her meeting with the consul. At the beginning, she had only been interested in returning the photos to the suitcase. But after learning that the suitcase belonged to Eleanor and that she had worked for the British government, Grace's questions had multiplied: Who were the girls in the photos and how were they connected to Eleanor? Could the answers possibly be in some files in Washington? The likelihood of finding anything seemed increasingly remote, and her doubts about going there to meet Mark grew stronger as the hours passed.

She hadn't mentioned needing time off to Frankie until the end of the day. "Is everything all right?" he asked when she finally made the request. The lines on his brow deepened with concern. Grace understood his reaction; she hadn't missed a single day in all of the time she had been working for him.

"Fine, fine," she reassured. "Just a family matter," she added with a firmness that she hoped would ward off any further questions.

"You know working, keeping busy, that's the best thing," he offered. Grace's guilt rose. He thought that she was taking time because of her grief over Tom. Instead, she was jetting out of town to chase a mystery that was none of her business with a man she should never see again. "You'll be back the day after tomorrow?" Frankie asked. It was both question and plea.

"I hope so." She couldn't see the trip taking longer than that.

"Good." He smiled. "'Cause I've gotten kinda used to having you around."

Grace smiled inwardly at the begrudging admission that Frankie had come to depend on her. "Thank you," she replied. It was more than just the time off for which she was grateful. It was his making a place for her here and holding it. His understanding. "I'll hurry back. I promise."

The train, a sleek blue Congressional Limited, whooshed across the wide expanse of the Chesapeake. Grace looked around the railcar. The seats were straight-backed, but made with a comfortable leather. The gleaming plate glass windows offered a splendid view of the sun-dappled water. A boy came through with his cart, selling coffee and snacks. Grace shook her head; she was cautious with money, not knowing how much things on the trip would cost. Instead, she pulled out the egg salad sandwich she'd packed.

As she unwrapped the sandwich, Grace peered out the window at a Maryland suburb, freshly built ranch houses in neat culs-de-sac. Manufactured towns like this one seemed to be springing up like weeds everywhere since the men had come home from the war and couples moved out of the cities to start families. Grace imagined women in each house, doing dishes and straightening up after the children had gone to school. She was mixed with equal parts guilt and longing and relief at not being one of them.

When she finished her sandwich, Grace balled up the wax paper. She took out the photographs of the girls, studying the mystery their eyes now seemed to hold. Each had a name written on the back in the same flowing script. *Josie. Brya.* Grace wondered if it was Eleanor's handwriting or someone else's.

It was after eleven o'clock when the train pulled into Union Station. Mark met her on the platform, freshly shaven in a crisp white shirt and sport coat, holding a smart gray fedora rather than wearing it. Seeing her, he seemed almost surprised. He had thought she might not come, she realized, as he kissed her cheek in a gesture that was at the same time too familiar and yet not at all enough. She savored the familiar scent of his aftershave in spite of herself. "Smooth trip?" he asked.

She nodded, stepping away from him with effort. "So what's our plan?" she asked as he led her across the vast marble lobby of the station. She marveled at the high-arched ceiling, which was adorned with an octagonal pattern, gold leafing in the center of each plaster coffer.

"I did some checking on the SOE files," he replied. They walked outside the station. The air was a hint warmer than it had been in New York. Above a cluster of bare trees, Grace could make out the dome of the US Capitol. She had seen it only once before as a girl on a trip with her family. She paused now, admiring its quiet majesty.

He led her to a waiting taxi and held the door. "Tell me," she said, when he had climbed in and closed the door behind him.

"Remember we discussed that SOE was a British agency that sent its people into Europe undercover during the war?"

"I do. What were they sent into Europe to do? Were they spies?"

"Not exactly. They were deployed to help the French partisans, supply weapons, sabotage German operations, that sort of thing." *Whatever could Eleanor have to do with that?* Grace wondered. Mark continued, "Anyway, I did some checking. An old army pal of mine, Tony, has a sister who works at the Pentagon. She confirmed what the consul said—some of SOE's files were transferred here after the war."

"That seems odd."

He shrugged. "Not a whole lot was making sense right after the war ended. But maybe there's something about Eleanor in those files."

"Or about the girls in the photos," Grace added. "Perhaps they had something to do with SOE as well." The whole thing had become about something larger than just Eleanor now. She pulled the photographs from her bag.

He moved closer to have a look. "May I?"

She handed him the photos. "If we can find out who they were…" Doubts nagged at her. "But how can we get access to the files? Surely they won't just let us walk in…" She exhaled sharply so that her breath blew her bangs upward.

Mark smiled. "I like it when you do that." Grace could feel her cheeks flush. This was about Eleanor and the girls, she reminded herself sternly. Otherwise, she would not be here at all.

"No, it's true the records have not been made public," he continued. "But Tony said his sister can get us access."

"You think she can do it?"

"I guess we'll find out."

The taxi navigated the wide circle in front of Union Station, weaving between the streetcars as it merged onto a wider thoroughfare. Though the war had been over for months, the signs around the city were still visible, from sandbags stacked against the base of a building to bits of blackout tape still clinging to the windows. Men in tired suits smoked on the curbs in front of nondescript government buildings. There were boys in winter coats playing baseball on the wide expanse of the Mall, tourists walking between the museums—little signs of the city coming back to life.

The cab began to climb the expanse of a long bridge across the Potomac, carrying them into Virginia. The Pentagon came into view. Grace had seen pictures of it in the newspaper, built to accommodate the massive Department of the Army that had grown out of the war. As they drew close, she was awed by the sheer size: each side was the length of several city blocks. A construction crane still hovered over scaffolding on one part of the building. Did they really need all of this now that the war was over?

The taxi pulled through the massive parking lot and stopped close to the door on one side of the Pentagon. Mark paid the driver and stepped out of the car. Looking up at the American flag waving high over the entranceway, Grace faltered; she had no business being here. But Mark came around and opened her door. "Do you want to know about Eleanor Trigg or not?" He had a quiet confidence about him, a sure-handedness that made her feel more certain of herself. She stepped from the car.

Inside, Mark took off his hat and gave his name to the soldier standing behind the desk. Grace peered around the official-looking entranceway and wondered if they would be turned away.

But a few minutes later, a shapely brunette in a pencil skirt appeared. Maybe a year or two younger than Grace, she was impossibly chic, in a way that Grace herself could never quite manage. She wore her dark hair in a sleek cap, the latest style. Her mouth was a perfect red bow. A curvier Ava Gardner. As she brushed past Grace to extend her hand to Mark, there was a faint hint of jasmine.

"I'm Raquel. You must be Mark."

"Guilty," he quipped, with the same twinkle in his eye that Grace had seen the night they met. "Tony has told me so much about you."

"He lies," Raquel quipped back. Good Lord, Grace thought,

with a tug of jealousy she had no right to feel. Were they flirting right in front of her?

"You must be Grace," Raquel added, making it sound like an afterthought. But at least Raquel was expecting her as well. Before Grace could respond, Raquel turned back to Mark. "Follow me." She pivoted on one foot. Her heels clicked against the floor as she led them down a hallway along an endless row of identical doors. They passed several men in uniform, their chests crowded with badges and medals, expressions grave. Tom would have been awed by the whole thing, Grace thought, with a note of sadness. She was suddenly homesick for New York and the messy comfort of Frankie's tiny office.

"We don't have long," Raquel said in a low voice when the men had passed and they were alone in the corridor once more. "Brian—he's the archivist—is at lunch. We have maybe an hour, tops, before he gets back." Grace hesitated. She hadn't realized that they would be sneaking in. But it was too late to back out now. Raquel had opened a door and was ushering them down a back staircase.

"The files aren't classified?" Mark asked.

Raquel shook her head. "Not really public either." The consul had said that the records would be sealed, Grace remembered, wondering if these were the right ones. "Brian said they arrived without notice from London earlier this year. He doesn't think anyone has gone through them."

"Why were the files brought here?" Grace asked, as they reached a landing and started down a second staircase. It was the question that had been nagging at her. Why had they shipped British documents all the way across the Atlantic?

"I have no idea," Raquel replied. When they reached the bottom floor, she led them into a storeroom with boxes piled high behind a chain-link gate. "The ones you're looking for should be somewhere over there." Raquel gestured vaguely toward the right side of the room, where about a dozen boxes were stacked on shelves. "Just be sure to put everything back as you found it. I'll be back in half an hour." Raquel turned and went, leaving them alone in the room full of boxes.

Grace looked at Mark questioningly. "There's no way to get through all of this in such a short time. How do we begin?"

Mark ran his hand over one of the boxes, clearing some dust. "We'll each take half. We just need to figure out how they're organized."

She studied the side of the boxes. Each bore a single letter, handwritten and circled. "What do you suppose that means?" He shrugged. She thought then of the photographs in her bag. Quickly she pulled them out. There was a small notation on the bottom of each picture. "I remember that the consul said something about Eleanor working for a section of SOE." Sure enough, on the bottom of each photo there was a small plate bearing the phrase *F Section*.

Mark was already ahead of her, moving through the boxes and stacks to a place on a shelf. "Here." She followed him and looked up. At least five of the boxes were marked with an *F*.

"Same letter as on the box," she remarked. "I wonder what it stands for."

Mark pulled two boxes off the shelf and set them on the ground. As he knelt to open one of them, Grace found her eyes drawn to the spot where his collar had pulled back to reveal a pale bit of skin, his brown hair curling against his neck. *Stop*, she scolded silently. Whatever madness had happened between them in New York, that was all in the past. He was Tom's friend, doing her a favor by helping her to gain access to the files. That was all.

Grace knelt before the other box on the ground, swiping at a handful of dust and coughing. She opened it. There were files, each bearing a surname on the label. She opened the top file. It contained a black-and-white photo like the ones Eleanor had been carrying, only this one was of a man. The file detailed locations and missions in Occupied Europe, presumably which the agent had undertaken for SOE. "The *F* is for French section," Mark called. "It looks like these are all people who were deployed to France during the war."

She flipped to the next file, then another. "But mine are all men."

"Mine, too."

That made sense, Grace reflected. The kind of work Mark had described SOE doing would have been done by men. And except for the *F* notation on the boxes and photos, there did not seem to be any connection to Eleanor. Grace wondered for a second if the trip to Washington had been all for nothing. She would get a train back to New York tonight and return to work in the morning.

"Here!" Mark called, interrupting her thoughts. As she stood and walked over to where he stood by the shelf, he pulled a thick stack of files from one of the boxes. "Regina Angell," he read aloud from the top of the file. Then he flipped to another. "Tracy Edmonds. Stephanie Turnow." She took one of the files from Mark and opened it. Inside was a photo like the ones Eleanor had carried. The name beneath the image was written in the same neat handwriting that Grace recognized from Eleanor's photos. Some of the SOE agents had been women after all.

But none of the names on the files were the same as the ones on the photos, Grace realized as she thumbed quickly through the box. Her shoulders slumped with disappointment. "The names don't match. These aren't the right ones."

"I wonder how many girls worked for SOE."

"There are about thirty here," Grace replied, thumbing through the files. "Plus another dozen if the ones in Eleanor's photos actually worked for SOE as well." She was surprised there had been so many female agents. She lifted one of the files. Sally Rider, the label read. Inside it was a personnel file or dossier of some sort, a page of background with a photo, then notes about training. The detail was impressive, line after line about the various schools the girl had been through, how she had performed at various tests and drills, all in that same handwritten script.

Grace scanned the file. Born in Herefordshire, it said. It contained a last known contact, not in England, but America. Impulsively, Grace pulled out a pencil and a scrap of paper and scribbled down the phone number in the file. Then there was a list of places: Paris, Lille. The women had been deployed for SOE to undertake various missions in Occupied Europe. The last entry was for Chartres in 1944. Nothing after that.

Grace closed the file and began thumbing through the others. Each had the same basic information, hometown, contact information. It was the list of whereabouts that was most interesting: Amiens, Beauvais. The missions had taken them to all corners of France.

There was something else she noticed, too: lots of lines blacked out. "Someone redacted the hell out of them," Mark observed over her shoulder.

"Maybe the files on the girls in the photos are in another box?"

But Mark shook his head. "There are seven boxes on F Section in all. The files in the others are all on men." He reached around Grace to thumb through the box she had been searching. "What's this?" He pulled out a thin manila folder that had been wedged between two of the personnel files. "This is odd," he remarked, paging through it.

"What is it?"

"Wireless transmissions. Some interoffice documents and telegrams, too. But it doesn't look like it belongs in this box with the personnel files. Someone must have packed it there by mistake." Grace reached for the file, wondering if it would shed some more light on the girls in the photos. She noticed that several of the documents had been issued on the same letterhead: "From the Desk of the Recruitment and Logistics Officer, E. Trigg."

Eleanor wasn't just a secretary. She was running things.

There was a clattering at the door to the archive. Grace turned to see Raquel in the doorway. "Raquel," Mark said. "We weren't expecting you back so soon." They could not have been in the archive for more than fifteen minutes.

"I saw Brian walking across the parking lot," Raquel stammered. The archivist must have come back from lunch early. "Come quickly." She led them out a back doorway and up a different flight of stairs. A few minutes later, she let them out onto a loading dock. "I'll phone you a cab. I never should have let you in here. I could lose my job."

"Thank you," Mark began, putting his hat on once more. "Tell Tony…" But Raquel had closed the door and was already gone.

"I'm sorry that wasn't more helpful," Mark said a few minutes later when they were seated in the cab. "A whole trip to DC for a few minutes in the archives. We could have used hours in there."

"Agreed. But at least we have this." She reached in her coat and pulled out the narrow file containing the wireless transmissions.

He stared, stunned by her audacity. "You took it."

"Borrowed, let us say. I didn't mean to. I was just startled when Raquel came back early, and I did it before I could think." Just like with the photos in the station. Hadn't she created enough of a mess by taking something that wasn't hers already? "I'm sorry. I shouldn't have." It was his friend who had given her access to the files and she hoped he wouldn't be mad.

But he smiled. "That was nervy. I'm impressed. Can I see?" He moved closer across the seat. She handed the file to him. He skipped the first few sheets, which he had seen when they were in the archives. "Eleanor's name is all over these papers," he remarked. "It seems like she was in charge, or pretty close to it."

"Not at all the clerk that the consul had described her to be," Grace replied. She wondered what else Sir Meacham might have been wrong—or lied—about. "But I still wonder about the girls in the photos. If there were no files on them, could they still have been agents, too?"

Mark pulled out two papers that were stapled together, scanning them. "This is a full list of all of the female agents, or at least it seems to be."

"Are the girls in the photos on there?"

He nodded and pointed to one of the familiar names, Eileen Nearne, then another, Josie Watkins. They had surnames now, had become whole people. "So they were on the list, but there were no personnel files for them," she mused. "I wonder what that means." There was a little notation next to about a dozen of the names—the same ones that were on the photos: *NN.*

"What does that stand for?"

Mark flipped over to the second page where there was a small legend. "'Nacht und Nebel,'" he read. "Night and Fog."

"But what does it mean?"

"It was a German program, designed to make people quite literally disappear." He closed the file. Then he turned to Grace, his expression somber. "I'm sorry, Gracie," he said gently, putting his arm around her shoulder. "But it means that all of the girls in the photos are dead."

CHAPTER THIRTEEN

ELEANOR

London, 1944

The first thing that should have tipped Eleanor off was the lack of mistakes.

She was alone in her office at Norgeby House, flipping through the roller deck of cards again and again like some movie she had seen a thousand times. Each three-by-five index card contained details for one of the girls, her background, strengths and liabilities, last known whereabouts. She didn't need to read them; she knew them all by heart. Her complete recall was not something she tried to do. Rather, once she saw a detail about an agent or a bit of news from France, it was seared indelibly on her brain.

Eleanor rubbed her eyes, then looked up around the office. It was a generous term for the windowless former broom closet. It was the only spot available, the clerk had claimed when she had turned up at the administrative office at headquarters with the note from the Director requisitioning a place for her unit.

Though Eleanor doubted this was true, she had no way to prove it and she took the space in the cellar, which was scarcely big enough to hold a desk. The air was so heavy with the smell of cleanser, it somedays threatened to overpower her. But the location was good, close to the radio room where transmissions were sent and received. The endless clacking of the teletype in the background was a now-familiar lullaby, one she was destined to hear even in her dreams.

Or would be, if she ever slept. Eleanor had practically lived in the office at Norgeby House in the months since she had started sending girls into the field, only going home briefly every few days to change clothes and reassure her mother that she was fine. Belle Tottenberg, who had changed her surname to Trigg upon arrival from Pinsk nearly twenty-five years earlier in order to fit in with the English circles she aspired to join, had never approved of what she referred to as her daughter's "boring little office job." If Eleanor had to work, she'd often said, it might as well be at Harrods or Selfridges. Eleanor had considered more than once telling her about the girls she recruited and the way they reminded her of Tatiana. But even if she could share such matters, Eleanor knew the meaning would be lost on her mother, who had buried her grief in a whirlwind of teas and plays, putting behind her the dark years that Eleanor herself could never seem to outrun.

Eleanor remained at Norgeby House nearly around the clock by choice, catching short naps at her desk in between the times when transmissions were scheduled and they were expecting messages from the field. She didn't have to stay; the wireless transmissions, which almost always came at night, would have been sorted and decoded and delivered to her in the morning. But she liked to study the messages as they came in to recognize the patterns in the text and ways the girls transmitted. By receiving the messages in real time, it felt almost like the girls were speaking to her directly.

Eleanor stood up from her desk and started toward the radio room. In the hallway, two uniformed men were talking in low voices. They averted their eyes as she passed. The male officers who had voiced such skepticism about her heading up the women's sector had not warmed to her. There was a hesitation when she entered the room for the morning briefing now, an almost whisper. As long as they didn't interfere with her doing her job and looking out for her girls, Eleanor didn't care.

Eleanor walked into the radio room. The air was thick with the smell of cigarette smoke and burned coffee. A half-dozen or so operators, all women younger than herself, clacked out messages or hunched over papers, decoding electric signals from the field, which were received at the transmission station at Grendon Underwood, then sent to Norgeby House by teleprinter. Fairy godmothers, the women at London headquarters were called by agents in the field. Each assigned to a specific agent or three or five, they waited loyally for the broadcast like a dog waiting for its master to come home.

Eleanor studied the blackboard that covered the front wall of the room, scanning the names chalked on it for her girls. The radio transmissions were scheduled for twice weekly at regular intervals, exchanges where London could send information about drops of personnel or equipment and receive correspondence from the field. They might come more often, if there was an urgent matter, or less if it was not safe for an operator to transmit. Ruth, whom they'd poached from the codebreakers at Bletchley Park, was on the schedule, as was Hannah, who had lost a child in the Blitz.

Marie's name was up on the blackboard, too, signaling that a transmission was expected this evening. It had been a week since Marie had dropped blind into that field north of Paris. There had been an initial communication from another W/T in a neighboring circuit, saying that Marie landed. Marie had missed her first scheduled broadcast three days earlier. A few hours' delay in a transmission was not uncommon. The Germans might have isolated her signal and blocked it. But three days might mean something more.

Eleanor felt her panic rise, then pressed it down neatly again into faint concern. Early on, she had learned not to get attached to the girls. Eleanor knew each of them personally, their background and history, their strengths and weaknesses. She remembered the first time she deployed one of the girls, a young Scottish girl called Angie who was to be dropped into Alsace-Lorraine. In that moment everything they had planned and prepared for was actually being set in motion, all of her plans and work come to fruition. The reality hit Eleanor then: the girl would no longer be under her control. Eleanor grew nervous, almost panicked and ready to call it all off. Something washed over her, a protectiveness. A maternal instinct, she might have called it, if she had any idea what that felt like. It had taken everything she had to go through with sending the girl.

The exercise of deploying the girls hadn't gotten any easier with time. She felt a sense of ownership, was vested in their well-being. She also knew the statistics, though, the very great odds that some would not survive. The practical reality was that some of them might not be coming back. Sentimentality would only cloud her judgment.

"Ma'am?" said one of the girls, an earnest, ginger-haired operator called Jane. Eleanor looked up from the pouch. "There's a transmission. From Marie." Eleanor leaped to her feet and sprinted to Jane's station. There was Marie's code name, Angel, at the bottom of the page. Eleanor had never liked it for the way that it bespoke death. She had meant to change it, but things had gotten busy and there hadn't been time.

"You have the worked-out key?" Jane nodded, then handed Eleanor the slip of paper containing the cipher that Marie would have used to code the message in the field.

As she began to decode the message, Eleanor wondered if it

might be garbled, as the girls' transmissions so often were, owing to weather interfering with the radio signals or circumstances forcing the W/Ts to rush. But the message was neat and clean. "In the Cardinal's nest. Eggs safe." Eleanor ran her fingers over the page, hearing Marie's voice in the text typed across the page. "The Cardinal" was a reference to Vesper, and "eggs" meant her radio had arrived intact.

The text was unremarkable and smooth, indistinct. It might have been written by anyone. Marie's heaviness on the first letter, the hallmark of her fist print, was lighter than usual.

Eleanor scanned the message for Marie's security checks, the mistakes she had been trained to include to verify her identity. She knew Marie's bluff check was to substitute a *p* for the thirty-fifth letter, but the message wasn't long enough for that. Nor did it contain a *c* where she should have substituted for a *k*, her true check. Eleanor cursed the code instructor who, in trying to create unique checks that would not be easily detected, had gotten too sophisticated and failed to give Marie checks that would have been usable in every transmission.

Eleanor studied the paper once more. Something felt off. She turned to Jane. "What do you think?"

Jane read the message through horn-rimmed glasses once, then again. "I'm not certain," she said slowly. But Eleanor could tell from Jane's face that she was worried, too.

"Is it her?" Eleanor pressed. She pictured Marie that night at Tangmere. Marie had seemed nervous, as if having doubts, Eleanor could see. But they all had doubts right before going. Good God, how could they not?

"I think so," Jane said, her voice more hopeful than definite. "The message is so brief. Maybe she was just rushed."

"Maybe," Eleanor repeated without conviction. Other than the fist print being a bit light, there was nothing else to support her uneasiness. But she felt it nevertheless.

"What do you want to do?" Jane asked, returning to her

own desk. They had at best a few minutes to transmit back to Marie. Eleanor needed Jane to send a message to Marie about the arms drop that was scheduled for the following Tuesday so that the Vesper circuit could organize a reception committee, locals who would receive the munitions and store them for the partisans. But if Marie had been somehow compromised, the information would fall into the wrong hands.

I need to send her a personal message, Eleanor thought. Something that only Marie would know. She hesitated. Airtime was scarce and precious and it was risky to keep an operator transmitting any longer than absolutely necessary. But she needed to confirm with Marie that it was really her—and nothing was amiss. "Tell her I'm holding the butterfly." It was a veiled reference to Marie's locket necklace, the one that she had confiscated the night Marie left. Though she wasn't quite sure, she sensed the necklace had meant a great deal to Marie. Something to do with her daughter, perhaps. Surely the message would prompt a personal response.

Eleanor held her breath as Jane coded and sent the message. Two minutes passed, then three. She imagined Marie receiving it, willed the girl to say something to reassure them it was her. The message came: "Thank you for the information." No recognition of the personal reference, nothing to confirm that it was really Marie. Eleanor's heart sank.

But the fist print was familiar now, heavy on the first word now like Marie's. "It looks like her this time, doesn't it?" Jane said, seeking reassurance.

"Yes," she replied. Marie had been told time and again in training not to talk about herself or her background, or to broadcast personal information. Perhaps in replying generically to Eleanor's message, she was just following orders.

"So what should we do?" Jane looked up at Eleanor uncertainly, asking whether to transmit the information about the next arms drop.

Eleanor hesitated. She had trained the girls, backed them with everything they had. But she was just being overly cautious now, and it wasn't like her. She had to believe that they were up to the job and would make the right decisions. Otherwise, none of this would work and the whole thing would fall apart.

Eleanor had to make the call. She stared at the radio, as though she might actually be able to hear Marie's voice and know it was her. Eleanor believed that, despite Marie's difficulties while training at Arisaig House, the girl was strong and smart enough and had grown sufficiently in training to rise to the challenges of the field; she would have otherwise never sent her into such dangerous territory. She had to trust now that Marie would never let anything happen to her wireless. And stopping the transmission would mean delaying operations. It was this or nothing.

She lifted her chin defiantly. "Send it," she instructed Jane. Then she walked from the room.

CHAPTER FOURTEEN

MARIE

France, 1944

Marie sat alone in the garret, waiting for the hours to pass so that she could transmit and trying not to think about the German on the other side of the wall.

It had been over a week since Julian brought her to Rosny-sur-Seine. He had not come again and she wondered where he had gone in the days he had left her. The tiny flat was pleasant enough, with two paned glass windows, one on the front overlooking the street and a second at the rear facing the canal. Late-day sunlight shone through the latter now, causing funny-shaped patterns to dance across the worn duvet on the bed.

It had turned out that the Germans did not just frequent the café downstairs. They were billeted in the same building, including one in the adjacent flat, which occupied the other half of the top floor, others below. When Marie had first discovered this, on a late-night trip to the toilet down the hall, she had thought Julian mad. Or perhaps he simply did not care if she was caught. But she had come to see that it was the perfect safe house because they never would have expected anything so close. And she took a peculiar satisfaction in transmitting quite literally under the Germans' noses.

Marie looked up at the clock. Five fifteen. Nearly time to transmit the message that a courier she did not recognize had brought her earlier. It was the waiting that was the hardest—and the part nobody had told her about in training. Each day she waited for instructions to transmit. At night she listened to the radio, hoping the BBC broadcast might contain at the end *messages personnel* that signaled an agent's arrival, or might secretly announce that the invasion was coming. She had left the flat once to go to the market on the square on Tuesday and another time to the patisserie shop, little errands so the locals wouldn't talk about that strange woman closed up in the apartment on Rue Anton. She'd been out so little that, except for in a few brief encounters with the landlady, she hadn't needed to use her alias or cover story at all.

Gazing out the window at the meadows bathed in soft light, she thought longingly of Tess and hoped the weather was nice enough in East Anglia to take advantage of the lengthening days and play outside after supper. If only she had been allowed to bring a photo of Tess with her. The image of the child was still crisp in her mind, though she had probably changed since Marie saw her last.

Marie moved her chair close to the low table in the corner where her radio sat, thinly disguised as a gramophone, with a top that inverted to quickly disguise the device. She pulled from her slip the tiny paper the courier had delivered earlier bearing Vesper's now-familiar handwriting. First she had to code the message. She felt in the lining of her shoe for the worked-out code, a small slip of silk bearing a cipher. The message was barely intelligible to Marie, filled with cryptic terms and messages that only made sense to Vesper and, hopefully, whoever was receiving it back at Norgeby House. She wondered if Eleanor might be there. Marie read the coded text she was to transmit several times to make sure she had it just right. Then she burned the original, uncoded message over the candle in front of her, dropping the last bit so her fingers would not get singed.

She selected from the spare parts pocket the crystal that would enable her to transmit on the proper frequency. After inserting the crystal, she began to type the message that she had coded. The wireless key clicked under her fingertips with satisfying purpose. Her radio touch was light and deft. She had noticed her own improvement during her short time in the field, like a foreign language she had once learned in the classroom now becoming fluent in-country. She could weave together a message quickly without wasting a single word.

A loud burst of laughter and song erupted from below, causing Marie to pause. She stood and walked to the rear window of the flat. The noise had come not from outside, but from the café below. She noticed outside the window, though, that the aerial wire she'd secretly hung the night after she arrived had dropped from where she had fixed it among the branches. Without the proper placement, her signal might not be sent. She opened the window and started to reach out.

Then she froze, hand suspended in midair. On the balcony of the room below stood a German soldier, watching her with interest.

Marie managed a smile, waved as though she was simply hanging wash. "Bonsoir," she called, trying to keep her voice light. She pulled her arm back inside, then closed the window with shaking hands.

She should stop typing, she knew. The German had seemed not to suspect anything, but he could be reporting her right now. She had to get this message out, though, and there were only a few more keystrokes. She tapped furiously and then stopped, her heart beating louder than the keys. She turned the radio top back over to disguise it as a gramophone, hoping that it had not been too late.

Marie heard the footsteps on the stairs. Someone was coming. Had her transmission been detected? *Destroy the radio, and if you cannot, then at least the crystals.* The instructions she had received in training played hurriedly in her mind, but she found herself unable to follow them. She sat like an animal trapped in headlights.

The footsteps grew louder. Would they split the door or knock, forcing her to answer? She gripped the necklace containing the cyanide capsule in her hand. "Chew it quickly," Eleanor had said. Tess appeared in her mind, left behind without parents at the age of five. The guilt that Marie had buried all these months sprung forward. She was a mother of a small child who needed her, and who would pay the price if anything happened. Being here was simply irresponsible.

The footsteps stopped in front of her door. Marie counted: *seven, eight, nine.* There was a knock at the door.

Marie looked desperately over her shoulder, wishing there was another way to escape. Hiding in the tiny flat was impossible. The knock came again. Reluctantly, she walked to the door and opened it.

She was surprised to see the pilot Will standing on the other side. "You scared me to death," she said.

His expression was serious. "Then stop transmitting sooner. I could hear your tapping all the way down the corridor." His Irish accent seemed stronger now, hard on the *r*s. "You'll do none of us any good if you're caught." Then his brown eyes softened. "How are you?"

Bored and lonely and nervous living surrounded by Germans, she wanted to say. But it felt petty to complain. "What are you doing here?" she asked instead, as her fear receded. "I'm not scheduled to transmit again until Thursday."

"I didn't come to bring you a message."

"Then what?"

"Julian needs your help."

Her ears pricked. "To translate again?"

He shook his head. "Something different."

Remembering her last failed mission for Julian with the bookseller, she was suddenly nervous. "What does he want?"

"Enough with the questions," he said. "Come."

Marie donned her coat and hat hurriedly, then picked up her purse. But she couldn't resist one more question. "If Julian needs me, why didn't he get me himself?"

"It wasn't safe for him to come." *Not safe.* Concern rose in her as she wondered what might have happened. As the leader of F Section, Julian was one of the most visible targets in northern France. There was little the Germans wouldn't do to find him. The dangers outside loomed all the more real. Suddenly staying here and being bored didn't seem like the worst thing in the world.

Will led Marie down the front stairs to a Peugeot parked at the curb and held open the door. "Get in."

On the street, the shops were closing for the night. The bookseller, drawing his shutters closed, looked up but did not acknowledge her. The café below her flat was just getting crowded, Germans clustering around the bar and tables. She hoped they would not notice her.

Will started the car and began to drive from the village without speaking. She studied him out of the corner of her eye. "Julian tells me you're the air movements officer."

He chuckled. "That's a very big name for what I do."

But really, she knew, his job was vast. He was the head of Moon Squadron, the ragtag bunch of pilots who, along with the RAF, made the drops into Occupied France. He controlled when the flights came and where they landed, who was on them and who left. And he handled virtually all of the mail that went between F Section and London. "My cousin exaggerates," he added.

"Josie mentioned you're related."

"We were raised like brothers on Julian's family farm in Cornwall," he explained. "My mum was a single mother." *Like me*, Marie thought, though she wasn't ready to say as much to Will. "She left me with her sister for long stretches because she had to work. And she died of flu when I was eleven." Will spoke easily, so unlike the tight-lipped manner in which the agents had been trained. "So Julian and I grew up together. And now we are all we have left."

"You don't have any family back home?"

Will shook his head. "I've always been alone. Julian's kind of everyone's and no one's at all. He was married, though," he offered, deflecting attention from himself. His face grew somber. "His wife and children were on a passenger ship, the *Athenia*, that was torpedoed by the Germans. There were no survivors."

"Oh, goodness," Marie said. She had no idea Julian was hiding such pain beneath his intensity and focus. She was amazed he was still living and walking at all. She thought of Tess with a giant pang in her heart. If anything happened to her daughter, she would not live to see the sun rise the next day.

"So it's just him and me now, and I would do anything for him. Even though sometimes he's dead wrong."

"You mean about warning the locals?" she asked, recalling his disagreement with Julian the morning she'd arrived.

He nodded. "There are people who have risen from all corners of France to help us. The dry cleaner who uses his solvents to make false papers. An owner of a brothel on Rue Malebranche in Paris that hides us when no one else will. And the *maquisards*. These people will pay with their lives for what we are doing. They deserve to know what is to come so they can try to protect themselves and their families."

He pulled up in front of the small rail station where she and

Julian had fetched the bike the morning after she had arrived. "Delivering me again," she mused.

Will smiled. "That seems to be my lot in life." One day, perhaps, he would also deliver her home. The thought was too dear to speak aloud. "Your train will be coming in ten minutes."

"My train?" She felt a nag of disappointment. When Will said Julian needed her, she thought that she would be seeing him and that they would be going somewhere together. "I don't understand. Where am I headed? And where is Julian?"

"He will meet you after," Will replied. After what? Marie wondered. But before she could ask, Will pulled out a piece of paper. "Memorize this address." She read it: 273 Rue Hermel, Montmartre.

She turned to him in disbelief. "Montmartre?"

"Yes. Julian said to tell you it is time you saw Paris."

Three hours later, Marie emerged from the metro station at Clignancourt and stepped out onto the steeply sloping Montmartre street. It was drizzling faintly and the damp pavement seemed to glow in the moonlight. The white dome of Sacré Cœur Basilica loomed overhead to the south, defiant and dazzling against the night sky. Dank smells rose from the sewers.

She had followed Will's instructions and taken the night train into Gare du Nord, made her way from the rail station to the north Paris neighborhood, a tangle of narrow, winding cobblestone streets lined with bustling cafés and art galleries.

Go to the address she'd memorized, he said, and ask for Andreas; take the package he would give her and meet Julian at the Gare Saint-Lazare before the last train at eleven. "The package is absolutely critical to the mission," he'd said. Then what on earth had made Julian send her, a radio operator with no experience as a courier who had been in-country all of a week? "The address you are looking for is a café and it will have a canary cage in the window. If there is no bird in the cage, that means it isn't safe to approach."

The address Will had given her was a sloping row house with a café on the ground floor. *L'ambassadeur*, read the gnarled wooden sign that jutted from the window beneath a striped awning. She searched for the birdcage but did not see it. Panic rose in her. An empty birdcage meant that it was not safe to enter, Will had said. He had not told her what to do if there was no birdcage at all.

Seeing no other choice, Marie walked into the café. It was almost empty, save for a group of men playing cards at the rear. The legendary singer Marie Dubas warbled "Mon Légionnaire" from an unseen gramophone. Behind the mirrored bar, a man in a white apron was drying glasses. He did not look up. What now?

She took a seat at one of the tables and placed her gloves atop the newspaper, fingers facing out, a signal of the resistance she had learned in training. A few minutes later, a waiter came over and placed a menu in front of her. Marie hesitated, confused. Will had said nothing about this part of the plan. She opened the menu, and inside was a small skeleton key. She looked up at the waiter. He gestured slightly with his head to the rear of the restaurant.

Clearly he meant for her to go there. But then what? Palming the key, Marie stood and walked nervously past the men who were playing cards. One of the men flicked his eyes upward and she held her breath as she passed, waiting for him to say something. But he was merely taking her in, appraising her in that way Frenchmen seemed to do. Not meeting his stare, she continued down a short corridor, past the kitchen and toilets. She found herself in a storeroom with a narrow set of stairs at the rear. Her nerves prickled; was this some sort of a trap? She looked back over her shoulder, but did not see the waiter who had sent her here.

Steeling herself, she climbed the stairs. The door at the top was locked. She inserted the key the waiter had given her. It slipped in the lock, twirling around but not working. Finally it caught, and she pushed the door open.

On the other side was a narrow, nearly dark room, an attic or warehouse of some sort. At the rear, an elderly man sat beneath a lone desk light, head bowed beneath a visor. Cigarette smoke plumed above him. Why had he not simply let her in?

Closer, she saw that he was working on some sort of device, meticulously connecting wires. He did not acknowledge her and she wondered if she should say something. She knew from training not to give her alias unless prompted. One minute passed, then another. Finally he looked up. "Raise your shirt."

"Excuse me?" she replied indignantly.

The man produced a package wrapped in brown paper, about the size of an envelope and an inch thick. Then he pulled out a roll of duct tape. "I need to secure this to you." She raised her arms and lifted her shirt. Then she turned her head away, mortified by the indignity. He was businesslike, though, taking care not to touch more than was necessary as he secured it to her body. "You'll want to move slowly," he said. "Don't let it get wet, or it won't work. And whatever you do, don't stumble."

"Why?"

"Because you'll kill yourself and whoever is around you as well. The package contains TNT."

Marie froze, recalling from Arisaig House the detonations that happened all too easily. There had been rumors of one agent in training who had been careless and lost a finger. Julian could not possibly expect her to transport dynamite out of Paris.

The man took a long drag from the cigarette that seemed decidedly a bad idea around the explosive. "Go," he said, dismissing her.

In the distance, a clock chimed ten. She needed to leave now if she was to meet Julian in time and make it out of the city before curfew.

Marie took one step, holding her breath, then another, backing out of the room as one might ease away from a dangerous animal. She started down the stairs, each step feeling as though it would be her last. She forced herself to walk normally through the café past the men. Sweat coursed down her body and she tried not to think about what might happen if the TNT got wet.

At the street, she stumbled, nearly falling. She braced, waiting for the explosion that would mean her end. But the package remained still.

Thirty minutes later she stood at the entrance to the Gare Saint-Lazare. The journey had taken longer than it should with the dangerous package that she dared not jostle or drop. Even at the late hour, the station was packed with travelers, families with sleepy children and too many bags, soldiers who pushed past them importantly. Marie consulted the board and saw that the next train back left in fifteen minutes from platform eight. She started for it.

She scanned the crowd, looking for Julian, eager to give him this package and be done with it. At last she spotted him, maybe twenty meters ahead, waiting for her on the platform. She raised her hand to get his attention. His eyes met hers, but he did not smile. His face remained solemn. Then she saw why: French police stood between them, inspecting the passengers individually as they approached the platform.

Marie panicked. There was a crush of passengers behind her, jostling into a rough queue as they neared the police. She couldn't get out of line without avoiding detection. But the package was bulky, impossible to hide or disguise if someone felt her midsection. She eyed a trash bin, wishing she could deposit the package there. Or perhaps in the toilet. But the line had moved forward now and she was nearly at the checkpoint. There was no way to remove the TNT from her body.

She reached the front of the line. "Papers," a policeman ordered and she delayed, unable to open her coat and access her purse without revealing the package. Travelers waiting behind her began to grumble at the delay. "Out of line!" the policeman shouted, losing patience. He waved her over to another officer who was doing more thorough inspections.

"Toilet?" she asked desperately, expecting the second officer to refuse. *"Les regles,"* she said, gesturing downward and using the French term for her period. She hoped that the crude reference would, at a minimum, help her avoid a close inspection. The officer looked horrified and waved her quickly into an adjacent ladies' room. Inside Marie pulled her shirt up, knowing that she only had seconds to stay in the toilet without attracting attention. She pulled the TNT carefully from her body, fighting the urge to cry out where it ripped her skin, causing it to bleed. For a moment, she considered leaving the package in the toilet, rather than risk being caught with it. But Will had said it was critical to the mission. Instead, she wedged it into the secret compartment at the bottom of her purse, squeezing the edges too tightly in order to make it fit.

She stepped from the bathroom and into the inspection queue once more, feeling Julian's eyes still on her. A few minutes later, she reached the front of the line. The police officer reached to pat her down and she fought not to recoil. Resisting would surely only make things worse. The man's hands were on her body, in all the places that they shouldn't have been, bringing back childhood nightmares, worse than the kicks and blows, which she thought she had buried forever. She gritted her teeth, willing herself not to feel the cold, invasive touch, taking from her as much as it could. It did not matter at all, she told herself, as long as it kept him away from the satchel.

Julian was watching the assault on the other side of the checkpoint. His face seethed with anger and his fists were clenched. She saw him reach for his gun. She pleaded with him with her eyes to be still and not react. It would destroy the mission and mean arrest or worse for both of them.

After what seemed an eternity, the policeman removed his filthy hands from her body. He reached for the bag and looked in the main compartment. His search was thorough, determined. In a moment, he would surely find the hidden package.

"Darling!" Julian stepped forward before the policeman could stop him, placing himself between the officer and Marie. "My wife is pregnant," he said, breaking his own rule of not trying to use his piteous French. He managed the words somehow, but his accent was abysmal. Marie froze. Just a second ago she had told the guard that she had her period; Julian hadn't heard and his story directly contradicted hers. She waited for the policeman to realize the lie.

"I feel ill," she chimed in, starting to double over.

The policeman stepped back. "Go!" he ordered. Julian held up his own papers, waving her through the gate.

"Keep walking," Julian murmured and she did, not looking back, terrified they were going to be stopped at any second.

On the train, he helped her into her seat, then kept a protective arm around her. Her heart was pounding so hard she wondered if he could feel it through the back of her dress. She held her breath, expecting the police to burst into the railcar and arrest them. The train sat still for what seemed an eternity and she prayed for it to go. At last it began to snake with painstaking slowness from the station. Neither of them moved as the train left the station.

There were no lights on the train and as Paris faded behind them, the darkness of the countryside seemed to envelop the railcar. Marie looked up at Julian, his face just visible in the faint moonlight. He was gazing down at her. His eyes conveyed a mixture of worry and relief, and perhaps something more, though she might have imagined it. Her eyes met his, held. She desperately wanted to speak with him, but they dared not talk in English. Finally, when she could bear it no longer, she broke from his gaze and looked away. He kept his arm around her and she let herself rest her head on his shoulder.

It was close to two o'clock in the morning when the train pulled into the same station where Will had dropped her earlier. The car he had been driving was left there, and Julian found where his cousin had hidden the key. He navigated the dark roads expertly to the village. Still neither spoke, as though afraid someone might still be listening even now.

At last they reached Marie's flat. "Thank God. I thought we were done for," Julian said in a low voice, mindful of the Germans.

"Because you decided to strap a bomb to my midsection without so much as telling me?" Marie said, her own relief quickly turning to anger. She took the package of TNT from the bottom compartment of her purse and handed it to him.

"I was worried that if I told you, you would be too afraid to go through with it. You did brilliantly."

She took little comfort in the praise. "I'm not a child. If you're going to risk my life, I at least deserve to know why."

"I'm sorry." He raised his hands. "Never again, okay? I promise. Let me explain everything now. We are to blow up the railway bridge just south of Mantes-la-Jolie," he said in a low voice. She had earned his trust and he was letting her in on the full scope of the plan at last. He pulled a map from his coat and spread it on the table in front of them. "The bridge is here." He pointed to a narrow strip of river. "It's a critical transit point for German tanks and destroying it will hurt their ability to fortify their defenses at Normandy. But we can't do it too soon or they will have time to repair." Timing, it seemed, was everything. "So we're gathering explosives. The piece you retrieved tonight is just one of a dozen we need. All of the work we have done so far, all of the arming and sabotage, pales in comparison to this mission."

"In what way?"

"The magnitude of the operation, its potential effect—and its danger. Once it works, if it works, we won't be able to hide in the shadows anymore."

"And what happens after?" He cocked his head, seeming not to understand. "If we will be out of the shadows, revealed, then how do we continue our work? Is it over?"

"It's never over," he replied firmly, snuffing out her hope. "We lie low for a few weeks, go to ground and hide in the safe houses away from the region. We shift our base of operations to other locations." She admired his single-mindedness and resolve.

"This can't go on forever," she said gently.

"No, of course not," he replied quickly. "No one can go on forever out here." She wondered if he really believed that. "But if we are taken, then scores of others will rise up to take our place."

"Then when is it over?"

"When the war is won." His face was resolute. In his mind, it could not have been otherwise.

"I could have been killed," she said, her anger returning.

"That was part of the bargain when you signed up, wasn't it?" Marie bit her lip, feeling that he was wrong but not quite sure how. "This particular type of TNT is actually rather stable," he added.

"You might have told me that ahead of time," she said, relaxing somewhat.

"I know, and I'm sorry. Anyway, sending you gave me the chance to see you again," he said. She was caught off guard by his sudden warmth. She felt herself unexpectedly drawn to him as well. Seeing Julian now, she realized she had missed him in the days since their last meeting, which seemed odd, since in the beginning she really hadn't liked him at all.

"That was a lucky break at the station, getting out of the queue just before inspection," he remarked, shifting topics abruptly. "How did you manage it?"

"I told him I had my period," she admitted uneasily. "Josie

taught me that in training. She said Eleanor had told her that the surest way to get a man to leave you alone is to mention the time of the month."

"Clever," he said, a touch of admiration in his voice. "I've heard quite a bit about Eleanor. She's meant to be very good at her job."

"Yes. She recruited Josie, and me as well. She's very stern. Not all of the girls like her."

"But you do?"

"I suppose I admire her. She selected me and I want her to think I've been up to the task."

Marie took off her coat and went to hang it on the rack. "You're bleeding," Julian said, moving closer.

She looked down and saw the red that had seeped through her blouse. "From where I tore the tape off," she said.

He walked to the basin and wet a cloth, then came over to her. "It needs to be cleaned. May I?" She nodded, then lifted her shirt slightly and looked away. He washed the wound tenderly, the pads of his fingers warm, almost hot, against her raw skin. "This needs a dressing," he fretted. "Or it could get infected." His hand shook worse than she had seen previously as he tended to her.

"Your tremors..."

"Worse when I'm tired," he explained.

"Rest then."

"Easier said than done." He shook his head. "I have to keep going."

"Rest here," she said in a firm voice that she hoped would ward off any argument.

Of course it did not. "I have to go. I'm expected at the airfield at daybreak." She wondered why; there had been no radio transmission announcing a drop. But she didn't want to tire him with more questions.

"That's still hours away. Now sleep," she said sternly. She pointed to the bed.

He smiled. "Yes, ma'am." But he sat down in the chair next to it, leaning back and resting his head against the wall. "Just for a bit."

"You'll be no good to anyone if you're dead from exhaustion." She meant this as a joke, but the words hung hollow between them, too close to the truth. Death, whether by flu or German arrest, was always just steps behind them, pursuing. She offered him her blanket. "I'm afraid this is all I have."

He waved it away. "I've slept in much worse places, I assure you. Rowboats and swamp beds. Once even a sewer. I was in a barn in the countryside last night."

She turned out the lamp and lay down on the bed. She desperately wanted to go and bathe and scrub off the memory of the day, but she didn't dare run the water at this hour and risk drawing the attention of the Germans billeted in the house. Neither of them spoke for several seconds. "Don't you get tired of it?" she asked. "All of the moving around."

"I don't mind it much. I don't really have a place I call home." There was unmistakable sadness in his voice.

"Will told me about your family," she said, then hoped he wouldn't take offense. "I'm so sorry."

"I met Reba when I was sixteen. I've never loved another. I put them on that boat," he said stiffly. "They had been living in Guernsey. I thought it best to get them out of Europe altogether because of the work I was doing. So I arranged for them to go live with Reba's sister in Canada. That's where they were going when the ship went down. I sent them to their deaths."

"You can't blame yourself. You were trying to keep them safe."

"Doesn't matter in the end, does it? They're dead—as surely as if they had gone to the camps. I like to imagine they were together at the end, Reba holding the boys. But I'll never know for sure." Marie struggled for the right words, but found none. He cleared his throat. "And you? What does your husband think of you signing up for this?"

"I'm not married," she blurted out. "That is, I know the files say I am, but the truth is my husband isn't missing in action. He left five years ago after our daughter, Tess, was born."

She studied his face in the semidarkness to see if he was angry at the lie. "You've raised her alone all of this time?" he asked. She nodded. "Then this mission should be a piece of cake." For the first time since she'd met him, she heard humor in his voice.

Then he reached over and touched her hand. "Your daughter will be very proud when she is old enough to understand." His fingers curled around hers, stayed. He tilted his head back and closed his eyes. His breathing grew longer and even. Watching him rest, his face calm and peaceful, a tenderness rose in her. She stopped, surprised. She could not have feelings for him. She had buried that part of herself away long ago, when Richard left. And she had spent years keeping to herself, so that such a thing could not happen again. But as she lay close to Julian, his hand warm on hers in the darkness, she knew what she felt was undeniably real.

She remembered then the way he had gazed fondly at her on the train. Was it possible that the attraction she felt to Julian was mutual? It was just loneliness, she told herself, the weeks and months he had spent on the move by himself. There couldn't be more. Josie had joked about "things happening out in the field." She could not have meant Julian, though. His only focus was the mission. He wouldn't let anything interfere with that.

Nor would she, Marie thought, sleepily now. She was here to do the job and get back to Tess. She couldn't afford to let anything get in the way of that. She considered pulling her hand from Julian's, then decided against it. Instead, lulled by the warm comfort of his touch, she let herself drift off to sleep.

Sometime later her eyes fluttered open. Through the window the sky was turning from gray to pink. Marie sat up, cursing herself for oversleeping when Julian said he needed to go before dawn. She wondered if he had slept too long as well. But when she looked up, he was awake, watching her. Her eyes met his and held as they had on the train. But it was daylight now, their feelings unmasked and out of the shadows.

She forced her gaze away. “What time is it?”

“Nearly dawn,” he said, reading the hour by the color of the sky.

“I should never have fallen asleep,” Marie said, jumping up.

He stood. “It’s all right.” He had been awake and could have gone sooner. But he had not. “That’s the first real sleep I’ve had in weeks.”

There was a rustling sound from the door. When Marie opened it, Will stood there, shifting uncomfortably, staring hard into the space between them. He sensed it, too, she could tell, the growing attraction between his cousin and Marie. “You didn’t come to the airfield,” he said to Julian. “I was worried. We have to go now.”

She turned to Julian. “Go where?”

“I’ve been recalled to England.”

She gasped involuntarily. “When?”

“I leave this morning. I’m sorry I didn’t tell you,” he said quickly, seeming to recall his promise the previous evening not to keep secrets from her anymore. “Only no one is meant to know. It’s only for a few days,” he added hastily. “A week at most.” There was a note of wistfulness in his voice…

“But what about the bridge?”

“Detonation isn’t scheduled for two weeks. I’ll be back by then.” His voice sounded uncertain and she wasn’t sure whether he believed it.

Knowing he was leaving, the feelings she had tried to ignore the night before threatened to burst forth. “Must you go?” she asked in a low voice, already knowing the answer.

"We're going to have to attempt a daylight takeoff at this point," Will interrupted before Julian could answer. "We have to hurry."

"Shall I come with you to the airfield?" she asked, trying to find a reason she might be needed.

But Julian shook his head. "The fewer the better," he said. "Especially when it isn't dark." It was just as well. She couldn't bear to see the Lysander swoop in and pluck him from their world. "Be safe until I return."

He turned to his cousin. "Take care of her." Will nodded solemnly. Marie wanted to protest that she did not need anyone to take care of her. She was an agent, for goodness sake, not some piece of property or someone's girl. But it was a solemn bond between the two of them and it seemed to be about something much bigger than her.

Suddenly she was struck with an uneasy feeling that he should not leave. "Do you really have to go? That is, the flying out and back again. It's so dangerous."

"There's no other way," he replied, his feet firmly set on the path. "I'll be back in a week," he promised, then started from the room. But as she watched him walk away with his cousin, she could not help but feel that she had lost him forever.

CHAPTER FIFTEEN

GRACE

Washington, 1946

"The girls are dead," Grace repeated aloud, as the taxi-cab crossed the bridge back into Washington. The idea was unthinkable. Each could not have been more than twenty, twenty-five at most. They should be married with small children or out having gay times with friends in postwar London. Not dead. "How?"

"Nacht und Nebel," Mark said, "means 'Night and Fog.' It was a German program to make people disappear, never to be heard from again."

"How do you know so much about it?"

He shifted uncomfortably. "I spent some time working for the prosecution at the War Crimes Tribunal last year, just after the war ended."

"Why didn't you say anything about that before?" That must have been how he knew so much about SOE. "Mark, that's such important work."

"My time there did not end well." Though his tone was neutral, she sensed pain beneath his words. "I'd rather not discuss it—at least not now."

"Okay," she relented. "Tell me more about Night and Fog."

"It was an odd program, very secret. Normally the Germans kept such meticulous records. Here, the Nazis wanted to make people disappear without a trace," Mark said.

"Including the girls."

He nodded. "Hitler personally issued an order that captured agents were to be 'slaughtered to the last man.'" Or woman, Grace thought. "He wanted no evidence of their existence left behind. I'm sorry we didn't find better news. What else is in the file?"

She pulled out the remaining documents, about a half dozen in all, typed in the blocky lettering. Each bore the letterhead at the top: "SOE, F Section." "What do you make of these?"

"Interoffice correspondence at headquarters." He pointed to one page, which contained schedules, with the girls' last names listed beside dates and times. "These look like they have to do with broadcasts or transmissions of some sort." As he pulled his hand back, their fingers brushed lightly.

"So what now?" she asked.

"I'm not sure what you mean. I think we've learned all we can."

"Not at all," Grace replied. "I mean, we know that the girls in the photos worked with Eleanor at SOE, and that those in the photos died. But we still have no idea why those girls' personnel files weren't in the boxes with the others. And we still have no idea why Eleanor came to New York." The whole thing swirled in Grace's mind, a giant knot that she couldn't untangle.

"We've reached a bit of a dead end," Mark conceded.

But Grace wasn't ready to give up, not yet. The cab was winding its way through Capitol Hill now, headed for Union Station and the train that would return her to New York. She pulled out the scrap of paper she'd been scribbling on when going through the files. "Some of the records had contact information for the girls or their families. I jotted down what I could."

"That was smart. I should have done the same. But, Gracie, that information could be outdated. And their contacts would have been in London, or overseas."

"Not all of them. One of them listed a Maryland number. Perhaps if I call, I might be able to speak with someone, even one of the girls who survived the war."

"You can certainly try. Let's go to my place and you can use the phone," he suggested. Grace hesitated, suddenly aware of him sitting beside her, too close. She was not sure that it was a good idea. But Mark was already giving the driver his address. The cab turned sharply left, starting in a new direction.

The taxi continued through neighborhoods that were unfamiliar to Grace, the large granite buildings giving way to neighborhoods with town houses and shops. "Georgetown," he explained, as the road inclined slightly upward. "I live just off the towpath, not far from the Potomac." She nodded as though this meant something to her.

A few minutes later, the cab turned onto an upscale street and stopped in front of a narrow brick row house. Mark paid the driver and then opened the door.

Inside the house was neat, with oak floors and a lack of photos or other personal items, except for an old-fashioned gramophone in the corner. Grace looked for signs of a woman's touch, but found none. It didn't look as though Mark had spent much time there at all. He led her into a study with a phone on the wall. "I'm going to make us some coffee," he said before leaving her alone.

Grace walked to the desk, then pulled out the piece of paper where she'd jotted down the number. She dialed and recited it to the operator. The radiator behind Mark's desk hissed softly as she waited.

The line rang once, then again. This wasn't going to work, Grace thought with a sinking feeling as the phone rang on and on. She started to hang up. But just before the receiver reached the cradle, there was a noise on the other end. Grace brought it back hurriedly to her ear. "Hello? I'm trying to reach Miss Annie Rider."

"One moment." There was a thud as the phone was set down or dropped, then footsteps, which started loud and faded. Grace imagined a rooming house like her own in New York, a landlady fetching her tenant.

"Yes?" A different woman's voice, scratchy this time and decidedly English, came across the line.

"Miss Rider?"

"Who's asking?"

Grace cleared her throat. "My name is Grace Healey. I'm so sorry to bother you, but I am trying to locate Sally Rider. Annie Rider was given as a contact."

"Sally?" The woman's voice rose with surprise. "What about her?"

"I was trying to reach her. I thought you might know where she is."

"Sally was my sister."

Was. "I'm sorry, I didn't realize she had passed." Sally had not been listed among the girls who had gone missing under Night and Fog. "Was she killed during the war?"

"She wasn't. She died after the war, in a car accident." Like Tom. Grace's stomach tightened.

Grace forced herself to focus on the call. "I'm sorry to trouble you. I had some questions about the work your sister did during the war." She paused. It seemed too intimate to ask over the phone. "I'm in Washington now, not terribly far away from you. Do you suppose we could meet?"

"I don't know..." There was a hesitation in the woman's voice.

"Please, it's very important. I can come to you if it's easier."

"No," the woman said quickly, as if the intrusion into her home would be unwelcome. "I have to be at The Willard tonight. If you'd like, we could meet in the bar at seven."

Grace hesitated. Meeting tonight might mean missing the last train back to New York and staying over—something she hadn't contemplated at all. But it was her only option if she wanted to learn more about the girls.

"Thank you. I'll be there."

As she hung up Grace cringed, thinking of Frankie and missing a second day of work. She considered asking Mark if she could make another call, then decided he wouldn't mind and dialed the operator again to place it. Frankie might be gone for the day, she realized, as the line to the office rang twice with no answer. But a moment later his voice filled the line. "Bleeker & Sons."

"Frankie, it's me." She did not have to say her name.

"Kiddo, how are you?" His voice sounded distant. The slight slur to his words made her wonder if he had been drinking.

"Frankie, you don't sound good. What's wrong?"

There was silence, dead air over the line. "It's Sammy. He came back. There was an older kid at his cousin's place who tried to take the money I gave Sammy. Sammy fought back and he got beat up."

"Oh, no! Is he okay?"

"Yeah, he's got a shiner and a busted lip. He'll live." Her heart screamed out at the idea that the little boy, who had been through so much, had now suffered this as well. "But he can't go back there. You were right, kiddo. He shouldn't be on his own so young. I'm filing papers to get him in the state system."

Poor Sammy would wind up in a boys' home after all. "I'm sorry, Frankie. It's so hard getting involved. Maybe we can figure out something else."

"I think we're out of options here. But we can talk about it when you get back tomorrow."

She hesitated. "About that… I need another day."

There was an audible sigh on the other end of the line and she could almost see his face, crestfallen. "Where are you, kiddo? I think I deserve to know."

She thought so, too. "I'm in Washington," she confessed.

"What on earth are you doing there?"

"I'm trying to find out some information on a woman named Eleanor Trigg. She's the one who was hit by a car in front of Grand Central the other day."

"Why? Did you know her?"

"I didn't."

"Then what was she to you?"

Good question, Grace thought. "It's complicated, Frankie. I found a suitcase of hers with some photographs of about a dozen young women. I took the photos, and when I went to return them, the suitcase was gone. I'm trying to figure out who she was and who the girls were and give the photos back. I'll be back in a day and I promise I'll explain more then, okay? I'm sorry I didn't tell you about the trip," she added, genuinely contrite. Frankie had been so good to her; she should have let him in on the whole thing from the start.

"It's all right," he said, forgiving her instantly. "If you need help, I could come down. I'm good at navigating the bureaucrats."

She smiled. "I know you are," she said, loving him for the offer. She had to see this through for herself, though. "But I think our clients need you there more." Grace was suddenly struck with an idea. "There is one thing. Eleanor came from England to New York at some point before the accident. Can you check with your friends over at immigration and customs and see if they have anything on her? You know, when she got here, what she put on the forms, that sort of thing." It was nervy, she knew, asking for another favor in addition to the extra time off. But Frankie wouldn't say no.

"You've got it, kiddo. Consider it done. Just hurry back—and be careful."

Grace placed the receiver back on the cradle, then returned to the living room. "I've managed a meeting with a sister of one of the girls tonight."

Mark smiled and handed her a warm mug of coffee. "So you'll be staying until tomorrow?"

She took a sip. "Most likely. I don't think there will be a train by the time I've finished seeing her. I'll find a hotel for the night." She tried to calculate what that might cost.

"Stay here. I can understand why after what happened you might not want to," he added quickly. "But I have a guest room, so it's all on the up-and-up."

She scrutinized Mark, wondering if he had other intentions. "That would hardly be appropriate."

He raised his hands. "Your decision, but it's a perfectly good room. I rented it out during the war when all of the government workers were here and housing was short. Unless you don't think you can behave yourself."

"I can..." she started, before realizing he was teasing. Her cheeks flushed. "That would be lovely. Thank you."

That night at seven, they stepped out of a cab in front of The Willard. Across Lafayette Park, the sky behind the White House was dusky. Mark helped her from the car, his hand warm and sure against the small of her back. Inside, the lobby was opulent. The floor was a mosaic of rosettes and the ceiling was elaborately painted with the seals of all forty-eight states. Marble columns ran from floor to ceiling. The chandeliers were fantastic globes, each wrapped by four bronze female figures. The chairs were upholstered in fine leather and oversize palms sat in pots. Grace wished she'd brought a nicer dress to wear.

At the entrance to the bar, she stopped, scanning the room uncertainly. It was a sea of men in business suits, puffing on cigars or cigarettes, with only a handful of women interspersed among them. Was one of them Annie? She hadn't thought to ask for a description.

Grace spied the bar at the far corner of the lobby and started toward it. Mark began to follow. She turned to him. "Mark, I'm so grateful for everything that you are doing, but..."

"You want to talk to Annie by yourself," he finished for her.

"Do you mind?"

He smiled. "Not at all. I mean, I feel vested at this point, but I understand."

"I just think she's more likely to talk to me if I'm alone."

He nodded. "Agreed." He dropped into one of the plush leather chairs. "I'll be waiting right here."

Grace started toward the bar once more, feeling Mark watch her as she went. Heat rose in her. What was it about him that had this effect on her? It wasn't like her to be swoony and it needed to stop. Grace walked to the maître d', wondering if Annie had a reservation. "I'm looking for a woman named Annie Rider."

He pointed in the direction of the bar without hesitation. "She's over there in the Round Robin Bar." Between two men, she could make out a female figure in a cocktail server's uniform. Annie was not a patron of The Willard. She worked here. Grace felt foolish for having thought otherwise. But how could she have possibly known?

The bar was filled with men and clouds of cigar smoke, and for a moment she wished she had taken Mark up on his offer to come with her. But she pressed forward alone. "Excuse me," she said, and a burly man moved out of the way to make space for her. She raised her hand and Annie came over. "I'm Grace Healey. We spoke on the phone." Annie could not have been more than thirty. But closer now, her face was careworn, with deep lines beneath the powdery makeup and penciled eyebrows.

Annie looked suddenly uneasy, and Grace wondered if she might decide not to talk to her. "Just give me a few minutes until I can take my break. You can wait in there." She pointed to a door at the side of the bar. Grace walked through it. She was in a storeroom just off the kitchen containing shelves stacked high with food and a few wooden stools. Watching a mouse scurry between boxes, Grace made a mental note not to eat at The Willard if she ever had the chance.

A moment later, Annie joined her. She sat down on one of the stools and gestured for Grace to do the same. "You said you had questions about my sister."

"Yes. And about a woman she worked with—Eleanor Trigg."

Annie's eyes narrowed, her brows drawing close like an odd punctuation mark. "Worked *for*," she corrected sharply. "Eleanor was in charge of it all." She stood, as if to leave.

"Wait!" Grace said. "I'm sorry if I upset you."

Annie sat back down slowly. "Bloody Eleanor," she muttered just under her breath.

Grace wondered what about Eleanor had set her off, but decided that it would be best to change the subject. She pulled the photographs from her bag. "Do you know any of these women?" Grace asked.

"I saw a few of them during my time at SOE."

"You worked at SOE as well?"

"Yes, as a clerk. I wanted to go over as an agent, too, but Eleanor said I didn't have it in me." Annie smiled ruefully. "She was right. Mostly I knew the girls in the field by name." She pointed to the photos. "Those were some of Eleanor's girls."

"What do you mean when you say they were hers?" Grace asked, veering gently back near the sensitive subject.

Annie pulled a pack of cigarettes out of her bag. "Eleanor ran the women's operation for SOE. They were sending the women into Europe, you know. They were messengers and radio operators." Annie lit the cigarette and took a drag. She reached for the photos with her free hand. "This one, they called her Josie. She was only seventeen when she started." Grace imagined herself at seventeen—she had been concerned with coming-out parties and summers at the beach. She could not have navigated her way across Manhattan at that point. Yet these girls were on their own in France battling the Nazis. Grace was overcome with awe and inadequacy at the same time.

"About how many women agents were there?"

"A few dozen," Annie replied. "Not more than fifty, tops."

"Then why photos of these twelve?" Grace asked.

"These were the ones who didn't come back."

"How did they die?"

"Awful ways, really. Executions. Injections." The women should have been treated like prisoners of war. Instead, they had been slaughtered.

But under Nacht und Nebel, the Germans hadn't wanted anyone to know what had become of the girls. "How did you find out?"

"Word trickled back to headquarters," Annie replied. She exhaled sharply, sending a cloud of smoke billowing upward. "Not official word, in most cases. But from other agents who had seen one of the girls in the camps or heard by word of mouth. By the end of the war, it was no secret that they had been killed."

A clock in the hotel lobby chimed eight; Annie's break would surely be over soon. "Tell me more about Eleanor," Grace said tentatively. "Who was she?"

"She wasn't like the others," Annie said. "She was older. Foreign. From Russia, or Poland maybe, somewhere eastern." The name *Trigg* didn't suggest that, Grace noted. Had she changed it deliberately? "She had come to SOE as a secretary," Annie added.

"Yet she wound up heading up a group for SOE," Grace interjected. "She must have been very good."

"The best. Eleanor had a mind like an encyclopedia, knew everyone's history and details from memory. And she could read people, tell from the start whether someone was cut out for the Racket. And Eleanor was different, cagey. You always got a sense that she was keeping a secret. I suppose she was just doing her job."

"Did you like her?" Grace asked.

Annie shook her head emphatically. "No one liked Eleanor. But we all respected her. She was the person you'd want looking after you if you were in the field. She wasn't someone you would want to have a drink with, though, if you know what I mean. She was an odd bird, awkward, stern, not easy to chat with. I wonder what she's gotten up to now."

Grace cleared her throat. "I'm sorry to tell you, but she's passed." She decided to spare Annie the grim details. "A few days ago in New York."

"New York?" Annie repeated, seeming more surprised than upset. "What was she doing in the States?"

"I was hoping you might know," she replied. "The man at the consulate said they were trying to find family, someone to claim Eleanor."

Annie ground out her cigarette in an ashtray, which sat on the edge of one of the shelves, leaving a perfect ring of lipstick around the edge. "They won't. Find anyone, that is. Eleanor was alone, at least after her mother passed. She had no one."

"But what about her personal life?"

"None. She didn't socialize or share much. She didn't seem interested in men, and I don't mean that in the way it sounds. She wasn't interested in women either. Only the work. She was an island unto herself. Very private. One got the sense…that there might have been something more to her than met the eye."

"Tell me more about Special Operations."

"There were problems from the start," Annie replied. "You can't take a bunch of young girls with no experience and think that because you ran them up and down the Scottish Highlands for a few weeks and showed them how to shoot they will manage in a war zone. It takes years to develop the instinct and the nerve to survive. You can't teach that."

Annie continued, "And then there was the size. Everyone knows that a covert operation with three people is less safe than one with two. But take Vesper circuit, for example. That was the big one, the unit operating in and around Paris. It was headed up by Vesper, or the Cardinal, I think he was called in code. He must have had dozens, maybe hundreds of agents under his control. The bigger the network got, the greater the risk for betrayal and leaks."

"I'm sorry," Grace said. "What do you mean betrayal?"

"Betrayal of the girls, of course." The room seemed to shift slightly under Grace. "You didn't think so many of them were arrested on their own, did you? No," Annie said, answering her own question. "Someone must have given them up." Though Grace was surprised, she managed not to react; she did not want Annie to stop talking. "They were caught by the SD, the Sicherheitsdienst, or German intelligence, mostly in the weeks just before D-Day. And not just in Paris, but all over France. Someone gave them up. At least that's what Eleanor thought."

"Eleanor? How do you know?"

"I saw her once, after the war. She came to see Sally, asked to talk to her privately. I wasn't supposed to be in the room, but I listened in. I had to look out for my sister, you see. Sally had come back from the war in such a fragile state and she didn't need Eleanor stirring up trouble for her again. She had dozens of questions about the girls who had gone missing during the war. Kind of like you." Grace's guilt rose; talking about the war and the work her sister had done could not have been easy for Annie. "A week later my sister was killed in the wreck."

"So Eleanor wanted to talk about what happened to the girls?" Grace asked.

"Not what happened, but how. It was all she could talk about. She said that it had something to do with the radios, someone transmitting and pretending to be one of the wireless operators. She wanted to know if Sally knew anything about it. Sally didn't, of course. Eleanor was determined to find out what had happened to the girls—and who had sold them out."

Grace's breath caught at this last part. Could that have possibly been what had brought Eleanor to New York?

"I have to get back to work," Annie said, standing.

"Thank you," Grace replied. "I know this couldn't have been easy."

"It wasn't. But if you find out anything more, it will have been worth it. You'll let me know, won't you?" Annie asked.

Grace nodded. "I will. I promise."

"Thank you. Those girls were like sisters to Sally." It should really be her thanking Annie, Grace thought, and not the other way around. But before Grace could do so, Annie shook her hand firmly and returned to her job behind the bar.

CHAPTER SIXTEEN

ELEANOR

London, 1944

Eleanor stood in the door of the Director's office, paper clutched in her hand. "Sir, something isn't right."

Ten minutes earlier, a message had come across the wireless. "It's Marie," the operator Jane had said. Eleanor raced across the room as Jane decoded the message.

It was not that Marie's message was overdue, as had been the case after her arrival. The girl had been broadcasting regularly—in some cases more often than expected. And some of her messages sounded just fine. But that first message, which had seemed somehow off, still rankled. Eleanor had tried to tell herself that it was just Marie's newness in the field, nerves making her typing less than smooth. There would not, could not, be further problems.

But as she scanned the paper now, her heart sank. The message purported to be from Angel. But the substance of what she was asking was wrong: "Awaiting weapons for the Maquis.

Please advise the location of the next arms drop." The message, too unguarded and overt, was not something a trained operator would ask.

And it was not just the content of the message; the stamp at the top of the message, "Security Check Assent," which would have signaled that Marie's bluff and true checks were both present in the coded transmission, was missing.

"Bloody hell!" Eleanor swore, crumpling the message into a ball. Jane blinked at Eleanor's unusual loss of composure. The problem was not just Marie for which she was concerned; a compromised radio could mean a much bigger leak or breach.

Eleanor started to throw the message away. Then, thinking better of it, she smoothed out the paper and started for the Director's office.

As she approached the Director's door, she could tell from his hunched posture that it was not a good time and that the intrusion would not be welcome. But he would not turn her away. He looked up wearily now from the report he had been reading and set his pipe down. "Trigg?"

"It's about one of the girls, sir." Of course, for her it was always about the girls. "That is, her radio transmissions." Eleanor normally hated to create any needless intrusion and risk the Director's impatience. She wanted to be self-sufficient, capable of running the unit she'd created. But now she was too worried to care. "Look here," she said, nearing his desk and placing the paper in front of him.

"It's from Roux," he observed. "A few weeks back, you were worried because she wasn't transmitting. This is good news, isn't it?"

"I'm afraid not, sir." Eleanor ran her finger under the last line of the transmission: "Please advise the location of the next arms drop." "Marie would never ask that directly, nor would Vesper, or anyone else for whom she might be transmitting."

The Director looked up from the paper skeptically. "You always said the girl was green. Maybe she made a mistake, or was rushed."

"I said she was innocent, perhaps even naive. Not careless. It's more than that, sir." He looked at her expectantly as she faltered to find more evidence to support her claim. "Something isn't right. This message makes no sense. And her security checks weren't present."

"What about the other girls' transmissions? Anything amiss?"

"Only hers." Eleanor hesitated. "The rest seem fine. But if something is wrong with Marie, it could affect the whole circuit. Information might not be getting through or back to us. There could be some sort of a disruption, even a leak."

"Maybe it's the machine," the Director said. "If we send orders to recalibrate..."

"That can't be it, sir. The transmissions are technically fine. It's something about the messages themselves. The *way* that the girl is transmitting."

"What do you make of it?"

"Honestly, I don't know." Eleanor hated to admit her uncertainty. "Either she's broadcasting under dire circumstances or under duress or..." She faltered, the words almost too unbelievable to say. "Or it isn't Marie who is actually broadcasting." She took a deep breath. "I'm worried, sir, that we've been compromised."

His eyes widened. "How is that even possible? We run that scenario a hundred times in setting up the radios. Even if one of the machines was captured, the Germans would need the crystals and the codes and the security checks. No agent worth his salt would ever give that up."

Or her salt, Eleanor thought, hoping that he was right. "Whoever it is might not have the security checks, if this message is any indication. But the radio and the crystals, if taken together, are a real possibility."

"You're trying to read tea leaves, Trigg. We need to stick to facts, what we know." Eleanor so often wished for a crystal ball like the one the witch had in that American film, *The Wizard of Oz*, to see what was happening in the field. Once she'd even dreamed she had one, but it was clouded and dark.

The Director leaned back in his chair, puffing on his pipe. "Even if you are correct, what do you want me to do about it? Are you suggesting that we stop transmitting altogether?"

Eleanor faltered. Doing that would mean leaving the agents out in the field with no connection or lifeline back to headquarters—alone. "No, sir."

"Then what?"

"I think Marie's radio should be shut down until it can be fully verified."

"But she broadcasts for Vesper network, which is the largest in-country. We'd be crippled. It would shut down operations." Eleanor noted with a bit of pride how integral the women had become to the fight in such a short amount of time. A year ago the men had doubted the women could help at all—now they could not function without them.

"I thought you said the girls were up to the task, Trigg. I believed you, staked my name on it." There was an accusatory note in his voice. The men made mistakes, too, Eleanor wanted to point out; it was what had given rise to the need for the women's unit in the first place. But the women had taken over the radio operator duties with increasing frequency in the past year, making this look very much like their problem.

"They were, sir. That is, they are." For the first time in as long as she could remember, Eleanor felt unsure of herself. "It's not the girls. Something is wrong over there."

The Director continued, "News of your unit has reached Churchill, you know. He's dead pleased about it." For the prime minister, that was high praise.

But it did not make the problem go away. "Sir, as it is, we have no way to know if the information we are sending is actually being retrieved by our agents. If we can't shut them down to verify, then I think someone should go over and check. Visit the units personally."

"I suppose you think it should be you."

"I do want to go," Eleanor admitted.

"We've been through all this before, Trigg," the Director huffed. "With your renewed citizenship application pending, I can't get your papers through. Even if I could, I wouldn't send you into the field. You know too much."

"Send me anyway," Eleanor pleaded again. The Director blinked with surprise. Eleanor was usually so rational and detached. There was a note of desperation in her voice now. She needed to see what was really going on over there, whether or not the girls were all right. She realized her own misstep. She had gotten too close—and for that reason alone, he would say no.

"It's out of the question," he said firmly.

"I have to see what went wrong. If you won't send me, at least shut down her set until we can verify matters." He did not respond. "When I took this on, you promised me complete control."

"Over your girls, yes. But not the whole bloody war. This is part of something much bigger. The invasion is coming and every day of the full moon that we don't drop personnel and supplies is an opportunity missed."

"But, sir, if the information about the drops are conveyed over the compromised radio, our agents and supplies could land in the wrong hands. We have to stop this!" Her voice rose, breaking at the end.

"I can't shut down the entire operation on an unsubstantiated hunch," he countered. "Everything must go forward." He leaned in, lowering his voice. "The invasion is weeks—no, days away. We can't afford distractions."

Eleanor's frustration boiled over and she struggled to maintain her composure. "I'll go to the War Office," she threatened, too far gone to stop herself.

The Director's face reddened. "You would go above me?" To him this was the ultimate betrayal. Then his expression softened. "You wouldn't." It was a bluff and he knew it. "I've supported you, Trigg, in more ways than one."

And I've supported you, she wanted to say. But she restrained herself. She couldn't risk going against him. Involving Whitehall would bring in the very people who thought the girls couldn't do this in the first place, prove the doubters right. It was more than just her pride that was at stake. The Director held the fate of her citizenship application, which she so desperately needed, in the palm of his hand.

There was nothing to do but watch and wait.

Eleanor stormed out of the Director's office without speaking further. She looked over her shoulder, wanting to go back there one more time and beseech him to intervene, demand that he act on her concerns. But she knew that he would not be swayed. He had shut her down entirely. It wasn't like him. Was he losing confidence in her? Most likely not, she knew. Rather, he was receiving pressure to step up operations. Slowing them for any reason was unthinkable.

Instead of returning to her office, she stepped out into the back alley of Norgeby House. She was eager for fresh air, but the tall, narrow buildings that surrounded it seemed to lean in, too close. She reached for the ladder of the fire escape and began to climb, one floor, then another.

She reached the flat rooftop. Though not tall enough for a proper view of London, she could make out the top of St. Paul's dome and a bit of London Bridge. Sooty chimneys jutted upward in the foreground like an endless candelabra, seeming to light the unusually fiery sunset.

Eleanor inhaled deeply. The damp air burned with the mix of coal and petrol that was always present. She felt herself trembling with rage and helplessness, the full adrenaline of her disagreement with the Director now set loose. Something was wrong over there; she knew it. Her girls were lost and alone and she was failing them as surely as she had failed her sister. But no one, even the Director, would listen.

Then came a shuffling sound behind her, the gravelly scuffing of footsteps. Eleanor jumped and spun around. At the far corner of the roof, a man stood, half-facing away from her toward the view of south London. Taking him in, the profile was somehow familiar, but she couldn't place it. Then she stifled a gasp.

"Vesper." He did not nod or otherwise acknowledge his identity, but his silence signaled assent. She had only known Vesper by reputation, having heard his name and exploits whispered throughout the halls of Baker Street from the day she'd arrived. She'd seen a lone photo of him in his personnel file and though he looked different here, more rugged, she knew his craggy features on sight. She studied the man about whom she had heard so much. He was tall and leonine, with a strong jawline and broad shoulders befitting all that he seemed to carry on them. He was much younger than she had imagined, though, for someone shrouded in such greatness.

The closest direct link to one of her girls was standing right before her. She could hardly believe it.

Eleanor moved closer. "What are you doing here?" she asked before realizing her mistake. He had no reason to answer a total stranger. "I'm Eleanor Trigg." She studied his face, wondering if he would recognize her name. But his expression did not change. "I'm in charge of the women's unit."

"I know. Marie speaks highly of you." Eleanor cringed as she imagined Marie saying too much and breaking protocol. At the same time, Eleanor could not help but feel a tug of pride. Though she had been hard on Marie for good reason, Eleanor had often worried that it would cause the girl to hate her. It might be the first time in her life she had ever worried about such a thing. "How is she?"

He smiled reluctantly. "Brilliant. Charming. Infuriating."

Eleanor stifled a laugh, remembering the girl who had asked questions constantly in training. She had been asking about Marie's work, though—and Vesper's answer suggested something else entirely. Vesper's reputation in the field was that of a lone wolf who isolated himself somewhat from his agents in order to lead. She wondered if he had developed feelings for Marie.

"And the others?"

"Only a few of your girls are with my circuit." Eleanor nodded. "Josie's unstoppable. She's out in the field right now with the *maquisards*. Le Petit, they call her." The Little One. "But I think they're afraid of her. She can outshoot any of them. They trust her more than most of the men at this point."

"What are you doing in London?" Eleanor asked. He had left his agents alone in the field to come; it must have been vitally important. She noted, with annoyance but not surprise, that she should have been notified he was coming. Had the Director kept Vesper's visit from her on purpose? Or perhaps he himself had not known.

"Not here," he said, gesturing around the corner to the part of the roof far from the windows where others might hear. She followed. "I was recalled to report in for meetings at headquarters," he said, returning to her original question about the purpose of his visit.

"Why?"

"I really can't talk about it." It was not her area of responsibility; he did not report to her, and she did not need to know.

But she persisted anyway. "Marie and those other girls, they're mine. That is, I recruited and trained them. I need to know what is going on." Vesper nodded, respecting her as an equal, but still offering nothing. "How are your operations?" she asked, trying a different tack.

"Things are going well, I think. Not perfectly, of course, but as well as can be expected." She wondered if this was true or if he was putting a brave face on it for headquarters. "We had a setback with a depot sabotage last winter, but we've recovered. Right now the whole focus is blowing up the bridge at Mantes-la-Jolie." Eleanor nodded. She'd heard about it in their daily briefings at headquarters; preparations for it were the reason she had agreed to deploy Josie early. The bridge was a key choke point for holding up the German tanks as they moved toward the coast for the invasion. But blowing it up was dangerous—and it would put the whole circuit at risk.

"You have what you need to do it?"

"We were lacking in explosives. But an agent from Marseille passed through a few weeks ago to establish contact. He was able to get us what we need, additional TNT in exchange for some munitions storehouses. We're managing."

"Is there any chance you've been compromised?" she asked bluntly. The question was too abrupt, out of left field, but it was what she most needed to know in order to determine what was going on with Marie's transmissions and there was no point in hiding it.

He bristled. "Not at all," he replied, too quickly. But he did not seem as surprised by the suggestion as Eleanor might had thought.

"You've considered the possibility, though, haven't you?"

"It's always a possibility," he countered, unwilling to admit more.

Then all of the concerns of the past weeks about the infrequencies of the transmissions and the way they didn't sound quite like Marie came rushing back. "Her transmissions," Eleanor ventured. "Some of her messages just don't sound like Marie."

"I'm sure it's just nerves, the newness of being in the field," he replied. "She's fine—or at least she was when I last saw her a few days ago." There was a warmth in his voice when he spoke of seeing Marie that answered Eleanor's question about his feelings for the girl. She wondered whether Marie felt the same, and whether anything had come of it. "She retrieved a package for me from Montmartre," he added.

Paris. "Good Lord! You aren't using her as a courier, are you?" Marie had the language skills, but she was so green. Her clandestine skills, how to blend in and not make the kind of mistakes that would get her caught, were simply undeveloped.

"She's better than you know."

"Perhaps." Eleanor bristled at the notion that anyone knew her girls better than she did.

"Anyway, we have to be fluid in the field, send people where they are needed."

Eleanor turned back to the question that had been nagging at her. "But her transmissions have been erratic. What's really going on out there?"

He looked down at his boots, not answering right away. "I don't know. Marie is fine. But there's something different about this mission. Something not right."

"Have you told headquarters?"

"They won't listen to me. They think I'm cracked from being in the field too long, my judgment clouded. It was all I could do to persuade them to let me go back at all. But you know it as well. Why haven't you said anything?"

"I've tried. But they won't listen to me either." The full scope of her powerlessness unfurled before her and her frustration bubbled over. Those in power were only interested in one thing now: the invasion. They wouldn't hear any voices that might slow it, or stand in the way—including the safety of the agents. Eleanor realized then that her girls were in much greater danger than she had imagined.

"So what now?" she asked.

"Get back to France, try to figure it out on my own."

"You could abort." For a fleeting second hope rose in her.

Cancel it all, extract the girls and bring them back safely. It wouldn't be a failure exactly, but a delay. They could regroup. Try again.

"I can't." Of course not. Too close to the invasion—just like the Director had said. "It's like a freight train too fast and strong for anything to stop. And if I don't do it, no one else will." He started back across the roof. "I need to get back to France as quickly as possible."

"I can help with that," she called after him. He turned back. "If your travel orders are ready, I will be glad to arrange the drop personally." Eleanor could use her position to jump the queue of transmissions and arrange for Vesper to go immediately.

"Thank you." She wasn't just doing it for him, though. The agents in the field needed him to survive.

"Wait!" she called as he started to leave once more. She wanted to send a message to her girls, something that would help them to survive whatever ordeals they were facing, or at least to let them know that she was working tirelessly back at headquarters for their safe return. That she had not given up on them. She struggled to find the message that would sum it all up at once, her care and concern, her praise and her warning. But words failed her.

"Tell Marie," she began. Of all the girls, he was most certain to see her. "Tell Marie I'm worried because her transmissions don't look right. They won't let me stop broadcasting or shut down her set, but tell her I'm worried." She tried to find words, not just of caution, but advice to help the girl survive whatever treacherous waters she might be navigating. But there did not seem to be any more to say.

And Vesper was already gone.

CHAPTER SEVENTEEN

MARIE

France, 1944

Julian had left them. "A week," he'd said. But it had been ten days. It might as well have been forever.

Marie drew her arms around herself and shivered, though it was in fact warm, the humid air more early summer than spring. The sky was unusually gray, the dark clouds carrying the promise of a storm. She imagined Tess by the old vicarage and hoped the joys of spring in the fens helped her think less about the weeks in which Mummy hadn't come.

She looked out over the field that stretched behind the safe house. She willed Julian's strong silhouette to appear on the horizon. But he was still a country away. She tried to imagine what he was doing right now in London. A few nights earlier, she'd dreamed that she had been walking along Kensington High Street and seen him, but he had not known her. The feelings that she had tried so hard to ignore when he was here had seemed to burst wide-open during his absence, and she knew there would be no denying them when he returned.

Marie waited faithfully by the wireless for a transmission from London, and listened to the BBC broadcast on the regular radio each night for the coded *messages personnel*, which were sometimes used as an alternate means of signaling a drop, praying for the signal to be on standby for a Lysander. Nothing. She looked up carefully, judging if the moon had reached its fullness or if they might have a whole extra night until its peak. Seven days on either side were bright enough for flying. If Julian didn't come, he might have to wait until next month. The thought was unbearable.

She was not the only one who missed him; Julian's absence left a void in the circuit. She could sense it from the messages the couriers brought for her to transmit, fewer now, less certain in tone. He was their leader and they couldn't fully function without him. Julian's absence wasn't the only problem either. Things were getting worse throughout northern France. There were rumors, whispered by the agents who brought her instructions: another arrest in Auvergne. A courier who had not turned up. Little pieces that, when put together, suggested that things were getting worse, the Sicherheitsdienst drawing closer, noose tightening. And all this right as they were about to undertake their most dangerous mission to date: blowing up the bridge.

There was a clattering below. Marie stood, her eyes darting across the flat to make sure everything was hidden, and that the radio was inverted into the gramophone, in case the police had come. She opened the door to find the corridor empty.

A moment later, Will's head appeared over the railing. She was surprised to see him; he hadn't come personally since the morning he had retrieved Julian for the flight. He stepped into the flat uninvited now and closed the door. His expression was unusually solemn and she held her breath, bracing for bad news. Was it about Julian or something else? "There's a personnel drop expected tonight," he announced without greeting. His brown eyes were solemn.

She jumped up with a surge of anticipation. But there had been nothing on the radio about a delivery. "How do you know?"

"Word was couriered over from the Acolyte circuit."

It seemed odd that the message had come from a network of agents to the east and not through her wireless. "Is it Julian?"

Will's brow furrowed with uncertainty. "They said the message was garbled, but he's the only one expected. It must be him. If I was flying him back myself, I would know."

"You asked to fly him?"

"Of course. Repeatedly. My request was denied." Will scowled. Perhaps that explained his dark mood. "They said I was needed here on the ground while Julian is in London," he added. Will had evolved somehow into a second-in-command, a leader while his cousin was away. He was normally a lone wolf, and it was not a role he wore comfortably.

"Well, Julian will be back tonight and you can get back to flying," she said brightly.

But his face remained grave. "Marie, there's something else." His voice was somber. "You know about the railway bridge?"

She nodded. "Of course." Everything they had done, including her life-threatening trip back from Montmartre with the TNT, had led up to this.

"The detonation is scheduled for tomorrow night."

"So soon?"

"We've received word that a large German convoy is to cross it the day after next. So we had to move it up."

"But Julian said not to proceed without him."

"We won't be. We will lay the charge and then retrieve him from the landing site before it explodes. It shouldn't be a problem."

She did not understand why his tone was so grave. "Then what's the matter?"

He hesitated. "The agent who was to lay the charge at the bridge tomorrow, she's gone missing."

She. There was only one woman in the network capable of undertaking such a task. Marie sank to the edge of the bed, praying that she had heard him wrong. "Will," she said slowly, "who is it?"

"Josie is missing," he confirmed bluntly, sitting down beside her. "She and Albert and one of the partisans, Marcin, were delivering guns to the Maquis when they went dark four days ago. We don't actually know if they were arrested," he added quickly. "They could just be lying low."

"Or injured or dead," Marie said, the awful possibilities flowing from her. "Have they checked the location of her last transmission? What about the town where she was last seen? We must send word to headquarters..." If Julian knew, he could make inquiries in London.

"We have. And a reconnaissance team is doing everything they can." Marie knew from the sound of his voice that it was futile. If Josie was all right, she would have found a way to get back or at least to be in touch. No, the only one thing that would have kept Josie from completing the mission was if she had been arrested—or killed.

She saw Josie at Arisaig House, so strong and defiant. Tears filled Marie's eyes as she turned to Will. "How could this have happened?" She leaned into him and cried then into the front of his shirt. It wasn't just for Josie she mourned, but for all of them. Josie had been unbreakable. If the Germans had gotten her, then what chance did Marie or the others have?

Marie felt paralyzed by her sadness, ready to give up then and there. But Josie would not have stood for her falling apart like this. She forced herself to breathe more calmly, and her sobs began to subside. A few minutes later, she straightened, dried her eyes.

"There is nothing we can do from here but wait," Will added.

"And destroy the railway bridge," she managed, forcing herself to focus on the task at hand. Julian had said the operation must go ahead at all costs. "Who's going to lay the charge now?"

"I don't know. I'm going to a few of the safe houses to see who's nearby that might be a good fit. Worst case, I'll do it myself."

"I'll do it." The words came out before she realized it. What on earth was she thinking? He looked at her for several seconds, as if not comprehending. "Lay the charge. I can do it."

"Marie, no. You aren't trained for this. You're a radio operator." She'd only had the most cursory training in explosives at Arisaig House. To actually lay the charge for the entire detonation was something else entirely. "Julian would never allow it," he added.

"Why?"

Will shrugged. "He's very protective." *Of me*, she wanted to ask, *or all the female agents?* He had been perfectly willing to let Marie risk herself with the trip into Paris to fetch the explosives. What had changed? She remembered the closeness between them the night before he left for London. She wondered whether Will had sensed it the next morning. Or perhaps Julian had said something to his cousin about her before he had gone.

But that had nothing to do with the question at hand. "Julian isn't here now. And there's no one else to do it. You need to be at the airfield. You go to receive him," she continued, a plan forming in her mind. "I'll lay the charge and meet you. Julian knows how to find the underground routes out of the region. We will get Julian and by the time the charge has detonated, we will all be long gone."

Will hesitated. Julian would have fought this plan to the last, and they both knew it. But Will's expression seemed to fold as he realized she was right. And even if she was wrong, there was no time to find an alternative.

"Very well. Quickly, follow me." They started out of the flat and down the stairs, across the town, going this time on foot. Will was as hard to keep up with as his cousin, legs shorter but steps rapid-fire.

"What do I do?" she asked. "I mean, after I set the charge."

"You'll need to cross the bridge to get to the rendezvous spot. Follow the riverbank south to the bend I showed you on the map, then east to the field where I dropped you the night you came." He made it all sound so easy. "Can you find it?" She nodded.

They pressed on in silence. "What did you do before the war?" she asked finally.

She expected him to chastise, as Julian might have done, for talking needlessly and risking detection. "I raced."

"Cars?" She was surprised.

"Motorbikes, actually." Somehow given his love of flying, it made sense. The excitement of the two seemed somehow the same. "Completely frivolous, I know. But true." They had all been such different people before the war, she realized.

Soon the woods began to thin. A railway bridge appeared ahead, looming like a giant skeleton. Marie's heartbeat quickened. It was so much larger than she imagined. "Do we have enough explosives to bring it down?"

"There's TNT positioned in at least a dozen spots along the bridge," he said. "We don't have to take the whole thing, just enough to make it unpassable. You remember how to set the charge from training?"

"Yes…" Marie faltered. She had not paid attention to explosives as well as she might have. She had been sent as a radio operator; blowing things up was simply not a job she had ever expected to do.

"It's not too late to change your mind," he said, seeming to read her doubts.

She lifted her chin defiantly. "I can do this."

He pulled the detonator from his bag, then pointed at the

corner of the bridge. "You'll need to lodge it up there in the joint. Wait until it's completely dark. I wish that I could do it for you," he added.

She shook her head. She was smaller and less easily seen. And her French would help if she got caught. "You need to go prepare the landing site for Julian."

"You must be there to meet me before Julian arrives," he fretted, seeing now all the weaknesses in their hastily constructed plan. "As soon as the plane lands, we have to pull up the torches and run."

"I know." She put one hand on each shoulder, looking squarely into his eyes. "I'll be there."

"You'd better," he grumbled. "My cousin would kill me if anything happened to you."

"Will..." She felt as though she should apologize for, or at least acknowledge, what seemed to have developed between her and Julian. But how could she explain what she didn't at all understand herself?

He waved his hand. "It doesn't matter." His voice sounded awkward. "Just get the job done."

"I will. Trust me," she said firmly. "Now go."

After Will had disappeared into the darkness of the woods, Marie's confidence faded. What on earth was she doing here? In the sky above she saw the faces of those who had doubted her all her life, first her father, then Richard. Those who made her believe she could never be enough. Pushing down her doubts, she instead imagined Julian boarding the Lysander, eager to return to his agents. She could not believe in just hours she would see him again.

The wait for darkness seemed an eternity, dusk lingering even longer than usual. When night fell at last, Marie crept from her hiding place and moved low and silent along the edge of the gently winding river. Its sleepy banks gave no indication of its significance for the war.

As she crept closer, Marie offered silent thanks that she did not have to carry the actual TNT again. Of course, laying the charge was no small thing. The joint where Will told her to place it was nearly twenty feet above. For Josie, who scaled the hills and climbed rocks so easily at Arisaig, this would have not been a problem, but to Marie it looked like a mountain. She crept along under the bridge to the spot Will had indicated, near one of the major joints. Cold water from the low-lying river seeped unpleasantly into her boots. She felt for the crude bolts, which jutted out from the steel, forming a haphazard climbing wall. She tucked the detonator into the top of her blouse and began to climb.

As she reached for a higher bolt, her foot slipped and the sharp metal cut into her ankle. She cried out from the pain in spite of herself, the sound cutting too loudly through the still air. Biting her lip, she struggled to reach for the bolt again and not fall.

At last she reached the spot under the railway bridge where the joints met. Clinging fiercely to the bridge with one hand, she managed to get the detonator from her blouse. She studied it, trying to recall everything she'd learned about detonators in training. With shaking hands, she connected the detonator wires. She said a quiet prayer that she had done it properly and it would all work.

She slid the charge in place. As she did, she felt a rumbling in the distance. An air raid, she thought, reminded of the years of terror in London. But as the sound grew louder and the bridge began to shake, she realized that a train was coming. There was no time to climb down. It was nearing now, shaking the entire bridge and threatening to knock the detonator from its place. Marie clung to the detonator with one hand and a bolt with the other, trying desperately not to let go. For once in her life, she would not run away or be afraid. The train roared overhead. She squeezed her eyes shut, praying she could hang on.

At last the train crossed the bridge and the shaking subsided.

Marie rechecked that the detonator was secure, and climbed down from the bridge with shaking legs. At the base, she paused to catch her breath. She looked in both directions and started across the bridge. She should go slowly, she knew, staying in the shadow of the pylons to avoid being seen. There was no path for pedestrians, though, and a train might come at any time. She ran along the track, feeling naked and exposed, reaching for the other side.

She made it to the landing field on time.

When Marie reached the flat, barren strip of land, it appeared deserted and she wondered if she was too late and Will had retrieved Julian and gone on without her. But there were small stakes in the ground, ready to be lit as soon as the plane neared. She saw Will then by the cover of the trees.

"Any sign?" she asked as she neared. Will shook his head. She was flooded with disappointment. Julian might have been here by now. Marie pushed down the feeling of uneasiness that formed in her throat. A few hours did not mean anything. There was a window of time when a plane might be able to land. The pilot might have been delayed, or circled around due to fog or fear of detection.

"We should wait out of sight." He led her from the open field of trees. One had fallen and behind it the ground was hollowed out to form a small ravine. He sunk to the ground and gestured for her to do the same.

A chill came into the air, and she shivered, feeling the wetness from the river that lingered in her boots. She wished for a fire, though, of course, that was impossible. She moved closer to Will, not caring if he minded. She stared out across the darkened field, wishing for a sign of Julian. He wasn't there. She could almost see his silhouette stepping from the shadows, smile cocked even as his eyes were terse and alert. But it was a mirage, a figment of her mind. Ten minutes passed, then fifteen, and hope turned to disappointment, then to worry.

She leaned against a tree and closed her eyes, too nervous to sleep. Then she sat up with a start as there came a noise from above, something filmy seeming to fall from the night sky.

A parachute!

She leaped to her feet and ran heedlessly into the field. They must have dropped him because it wasn't safe to land. As the parachute lowered, she sidestepped to avoid being crushed. "I told you I would come back," Julian said.

A buzzing sound overhead awoke her suddenly. Her eyes snapped open. She was still sleeping in the darkness of the woods. The reunion had been a dream. Still no Julian. She had shifted slightly from the tree trunk to leaning on Will's shoulder. He had put his arm around her for warmth. Hurriedly they straightened, separating. "Anything?" He shook his head.

The night sky remained dark but it was beginning to pinken at the horizon. It was too late now. Julian's plane wasn't going to show.

She looked into the blankness above, searching for answers about what happened. "Could the landing information have been mistaken?" she pressed.

"I've never known it to be. It was quite certain." Though he didn't say more, the fear in his eyes was unmistakable. Julian was supposed to be here. Something had gone horribly wrong.

Marie stared into the sky, which was turning to gray as dawn neared, willing the whole thing to be a bad dream. "Perhaps the plane will still come," she said, feigning hope.

But knowing the protocol and unwilling to pretend, Will shook his head. "Not enough fuel. Too close to dawn." He rattled off rapid-fire the reasons it was impossible.

"You said that the delivery was confirmed. What could have happened?"

"I don't know. Anyway, we can't wait any longer. If it wasn't safe for him to land, then it likely isn't safe for us to be here." Marie's skin prickled with fear. "We have to go." Will's voice was insistent.

He stood and started for the trees. *Leave and come back the next day at the same time*; that was the protocol when a scheduled drop or landing did not happen. Marie lingered behind a moment. Despite the danger, she did not want to leave the spot that was their best—and perhaps only—hope of reuniting with Julian. The hours until they could try again stretched out in front of her, dark and agonizing. Will was right, though. Every second here risked capture and death, not just for themselves but the other agents and the locals who helped them.

"Maybe he had orders to stay," Marie suggested, as she caught up with Will in the woods.

"That wouldn't stop Julian," Will replied firmly. "My cousin would always come back."

Only he hadn't. That could only mean that something was very, very wrong.

"He'll come at the second drop," Will said, trying to force confidence in his voice.

"But we can't wait," Marie realized. "The bridge. It's set to go off tonight." She saw the alarm behind Will's eyes. She had set the timer on the explosive, as instructed, to detonate at ten o'clock tonight, after nightfall. The plan had been to get Julian and he would lead them to ground.

Only now that was impossible. They couldn't flee without Julian; they didn't have his extensive knowledge of who could be trusted, where they could safely hide. "Go to the flat," Will instructed, seeming to form a plan as he spoke. "Make it look as though you never lived there. Destroy everything you cannot conceal or carry."

"Why?"

"Because I am flying you out of France tonight."

"But we can't just leave," she protested. "We have to be here to receive Julian."

"Marie, he isn't coming," Will said, acknowledging the truth to himself as he said it aloud for the first time.

"He might…" she persisted.

He stopped and turned to her, then grasped her firmly by the shoulders. "We can't afford to wait. Once the bridge blows, none of us will be safe. It's over, Marie. You've done your duty and more. Time to go back to your daughter while you still can."

"But how?" she asked numbly, overwhelmed.

"The Juggler circuit has a Lysander on the ground near Versailles that was damaged when it took on some flak during a landing a few months back, and they've been secretly working to fix it. If I can get there and make it airborne, I can fly us out tonight." He pointed in the opposite direction through the trees. "There's another landing site about five kilometers to the east. If you go due east through the woods, you will come to it. Stay hidden at the landing site until you see me. Meet me at nine thirty and I'll have us off the ground before the detonation." He made it all sound so easy.

Without waiting for a response, he turned and started to go. *Wait*, she wanted to call. She wanted to protest again that they could not leave the country if there was still a chance that Julian might return. But she knew she would get no further with the argument. And it was best for Will to leave now, she knew, under the cover of the darkness that remained. She watched him disappear into the woods.

That evening, after dusk had fallen, Marie stood in the doorway to the flat. The day had stretched slowly. Defying Will, she had decided against packing her few belongings. Best, if anyone came looking, to have it appear she had only gone out for a bit. She had tried to bring up London on the wireless to signal that she and Will were returning and to find out why Julian hadn't come. But there had been no response. There should have been an operator on the other end receiving, even though it wasn't her scheduled broadcast. She wondered if the Germans had managed to jam her signal. Or perhaps it was just the weather. It was no matter. By tomorrow they would be back in London. Surely Julian would be waiting for them and explain everything.

Her eyes lingered now in the corner where the radio was hidden inside the gramophone. She couldn't take it with her. Will meant for her to destroy it, she knew; she had learned as much in training. She walked to it and opened the case, then looked around for something hard. The iron pot by the fire was her best choice. She picked it up and raised it above the radio.

Then she stopped, pot hovering midair. She set it down again. She should try to reach London once more before going. Hurriedly she found her box of silks and selected the top worked-out key to encrypt the message. She pulled the crystals out of her pocket and inserted them into the radio, adjusting the transmittal knobs to find the right frequency. "Angel to House," she typed.

The reply came quickly. "House here." Marie started to type news of the detonation, but before she could, a second message came through: "Confirm receipt of the Cardinal."

As she decoded the message, a rock seemed to form in her stomach. The message was talking about Julian. London had sent him and wanted to confirm that he landed.

Only he hadn't. She hastily coded her reply: "Cardinal not received. Repeat Cardinal not received."

There was no further response. The signal was lost or jammed. She could not tell if her message had gone through or not.

Marie struggled to breathe as she processed the information. London thought Julian had landed. Where was he? Had something happened to him, midflight or on the ground? It was impossible to know, but one thing was certain: if there was a possibility that Julian had landed, there was no way she could leave France.

Marie wanted to wait to see if there was a response from

London, but she did not dare make Will sit in the plane on the ground any longer than necessary and risk capture. She looked at the radio once more. It was her only source of information about Julian now, and she couldn't bear to destroy it. No one could use it without the crystals anyway.

Grabbing the crystals and silks once more, she turned and raced from the flat to meet Will.

Outside Marie forced herself to walk normally, adjusting her sweater as she started down the street. "Mademoiselle!" a male voice called in a loud whisper. She froze, certain it was the police or one of the Germans. It was just the bookseller, though, beckoning to her from across the street.

Marie hesitated. She didn't have time to stop. She waved, hoping that would suffice. But he continued to gesture to her. Fearing someone else might see, Marie walked hurriedly to the shop.

"Bonsoir," she said politely, stepping inside the empty shop. She had gone into the bookstore once or twice since her arrival, looking for something to read to pass the endless hours alone. They had never exchanged a word about that first night, when she had asked him for help with the mission. What could he possibly want with her now?

He slipped her a Rudyard Kipling novel. But before she could express her confusion, he opened it to reveal an empty compartment instead. He was offering to help after all.

Only it was too late. She thought of telling him, then thought better of it. "That will be of great use," she said. The old man's face brightened and he stood a bit straighter, seemingly proud to help. "Thank you, monsieur." She clasped his hand, and then walked hurriedly from the shop.

She started out of town, crossing the bridge over the canal as she had the first night Julian had brought her here. An hour later she reached the landing site. A plane idled at the center of the field and for a moment she hoped it was Julian, returning. But Will stood in the doorway, hand over his eyes as he scanned the horizon for her. His face broke when he saw her, first to relief, then impatience. "Get in, quickly. The detonator is set to go off soon. We have to leave now."

He stepped aside to let her onto the plane, but she stood still, struggling to catch her breath from the sprint. "Will, wait. I received a transmission from London, saying that they delivered Julian."

"But that's impossible." His face registered a mix of surprise and dismay. "We were at the landing site at the right time."

"Unless he was dropped somewhere else."

"I set the location myself. How could that happen?"

"I don't know. Someone must have changed the location somehow. But it means Julian's in-country. He could be anywhere, hurt or arrested or…" She could not finish the thought. "I can't leave until we know what happened to him."

"You mean…" He stopped short. "You aren't planning to come with me?"

"I'll stay here and keep looking for him. You go to London and tell them he's missing. I tried to signal it, but I can't tell if it went through, or maybe they didn't believe me."

"Marie, it won't be safe here after the bridge is destroyed. No one cares about my cousin more than me, but this is crazy. Staying here is a death sentence."

Marie shook her head. "I'll take the next transport."

"There might not be another transport."

"You'll find a way to come back. You always do. And while you are gone, I can keep looking for Julian. I need to be here when he returns," she insisted. "Without a translator and a radio operator, he'll have nothing."

"He's the circuit leader, for Christ's sake!" Will exploded. "He managed for a long time before you were on the ground. He'll manage now."

"I can't leave until I find him—or at least know what happened."

"Julian would want you to go," Will pressed. "He couldn't go on if something happened to you. Julian has feelings for you," he added, saying aloud what she'd scarcely dared to acknowledge to herself. "He cares about you in a way he hasn't about anybody since he lost his wife." *Julian has feelings for you.* She heard the words over again in her mind. "And you have your daughter to think of. You made it, Marie. You lived. So many others cannot say that. Why can't you just take that gift?"

"Because I can't." She couldn't simply leave knowing that Julian had been dropped back into France. She had to find him. She met Will's eyes squarely. "And neither can you. Which is why you'll come back for me in a week."

"But where will you go?" He paused, thinking. "The brothel in the Latin Quarter. You've heard of it?"

"Julian mentioned it once. He said that the women there hide our agents."

"It's more than that. The whorehouse serves as a clearinghouse for all sorts of information. It's one of our most valuable safe houses in all of Occupied France, not to be used except in extreme emergencies." This, Marie thought, must surely qualify. "The proprietor, Lisette, knows half the men in Paris from her line of work. If anyone can make inquiries and help you find Julian, it's her."

"I'll go there straightaway," she promised.

But Will looked out across the horizon and frowned, still not satisfied. "There won't be more flights once the invasion starts." He turned back desperately toward the plane. She could tell he was torn about leaving without her.

"I know," she replied. "But it's another week, two at most."

"One week," he said firmly. "Find him or not, you're coming with me. Listen to the broadcasts in case I have to land on another field. And whatever you do, do not return to the flat."

"I have to go back and see if there is any further word from London over the radio about Julian," she argued.

"You can't. Once the bridge has detonated, it won't be safe any longer. You can't help Julian if you are arrested. Do you understand?" She nodded. "One week," he repeated. "I want you on this plane no matter what. Promise?"

"I promise." A shadow of doubt clouded his eyes. Did he think she would refuse to leave or did he simply not believe she would live out the week?

But there was no time to question. It was nearly ten o'clock. The bridge would blow any second.

Marie kissed him quickly once on the cheek and ran for the cover of the woods.

CHAPTER EIGHTEEN

ELEANOR

London, 1944

Eleanor stiffened, then sat up in bed, gasping for air. She felt for the nightstand lamp in the darkness and flicked it on, heedless of whether or not the blackout curtains were closed. She had the nightmare again where she was running from something. It was as if she was being chased, the space in front of her blackness.

Served her right, Eleanor thought, rubbing at her eyes. She swung her feet around to the floor, then stretched to ease the stiffness in her hips and shoulders. A few hours earlier, she had heeded the Director's order to go home and get some rest after an unbroken three-day stretch at Norgeby House. That was her first mistake. The nightmares never came when she napped at work because her head was too full of details and organizing the things that had to be done. Only here did she dream of crashes and arrests and a place where all the girls were somewhere dark and nameless, crying for her help, but she could not reach them.

Her internal clock told her it was after four. She stood and walked to the toilet, then started the hot water tap for the bath. It had been five days since she had raised her doubts to the Director, five days since he had turned her away. There had been no further messages from Marie.

And still the Director wouldn't listen. Though it seemed as if he did not care about the agents at all, Eleanor knew that wasn't true. Rather, they were simply expendable, collateral damage of a train that was barreling along the tracks, too fast and strong to stop. Her mind reeled back to her conversation on the roof with Vesper, his worry and frustration. If the men in power would not listen to the concerns of their most senior agent, who witnessed it all firsthand in the field, what hope did she have of convincing them?

Worrying would do no good. Pushing down her unease, Eleanor climbed into the bath. She'd run the water too long and it was now well above the four inches permitted by wartime regulations. She savored the excess with a mix of guilt and defiance. She did not linger, though, but washed quickly. Time to get back to Norgeby House, to begin her wait anew. It was not just Marie she was worried about. They'd had no word from Josie for two weeks and Brya's last transmission had been weak as well. It was as though the girls were sliding from her fingers, their voices growing weaker in the darkness of the storm.

Eleanor got out of the tub and dried, then reached for her robe. She had just started to dress when there was a knocking down below. She listened to see if it was one of the usual early morning sounds, the milkman swapping out the bottles, lorries making deliveries down the street. But it had been an actual knock at the door. There were voices, her mother's low and puzzled, a male one tense and urgent. Dodds, the butler at headquarters who also doubled as her driver. He was at least an hour ahead of schedule to pick her up—and he never got out of the car to fetch her. Eleanor dressed quickly, still buttoning as she went down the stairs.

For the first time, Dodds stood in the doorway, looking out of place and uncomfortable. "What is it?" Eleanor asked.

Dodds shook his head, not wanting to speak in front of Eleanor's mother, whose eyes were wide, realizing once and for all that her daughter did not have a job in one of the high street shops. Eleanor grabbed her bag from its peg by the door and raced out the door after Dodds without a word. Her hair flew out behind her and as she sat in the back of the car, she began rolling it into a knot with her fingers. "Tell me."

"The Director said to get you in a hurry. Something about the transmissions." Eleanor's heart stopped as she imagined a thousand different scenarios, all of the things that could have gone wrong. She kept coming back to just one.

"Bloody hell," she swore. She never should have left headquarters. She pressed her foot against the floor of the car, willing Dodds to go faster even as they skidded too quickly across the rain-slicked streets.

When the car pulled up in front of Norgeby House, the Director himself was waiting for her at the door—a sign more alarming than the predawn summons itself. "It's a message I don't quite understand," he said, casting aside his usual discretion and speaking in the corridor as they walked toward the radio room. "From one of the southern networks." Not Vesper's circuit, she realized with faint relief. "Something doesn't look right."

He handed her a piece of paper, an already decoded message asking for the details of an arms drop. But the W/T who sent it was male—not one of hers. Eleanor exhaled slightly. "I'm sorry, sir, but I'm not familiar with this operator." She wondered why the Director had called her in at this hour regarding a transmission that had nothing to do with her girls. "If you'd like, I can pull his file and compare the fist print."

The Director shook his head grimly. "No need. One of the radio operators flagged the message because it is supposed to be from an agent called Ray Tompkins."

"Tompkins was captured at a safe house outside Marseille nearly three weeks ago," Eleanor said, recognizing the name.

"Exactly. This message cannot possibly be from him."

A cold chill ran up Eleanor's spine as she looked at the note once more. "It could be someone else from his team," she ventured hollowly, knowing as she spoke that the words weren't true.

The Director shook his head. "The other two members of that circuit who knew how to transmit were arrested days earlier. No, I'm afraid we must assume the worst—someone else has gotten hold of the radio and is using it."

Eleanor let the reality sink in. One of their radios had been captured weeks ago, and someone (the Germans, presumably) had gotten the crystals and the codes to keep playing it back, as if it was still operational. But would the Germans really have dared to play back the radios of the captured agents, knowing they might not have the security checks quite right and risking detection? Yes, because it had worked. She thought back over the not-quite-right transmissions. They had been short at first, tentative questions. Only after she had responded had they began asking for the locations of arms drops and other valuable information. It was the thing she had feared most, though she had not quite understood it—or perhaps had not wanted to.

Eleanor studied the transmission, looking for answers that were not on the page. Her frustration rose. She had raised her concerns to the Director. Why hadn't he listened?

"There could be ramifications across all of F Section," the Director said. "I need your help assessing the damage, and figuring out how to mitigate it."

Eleanor thought wildly about the messages that London might

have sent to the field across that wireless set during that time, the information that they had unwittingly put into the Germans' hands. They might have revealed safe houses, weapons caches—or worse yet, the identities of agents themselves. The southern circuits were less familiar to her because none of her girls had deployed to them. She would have to comb through the files. It would take hours—no, days.

Her blood chilled as she remembered her conversation with Vesper that night on the roof. He had mentioned a Marseille agent who had contacted the circuit, aided them in getting TNT. If the Marseille circuit had been compromised and had reached out to Vesper, the latter network might be compromised as well.

She had to warn them. Eleanor broke into a run. "Wait…" the Director called after her. But Eleanor didn't stop as she sprinted down the stairs to the radio room.

"Marie Roux," she ordered. "I need to send her a message."

Jane looked puzzled. "She isn't on the scheds for another twenty minutes." Protocol prohibited transmitting to agents in the field off schedule. If the agent wasn't at her radio, she wouldn't be able to receive the message at all.

But Eleanor, in her desperation, needed to try. "Do it."

Jane adjusted the set in front of her, set the frequency and crystals where she normally reached Marie. She sent a call over the wireless, testing if Marie was on the other line. There was only silence. "Nothing."

"Try again." Eleanor held her breath as Jane tried once, then again, to summon Marie over the radio.

A moment later, there came a clicking. "She's there," Jane said brightly.

Eleanor did not share her relief. "Ask her if there are parasols in Hyde Park." The message was code for whether an airdrop had been received. She wanted to ask more directly about Vesper and whether he had returned safely. But given her uncertainties, she didn't dare.

There was a pause as Jane used the worked-out key to code the message and send it, then more clicking. A moment later came the return. "The message says 'confirmed,'" Jane said slowly as she decoded the letters.

"That's it, just 'confirmed'?" Jane nodded. The response was alarmingly brief. Eleanor wanted something more to authenticate that it was really Marie. "How does her fist print look?" she asked.

Jane shrugged. "With such a short message, it is absolutely impossible to tell."

Of course. Eleanor hesitated. She needed to know more, but did not dare say much. "Ask if the parasols were red or blue." Blue meant people; red meant supplies. Jane coded the message and sent it swiftly. There was a hesitation in the return, and uneasiness crept over Eleanor like a cold chill. Something wasn't right.

"We're going to have to end the communication soon," Jane reminded. It wasn't safe for the agents to transmit for more than a few minutes.

But Eleanor couldn't stop. "Send this." She scribbled a message on a piece of paper and handed it to Jane, whose eyes widened. "Have you seen Arlene O'Toole?" the message read. Using actual names over the radio was forbidden. Arlene was a trainee who had dropped out of Arisaig without ever making it through the course, though. She wasn't in the field and they both knew it—as did Marie.

"Are you certain?" Jane asked. Eleanor nodded grimly and Jane began coding.

After she sent the message, the response came quickly. Eleanor read over Jane's shoulder as she decoded the text: "Have seen Arlene. All is well."

Eleanor's blood ran cold. The radio was being run by an impostor.

She looked back over her shoulder where the Director stood and their eyes connected, sharing the full scope of the horror. The radio had been compromised…but for how long? Eleanor racked her brain for the messages that had been sent to Vesper circuit recently, assessing the damage. A few arms drops, perhaps. There had not been many new agents deployed, fortunately.

Only the return of Julian. Her mind reeled back to the night she had seen him on the roof of Norgeby House. After promising him that she would send word of his return flight as a priority transmission, she had gone straight to the radio room. "I need to arrange for a drop. Tell Marie, *'Romeo embresse Juliette.'*" It was one of the prearranged codes to signal for the arrival of personnel.

Marie hadn't been on the radio at the time. But a few hours later the return message had come: "Do not use the usual site. Land at the field outside Les Mureaux instead. Original location compromised." She wanted to ask what had happened to the original field. Les Mureaux was farther west than they typically dropped agents, not close to any safe house. But there was no way to do so safely or openly over the radio. Julian would find out when he returned.

Eleanor's mind raced now as she recalled the message changing the drop site. "Julian," she said aloud. The Director's eyes widened as he grasped the significance of the name. They had no confirmation he had arrived in France. Had they dropped Julian quite literally into the arms of the enemy?

"Ask if the Cardinal landed," she ordered now. Jane looked at her questioningly. The message was not discreet enough, too overt. But Eleanor did not care. "Send it!"

Jane coded then clacked the message. There was no response. A minute passed then another. "House to Angel," she typed, sending the beacon. "House to Angel." Jane tapped the code over and over again, pausing between each time, listening carefully. There was no sign of an answer.

Marie, or whoever had been impersonating her, was gone.

CHAPTER NINETEEN

MARIE

Paris, 1944

Five days. That was how long Marie had been in the cellar of the whorehouse. Marie looked around the tiny space, its dark, close confines reminiscent of the gardener's shed where Julian had left her that first night. She lay her head on the filthy, perfumed-soaked pillow, too tired to care who might have used the creaky mattress previously. Her clothes were grimy and she could smell her own stench beneath them. Across the room there was a laundry basket, a bustier with the nipples cut out carelessly strewn on top. How, Marie wondered, had she gotten here?

After leaving Will at the Lysander, she'd started back through the woods. A few minutes later, she'd heard a rumble, low and deep. The bridge. She'd turned back, daring to stop only for a second to see the way the explosion illuminated the night sky. The detonation had worked after all. She felt a moment's pride, quickly replaced by panic. The Germans would come swiftly after those they believed responsible. She had to keep moving.

Despite her promise to Will, Marie did not go immediately to the brothel in Paris. She needed to check the area for any sign of Julian. She had desperately wanted to return to the flat and try the radio again, but remembering his warning, she had not. Instead, she had gone back to the safe house where Julian had brought her the morning after she'd landed, hoping he might have gone there. But the château was deserted. The old library had been hastily abandoned, dirty plates still on the tables and spoiled food left out. There was a pile of ash in the fireplace where someone had burned papers. Marie put her hand on it, hoping it might still be warm. But the fire had gone out days ago. There were chairs overturned and she wondered if there might have been a raid by the Germans. It appeared the other agents had simply disappeared.

Marie made her way to Paris then, taking a train to the outskirts of the city. She spent the sleepless hours between darkness and dawn hidden in an alley so she didn't get arrested for breaking curfew. The next morning she hitched a ride with a toothless lorry driver who was too interested in staring at her legs to ask questions.

At last, she reached the Left Bank, a tangle of narrow, crowded streets and leaning tall houses that seemed in itself the perfect place to disappear. If she'd had enough money, she might have stayed on her own and not gone to the unfamiliar brothel, as Will had instructed.

Finally she reached the whorehouse on Rue Malebranche and climbed the side stairs above the bistro. A woman no older than herself, wearing more makeup than she had ever seen, answered the door. "I'm Renee Demare," she began, using her cover. "Will sent me." She didn't have any sort of password and she hoped that his name would be enough. There was a flicker of recognition around the woman's eyes.

"Where is he?"

"He flew a plane back to London."

"You should have gone with him. Things are very dangerous now," the woman hissed. "I've had two other agents knock in the past day."

"Who were they?" Marie asked.

"Agents from Montreuil, seeking shelter. I had to turn them away." Marie expected to be sent packing as well. "I'm Lisette," she added.

"I need a place to stay for the next six days until Will comes back for me." Marie could see the woman calculating the risk, weighing it against whatever loyalty she owed to Will.

Finally, Lisette nodded. "Six days. No longer."

Lisette led her down to the cellar. "One more thing," Marie said. Lisette turned to her, arms folded. "Vesper didn't return as expected. But we think he's somewhere in-country. I need to find him."

"Impossible," Lisette snapped. "Do you have any idea what has happened out on the streets in the past twenty-four hours? More than a dozen agents have been arrested, and almost all of the safe houses have been discovered." Marie thought back to the deserted villa. Had the other agents been arrested there? If the Germans had that location, they might know about her flat as well. She regretted then leaving her radio intact, lest they come looking for her and discover it. "And the locals who were helping have grown scared and started turning folks in. It's a miracle you made it here," Lisette added. "To start asking questions now would be suicide for all of us."

"Please." Impulsively, Marie reached out and touched Lisette's arm. "You must understand—I didn't fly out with Will because I need to find Vesper. I can't simply sit here."

But Lisette shook her head emphatically. "If you stay here, you must stay out of sight. Otherwise you will risk this location—and my girls."

"Then I can't stay," Marie countered.

"All right," Lisette relented finally. "I will make inquiries for you. But you must stay hidden."

Marie wanted to argue that she herself had to go looking. But what chance did she have really, without connections or any link to the locals here? No, Lisette was her best and perhaps only chance of finding him. "Thank you," she said finally.

"I'll ask around for you. But don't get your hopes up," Lisette cautioned. "With all of the arrests, it's all but over now."

So Marie waited helplessly in the cellar for five days, her hope of finding Julian fading. Each night Lisette came back with nothing. No news of his whereabouts. Marie saw his face constantly, and she wondered where he was and whether he was hurt.

A creaking from above pulled Marie from her thoughts. Footsteps, too heavy to be Lisette's. One minute passed, then another. Then silence. A cold sweat broke out on Marie's skin. But the footsteps creaked again on the floor above, followed by a rattle and clink sound. She relaxed slightly. Probably Anders, the barkeep, setting out the clean glasses from the night prior. The whorehouse had a quiet rhythm during the day, silent preparations for the boisterous evening that always followed.

There was an unexpected, high-pitched ringing, the bells above the front door to the bar as it opened. Marie tensed once more. The girls all used the discreet back entrance and almost no one came here during the day. She crept up the stairs from the cellar and peeked through the crack in the door. Two gendarmes had entered the bar.

"Have you seen this woman?" Once of the policemen held up a photo. Anders's expression did not change, but Marie knew without a shadow of a doubt they were looking for her.

Anders shook his head. "She isn't one of our girls." Marie prayed the barman would keep her cover.

"Marie Roux," the policeman pressed. They knew who she was. But how?

"She isn't here," Anders said, and retrieved a bottle of expensive cognac from beneath the counter. "We're closed," he added, extending the bottle toward the man. Marie held her breath. Would the bribe work?

"We'll be back tonight," the policeman said ominously, taking the bottle Anders offered and starting back toward the door.

When the door had shut behind the gendarmes, Marie slumped against the door frame. But her relief was short-lived: hands grabbed her from behind and pulled her back into the cellar, nearly throwing her down the stairs. She struggled to escape the grasp.

It was Lisette, her face flushed with anger. "Idiot!" she growled, her voice angry and low. "What were you doing up there? Are you trying to get us all killed?" Marie searched for a good answer and found none. "Here." Lisette thrust a piece of hard baguette at her.

"Thank you," Marie said guiltily. She gobbled down the bread, not bothering with manners. She wanted to ask for water, but did not dare. "The policemen, they were looking for me. How could they possibly know who I am, or that I am here?"

Lisette shrugged. "They seem to know everything these days."

"And you've still had no word of Vesper?"

"*Non.* I've checked with all my usual sources. But it is as if he never landed." Or, Marie thought, perhaps he had somehow disappeared. "There's no sign of him anywhere and the others are all gone. Perhaps he didn't leave London."

Marie shook her head. "He did. There was a broadcast saying as much." Who knew how much of the transmissions could be trusted anymore? But that part at least seemed to ring true. Julian had come back for them but never made it. "I'm certain of it."

"You love him, don't you?" Lisette asked bluntly. Marie was caught off guard by the personal question from a woman she hardly knew. She prepared to deny it. But Lisette's expression was a mix of sadness and understanding; Marie wondered who the girl had lost, whether it was before she turned to this way of life.

"Yes." *Love* seemed a strong word for someone she had known such a short time. But hearing it aloud, she knew that it was the truth.

"Well, wherever he's gone, there's no trace. Things are more dangerous now than ever," Lisette said in a low voice. "Three students at the university were arrested yesterday. And the dry cleaner who once made documents for us, gone." Since coming to the brothel, Marie had been awed by the extent of Lisette's network, the way she was able to use her connections to get information and help the resistance. But Lisette's involvement only heightened the danger. The Germans were tightening the noose and it was just a matter of time until they figured out Marie was hiding here.

"Now that you have food, stay downstairs and out of sight," Lisette ordered. "Or was there something more?"

Marie hesitated. Lisette had seen it in her before she had even seen it in herself. "I have to go," she said.

"Go? But the Lysander isn't scheduled for another day."

"I can't stay here anymore. I'm bringing too much danger to you all."

"Where can you possibly go?"

"I have to go back to the flat."

"You foolish girl, it isn't safe now. And you are risking the lives of everyone who helped you if you are caught."

"I don't have a choice. My radio is still there. I should have destroyed it before I left, but when I decided to stay and look for Julian, I left it intact in case there was further word from London about him. Now that I'm going for good, I have to destroy it." She waited for Lisette to argue further, but she did not. "Thank you for all you have done."

Lisette followed her to the cellar stairs. "Godspeed. And be careful. Vesper would never forgive me if something happened to you."

Marie stepped out, squinting in the daylight, the brightest she had seen in almost a week. She hesitated, wondering if it would have been wiser to wait until after dark. But getting around after curfew was even harder. And if she didn't go now, she knew she might never leave at all.

She smoothed her hair, hoping her bedraggled appearance would not cause her to stand out. But the pedestrians here were students and artists, their clothes an eclectic mix. Then she started down the boulevard, taking in the sloping houses of the Latin Quarter. She passed a cathedral, its doors wide-open. The familiar musty smell of the damp, ancient stones filled her nose. Marie paused. Once, she and Tess had gone faithfully every Sunday, hand in hand, to Saint Thomas More in Swiss Cottage. Now she entered the church and fell to her knees, feeling the cold, hard stone beneath her. Prayer flowed from her like water, for Julian and the other agents who might still be at large, for her family.

A moment later, she stood and started for the door, wishing there was time to light a candle in one of the darkened naves. But taking the time to stop and pray had been frivolous enough. Instead, somewhat fortified, she pressed on.

It was midafternoon by the time she reached Rosny-sur-Seine. The clustered houses seemed tiny and claustrophobic after the teeming streets of Paris. But as she neared the safe house, a feeling of warmth overtook her. Somehow, in the weeks she had been here in the village, it had become her home.

There was no time for sentiment, though. As she eyed the shuttered café on the ground floor of the house, Marie's doubts grew. She should not be here. She hurried across the street, nodding to the bookseller through the plate glass window of his shop. Had she imagined it, or was his expression more uneasy than usual? She paused before the safe house. The café on the ground floor was nearly empty, the Germans who frequented in the evening still sleeping off the previous night's drink. The window shutters of the landlord's flat on the floor above, usually flung wide-open, were drawn. She walked around the back of the house, then stopped again.

The back door was ajar.

Run, a voice inside her screamed. Instead, she studied the ground. There was thick brown dirt, creased like the sole of a man's shoe, looking out of place on the stoop, which the landlady, Madame Turout, always kept so meticulously clean. The dirt was fresh; someone had been there within the hour.

Marie looked over her shoulder. She should turn around and leave, she knew. Will was right; coming back was too dangerous. But she could not desert the radio and risk having it found. She started up the steps.

When she reached the top, she pulled out the skeleton key and promptly dropped it. It clattered noisily to the wood floor. Hurriedly, she picked it up and tried again to insert it in the lock with shaking fingers. She slipped inside the flat, wondering as she did if she was too late.

The flat appeared as she had left it a week earlier, seemingly untouched. The gramophone containing the radio looked as ordinary as a toaster or other household appliance. Studying the radio, an idea came to her suddenly: she should send one quick last message to London, signaling to Eleanor that Julian was still missing and that she was coming home. Marie knew she should not linger here. But she had to try.

She put the crystals in and turned the dial. Nothing. Her body broke out in a sweat. It wasn't going to work. She checked the back of the radio, wondering if someone had tampered with it. Everything she knew about fixing the wireless set ran through her mind. But there simply wasn't time. She needed to go. And she couldn't take it with her without attracting attention. No, if she couldn't transmit one last time, she would simply destroy the radio so that no one else could use it. She reached for the iron pot she'd nearly used to wreck it a week earlier, raised it above her head.

There was a quiet knock. Marie froze. Someone was here.

She looked from the door to the fourth-floor window, wishing the tree outside was heavy enough to support her. But there was no means of escape. The knock came again. "Yes?" she managed, setting down the iron pot.

"Mademoiselle?" a high-pitched voice said on the other side of the door. Marie relaxed, recognizing the landlady's seven-year-old son, Claude. "There's a message for you downstairs."

Marie's heart lifted; could it be a message from Julian? *"Moment, s'il vous plaît,"* she said, setting down the pot. She closed the wireless case and picked it up, starting for the door. "Claude, would you please tell your mother…" she began as she opened the door.

Pointed at her chest was the barrel of a policeman's gun.

"Marie Roux," said the officer who was holding the gun. "You are under arrest." A second *milice* pushed past her and began to search the flat.

She raised one hand to indicate surrender. With her other, she tried to set down the radio case behind the door. But the second officer kicked it with his foot.

"Easy," his colleague admonished. He smiled coldly at Marie. "I'm told you'll be needing that."

CHAPTER TWENTY

GRACE

Washington, 1946

"Come," Mark said, leading her from The Willard when her meeting with Annie was over. Outside, Grace inhaled the fresh air, trying to clear the cigarette smoke from her lungs.

Mark started for the taxi line, but Grace reached out and touched his arm. "Wait," she said, pulling back. "Do you mind if we walk for a bit?" It was a habit she had formed in New York, strolling great swaths of the city, block after block, when she was sad or wanted to think things through.

He smiled. "I'd love to. Have you ever seen the monuments at night?" She shook her head. "You must." She wanted to protest—it seemed too far, too late. More than she had intended. But the air was crisp and lovely and the Washington Monument beckoned in the distance. "I did this all the time in law school," he added, as they walked past the darkened government buildings. "But then with the blackout and curfew, I wasn't able to for years."

He led her south on Fifteenth Street along the edge of the Ellipse. "So, was talking to Annie helpful?"

"In a sense. She confirmed what we thought from the archives—Eleanor ran the women's unit for SOE. But there was something else." Grace stopped, turning to Mark. "She said that someone betrayed the girls."

"Betrayed how?"

"She didn't know."

"That seems fairly incredible," Mark replied.

"Maybe, but she seemed quite sure about it. And she said Eleanor came to see her sister, asking questions because she was convinced of the same thing. You don't believe it?"

Mark shrugged. "I don't know. I mean, everyone loves a good conspiracy theory, right? For those who lost loved ones, like Annie's sister or even Eleanor, it might be easier to accept than the truth."

"The girls disappeared during the war," Grace mused, a picture beginning to form in her mind. "And Eleanor, who had recruited them, went looking for answers." She had surely found, as they had, that the girls had died in Nacht und Nebel. But she had learned something else, too, that made her suspect a betrayal. That was the piece they were missing.

"In New York?" Mark asked, with more than a note of doubt in his voice. They skirted the edge of the temporary government buildings erected on the West Mall to accommodate the influx of workers during the war. Mark took her elbow to help her around a broken curb. "It doesn't seem terribly likely that she'd find what she was looking for in New York."

"It's as likely as us finding what we are looking for in Washington." Nothing, it seemed, was where it should be anymore. "Anyway, it might have not been her first stop."

They were on the edge of the Mall now. Mark held out his arm and she took it, the scratchy wool of his overcoat brushing against the back of her hand. He led her to the right, toward the Lincoln Memorial.

"You don't want to leave it alone, do you?" he asked.

Grace shook her head. "I can't." Somewhere along the way it had gone from curiosity to quest. It had become personal.

"What is it exactly that you want to know? The girls died. Isn't that enough?"

"That's the thing. Eleanor knew that, too, and it wasn't enough for her. She kept searching. She wasn't just looking for what happened to them. She was looking for *why*."

"Does the 'why' matter?"

"Those girls never came home to their families, Mark," Grace said, her voice rising. She pulled her arm from his. "Of course it matters. Maybe there's more to the story, something important or even heroic. If we could tell even one of these families what led to their daughter's death or that her life was not lost in vain, well, then, that would be something, wouldn't it?"

"You wish that about Tom, don't you?" Mark asked. "That someone could tell you his death wasn't for nothing." Mark's words cut through her like a knife.

Frustrated, Grace turned and started away from him, up the stairs of the Lincoln Memorial. She reached the massive statue of the president seated at the top, seeming to watch sentry over the capital and the nation. Her lungs burned from the climb.

A moment later Mark caught up with her. Grace turned away, taking in the panorama of the Mall below, the long stretch of the Reflecting Pool leading to the Washington Monument, the Jefferson smaller but visible just to the south. Neither of them spoke. Mark stepped close behind her, his coat brushing hers, and put his arms around her lightly. Grace shivered. But didn't step away. She liked him, she admitted to herself—more than she should for the short time they had spent together and more than she wanted. There was a calmness about him that seemed to center her. But there wasn't space in her life for that now.

"I was still in school during the war," he said finally, his breath warm on her hair. "But I lost two brothers at Normandy."

"Oh, Mark." She pulled away and turned to face him. "I'm so sorry."

"So I have some idea of how you are hurting," he added.

"I suppose," she replied. But the truth was when it came to grief, each person was an island, alone. She'd learned that the hard way. She had tried to join a war widows group in New York shortly after she had arrived. She'd hoped she would find some connection that would help her break through the wall that seemed to have formed around her heart, but as she sat among those sorry women who had supposedly known what she had gone through, she had never felt more alone.

But she did not want the conversation to turn to her. "I'm exhausted," she said finally.

"It's been a long day," he agreed. "And it's late. Let's go."

Half an hour later the taxi they had hailed at the edge of the Mall dropped them back at Mark's house in Georgetown. Inside, he made a fire in the grate and poured them each a brandy, just as she'd had at the restaurant the night they met. "Wait here," he said, leaving her to sit and think. She sat in the oversize leather chair and took a large sip of her drink, welcoming the burn.

He returned a few minutes later with two plates, each holding a ham-and-cheese sandwich. "That looks delicious," she remarked, suddenly realizing how hungry she actually was.

"It's nothing fancy," he said, passing her a napkin. "But I've learned to make due with what's in the icebox, being on my own and all."

"Has it always been that way?" she asked. "Just you, I mean." The question was too personal.

He shrugged. "More or less. I dated a few girls in college and law school, but I never got stuck on one girl the way Tom did on you." Grace felt flattered and sad at the same time. "After graduation, I went right to the War Crimes Office and then here. Life just seems to carry me too quickly to settle down, and I haven't found a girl who can keep up—at least not yet. Really it's just me and my work all the time." He smiled. "At least until now," he added bluntly.

Grace looked away, caught off guard by the admission. She had sensed, of course, that Mark had feelings for her. There was something between them that went well beyond the night they had spent together, or even their shared connection with Tom. But it was that connection that made it so very hard to contemplate.

Why now? she wondered. A year was a respectable time for a widow to wait before dating. Tom would have wanted her to move on and be happy, or at least she thought so; he had died so young and so suddenly, they never had the chance to discuss such things. And he thought the world of Mark. No, it wasn't Tom's memory that held her up. She had built her own little world in New York, a kind of fortress where she only depended on herself. She wasn't ready to let anyone else in.

"And you? What did you do during the war?" he asked.

Grace relaxed slightly, blotting at her mouth with the napkin. "I was a postal censor near Westport, where my parents live. Just something to keep me busy while Tom was off fighting. We were supposed to move to Boston and buy a house when he came back." Those dreams seemed so distant, like tissue paper crumpled and thrown away without a second thought. She cleared her throat.

"And now you're living in New York."

"I am." She could not have imagined that the city would suit her so.

"Does your family mind?"

"They don't know I'm there," she confessed. "They think I'm with my girlfriend Marcia at her family's place in the Hamptons, recovering." Because that is what a good widow would do—and Grace had always been the good girl.

"So you ran away?"

"Yes." It wasn't as if she had done anything wrong. She was an adult, no children to care for and no husband. She simply picked up and left. "And I don't want to go back."

"Were things so very bad at home?"

"No." That was the thing of it. They hadn't been bad at all, really. "Just not right for me. I went right from my parents' home to Tom without ever thinking about what I wanted for me." And when Tom died, she realized guiltily, it felt like a fresh start.

Suddenly it was all too much. "I'm rather tired. I'm going to turn in," Grace said, heading for the guest room down the hall he'd pointed out earlier.

Grace closed the door and lay down in the unfamiliar bed, still dressed, the sheets cool and crisp. The headlights from passing cars caused patterns to dance on the ceiling. She heard water running, the sounds of Mark washing. A creak as he lay down in his own bed.

Grace closed her eyes and tried to rest. She saw Eleanor and the girls then in her mind, seeming to call to her, wanting to tell her something. A betrayal, Annie had said. Someone had given up the girls to the Germans. It might have been another agent in the field. But the girls who had been caught were not all operating near Paris as part of the Vesper circuit, or even the adjacent networks. They had been scattered all over France. To have information on all of them, one would have to have been very high up—or even in charge of it all.

Grace sat up with a jolt. She leaped from bed and raced from the room, feeling propelled by something other than herself. A moment later, she found herself standing in the doorway to Mark's bedroom. She knocked. *Turn away*, she thought, panicking. But it was too late. He had opened the door and stood before her, shirt half unbuttoned. "Is everything all right? Did you need something?"

"Eleanor," she said, jumping right in. "We've been assuming all the time that she was looking for answers about the girls. What if she had already found out the truth?" She took a deep breath. "Or what if she already knew because she was the one who betrayed them?"

He hesitated for several seconds, considering the idea. "Do you want to come in?" Grace nodded.

His bedroom was cluttered. Clothes covered the sofa and overflowed from the dresser. He cleared a spot for her on the lone chair, moving his briefcase to the ottoman in front of it.

"So you think Eleanor betrayed the girls?" he asked as she sat.

"I don't know. But if she did, she might have been trying to hide the truth, rather than find it."

"It's a theory, isn't it? Annie said that Eleanor had a mysterious past and no friends. She was from Eastern Europe. What if she was working for the Germans?"

Grace's mind spun. She didn't want to consider the idea, but she couldn't look away.

"It's mind-boggling," she said. "What if Eleanor from the start had been a traitor, sent to infiltrate SOE? She would have used the girls as chess pieces to help the Germans get information. Instead of their protector, she had sent them to their deaths." She paused, trying to fit the pieces together. "But Annie said Eleanor came to her sister after the war, asking questions. If she was the one who betrayed the girls, why would she have done that?"

"Who knows? Maybe she wanted to make sure no one suspected her." Suddenly, nothing was as it had appeared to be. Even Eleanor's death, a simple car accident, seemed shrouded in mystery. Could Eleanor, guilt stricken about what she had done, have deliberately stepped out to be killed?

"I just can't believe Eleanor would have betrayed the girls," Grace said. The woman was a stranger, though; anything was possible. "I can't think about it anymore tonight. I should go," she said wearily. But she remained seated.

A look of understanding crossed his face. "Sometimes," he

said, "you just don't want to be alone." He crossed the room and sat down beside her, too close. Their faces turned toward one another. She closed her eyes, certain that he would try to kiss her and almost wanting him to. He did not. Instead, he ran a thumb along her cheekbone, catching a tear that she had not known had fallen.

A moment later he stood and went to the dresser. He returned with a flannel shirt, which he handed to her. She went into the bathroom to change, smelling him in the fabric even through the fresh scent of the laundry detergent.

When she came out of the bathroom, swimming in the oversize nightshirt, he was arranging sheets on the chair and ottoman, and she assumed that he meant for her to sleep there. But he stretched out on the chair, adjusting his lanky frame to the cramped space.

"I couldn't possibly take your bed," she protested.

"I insist. I can sleep anywhere." She sat on the edge of the bed, overwhelmed by the impropriety of the situation and yet not caring at all. Part of her wished he would join her.

She leaned back against the headboard. "What I said earlier about my life before the war… I loved Tom." It felt odd to be talking about her husband here, in his best friend's bedroom, but she felt as though she had to explain. "I still do. It was just the life, you know, married, in the suburbs. I never quite fit in."

"I understand," Mark replied. "It was like me, at Yale." Grace was surprised; she had always thought of Mark as one of the guys. "I was there on scholarship. I don't suppose Tom ever mentioned it." Grace shook her head. "No, he wouldn't have, of course. I was always working, waiting tables in the dining hall, doing whatever I needed to earn extra money and make ends meet. Tom never minded, but some of the fellas made sure I knew I would never be one of them. It doesn't matter in the end. I've done fine for myself," he added, gesturing around the room. "The ink on my diploma is the same as theirs. But I'll never forget that feeling."

Grace shook her head. "It was more than just the not fitting in. When Tom was finishing officers' school, he wanted me to come down to Georgia for the graduation and have a few days together before he shipped out. But I didn't. I made some excuses about needing to be in Westport for work. But really it just seemed too much, the trip down there. And being among all of those officers and their wives, it was everything I hated about married life, only more so. When I said I couldn't go, Tom arranged to come to New York and see me before he left. That's why he was in the jeep. That's why he was killed." Not going to Georgia had been the worst mistake of her life.

Mark sat beside her and put his arm around her shoulder. "You didn't know, Gracie. We just never know." They sat together without speaking for several minutes. Finally, he stretched out beside her on the bed. They didn't touch but he held her hand firmly in his.

Neither of them spoke further. Several minutes passed, broken by the quiet ticking of a clock on his nightstand. She turned to look at him. He lay just inches from her, legs flung over the edge. His eyes were closed and his breathing had grown long and even, signaling sleep. Longing rose up in her. She reached out her hand, wanting to wake him.

Then she stopped herself. What had happened in New York had been bad enough, but this...this longing, was a whole other thing entirely. It had to stop.

She was suddenly racked with guilt and doubt. What was she doing here? She had come to find out what she could about Eleanor and the girls, and now she knew. There was nothing more to be learned here. There was no reason to stay. It was time to get back to New York and her work with Frankie and figuring out the life that awaited her.

Grace quietly sat up and stepped out of the bed. She moved

closer to Mark in spite of herself. Her hand lingered close to his neck. Sensing her there, he shifted in his sleep. She was seized once more with the urge to wake him for all the wrong reasons. No, she had to leave now.

Still wearing his flannel shirt, Grace picked up her clothes and tiptoed from the room. She changed in the bathroom, then went to the office to phone a cab. Her purse was there, the papers she had taken from the Pentagon just beneath them. She should leave those here, for Mark to return to the archive. But she picked up the file and opened it.

The documents, wireless transmissions and interoffice memos were the same ones she and Mark had looked at earlier in the taxi back from the Pentagon. But now she viewed them with a fresh eye. Could there be evidence among them that Eleanor had betrayed her girls?

There was an incoming telegram. "Thank you for your collaboration and for the weapons you sent us. SD." Grace felt a tightening in her chest. SD stood for Sicherheitsdienst, the German intelligence service. The message was clear confirmation that the Germans had been operating one of the wireless radios, and that they had brazenly, foolishly perhaps, let London know.

There was a second sheet attached, from the desk of E. Trigg. "Message not authenticated," it said. "Continue transmissions." The memo was dated May 8, 1944—right around the time the arrests of Eleanor's girls had begun.

There it was in black-and-white—proof that Eleanor had known the radios were compromised and she continued to transmit critical information that enabled the Germans to arrest the girls. Grace stared at the paper. It was Eleanor's own confession, as surely as if it had been signed.

"No..." Grace whispered under her breath. Just minutes earlier, the notion that Eleanor had betrayed the girls had seemed impossible. Now, undeniable proof was right before her.

She thought of waking Mark, telling him the truth about

Eleanor. But there was no point. Her worst suspicions about Eleanor, the ones she'd shared with him earlier, were in fact correct. She wished then that she had never come to Washington at all, that she had left it all alone and never found out the awful truth. Overwhelmed by it all, Grace tucked the folder underneath her arm.

Then, without looking back, she left.

CHAPTER TWENTY-ONE

MARIE

France, 1944

Marie had not resisted arrest.

As she stood in the doorway to her flat, muzzle of the gun pushing against her ribs, everything she learned at training ran through her head: *resist, fight, run.* Though she had not been good at the hand-to-hand combat drills, she had absorbed enough from working with Josie to know to kick at the groin and claw the face.

But little Claude had been standing in the corridor and she did not dare risk the child's injury in a scuffle. So she went with the police without argument.

They took her to Paris, not in a police car or a round-up wagon as she had always imagined, but in a black Renault with leather seats. One of the officers sat in the back beside her, reaching over to lock her door with an ominous click. As they wound silently through the streets of the Sixteenth Arrondissement, Marie fought the urge to scream out to the passersby on the street for help, women pushing prams and men walking home from work, unaware that she was being held prisoner in the car. Instead, she memorized the route the car was taking in hopes of escaping the prison to which they were surely taking her.

To her surprise, the car pulled up in front of a wide, elegant town house on the Avenue Foch. When they ushered her inside, Marie could see that it had once been a wealthy home, with brass furnishings and deep red curtains that someone had chosen to match the floral rugs just so. The air was heavy with stale cigarette smoke. A German corollary to Norgeby House, Marie thought, watching a messenger scurry between rooms, two uniformed men talking behind a half-closed door.

The policeman who had sat beside her in the car kept a firm grip on her elbow as he led her up one floor of the town house, then another. On the uppermost floor, the policeman unlocked a door to reveal a dormitory-style room with a sloped ceiling, a half-dozen army cots and a shelf full of books in the corner. Faded wallpaper with little yellow ducks suggested this had once been a nursery or playroom. The policeman threw her inside the empty room, the pretense of civility ebbing now that they were out of sight. Caught off guard by the unexpected roughness, Marie stumbled, banging her shin on the frame of one of the cots. She rubbed her leg to ease the throb, then looked around the space, which smelled faintly of sweat and waste. Others had been here clearly, prisoners like herself. But who?

The officer slammed the door, leaving her alone. Marie walked around the room for an escape. The door was locked. She raced to the window and tried to raise it. It was sealed shut, the nails painted over, as if it had been that way for years. She searched the room for other escape routes and found none. Then she walked to the window once more, and looked across the way at the grand houses where people still lived. There was an elderly couple in one of them and she considered trying to get their attention. Did they know people were being held prisoner here? Perhaps they did not care. Through another window, she saw a young woman, an au pair perhaps, serving dinner to several small uniformed girls at a long table. A lump formed in Marie's throat as she wondered whether she would ever see her daughter again.

Male voices from below pulled Marie from her thoughts. She knelt and pressed her ear close to the heater, trying to hear the sounds that rose through the pipes. A voice with a German accent, asking something. Demanding. The voice that responded was deeper. English. It somehow sounded familiar to her.

Her heart quickened as she tried to calm herself. The German voice came again, then the Englishman. The exchange between the men reminded Marie of a Ping-Pong match, the German asking a question, the Brit saying no. There were several seconds of silence, followed by a sickening thud. Marie held her breath as she waited to hear the voice of the Englishman again. When it came it was desperate and broken, almost a sob.

Marie's terror grew as she wondered what the German had done to the man, and whether the same fate awaited her. Her panic rose. She raced to the attic door and tried the knob again, desperate to escape, but it was locked. She tried the window once more. The situation crashed down on her then: she was trapped at the headquarters of Nazi intelligence, her cover blown. The Germans knew who she was and that she worked a radio for SOE, perhaps that she had set the charge as well. No one from SOE, either in Paris or in London, knew she was here and she had no way to call for help. The stories she'd heard at training of interrogation and torture filled her mind. Whatever dreadful fate the man downstairs was suffering, she would surely face it next. She would never make it out of here alive or see Tess again.

The door to the room opened suddenly and Marie leaped back so as not to be struck. A different man, German this time, stood in the doorway. "Madame Roux," he said with mock deference. Marie's blood chilled.

The German led her down the stairs to the floor below. He opened a door to an office, then stepped aside to let her in. Marie let out a yelp.

Seated in a chair in the middle of the room, with his hands and legs bound, was Julian.

Marie knew then why he hadn't come back to them as he had promised. The Germans had already arrested him.

"You have five minutes," the German snarled, before slamming the door behind him.

"Vesper," Marie said, not daring to use his real name here. What had they done to him? His face was nearly unrecognizable from all of the beatings. A long gash now marred his cheek and his left eye was swollen shut. His nose was off-kilter, too, broken badly. But she had found him. Marie ran to him as joy and relief and terror overtook her all at once. She threw her arms around him so hard the chair threatened to topple.

He leaned his head in her direction, unable to do more because his hands were bound. "Are you all right? They didn't hurt you, did they?"

"I'm fine," she reassured him, feeling guilty that he should worry about her when his own condition was so much worse.

"The bridge?" he whispered. "Did it work?"

She nodded. "Blown."

He sat back. "Thank God. They were trying to get it from me, the timing and details. I held out as long as I could, but I didn't know if it would be enough." His face was a map of lacerations and bruises, his sacrifice so that the mission could proceed.

"The operation went smoothly. I set the detonator myself." A note of pride crept into her voice.

"You did what?" Surprise, then anger, registered across his battered face. "Bloody Will! I never should have left him in charge."

"There was no other way," she replied. "Josie's gone missing. There's been no word of her." Marie's eyes filled with tears. If she and Julian had been arrested, was there any real hope that Josie might have somehow escaped?

"And Will?" Julian asked. She could see the concern in his eyes for his cousin.

"Fine, too, as far as I know. He went to London to notify headquarters you hadn't returned. He's supposed to be coming back for me tomorrow." Only now she wouldn't be there. "He wanted me to go with him, but I stayed."

"He never should have let you."

"It wasn't his choice. I insisted."

"Why?"

She faltered. "I needed to find you." Their eyes met then. Here, in what might be their last moments together, there was no possibility of hiding what was between them. He tilted his head toward her once more, stopped by the bonds that held him. She leaned in, meeting him, and their lips touched. She kissed him softly, not wanting to worsen the pain of his wounds, but he pressed for more, seemingly heedless.

A moment later, she pulled away. "How did they get you?"

"They were waiting for me at the landing. They had the location and time of the flight. Why did you change the site?"

"We didn't," she said incredulously. "That is, we received word from London..."

He shook his head. "London said they received word from you."

The realization passed between them then. The Germans had intercepted one of the radios and was transmitting to London, impersonating an agent. "That must be how they knew. Not just about me. They have everything, Marie. Our notes, our records." A look of realization dawned in his eyes. "Eleanor suspected as much. She wanted me to warn you that the radio was compromised and to be on guard. Only now it's too late."

Her mind reeled. "But if they already have everything, then what do they want from me?"

"They want you to..." Before he could finish his answer, noise came from the corridor. Footsteps, followed by a turning of a key in the lock. Two uniformed men walked in. The younger one, who had brought her downstairs earlier, untied Julian from the chair and dragged him from the room. Marie wanted to cry out. But remembering her training, she did not. She turned to face the second man, whom she had not seen before. He was older, with horn-rimmed glasses. The breast of his uniform was adorned by a sea of metals and she wondered what he had done to earn them.

"I'm Sturmbannführer Kriegler of the Sicherheitsdienst." Her terror grew as she recognized the name of the SD leader, known for his sheer brutality. "Can I get you anything?"

For you to let us free, she thought, *and then to drop dead*. "Perhaps some tea?" she asked, scarcely believing the audacity of her own voice. She lifted her head to meet his eyes.

He paused, then stood and started for the door and opened it. "Tea, *bitte*," he called to someone on the other side. Kriegler waited in the doorway. Marie's eyes darted around the room. The request had bought her some time. But there was simply nowhere to go.

A moment later, Kriegler returned and handed her the teacup. She held it, not drinking. "Now let's get to work," he said. He gestured for her to follow him to a small room off the rear of the office.

Walking into the annex, her heart sank. There, sitting on the table, was her radio.

But as she walked closer, she saw that this was not the radio they had confiscated from her flat; the markings on the case were different. She wondered whose it was, and how long they'd had it. The Germans had been broadcasting to London, acting as one of their own—and London believed it. It all came together then—how the Germans had impersonated the agents and fooled

London into sharing critical information. The radio, which had been their lifeline, had also now proved their undoing.

"But you already have the radio," she managed. "What do you want from me?"

"We need you to talk to London to authenticate the messages." There must be something about their transmissions, Marie realized, and they wanted her to validate them. Julian couldn't have done it, even if he was willing. She understood then they needed her. If she helped them, she might save her life—and Julian's. But if she refused and London realized that something was amiss, she might put an end to the radio game once and for all.

She saw Josie's face in the sky above her, foreboding, beseeching her to be strong. She saw Eleanor, who would expect better. "No," she said aloud. She would not do it.

Kriegler walked around the front of the desk and stood before her. Without speaking, he slapped her across the mouth so hard she was lifted from the chair. She fell backward and clattered to the floor, her head slamming against the ground. The teacup shattered, spraying hot liquid and shards of porcelain everywhere.

But what Kriegler did not know was that it was not the first time in Marie's life she had been hit. Marie's father had been a violent drunk. When he'd come home from the pub, Marie or her mother, whoever was closest, were the collateral damage of his rage. Blows and fists; once he'd slammed her head into the wall. She'd escaped her father's wrath; he hadn't defeated her, and she wasn't going to let Kriegler defeat her now.

So as Marie lay on the floor of the office of Avenue Foch, seeing her father in this monster standing before her, something inside her hardened. Kriegler was going to have to kill her—because she would never talk.

Kriegler reached down and, with unexpected civility, helped

her back into the chair. Warm wetness bubbled at her lip where it had split.

When she looked up, Kriegler was holding a list, which he passed to her. She turned away, but he pushed it forcibly, the paper scraping against her face. Finally she could avoid it no longer. The paper contained not just scraps of information but what appeared to be a list of every single agent in the region, their aliases and their actual names. They had the names of all of their French contacts, too, and their addresses. The safe houses and the storehouses where munitions and so much else were hidden.

She stared at the paper. Someone had given them up; Julian had confirmed that moments earlier. But the scope of the betrayal, before her on this paper, was staggering. Who among them could have possibly been such a traitor?

"We have everything," Kriegler said smugly.

"Then I suppose," she said, lifting her chin defiantly, "you don't need me."

Kriegler's open palm slammed into her again. She fell to the floor and when he lifted her this time, it was by the hair. The blows rained down quicker now, one after the other. For the first time in her life, she prayed for death to come quickly. She saw Tess's face in her mind and locked on it, transporting herself from this horrible place. She held her breath and counted, willing herself not to scream.

Kriegler suddenly stopped. Just as abruptly as it had started, the beating was over. She tried to see through her swollen eyes, to breathe and brace herself for whatever was coming next.

A door opened and shut again. A guard threw Julian into the annex and he fell to the floor, too weak and beaten to stand.

Seeing her mangled face, he let out an anguished cry. She sat up and tried to go to him. Kriegler stepped between them and put the gun to Julian's head. "Do it or he dies." His eyes were steely, no sign of life behind them. She knew he would kill Julian without a shred of hesitation.

"Marie, don't..." Julian pleaded.

Marie faltered; her own life was one thing, but Julian was their leader and she had to make sure nothing happened to him. This was not about her feelings for him. The survival of the Vesper circuit, or whatever remained of it, depended on him. "All right," she said finally. She spat away the blood that had pooled in her mouth. "I'll do it." It was against everything she had learned and trained for—but she would do it to save his life.

The guard wrenched her from Julian and dragged her over to the machine. She started to reach for the radio, but Kriegler shooed her away and set up the transmission himself, as expertly as any operator who had trained with her at Arisaig House.

Kriegler pulled out her box of worked-out keys, which they had confiscated from her upon arrest. "Send a message, letting them know that it is you and that everything is fine. Then send this." He handed her a message and a slip of silk bearing one of the ciphers. The message was requesting another drop of supplies to a specific location. If she did as Kriegler was demanding, the ruse would go on and on. SOE would keep sending agents and arms right into the waiting hands of the Germans.

Marie transcribed the message into code, then found her frequency with shaking hands. She finished the message and showed it to Kriegler. "Your security check," Kriegler said. He jammed the gun into the wound beneath Julian's jaw, and Julian grunted to keep from crying out in pain. "What is it?" Kriegler demanded.

Marie hesitated. If she gave up the information too easily, Kriegler would know it was a bluff. "Changing the thirty-fifth letter of the message to *p*," she explained slowly, pointing. "I did it right there." She didn't mention the second check, the one she had left out. She prayed he did not know about it and would not notice.

"Send it," he growled. Back in London, Eleanor would be

reading the message. Surely she would notice the absence of the second security check and realize that something was amiss.

A message came back over the line and she wrote it down. As she decoded it with the silk, her terror grew. It was the one she most dreaded, the one she never thought they would send: "True check missing."

As she decoded the message, Marie stiffened with dread. The operator in London had just told Kriegler that Marie had tried to dupe him. But that was exactly what the second check was supposed to convey, that something was amiss with the transmission. How could the operator back in London not know that? Marie was flooded with despair. Behind her, she could sense Kriegler's growing rage. "Wait, I..." She turned toward him, trying to find an explanation.

He grabbed her by the nape of her neck, pulling at her hair until her scalp screamed. Then, just as abruptly, he let her go. "Your second check," Kriegler hissed, cocking his revolver against Julian's head.

"Marie, don't do it!" Julian cried out. "They'll kill us anyway."

But she had lost him once; she could not bear to lose him again, this time for good. "*K* instead of *c*," she blurted desperately. "Every other time." Now the Germans had exactly what they needed to transmit as her without detection.

"Fix it!" Kriegler ordered. She recoded the message and sent it again.

The response came and she used the worked-out key to decode it hurriedly: "Check verified. Information forthcoming."

"There..." she began, turning back toward Kriegler. His gun was pointed at her now. She saw Tess's face hovering above her, said farewell as she prepared to die.

"You should have helped us the first time." He swung his arm sideways toward Julian.

"Don't!"

It was too late. A shot rang out. Julian jerked, then slumped onto the floor.

"No!" she screamed, running toward him.

She knelt where he had fallen and took him in her arms. Kriegler had fired with deadly accuracy. The bullet had entered between Julian's temple and cheekbone, lodged somewhere. The rational part of her knew that there was no way he could survive such a wound. But in her heart, she could not believe it. "Hold on, Julian," she pleaded. His eyes were still open. But they drifted upward, the light fading from them.

"I love you," he breathed. There it was, the feelings between them realized at last. Or perhaps he simply thought she was Reba, his wife. But he grabbed her arm. "We should have been together, Marie." She heard in his words all that might have been between them if things had been different. "I love you," he repeated.

"And I, you," she said, holding him close. There was no denying what was between them anymore. She kissed him again, for what she knew would be the last time.

His body went slack then and she pulled away. "I see them," he whispered. He had almost no voice left at all. "My wife and boys." His hand reached out to the invisible image in front of him.

"Don't leave me," she begged, selfish where she should have been strong. She did not know how she could face whatever would come next without him. "This is not the end." She remembered what he had once said about scores of others rising up to take their place. She saw it now in the light behind his eyes. He grimaced and then his face relaxed, the calmest she had ever seen him. His breathing stilled. She buried her face in his chest.

And then he was gone.

She set his head down gently. "Why?" she screamed, lunging at Kriegler. She gouged his face with her nails.

"Bitch!" he swore, raising his hand to where she had drawn blood. He gestured for the guard to take her.

"We did what you wanted!" she screamed, unhinged now as the guard dragged her from the room. "We did what you asked. We are prisoners of war under the Geneva Convention. You cannot do this!"

"Prisoners of war?" he laughed with contempt. "Fräulein, where you are going, you don't even exist."

CHAPTER TWENTY-TWO

ELEANOR

London, 1944

Eleanor sat at her desk in Norgeby House, poring over the old transmissions.

She was still reeling over the awful truth about the radio being compromised. There was still no word about Julian or Marie. She studied the past messages from Vesper circuit, looking for more signs of the breach and trying to assess the damage that might have been done. How could she have let this happen? Protecting the girls was everything, her life's work. Yet she had failed them, just as surely as she had failed her sister decades earlier.

Rubbing her eyes, she stood and walked into the radio room. The operators were sitting more quietly than usual, the clacking of a lone wireless set the only sound.

"Is everything all right?" she asked Jane. The question was a foolish one; Jane had taken the compromise of Marie's radio every bit as hard as Eleanor herself. The girl looked pale and drawn from the long hours of waiting and worrying since the false transmission that purported to be from Marie.

Jane shook her head. "Margaret didn't broadcast as scheduled."

"Nor has Maureen," another operator chimed in.

"Perhaps there's a problem with the transmissions," she said, wanting to comfort them. But the words hung hollow in the air. Something larger was amiss.

Eleanor started down the street for the Director's office, bypassing his secretary and not bothering to knock. "Sir?"

The Director raised his eyebrows. "Trigg? Come in. I was just about to come see you." This seemed odd when he had not summoned her; in fact, he had not expected her at all.

"Two more radios have gone silent."

He pursed his lips beneath his moustache, but did not seem surprised. "There have been rumors of more arrests outside Paris." Eleanor's stomach twisted. "Two agents taken at a safe house outside Paris. Others to the east and south."

It was not just the destruction of the bridge that had set off the wave of arrests, she knew. Although the detonations had set off the round of reprisals that had come swiftly in its wake, it was more than that. Kriegler and the SD seemed to suddenly know all too well where to find the agents they were seeking. They must have been playing along for months, Eleanor suspected, letting the agents operate as long as the radio ruse had worked. Once they knew that they had been detected, the Germans had nothing more to lose. They had taken the gloves off, acted on the intelligence that they had amassed and began a dragnet to catch all of the agents. Though there had been no word of Marie or Julian, it seemed inevitable that they had been taken as well.

"Were the arrested agents men or women?" she asked.

"Maybe both," the Director replied. "I don't have the names yet." With sinking dread, Eleanor felt certain that Margaret and Maureen would be among them.

"Sir, we have to do something." They had sent word to all

of the circuits in France, telling them to go to ground. It wasn't enough. The agents should have been recalled; Eleanor had demanded it. But it was just days before the invasion, and they were not about to start a mass evacuation that would raise questions.

"We are going to do something." He paused. "We're bringing them home as you suggested." Things must be very bad if they were actually going through with the withdrawal of agents. "Orders to extract those that remain have already been sent." Eleanor felt as though she had been slapped. Why hadn't those orders been sent through her? "It will take a bit longer than we hoped," he added.

"How long?" she demanded. Another week and there might not be any agents left at all.

"I don't know. Will Rourke, the pilot who organized Moon Squadron, has gone missing. There's word of a plane shot down over Brittany, which might be his. But we'll get them home as quickly as possible."

Relief flooded Eleanor, quickly replaced by confusion. "All of the agents?"

He shook his head. "Just the girls. They're shutting you down." *You*, she noticed. Not *us*. "I'm afraid they're writing off the women's unit as a failed experiment."

Failed experiment. Eleanor seethed at the words. The girls had done great things, accomplished their missions, done everything that was asked of them. No, the failure was not the girls, or even the agents, but headquarters.

Eleanor's brain screamed with disbelief. "But the invasion is just days away. Surely our work there is more important than ever."

"The circuits are being regrouped, in some cases eliminated. The work will be done by the men."

"Have you accounted for all of them?" she asked, already knowing the answer. "The girls, I mean."

"All but twelve." The number was so much larger than she

had anticipated. He handed her a piece of paper with the names. Josie was on it, Marie, too. Twelve of her girls were still missing.

And it was in no small part her own fault. Bringing women into F Section had been her idea in the first place. Eleanor had recruited those girls, overseen their training and personally deployed them to Occupied Europe. And she had seen that there were problems, yet failed to insist that more be done. No, she alone was responsible for those who went missing and would never return.

"There are men missing, too," he pointed out.

"Yes, of course." Eleanor swatted at the argument she had heard a dozen times. "But the men have commissions. And they are to be treated as POWs if captured." It was not that she didn't care about the men. But they had army titles, ranks—and the protections of the Geneva Convention. The government would look for them. Remember them. Not her girls.

"I have to go see for myself what went wrong on the ground."

"You mean to find the girls? I'm afraid that is quite impossible."

"But, sir, a dozen are still missing," she protested. "We can't simply give up."

He lowered his voice. "Eleanor, you must stop asking about the girls. There will be repercussions for yourself and for others. You have much to lose right now. And if not for yourself, you have to let it go for the families of the girls. You know as well as I do that if the Germans have caught them, they are likely gone. Your questions will only bring their families more pain."

The Director picked up his pipe. "The investigation is classified, and being handled at the highest levels." That, Eleanor knew, was a lie. If anyone at all was looking for the girls, they would have come and spoken to her. No, the matter had been *shelved* at the highest levels. "There is simply no need for you to know," he added, before she could call him on it.

"No need?" Her voice was incredulous. They were her girls.

She had recruited them, sent them over. "So you're ordering me to stop looking for them?" she asked with disbelief.

"It's more than that. The women's unit has ended. Your position has been eliminated."

"I'm being transferred then? Where am I to go?"

He looked away, not meeting her eyes. "I'm afraid we've been ordered to downsize." He spoke stiffly now, as if reading words from a document he had not himself written. "We are grateful for your service, but I regret to inform you that your tenure at SOE has ended."

She stared at him blankly. "Surely this is a mistake." She had been with SOE for months—no, years—before the women's unit was founded. They could not be getting rid of her now.

"We have no choice. You've been given thirty minutes to gather your personal belongings." She searched for words, found none. Her insides burned white-hot with anger. She stood and fled his office, starting back down the stairs to Norgeby House.

Eleanor went to her desk and started stacking files, pulling the photos of the girls who were missing and slipping them into her bag. She knew she did not have much time. A moment later, the Director appeared in the doorway. "I'll see you out," he said. She reached for another file, but he stilled her hand. "Leave everything as it is." She understood then why he had followed her. "You're to take your personal belongings only. No papers," he added, seeming to know before she did herself that she would not stop looking for the girls. A plan began to form in her mind.

"I can manage myself. You don't have to stay," she offered, hoping to buy a few minutes alone here to gather what she needed.

"We have orders to see you out," he said, awkwardness creeping into his voice. She stopped with surprise, her hand hovering midair. In just moments, her whole world had been turned upside down. She searched his face, looking for answers, or at least some sign of the mentor she thought she knew. But his eyes were blank.

She turned away blindly. "I have to organize the files." The thought of turning over her papers in less than perfect order was unthinkable.

"It isn't necessary," he added. "The military will be coming and packing everything up."

"Why?" she demanded. "Where are they taking it?"

He did not answer. She noticed then a military police officer standing at the door of her office, waiting to escort her out and make sure she left. Something inside her hardened. She was being cast out like a foreign invader from the very place she had created.

She stepped away from the desk, trembling with rage. The Director held out papers to her. "This is for you. They came through yesterday." Her citizenship papers—the one thing she had always wanted. They seemed now a sorry consolation prize for the girls she had lost. She pushed them back at him.

"I'm sorry," he said.

And then she was dismissed.

CHAPTER TWENTY-THREE

GRACE

New York, 1946

The next afternoon, Grace climbed the steps of the rooming house in Hell's Kitchen. She was exhausted, as much from everything that had happened in Washington as the trip itself, and she was glad to be back home. She was also eager to see Frankie and get back to the ordinary business of her life. It was late Friday, though, and she had already booked the day off. And it wasn't entirely a bad thing that she had the weekend to rest and sort herself out before returning to work.

Grace reached the top floor of the rooming house and turned her key in the lock to her apartment. She opened the door, then froze.

Sitting in the lone chair, clutching her black patent leather purse, was Grace's mother.

Her mind whirled. How had her mother found out where she lived? And how long had she been here? Grace's eyes darted from the unslept-in bed to her wrinkled clothes from the night prior. She searched for an explanation that would make the sight less awkward, but found none.

"The landlady let me in," her mother said in her birdlike voice, as though that explained everything. Her hair was swept back beneath a salmon velvet cloche hat that matched her Elever swing coat perfectly. Grace could imagine it, the charming smile, little tinkle of a laugh as she talked her way into the apartment.

"Darling, I know it's awful just to pop in like this," her mother continued, smoothing the gloves she'd laid neatly on top of her purse. "But you didn't answer my calls. I was so worried." Really, that was only part of the story. Grace's mother wanted to see what she was doing here, what her life was all about.

"How did you know I was here?"

"I went in to Hartford to do some shopping and I ran into Marcia in the dressing room at G. Fox." Grace flushed at the mention of Marcia's name—her alibi. She imagined the scene in the department store. Marcia would have been nervous, caught off guard by the unexpected encounter. It wouldn't have taken much pressing for Grace's mother to get the address, which Grace had given Marcia so she could forward mail.

"I'm sorry for not telling you myself," Grace said, perching on the edge of the bed.

"It's all right," her mother replied, putting her hand on Grace's. "We were just so worried." It hadn't been just about the appearance of things for her mother—she had genuinely cared. Somehow lost in the haze of her own problems, Grace had lost sight of that.

But that didn't mean she wanted to go home.

"So this is where you've been staying." Her mother looked around the tiny room, her nose wrinkling involuntarily with distaste. "If I help you pack, we can be gone in an hour. If you don't want to stay with your father and me, your sister Bernadette offered her spare room." Staying with her older sister and her three pugnacious children, Grace reflected, might be the only thing worse than going home.

"Mother, I can't just leave. I have a job."

Her mother waved her hand as though Grace's work was irrelevant. "You can send a note."

"It's not a cocktail party, it's a job. And also there's this." She reached past her mother and picked up the newspaper she'd left on the nightstand before her trip to Washington. "I saw this happen." She pointed at the story about Eleanor.

"That woman was killed by a car. How awful. The city is so dangerous. I don't know why on earth you would ever want to stay here."

"The woman who was killed left behind photographs of some girls who went missing during the war and I've been trying to find out what happened to them." She left out the part about going to Washington with Mark.

"And is this part of your job?"

Grace faltered. "Not exactly." She had shared the story hoping it would help to make sense of her staying in New York. But it just seemed to confuse things.

"If these girls have nothing to do with your job, then what are they to you?"

Her mother's question, a refrain of Frankie's on the phone a day earlier, nagged at Grace. She had no connection to the girls. They were strangers, really. Only she had been following this so intently, she had gotten wrapped up in their world and struggles and, for a little bit, had nearly forgotten about her own. Perhaps that was the attraction of it. "It's hard to explain. Anyway, it's over now."

"So you'll be coming with me then?"

"I didn't say that." Her words came out more snappishly than Grace intended.

"You belong with your family," her mother pressed. "It's time to come home."

"Mother, I don't *want* to." It was the first time she had said those words aloud to anyone but Mark. She watched the inevitable hurt that crossed her mother's face and waited for her to regroup for another argument. "I love it here. I have a job. And my own place." The flat wasn't much, but it was hers.

Her mother's face softened. "You know, part of me is jealous," her mother confessed. "I always wanted a life like this." Grace was surprised. She couldn't imagine her mother anywhere but the life she was in.

"I auditioned for a Broadway show once," she added. Grace tried to picture her reserved mother, who mouthed the words to "Happy Birthday" at parties instead of singing them, getting on stage. Suddenly she seemed like a whole other woman with a life and dreams of her own, someone Grace didn't know.

Neither of them spoke for several seconds. "You don't have to make the same choices as Bernadette or Helen," her mother said finally. "I just want you to be happy." It had always felt to Grace like her mother was disappointed that she hadn't been more like her sisters, hadn't fit into the life she expected for her. But maybe the expectation had been in her own mind.

"You know, when you were little and you got hurt or scared, I could make it all better with a hug or treat. But when your children get older, it becomes less and less easy to heal their wounds. And then when Tom..." Her mother paused, as if unable to say it. "I just felt so helpless, like I couldn't reach you at all."

Grace put her hand atop her mother's. "It wasn't your fault, Mom. No one could. It was just something I had to go through alone."

"I brought you these." Her mother picked up an arrangement of orange wax flowers from the table. It was everything Grace hated about home.

But it was also a gesture—and an acknowledgment that Grace might want to stay. "Thank you," she said, taking them.

"You'll come home to see us at the holidays," her mother said.

Grace nodded. "I will," she replied, trying to sound certain. Christmas was such a long time away. Who could say what would happen by then?

Her mother was really trying, though. "Maybe you could come back in a few weeks and we could go shopping," Grace suggested, wanting to make the effort, too. "Or we could visit the botanical gardens when it gets warmer."

Her mother smiled. "I would love that." She stood, buttoned her coat and adjusted her hat. She smoothed Grace's hair like she did when Grace was a child, and she kissed her daughter on the top of the head. "We'll be there when you're ready," she said. Then she walked from the apartment.

Watching her mother go, Grace was filled with gratitude and relief. She had permission to be who she wanted, to live life on her own terms. She felt a bit of sadness, too, that living the life she wanted might mean she and her mother would always be at a distance.

Grace sat alone in the silence of the apartment, which seemed larger somehow. She noticed then a white envelope lying on her bed. "Mom, wait…" She started after her mother to tell her she had forgotten something. But the envelope was addressed to Grace at her parents' house, from an unfamiliar office address in Washington, DC.

Inside there was a letter from a law firm regarding the estate of Thomas Healey, along with a check from his lawyer made out to her in the amount of ten thousand dollars. Tears formed in her eyes, causing the words to blur. She had not known that Tom had taken care of his affairs or provided for her. Where had this money even come from? She held the check, overwhelmed with sadness. Tom was looking out for her still, even after he was gone.

It seemed like somehow a sign: time to move on. She needed to put the matter of the girls behind her and focus on her job and her life here. Nothing to do but move forward.

She would return the photos to the consulate, Grace decided. She pulled them out to look at them a final time. She knew that the girls had been killed and that Eleanor had betrayed them. She would never know why, and she had taken the matter as far as she could. Her part in it was over. It would have to be enough.

On Monday morning at nine, Grace stood in front of the British consulate once more. Time to return the photos and get to work. Inside, the same receptionist sat at the desk. "Ah, Ms.…"

"Healey," Grace finished for her, not at all surprised that the woman did not remember her name.

"You're back," the receptionist noted, sounding none too pleased.

"Yes. I was wondering if you had learned anything more about Eleanor Trigg." Though Grace had come to return the photos, she could not help but be curious.

The receptionist hesitated, as if unsure whether to answer. "The police returned Miss Trigg's personal effects to us." Grace had been so focused on the suitcase and its contents, she hadn't considered any possessions Eleanor might have had on her when she died. "We're still looking for a next of kin."

A flicker of hope rose in Grace and she tried to tamp it down. She should go. It was time to walk away. But she had come this far; she needed to know. "Can I see them?" she asked in spite of herself. "Her effects, I mean." She expected the receptionist to refuse.

"Why? These are her personal belongings. You aren't a relative."

"Because I've spent the past several days trying to find out more about Eleanor. I'm not asking to take them, just to see what she was carrying." The receptionist looked unmoved and Grace was certain she would refuse. "Please. It will only take a minute. Perhaps I can help you figure out where they should go."

"Fine," the receptionist relented at last. "I suppose if you find someone, it will save us a lot of paperwork for the death certificate, that sort of thing." To her, Eleanor was still nothing more than a bureaucratic hassle. She produced a large envelope. "Put everything back just as you found it."

Grace opened the envelope. There were a few dollar bills and some reading glasses, shattered into pieces from the impact of the crash. A dark blue passport was nearly bent in two. Grace picked it up and paged through it carefully. The passport, despite the damage, looked relatively new. It bore entry stamps for France and Germany just weeks prior to Eleanor's arrival in America. Eleanor had been traveling in the days before she came here. But why?

"Thank you," Grace said, and returned the passport to the envelope. She pulled out the photographs and started to hand them to the receptionist. But something made her pause.

"Do you want to keep them?" the woman asked, noticing Grace's hesitation.

Grace shook her head. "They aren't mine anymore." But then she thought better of it. She handed over all but the picture of the dark-eyed girl, Josie, a souvenir from the journey she had never expected.

CHAPTER TWENTY-FOUR

ELEANOR

London, 1946

The knock came unexpectedly at the door to Eleanor's house before dawn. "There's a car here for you," her mother called. Eleanor's mother had said mercifully little about her daughter's departure more than a year and a half earlier from the government job she'd never thought suitable in the first place. Surprised, Eleanor peered out the window. At the sight of the familiar black Austin, her heartbeat quickened. She was being summoned back to headquarters. But why, after all this time?

Eleanor dressed carefully and quickly, fingers trembling as she buttoned the crisp white blouse that, along with her navy skirt, had served as an almost-uniform during her days at SOE. She approached the black Austin that idled silently at the curb outside her flat. A thin finger of smoke curled from the driver's-side window, mixing with the low fog. "Dodds," she said, using his name as greeting. She smiled at the familiar silhouette, black bowler hat drawn low over his white fringe of hair that she had not seen in more than a year and a half. "What on earth are you doing here?"

"The Director," he said simply, and that was enough for Eleanor. She climbed in the back seat and closed the door. The summons was a refrain of the last time Dodds had come unexpectedly for her. But the women's unit was gone now, relegated to a footnote in the history of SOE. She could not fathom what the Director might want.

Dodds put the car into gear. As ever, he did not speak, but kept his eyes squarely on the road, turning smartly at the red phone booth on the corner. The car wound silently down the shuttered streets of North London, deserted except for the occasional lorry driver packing his load for the early morning deliveries. Though the blackout had ended months ago, the streetlights were still dimmed, like a habit not easily shaken. It was January 4 and a few Christmas decorations still hung in the windows. The holidays had been a dismal affair—as though no one remembered how to celebrate in peacetime. Hard to feel festive, Eleanor supposed, when basic staples like coffee and sugar were still in such scarce supply—and when so many were observing the holidays without the loved one who had never come home.

It wasn't until they reached the corner of Baker Street that she saw it: Norgeby House had been destroyed in a fire. The slate roof was peeled back like an open can and the window frames stood hollow, spectacle rims charred with flame. Stone and wood smoldered on the ground, seeming to give off heat even through the closed window of the car.

"What on earth?" she said aloud, wondering when the fire had started, calculated whether the story would make the morning newspapers and decided it would not. Though Eleanor didn't know exactly what was going on, she had a keen understanding that it had to do with why the Director had summoned her so unexpectedly.

Eleanor desperately wanted to get out and have a closer look, but Dodds did not stop the car. Instead, he drove her down Baker Street to Number 64, the main headquarters building for SOE. He ushered her through the door of the building, which, although only slightly larger than Norgeby House, felt infinitely more austere. Inside the foyer, a cluster of senior army officers brushed by. Though some of their faces were familiar to Eleanor, none of the men acknowledged her.

Dodds led her up three flights of stairs to the anteroom of an office and closed the door behind her without a word, leaving her alone. Eleanor did not hang her coat on the stand in the corner, but folded it over her arm. A furnace hissed menacingly and a cigarette not quite extinguished gave off an acrid smell from an unseen ashtray. Eleanor walked to the window, which overlooked the rear of the building. Over the lip of the rooftop, she could just make out the remains of the burned house, the war room where they had met daily. Tattered bits of their maps and photographs, once closely guarded secrets, now fluttered through the broken window like confetti.

Had it really been a year and a half since she had last been here with her hat in her hand, asking to go find her girls? So much had happened since then, D-Day, victory in Europe and, finally, the end of the war. The last time she had been here, the Director had dismissed her, turned her out callously from the place that had once been hers. Even now, it made her insides ache to remember, the pain as fresh as though it had happened yesterday.

The click of the door jolted Eleanor from her memories. Imogen, the receptionist, eyed her coolly, as though they had never met. "He'll see you now."

"Eleanor." The Director did not stand as she entered. But there was a warmth in his eyes behind the businesslike exterior, acknowledging the bond they had once shared. The distance he had shown the day he'd dismissed her was gone, as if it had never existed. Eleanor relaxed slightly.

The Director gestured for her to sit. Closer now, she could

see the toll that the war had taken on him—as it had on herself. His sleeves were rolled up, his collar unbuttoned, and the stubble on his cheeks and chin said that he'd been there since the previous day. He'd always been impeccably groomed, but now he looked unhinged.

He followed her gaze out the window toward the smoldering remains of Norgeby House. "Olympus, it seems, has fallen." His voice was stiff with disbelief.

It wasn't her problem, she told herself. She had been cast out months ago. Her world had been destroyed, not in the burning of a dusty building off Baker Street, but somewhere in the darkness of Occupied France when she had failed her girls and lost so many of them for good. But Norgeby House was emblematic of the organization that she had given everything to build. And now it was gone. Her eyes burned.

She perched on the edge of the chair he'd indicated. "What happened?"

"A fire," he said, stating the obvious.

"It might have been an accident," she offered. Norgeby House, with its endless piles of papers and operators constantly smoking, had been a tinderbox waiting to go up in flames.

"Perhaps," he said, but she could tell by the tone of his voice that he was skeptical. "There will be an investigation."

Which did not, Eleanor reflected, mean that there would be answers. "Why did you call me, sir?"

"A bloody mess," he muttered, but was he talking about the fire or something more? He poured tea from the tray Imogen had left on the edge of his desk. "They're shutting us down. The whole of SOE. Orders straight from Whitehall. With the war over, they say they don't need us anymore. We've recalled all of the agents."

"All of the agents you can find," she corrected. "Have there been any word of the others? My girls, I mean."

"Seven of the girls have been accounted for," he said. For a moment, Eleanor's hopes rose. But then he shared the list with her and she saw the notations: Auschwitz, 1945, Ravensbrück, 1944. "Places where the girls have been confirmed dead."

Dead. Eleanor's grief and sense of responsibility for what had happened rose like a wave, threatening to drown her. "And the remaining five?"

"They've been given a disposition. Missing. Presumed dead," he said bluntly. It was an awful verdict, ominous yet uncertain.

"That isn't enough to tell the families. They were wives, daughters, mothers, for goodness sake." It was true that some of the families may have put it to rest, lowered empty coffins into the ground or had a memorial service to remember. But for others, the unanswered questions hit hard. Like Rhoda Hobbs's mother, who had sat sobbing when Eleanor had called on her with questions just days earlier. "Rhoda was a typist," her mother protested, when Eleanor had suggested that she might have been lost during the war. "The last time I spoke with her, she said she was just running papers down to Plymouth." Eleanor saw Rhoda in her mind's eye, boarding the Lysander that had taken her across the Channel, never to return.

Mothers like Rhoda's deserved to know of their daughters' valor—and what had become of them. Rage burned white-hot in her as she saw the girls, who had given everything for a promise, betrayed.

"And there's no word of them?"

"I'm not supposed to discuss such matters, now that your clearances have been revoked." Though not news to her, the statement felt like a blow. "But I suppose you deserve to know—there are reports from the camps. No records, of course, but eyewitness accounts. They say that the women were executed immediately." Eleanor turned away, sickened. "Other than that, there has been no indication that any are alive. I think hoping at this point is foolhardy. We must presume them dead." If he had sent her months earlier as she had asked, she might have found some of them alive. Now it was too late.

Eleanor tried to steady her hands. She took the cup of Earl Grey he offered and felt the warmth, waiting for him to say more. "We still don't know how they were caught. That is, how the Germans managed the radio game in the first place."

The Director cleared his throat. "You have notes, I assume, from your search?"

She shifted abruptly, and tea sloshed over the side of the cup, burning her skin. "Sir?" she asked, as though she did not know what he was referring to. She prepared to deny she still possessed any papers after she had been dismissed and told to leave matters alone. But, of course, Eleanor had not stopped looking. She had kept digging through old newspapers and files from the Public Records Office at Kew Gardens, making inquiries through government contacts. She had not just combed all of the records she could get her hands on; she had spoken to every last person in Britain who had any connection to the girls, including the agents who had come back and the families of those who had not. There were complicated stories of arrests, dozens of rabbit holes, but none of them shed any light about what happened to the missing girls, or the truth of how they had been caught in the first place.

Perhaps word of her inquiries had trickled back to the Director. She was a private citizen now, she thought. What right did they have to forbid her?

But there would be no fooling the Director. Eleanor set down her tea and pulled the file that she always carried with her from her messenger bag and studied it. She handed over the folder containing all the information she was not supposed to have—and that she knew he would want to see.

The Director thumbed through her notes and she could tell from his expression that they did not contain anything he didn't already know. "Like I've always said, it's a bloody shame about these girls." The Director handed back her file and Eleanor clutched it tightly, the sharp edge cutting into the scarred pads of her fingertips. "I'm prepared to send you."

She could not believe her own ears. "Sir?"

"If you're still keen to go, of course. To find out what became of the missing girls—and how they were all caught in the first place." He knew that she'd been more than keen to go. Those girls had consumed her, and she was desperate to find out about them.

A dozen questions circled in her mind. "Why now?" Eleanor managed finally. After the months of rejection and pain, she needed to understand.

"I'd been thinking about calling you for some time. For one thing, someone's been asking questions."

"Who?"

"Thogden Barnett." Violet's father. Eleanor had spoken with Barnett not two weeks earlier and had sensed among all of the parents that he was the angriest, the least likely to let it go. So she had fed him ever so subtly her doubts and questions about what had happened to the girls, let the ideas fester in his brain. An outsider, he could take it to his member of parliament and press the matter in a way that she could not. Apparently the gamble had paid off. "Most of the families have, as you know, tried to put the past behind them," the Director continued. "But Mr. Barnett has been asking questions about what happened to his daughter and how she died. When no one answered to his satisfaction, he brought the matter to his MP. They're threatening a parliamentary investigation. I need to be able to tell them how the girls died—or at least all of the ways we tried to find out."

But questions from a grieving parent would not have been enough reason for the Director to take the drastic step of sending her. "You said 'for one thing.' Is there another reason?"

"Yes, this business with the fire."

"I don't understand the connection."

"And maybe there isn't one. You remember how you were asked to leave the files?" he asked. Eleanor nodded. The orders had been clear: touch nothing. "They'd said the files would be packed up and taken. Well, for months, the files sat. No one came for them. It was almost as though they had been forgotten. Then a few days ago, I received a message that the files would be picked up this morning for the parliamentary investigation. And then this happened." He gestured in the direction of Norgeby House.

"You think someone set the fire deliberately to destroy the files?"

He grunted in tacit agreement. "The police say it was too many old papers in a tight space. But our inspectors found this." He held up a charred piece of metal. She recognized it as one of the timed incendiary devices they trained the field agents how to use.

"It wasn't just an ordinary fire," the Director continued. "It was planned. I want to know who did it and why." She understood then his sudden interest in having her go abroad. He thought that the fire, which went up just before her records were to be taken, might have something to do with the agents who had disappeared. Particularly the girls. Sending her to find answers about that might bring him answers as well.

"You think it has something to do with my girls?"

"I don't know. The fire happened right before we were to turn the files over to Parliament. I've got people investigating that here."

But the only way to find that out, Eleanor concluded silently, was in France, where the network had collapsed and the girls were arrested. "We need to know how they were caught, where they were taken, what happened to them," he said, rattling off the same questions she had been asking all along. But the biggest one was why.

"You were done with me," she said, unable to keep the recrimination from her voice.

"We had no reason to follow up," he replied, then gestured toward the smoldering remains of Norgeby House with his head. "Now we do."

The lives of twelve girls, Eleanor thought, should have been reason enough. "So you want to send me to find out what happened?"

"I can't." Her stomach sank. He was going to say no again. Was this some kind of a cruel joke? "At least not in any official capacity," he added hurriedly. "So if I send you, it's off the books. What do you say, Trigg?"

She faltered. These last lonely months of searching on her own, she had just about given up hope, accepted that she would never know the truth. Now he was dangling it in front of her. It was what she had wanted, had lobbied for. And now that she had it, she was terrified.

"All right," Eleanor said at last. "I'll go."

"I want answers. Find them," he said, "at any cost." His eyes were blazing, the gloves off. Now that they were being cast out, he simply had nothing left to lose. He scribbled something on a piece of paper. "I've managed to have you commissioned as a WAAF officer. I can get you a stipend and the necessary paperwork to travel. We've got two weeks until they shut us down. After that I won't be able to pay you—or give you the support you need," he added quickly, knowing that the money meant almost nothing to her.

She nodded. "I'll go tonight, if arrangements can be made."

He held out the British passport. "It's yours. You'll need this." She hesitated. British citizenship, which she had once wanted so badly, was little more than a reminder of all she had lost. But she would need it now. Pushing sentimentality aside, she took the passport from him.

"Where will you start?"

"Paris." She might have gone to Germany and started at the camps. But the girls had all been deployed to networks in or around the French capital. It was where they had operated, and it had all gone so horribly wrong. "And if I need to reach you, how should I wire?"

He shook his head. "Don't." The implication in his tone was clear. The lines were not to be trusted as secure. He stood. "Goodbye, Trigg." He shook her hand firmly. "And good luck."

Eleanor left his office and made her way down the stairs and out the front door of headquarters. At the corner, Dodds waited for her by the car. Turning swiftly in the other direction, she ducked between the row houses so he would not see her. She crept through the alley toward the remains of Norgeby House. The fire had gutted the upper floors. She walked through the remains of the ground floor where their meeting room had once stood, rubble still warm around her ankles. She reached the spot where the door to the basement had once been. The stairway that led down to her cellar office and the radio room was thankfully still intact.

She started tentatively down the stairs. Dirt fell from above, as though the whole thing might cave at any second. Eleanor was suddenly gripped with terror. It wasn't that she feared death, but rather she didn't want to lose it all now before she might get the answers she had been looking for.

Hurriedly, she stopped before what had been the closet in her office. She went to the file cabinet. The files were all gone. She pulled the drawer all the way out to reach the very back, where whoever had cleaned out her office hadn't thought to look. There was a steel box where she had left it, untouched by the fire. It was here the girls placed the things most dear to them before deploying. She should have taken the box with her that last day, but she had been ordered to pack and leave so abruptly that there hadn't been time. She picked up the box. The lid fell off and a tiny baby shoe fell out. Eleanor retrieved it, stifling a cry.

A voice came from above. "Is someone down there?" A flashlight licked the dark walls. Eleanor did not answer, but continued gathering what she had come for. Then she climbed the stairs once more.

A young policeman stood at the top, looking surprised to have actually found someone in the rubble. "Ma'am, you can't take that," he said, gesturing toward the box in her arms. "It's evidence for the fire investigation."

"So arrest me," she said, then walked away defiantly, her arms full.

It was the least she owed the girls after what she had done.

CHAPTER TWENTY-FIVE

ELEANOR

Paris, 1946

An onlooker would have wondered: Who was that woman who sat alone every evening at the bar at The Hotel Savoy, nursing a dry martini for four or even five hours on end? She might have been left waiting by a boyfriend or lover, but her face was not sad. Nor did she look ill at ease being a woman alone at a bar. She sat calmly, studying the after-work crowds as they flowed and waned through the revolving door.

It had been three weeks since Eleanor had stood in the Director's office and received his go-ahead. Though she had been desperate to get started, she had not been able to leave for Paris right away as she'd hoped; there had been paperwork and red tape, even for a mission that was not supposed to exist at all. Then she had to figure out how to get to Europe, jostling for a place amid all of the men and supplies being ferried across the Channel as part of the postwar recovery. Finally, she had secured passage on a transport ship. She'd stood on the deck, not minding the sea spray that kicked up at her face and dampened her dress. Imagining the girls who had dropped in by parachute or plane under cover of night, she marveled at the relative ease with which she was able to enter Europe now.

Since arriving, Eleanor had made the rounds of the government agencies and embassies, trying to get a lead on someone who might have known or heard of her girls, any of them. Marie and Josie, at least, had been deployed to the Paris region and had operated here. The arrest of British female agents would have been unusual, noteworthy. Surely someone would remember.

But the government agencies, still trying to reconstitute themselves after liberation, were in little position to help her. "I'm looking for records of German arrests here," she had said at the provisional government headquarters two days earlier. "From the Gestapo or German intelligence, perhaps?"

But the civil servant had shaken his head. "The Germans destroyed most of the records before the liberation of Paris. Even if we did have what you are asking for, the files would be classified. Off-limits to foreigners."

Coming up empty, Eleanor tried other places: the city coroner's office, a displaced persons' camp on the outskirts of the city. Nothing. It was more than her lack of status. (The card, which the Director had provided designating her as SOE representative of the War Crimes Investigative Unit, impressed no one.) The responses to her inquiries were cold, almost hostile. She had hoped that there might be some gratitude for the role the British agents had played in freeing their city. To the contrary, de Gaulle and his people wanted liberation remembered as a victory solely of the French resistance. A woman from Britain asking questions, reminding people of how much foreigners had helped, was simply not welcome.

Each night she came back to the hotel bar and she read over her notes and plotted the next day's assault. She had taken a room at The Savoy purposefully, though she knew the Director couldn't cover the cost. It wasn't the central location of the once-grand hotel, or the fact that it was one of the only hotels in Paris whose kitchen had returned to nearly a prewar menu. Rather, The Savoy had been known during the war as a meeting place for agents and resistance. She hoped that one or two might still frequent the bar.

There was no point in waiting in Paris any longer, she realized now, running through the list of leads she had exhausted. She had been here nearly a week and already the Director could no longer support her. She considered going home. But if she stopped searching, that would be it for the girls. Others would go on looking for the men; there were lists and commissions and inquests. Without her, the girls would disappear forever. No, she wouldn't give up, but she might need to look elsewhere, rent a car and travel north to the other regions outside Paris where the agents had also operated.

Across the bar, she noticed a man younger than herself with close-set eyes, wearing a gray wool blazer. He was pretending to read a *Le Monde. "Procès Pour Crimes de Guerre!"* the headline read. "War Crimes Trial." But Eleanor could feel the man watching her over the top of the page. Her muscles tensed. Knowing when one was being tailed was something they taught the agents at Arisaig House from the start, but this was the first time that Eleanor had to worry about it herself.

Eleanor quickly finished her drink and signed her tab, then started across the lobby to the elevator. She stepped inside her room, a once-elegant space that now suffered from a sagging bed and peeling wallpaper.

There was a knock at the door. Eleanor jumped, then looked through the peephole. The man from the bar. Rather overt for one who was tailing her, Eleanor thought. For a moment, she considered not answering. But the man had clearly seen her come upstairs, and he might have information she was looking for. She opened the door a crack. "Yes?"

"I'm Henri Duquet. I was with the French resistance." Once speaking such words aloud would have been a death sentence; now he wore it like a badge of honor.

She hesitated, still uncertain how he had found her or what he wanted. "I'm Eleanor Trigg," she offered cautiously, opening the door wider.

He stepped inside, setting down the newspaper he had been reading at the bar. He eyed her coolly. "I saw you over at the ministry where I work. You've been asking questions all over Paris. People are not happy about it."

"Which people?" He did not answer. "Did you know the agents of the Vesper circuit during the war?" she asked. "Vesper? Renee Demare?" She used the girl's code name as a reflex, then remembered it didn't matter anymore. "I mean, Marie Roux? Do you know what happened to them?" It could be a bluff. She tried not to get too excited. "If it is a question of money..." she began, calculating how much she could give him from her own funds and still have enough for the trip home.

"Non!" he said fiercely, and she worried that she had offended him. Suddenly, the man grabbed her arm. Looking into his seething eyes, she knew he was angry. "Come," he said. "I want to show you the blood that is on your hands."

Forty minutes later Eleanor found herself standing in the middle of Gestapo headquarters in Paris.

"Blood on my hands?" Eleanor had repeated questioningly as Henri Duquet had led her from the hotel. "I have no idea what you are talking about." Eleanor felt guilty, to be sure, that she had not acted sooner on the radio transmissions and forced the Director to listen. But this Frenchman could not possibly know that.

As he had led her toward an awaiting Renault, she had tensed. *Never let an assailant take you from the primary scene of encounter*; it was a cardinal rule of espionage. Once you were removed from your familiar territory, you were vulnerable and weak. She had no business going God knows where with this stranger who so clearly despised her.

"Where are you taking me?" she demanded. He didn't answer. She thought about resisting, even making a scene to stop him. But he might have information about her girls.

Henri did not speak as he drove through the streets of Paris at dusk. Eleanor hadn't really paid much attention to the city as she had rushed from one government building to another during her first few days of inquiries. Now she studied the scene outside the window, partly to calm her nerves and partly to make careful note of their route in case she had to find her way back in a hurry. The streets were brisk; fashionably clad couples chatted behind the wide café windows, shopkeepers drew down the awnings for the night. But there was a kind of haze from the war that seemed to linger over it all, muting the once-gay colors.

Finally, the car turned onto a wide residential street. *Avenue Foch*, a sign at the corner read. Eleanor knew immediately where they were going. Her stomach tensed. She had read about No. 84 Avenue Foch in the intelligence reports during the war. It had been the Paris headquarters of the Sicherheitsdienst, the German counterintelligence agency.

Easy, she thought, willing herself to breathe as the car came to a halt before a five-story town house with wrought iron balconies on every floor. The SD no longer existed. Henri Duquet was a member of the resistance. He was an ally, or at least he should have been once. Surely, he had brought her here for answers.

Eleanor stepped out of the car. The winter air was bitingly cold, a sharp wind whipping across and cutting into her as it sliced across the wide boulevards. The flagpole above the doorway, which had undoubtedly flown a swastika a year earlier, was bare. Henri unlocked the door to the building and she wondered how he had gotten such access. Inside, the foyer was still.

It looked like any other house that had been converted for office use, yet Eleanor had read, too often, of the atrocities that had taken place here while interrogating prisoners. She shuddered inwardly, steeling herself as she followed Henri up the stairs.

"Here." He opened a door on the first floor and allowed her to step through. It was an office, no bigger than the Director's back at headquarters, with a desk, plus a small table with chairs. The office had been abandoned by the Germans months ago but the walls still reeked of cigarette smoke and urine and something else metallic and rotten.

She saw it then in the corner, one of their own radio sets—undoubtedly the one that had caused their downfall. "The radio… How did they get it?"

"We believe there was a Marseille sector infiltrated by the Germans. After the agents from Marseille were arrested, the Germans obtained the wireless set. Then, by impersonating various wireless operators, they were able to get the locations of the drops of weapons and even personnel. More arrests and even more radios. This particular set, I think, came later."

"But how could they impersonate the agents? The radios had security features. There were the worked-out codes, the crystals and the security checks."

"I've spent a lot of time trying to figure that out. Some of the crystals overlapped in frequency. And the ciphers do not appear to have been unique. So it would be possible to broadcast as an agent, even if you didn't have her exact silks or crystals." It was a sloppy detail and Eleanor berated herself for not having fixed it when she had the chance. "And the security checks?"

"I don't know. You tell me."

Eleanor walked toward the radio. She ran her fingers over it. One of the radio keys was bent. Her mind reeled back to the day at Arisaig House when she had dismantled Marie's radio, testing her to see if she had what it took. She knew then without a shadow of a doubt that Marie had been arrested by the Germans.

"Did you see the operator?"

Henri shook his head. "I wasn't here personally. But we had a contact, a woman who cooked and cleaned for the Germans. She told us of an Englishwoman who had been brought here but refused to cooperate and transmit over the wireless. She held out as long as she could."

Eleanor cleared her throat. "Was Vesper here, too?"

At the mention of the name, Henri's face hardened. "Yes."

"Where were they kept?"

He led her out of the room, up a narrow flight of stairs, then another. A moment later she stood inside a tiny attic room. It was not at all what she expected for the holding cell at SD headquarters, where the most-wanted fugitives were brought for questioning. There were a half-dozen dormitory-style beds like the ones the girls had slept in during training at Arisaig House. A dusty, overflowing bookshelf sat in one corner. The room was bare now, no sheets or clothes or other personal effects. But there were little signs of those who had gone before, letters and other markings carved into the iron bed frames. The mattress of the bed closest to her was stained with blood. Eleanor looked out the window. The tip of the Eiffel Tower was just barely visible over the rooftops. She imagined what it was like for those who had spent their last days here, viewing the splendor of Paris from so close, yet trapped in his or her own despair.

"Here is where they were kept during questioning. A few days, maybe a week at most. Then the Germans were done with them."

"And from here?"

"Some went to Fresnes prison. Others, like Vesper, were killed here, shot in the head." He said this unflinchingly.

Eleanor knew that Vesper died, but until that moment had not known how. "And the radio operator?"

"I don't know. Fresnes, I'd imagine. When the prison was emptied, those held there were sent to Natzweiler," he added.

Eleanor shuddered at the name of the concentration camp on French soil where so many of the captured male agents had reportedly perished. But something puzzled her. "Why not Ravensbrück? Natzweiler was only for the men, wasn't it?"

"Perhaps because they didn't expect to keep them alive very long. The Germans killed them without records. Nacht und Nebel."

Night and Fog. Eleanor had heard of the program at headquarters, meant to make prisoners disappear without a trace. She pressed back the tears that burned heavy against her eyelids. "How long?" she asked Henri. "How long before the invasion were they taken from here?"

"Not more than a few weeks." She gasped. They had come so close to making it.

"You know they weren't the only ones who died," Henri said abruptly.

She nodded. "I know. You lost people as well." It was another reality of what had happened; even as the agents were working to liberate Europe, civilians had become caught in the cross fire. Not just partisans, but ordinary men, women and children. Some had been killed as collateral damage in the acts of sabotage—the factory workers when a bomb was set, or the driver of a train that had been derailed. Still others lost their lives through German reprisals against the resistance. Churchill had said to set Europe ablaze, but the hard truth was that innocents got burned.

Eleanor stood in the middle of the tiny attic space, seeing Marie here beneath the creaky rafters, cold and alone. Or had some of the others been here with her? Eleanor would never know.

How had she been arrested? Something had gone terribly wrong in the field, and no one had survived to tell about it. Eleanor stared hard at the walls, as though willing Marie to speak through time. But the room remained still. Perhaps Marie herself had died not knowing.

Or perhaps she had left some kind of clue. Eleanor scanned the room, looking for some sort of hiding place. She ran her hand along the paneled walls.

"We searched it thoroughly, I assure you," Henri said. Eleanor ignored him, continuing to feel along the floor, heedless of the dirt that blackened her hands. He didn't know the girls the way she did, nor understand the way they would have operated to conceal things. Her hands ran over an uneven floorboard and she pried it up to reveal a hollow space. She looked up at Henri, whose face registered surprise in spite of itself. But the compartment was empty.

She ran her hands along the edge of the bed frame, the rough lines where agents and other prisoners had carved things into the metal raised like scars. She knelt to examine it. Some had put tally marks as though counting off days, others their names. *Believe*, read a single word. She did not see Marie's name. She moved to the next bed frame where she found a word written in familiar handwriting. "Baudelaire." The French poet.

Eleanor recalled the report of Marie's recruitment, reading French poetry in a café. She walked to the bookshelf, scanning the titles that were mostly in French. She pulled out a book of French poetry and scanned the table of contents until she found a Baudelaire poem, "Fleurs du Mal." Eleanor turned quickly to the page where the poem began. Sure enough, certain letters had been underlined faintly. She followed the pattern they spelled out: *L-O-N-D-O-N.* Marie had tried to signal something about headquarters, but what? Once it would have seemed a cry for help. But now, hearing the echo of Henri's words, it seemed something altogether different: an accusation by Marie of those who had betrayed her and the other agents. Was she saying that someone in London was to blame?

Shuddering, she closed the book, then looked up at Henri. "Earlier you said the blood was on my hands." Henri seemed less angry than when they had first met, and she didn't want to stir it all up again. But she had to know. "What did you mean?"

"While I was working as a messenger, I often carried messages between here and Gestapo headquarters. The Germans were broadcasting to London so haphazardly. Why did no one notice and stop it? The Germans would not have been able to manage the radios on their own. They needed help, Miss Trigg. It had to be someone on your side. The way they were broadcasting and got the information so easily." His voice was almost pleading now. "Somebody had to know."

"Is that why you came to find me?" Henri, it seemed, had not come to help her, but had been looking for answers of his own.

"My brother was one of the resistance members taken in the sweeps right before D-Day, after Vesper circuit was broken. He never returned."

"I'm terribly sorry. But you can't possibly blame us for that."

"It's a funny thing, you asking about the girls," he continued. "I mean, you were in charge of them all. And with your background, it well could have been you. Maybe you were the one who knew all along."

"Excuse me?" Heat rose to Eleanor's cheeks. "You can't possibly think..." He was suggesting that not just London, but Eleanor personally, had sold out her girls. "I didn't betray them." But failing them was almost as bad. "I have to go," Eleanor said, suddenly needing to be away from Henri Duquet and his accusations. She fled down the stairs and from the house on Avenue Foch, ran without stopping down the rue. She looked back, relieved to see that Henri had not followed her.

Turning the corner, she slowed to a walk. It was dark now, streetlights casting yellow pools on the pavement. Eleanor's mind reeled. A betrayal at headquarters. The idea was almost unthinkable. But Vesper had suggested as much when he said he couldn't trust anyone in London with his suspicions for fear of a leak. And Marie had seemed to signal it in her last desperate message in the poetry book. Eleanor pictured the meetings at Norgeby House, the inner circle that so carefully planned for the agents in the field. Could one of them possibly be the traitor?

Eleanor neared the Arc de Triomphe. A lone cab was parked at the stand by Rue de Presbourg, and she climbed in and asked for The Savoy. If someone at headquarters had betrayed the girls, that would explain how they had been caught so neatly, one after another, their drop boxes and safe houses compromised. It might explain, too, why someone would have wanted Norgeby House and all of its records burned.

She reached the safety of her hotel room and sank down into a chair. Henri had confirmed that the radios were played back to London. But she still didn't know how the SD had been able to pull it off. They had to have had some sort of help. She had always known, of course, that her failure to push harder had stopped them from finding out before it was too late. But the idea that she had intentionally betrayed the girls cut through her like a knife. She was no closer to finding her answers than before.

On the chair in her room sat the newspaper Henri had been reading in the bar. She picked it up and scanned the story about the war crimes trial in Germany. She was surprised the French newspaper had given it such prominence; there had been so many they had become commonplace. But this one was different; the defendant was an SD officer who had terrorized northern France for months. Hans Kriegler. Kriegler had been the head of SD—and quite possibly the architect of F Section's downfall. She saw Kriegler's face in the files of Norgeby House, details of his sadistic treatment of prisoners.

Eleanor's grip on the paper tightened. Kriegler was alive and he was about to go on trial. Surely he knew Marie's fate—and the identity of her betrayer.

Eleanor was going to Germany to find out.

CHAPTER TWENTY-SIX

MARIE

France, 1944

Marie looked up from the hard concrete floor of Fresnes prison through a foggy haze, trying to focus. Her head pounded and her mouth was parched with thirst. There, to her amazement, stood Eleanor.

"Eleanor…" How had she found her? Eleanor held out a canteen and Marie drank from it, cool, fresh water splashing carelessly out the sides of her mouth as she gulped it down.

Marie bowed her head, feeling the ache of the fresh, unhealed wounds at the base of her neck where it met her back. "I failed you," she said softly. "I'm sorry."

"Get dressed. I'm taking you home."

The image faded as Marie's eyes opened. She reached her hand out, closing it around the emptiness before her. Eleanor was not there. Pain assaulted her as she realized where she was, and all that had happened to bring her here. The morning after the interrogation at Avenue Foch, she had been taken from the attic room and transported unceremoniously to the prison. She didn't know where they had taken Julian, what they had done with his body.

That was nearly a month ago. The dream of Eleanor rescuing her and bringing her home to her daughter was one she had almost every night since.

It was shouting that had roused her from sleep. *"Raus!"* voices barked. Not the usual French of the *milice* who ran Fresnes prison, but German. Something hard clanged against the metal bars of each cell as the doors opened.

Marie sat up quickly. What was happening? For a fleeting second, she wondered if they were being liberated. The invasion had come since her imprisonment, she'd learned, Allied troops inching toward Paris. But the faces around her were grim, pupils dark and dilated with fear. Throughout the large cell, emaciated women were gathering their few belongings, writing notes on tiny scraps of paper. One was feverishly attempting to swallow a piece of jewelry she had managed to keep. These were the last preparations each woman had rehearsed hundreds of times in her mind, knowing this day would come. The rumors they had heard of the prison being emptied were true.

Marie rose stiffly. She had been one of the last arrivals to the cell, and there were no more thin, straw mattresses left for her to sleep on. She had instead spent more than three weeks sleeping on the floor. She had consoled herself by thinking she might avoid nits by not lying on one of the filthy pallets. But it was inevitable with too many people in such a small space. Her scalp itched now with the tiny bugs, and she scratched her head, disgusted.

She watched the women scurry about, making the only preparations for deportation that they could, as though it would change anything at all. About a dozen in all, they had been here longer than she, and their bodies were skeletal, covered with sores from the bedbugs and bruises from where they had been beaten. Marie had come to learn that they were all French, resistance members and spouses of partisans, and ordinary women who had been caught helping to defy the Germans. Very few were Jews; those poor souls had already been sent east, but their presence lingered in the makeshift mezuzah one had scratched into the wall near the door.

The women moved swiftly now. They squeezed slips of paper through the thin slit prison windows, sending them cascading to the ground like confetti. They were notes, scribbles on whatever could be found, written in charcoal or sometimes blood, asking about relatives or trying to send word. Or simply *"Je suis là"* ("I am here"), followed by a name, because soon they would not be and someone needed to remember.

But Marie stood motionless, letting the activity swirl around her as she prepared to be taken, once again, against her will to points unknown. She considered refusing to go. The Germans would surely shoot her on the spot, as they had Julian. Her heart screamed as she remembered his last moments, life pouring from him. He had looked so peaceful. Without him, all hope was gone. Perhaps it would be for the best.

No, not all hope. If the Allies were closing in on Paris, surely the Germans would want the prisoners moved ahead of that. Liberation could not be far behind. If there was a chance of someday getting back to her daughter, Marie had to try.

The door to the cell, which had been locked since her arrival weeks earlier, now burst open with a clang. *"Raus!"* The women around her surged forward. No one wanted to face the consequences of being last. In the dank central corridor, women poured from the other cells, merging with them until the stream became a river of bodies, thick and warm.

As the crowd pushed her forward, Marie stumbled over something and nearly fell. It was a woman on the corridor floor, curled up in a ball, too sick or hurt to go on. Marie hesitated. She did not want to lag behind. But the woman would surely be killed if she remained on the ground. Marie knelt hurriedly and tried to help the woman. Then she let out a yelp of recognition.

It was Josie.

Marie froze, wondering if it was an illusion, or another dream. Then she dropped to her knees, embracing her friend. "You're alive!" Josie was a skeleton, though, hardly recognizable, not moving. "It's me, Marie," she added, when Josie did not respond or seem to know her.

Josie opened her mouth but no words came out. Despite the awful conditions, joy surged through Marie. Josie was alive. But how? She had been reported missing a month earlier, presumed dead. There were so many questions Marie wanted to ask, too, but Josie seemed to lack the strength to speak, much less describe the horrors she had been through. Marie wanted to tell her about everything that had happened, including Julian's death.

There was no time now. They were emptying the entire prison, ordering people forward, outside onto the trucks. It was either obey or be trampled or shot. "Come," she urged Josie to her feet. "We have to move."

"I can't," Josie rasped. Marie tried to lift her, but nearly buckled under the weight. Behind her, a shot rang out, reminding her what would happen if they refused to go.

"You can do this." Marie braced her knees and tried again to raise Josie. She recalled the day Josie had carried her down the Scottish hillside in that run that seemed a lifetime ago. Now it was Marie's turn to be strong.

"Come," she said to Josie. She could almost feel the crisp wind of the Highlands urging them forward. Together, they inched ahead toward the fate that awaited them.

Through the slatted boxcar window, Marie could make out the faintest light. Whether it was sunrise or sunset, she no longer knew. They had been brought from Fresnes to the Gare de Pantin in trucks, loaded into the railcar forty deep. The train stood idle in the station for hours, baking under the summer sun. When it finally left, it moved east at a glacial pace, at times stopping for hours on end, then starting again just as inexplicably. At some point, Marie assumed, they had crossed from France into Germany. The doors had opened once to pass in a bucket of water and some stale bread, not nearly enough for all of them. Marie's mouth was dry and cracked with thirst.

Some of the women moaned; others were silent, condemned to their fate. The air reeked of toilet smells and worse. Someone had died in the car, maybe more than one person, judging by the stench. Marie found it most bearable to stand high and press her nose close to the tiny window. But Josie slumped on the floor beside her.

Marie winced as her stomach cramped violently. There was a bucket on the far side of the railcar, which they were meant to use to relieve themselves. But even if she could make it in time, she did not dare leave Josie alone. For a moment, she feared she would soil herself. Then she felt the blood, rushing down her leg in a hot, humiliating stream. Her period. She bunched her dress closer between her legs, feeling the wetness seep through. There was simply nothing to be done about it.

She bent close to Josie and placed her hand in front of her friend's mouth to make sure she was still breathing. Josie was burning with fever now, heat seeming to radiate off her. Marie took the wet rag, which she had managed to soak when the bucket passed through the railcar earlier, and placed it on Josie's burning head. She didn't know what was wrong with her friend; there was no visible wound. Typhus maybe, or dysentery. She leaned closer, heedless of catching whatever Josie had herself. "Josie, you're alive. I'm so glad I found you. All of this time we thought…"

Josie smiled weakly. "I went to make contact with the Maquis…" She paused to lick her lips and draw a strained breath. "But it was a trap. The Germans knew I was coming there for a meeting and they were waiting. They knew who I was, my real identity and even the fact that I was half-Jewish. Whoever turned us in is still out there. We have to find a way to send word to Julian."

Josie did not know. For a second, Marie wanted to hide the truth from her, fearing that it would be too much. But she could not. "Julian's dead."

Josie winced. "You're certain?"

"I saw it myself." A tear burned Marie's cheeks. "I held him until he was gone. It was my fault," she confessed. "The SD had one of our radios and they wanted me to broadcast to London for them, so London wouldn't grow suspicious and would keep sending information. I tried to transmit without my security check so they would know it was a fake. But the Germans discovered what I did and killed Julian."

"You were doing exactly as you were trained," Josie managed, comforting Marie when in fact it should have been the reverse. "You mustn't blame yourself. It's what Julian would have wanted. He wouldn't want you to give up the operation for him."

Then Josie's face went stony. "It's over then," she said quietly. She lay back, the little strength she had mustered seemingly gone. Marie wanted to argue, but could not. She dropped to the floor of the railcar, squeezing into the spot beside her friend. Her fingers found Josie's and they sat without speaking amid the sounds of the train clacking over the rails and the piteous moans of women dying.

Josie closed her eyes, seeming to sleep. Watching her, something inside Marie broke. Josie had been the best of them. Yet she lay here, broken, a wizened and suffering near corpse. An eighteen-year-old girl should have young-girl dreams, not be facing the end of her days.

"We could be dancing in London right now," Marie mused aloud. It was an old joke, one they used to make after the worst days of training at Arisaig House. "A night at the Ritz with one of those American Joes."

Josie half opened her eyes and managed another faint smile, more of a grimace this time. She tried to speak, but no sound came out. Instead, there was a rattle in Josie's throat, the unmistakable sound that the end was drawing near.

"Josie…" There was so much Marie wanted to ask about her life and the things she had seen in the field. Josie would know how to move forward, to survive whatever awaited her. But she was already too far gone to answer.

Suddenly there came a rumbling in the distance. An explosion of some sort. A murmur rippled through the car. "Allied bombers," someone whispered. One woman cheered, another applauded. Could it really be the long-promised liberation? It had been rumored for so long, Marie hardly believed it anymore.

But their joy was short-lived. Another explosion hit, closer this time. Boards fell from the roof of the railcar. Marie covered Josie with her own body to shield her from the debris that rained down. "We've been hit!" someone cried. Not yet, Marie thought, but it was only a matter of time. The car wobbled and started to topple on its side, and Marie struggled to hold off the tide of bodies that cascaded toward them.

Then the explosions stopped and the railcar stilled, listing precariously at a tilted angle. The doors opened and the blast of cool air was a welcome relief. *"Raus! Mach schnell!"* came the order to evacuate. Marie was puzzled. Why should the Germans care if the railcar full of prisoners fell or was hit by a bomb? But as she raised herself up and peered out the window, she could see that the track ahead had been destroyed, making the line impassable.

The other women were clambering up the tilted incline of the railcar now, following orders to exit. But Josie lay on the floor, not moving. Was she dead? "Come, Josie," Marie pleaded, desperately afraid. She tried to drag Josie, but the sharp angle on which the railcar listed made it impossible.

Spying the two women still inside the railcar, one of the Germans climbed inside. "Out!" he barked, moving closer.

"She's sick and she can't move," Marie cried, pleading for clemency. She instantly realized her mistake. The frail and wounded were refuse to the Germans, deserving not of care but instant disposal.

The German lifted his foot to kick Josie and landed a fierce blow, nearly lifting her whole body. "No!" Marie cried, throwing herself over her friend.

"Go, or you'll face the same," the German ordered. Marie did not answer, but held on to Josie even more tightly. She would not abandon her to this fate. Marie felt a whoosh of air as the soldier's foot swept down again. Pain exploded in her ribs, which were still bruised from the beating she'd suffered at Avenue Foch. She curled into a ball over her friend, bracing herself for another blow, wondering how many she could take. She glanced out of the corner of her eye as the German reached for his gun. So this was how it was to end. At least she was with Josie and not alone.

"I'm sorry," Marie whispered, thinking of her daughter whom she never should have left at all.

There was a banging sound as another German climbed into the railcar. "Don't waste your ammunition," he said to the first. "If they want to die here in the air raid, let them."

But the first soldier persisted, grabbing Marie roughly and attempting to drag her off her friend. Marie fought, then felt movement beneath her. When she looked down, Josie's eyes were wide-open, her gaze clear and calm. Suddenly they were back in Scotland and it was just the two of them lying awake, talking in the darkness. Josie's lips formed a single word, unmistakable: *run*.

Marie felt it then, something round and hard between them. Josie was clutching a dark metal egg to her chest. A grenade, like the ones they had trained with at Arisaig House. She could not imagine how she had managed to keep it with her all of this time. But she knew Josie had saved it for exactly this moment—her last stand.

"No!" Marie cried, but it was too late. Josie had already pulled the pin.

Marie lifted herself from Josie and as though propelled by unseen hands, burst through the Germans who had clustered around.

She leaped for the door and the daylight beyond. She was powerless no more. She could do this. For Tess. For Julian. For Josie. For all of them.

The boxcar exploded, thrusting Marie forward in the darkness.

CHAPTER TWENTY-SEVEN

ELEANOR

Germany, 1946

Three days later, Eleanor pulled her rented jeep to a stop before the south entrance of the former concentration camp Dachau.

After leaving The Savoy, Eleanor had boarded a nearly empty train at Gare de l'Est and traveled all day and night to get across France. As they'd neared the German border in the darkness, she'd stiffened. Germany loomed large in her mind from the war, the source of so much suffering and evil. She had not been there since crossing through it as a girl when she had fled Poland with her mother and Tatiana. Now, as then, she'd felt chased, as if someone might come after her and stop her at any moment. But the border crossing was uneventful, a perfunctory passport check by a guard, who mercifully didn't ask why she was coming there.

She'd reached Stuttgart then transferred to another train to go south. The train had wound its way painstakingly through the pine-covered Bavarian hills, stopping often and detouring around tracks that had still not been repaired since the last Allied air raids. At last she disembarked at what had once been the train station in Munich, now a shell of a building with a lone rickety platform. She had read about the annihilation of Germany in the bombing campaign during the last days of the war, but nothing had prepared her for the magnitude of the devastation: block after block of bombed-out buildings, a wasteland of rubble that made the darkest days of the Blitz pale in comparison. She wanted to take some pleasure in the Germans' pain. After all, it was their country that had caused all of the suffering. But these were ordinary people, living on the street in deepest winter with nothing but thin clothing to keep out the chill. In particular, the children begging at the train station seared her heart in a way few things ever had. The powerful nation that had been the aggressor had been reduced to dust.

No one knew Eleanor was going to Germany. She had briefly considered wiring the Director the news to tell him where she was going and request that he authorize clearances. But he had said to remain dark. Even if he wanted to help her, he could hardly do so anymore. And he might have told her no. Asking questions in Paris was one thing; poking around the tribunals in Germany quite another.

But not telling him meant she had no official status here, Eleanor reflected as she sat in the idling jeep before the barbed wire fence at Dachau. The camp looked exactly as it had in the photos, acres and acres of low wooden buildings, now covered in a powdery snow. The sky was heavy and gray. Eleanor could almost see the victims who had been kept here less than a year ago, bald, skeletal men, women and children in thin, striped prison garb. Those who had survived had long since been liberated, but she could almost feel their sunken eyes staring at her, demanding to know why the world had not come sooner.

"Papers," the guard said.

Eleanor handed over the documents the Director had given her before she left London to the guard. She held her breath as he scanned them. "These expired yesterday."

"Did they?" Eleanor acted flustered. "Oh, my, I was sure today was the twenty-seventh." She attempted her sweetest smile. Feminine guile was an unfamiliar costume to her. "I'm sure if you check with your superior, you'll see everything is in order," she bluffed. The guard looked uncertainly behind him toward the massive brick building that spanned the entranceway to the camp. It was bisected by a wide arch with an ominous square tower rising above it. Dachau was a former factory site that had once produced munitions. As she had driven to the camp over the icy stone road built on peat bogs, she had marveled at the houses that flanked either side; she'd wondered what the people there had seen and known and thought during the war. What had they done about it?

The guard studied her papers, seemingly uncertain what to do. Whether he was daunted by the prospect of bothering his boss at dinnertime or the long snowy walk or leaving his post, she could not tell. "I'll tell you what," she offered. "Let me in and I'll check back with you first thing in the morning and we'll sort it out then." Eleanor wasn't exactly sure what she needed to do once she was inside, but she knew she had to get past the guard if she was going to find Kriegler.

"All right." Eleanor exhaled slightly as the guard started to hand back her papers. He was going to let her through after all.

But as she turned the key in the engine, another voice called out. "Stop right there!" A man walked up to the car and opened the door. "Out please, ma'am." His American accent was Southern, she recognized from the films. He was older than the guard, and the gold insignia on the shoulder of his uniform signaled major, an officer's rank. "Out," he repeated. She complied, swatting at the cloud of cigarette smoke swirling around her head. "Never let anyone who isn't cleared through," he admonished the guard. "Even a good-looking woman." Eleanor didn't know whether to be flattered or annoyed. "And always inspect the vehicle. Are we clear?"

"Yes, sir."

The major stamped the snow from his boots. Though it had to be ten below freezing, he wore no coat. "I'll take it from here." When the guard retreated into the hut, the major returned to Eleanor. "Who are you really?"

She could see from his piercing eyes that there was no point in lying. "Eleanor Trigg."

He scanned the papers she held out. "Well, these certainly have all the right stamps, even if they are rotten. I'm Mick Willis from the Investigations Section, War Crimes Group. I'm a haystack man." She cocked her head, not bothering to pretend that she understood. "Nazi hunters. They call us that because we can find a needle in a haystack. I hunt down the Nazi bastards, or at least I did. Now I'm detailed here from the US Army JAG helping get them ready for trial." His face was gruff and stubbled with a salt-and-pepper five o'clock shadow. "What is it that you want?"

"I'm British, from Special Operations Executive. I recruited and ran our agents out of London."

"I thought they were being shut down." His voice was keen, no-nonsense.

"Yes, but my former boss, Colonel Winslow, sent me to investigate." She reached in her bag and pulled out the photos. "Female agents, lost with no information on their whereabouts," she pressed. "I received a lead in France that some of them might have been sent here." She stopped short of the real reason she had come.

He threw his cigarette down, then ground it out with his heel. "There are no victims of the Reich left here. They've all been sent to the DP camps. But you already knew that." He looked at her evenly. "What is it you really want?"

Clearly, there was no fooling Mick Willis. "You have Hans Kriegler here. I want to speak with him to ask him about the girls."

"That's impossible. No one is allowed access to him by order of head prosecutor Charlie Denson himself." Eleanor's frustration rose. She'd been told no, first by the British, then the French, a dozen times or more. But the Americans were all recovery aid and good intentions; she thought she might have a shot with them.

"Look, you have to go, but there's no way for you to get back tonight. I can offer you a bed and a meal. Then first thing tomorrow, you're on your way. Got it?"

Eleanor opened her mouth to protest. She had no intention of leaving. She would speak with Kriegler. Nothing less would do. But she could see from Mick's grimly set jaw that he wasn't going to acquiesce. And a night here would give her time to figure something out. "That would be fine, thank you."

She thought he meant for her to follow on foot, but instead he walked around to the driver's side of the jeep. "May I?" She nodded and climbed in to the passenger side. "Our barracks are a good half mile from here," he explained, as he navigated the perimeter of the camp. "We're lodged in one of the former SS barracks." She was amazed by the size and scope of the camp that unfurled before her as he drove. It was so much bigger than she'd ever imagined.

He pulled up in front of a long, wooden, single-story building which, she was relieved to note, was outside the barbed wire of the camp. "Follow me." He led her inside. There was an office, dimly lit by a lone Anglepoise lamp on a metal desk. An overturned tin was filled with cigarette butts and ash. Someone had pinned up a rogue's gallery of photos, Germans who were still at large. "I'm going to see about getting you a room for the night. Wait here—and don't touch anything."

Eleanor stood awkwardly in the middle of the space. She desperately wanted to rifle through the papers on the desk and in the files, but she didn't dare.

A few minutes later, Mick returned. "They'll get a rack for you. Best grab some food before the mess closes." He started from the office without speaking and she assumed she was to follow. They entered a dining hall with long tables that reminded her of the training facility at Arisaig House. She could almost hear the laughter of the girls.

But the mess here was served cafeteria-style. Mick handed her a tray and led her through the line, where she was unceremoniously served some sort of meat and potatoes without being asked. "Our quarters aren't bad," Mick remarked as they found two spots at a table. "Anything beats the winter we spent in the foxholes near Bastogne. Of course, the food is still awful." Eleanor's stomach turned as she thought of the starving children she'd passed near the train station in Munich, so emaciated their bones showed through their pale skin. And that, she reflected, surely paled in comparison to the suffering Jews who had been imprisoned at Dachau, scarcely a quarter mile from where they now sat.

Mick tore into his food without hesitation. "I'm sorry for being rude earlier," he said between bites. "This whole operation has been completely messed up. While the big shots in Nuremberg prosecute the high-profile cases, the real beasts, the guards who did the actual killing, are down here. And we've got precious little to work with. We've got a trial starting next week and the work has been nonstop. We're all exhausted." He paused, looking her up and down. "You don't look so good yourself," he added bluntly.

She ignored the unintended offensiveness of his remark. "I've been traveling from Paris since yesterday morning. And now it seems, I'll be heading right back out."

"At first light," he agreed, still chewing. He wasn't trying to be rude, she realized. Rather he ate with the haste of one who had lived through combat, not knowing how long he had to finish the meal or when the next one would come. "Can't have anything interfering with trial prep." He paused. "I've heard of the female agents." Eleanor was impressed. Few beyond SOE would have heard about her program. "I read in the reports that some were arrested along with the men. I don't know if they were yours, of course," he added hastily.

"They were all mine. Tell me," she ordered, forgetting in her eagerness to be polite.

"We interviewed a guard who spoke of some women being brought in."

"When?"

He scratched his head. "June or early July of '44 maybe. It wasn't unusual to have women here. There was a whole barracks for them over the hill." He pointed toward the darkness outside. Eleanor's stomach turned. In coming for Kriegler, she hadn't realized that she'd stumbled upon the very spot some of the girls were lost forever. "But these women were never registered, never went into the barracks. They were taken straight to the interrogation cell." Eleanor shuddered. She had heard of such places of suffering before death. "No one ever saw them again. Except one prisoner who had worked in that block. We have his testimony."

"Can I see it?"

He hesitated. "I suppose it can't hurt if I just show the transcript to you. You're leaving tomorrow anyway. You can see them after we eat."

She slid the tray across the table and then pushed her chair back with a loud scrape. "I'm done."

Mick took one more bite, then stood and cleared the trays. He led her back to the office where she had waited earlier. There were papers stacked everywhere and it seemed to Eleanor, who had always kept her own records immaculate, that he might not be able to find anything after all. But he walked to the file cabinet and opened the drawer without hesitation. He pulled out a thin folder and handed it to her.

Eleanor opened it. It was witness testimony from a Pole who had been forced to work as a laborer at Dachau. She skimmed the pages of testimony about the awful job he had been forced to perform, putting bodies in the ovens after the prisoners had been murdered.

A line caught her eye. "Three women were brought in from a transport one night. They stood out and were very well dressed. One had red hair." *That would have been Maureen.* Eleanor continued reading:

"They did not show fear but walked arm in arm through the camp, even though they were followed with a gun at their backs. The women were not registered as prisoners, but were brought straight to the medical barracks, next to where I worked. A guard ordered them to undress for a physical. I heard a woman's voice asking, *'Pour quoi?'*"

For what? Eleanor translated in her head before reading on: "And the answer came, 'For typhus.' I heard nothing more after that, and then the bodies were brought to me."

Eleanor set down the file. They were injected with something, told that it was medicine. She had known that the girls were dead. But the picture of what exactly had happened was now painted before her. It was almost too much to take.

But she still didn't know how they had been caught in the first place. She forced her feelings down and focused on why she had come. "I need to see Kriegler."

"Damn it, Ellie," Mick swore. It was the first time in her life anyone had called her that. She considered telling him not to, then decided against it. "You're one pushy broad." Mick pulled out a pack of cigarettes and offered her one. She waved it away. She'd only smoked on the nights she put the girls on the planes to France; she hadn't taken a drag since. He lit one for himself. "I've already told you more than I should. Your girls were killed by the Germans. It's a damn shame, but at least you know for sure now. Isn't that enough?"

"Not for me. I want to know everything—including how they caught the girls in the first place. That's why I need to speak with Kriegler. Half an hour. That's all I'm asking. You claim to care about bringing these men to justice. But what about those against whom they committed the crimes?"

Mick took a drag of his cigarette, then exhaled hard. "The female agents had no official status and, other than the one report I showed you, there's so much we don't know about what happened. It's as if the evidence disappeared with them." Which was what the Germans wanted, Eleanor thought. Just another way justice had been denied to her girls. "I understand your loyalty to these girls and it's admirable," Mick continued. "But you have to see the bigger picture. These men murdered thousands—no, millions. And Kriegler is among the worst of them. I can't risk bringing him to justice just to help you. Especially when we aren't ready..." He stopped, as if realizing he'd said too much.

"That's it," Eleanor said. "Your case against Kriegler—it isn't strong enough, is it?"

"I have no idea what you're talking about." But there was a warble in his voice.

"Kriegler." Eleanor seized on it. "He won't talk. You don't have what you need to convict him, do you?"

"Even if that was true, the prosecution's case is classified. You know I couldn't say."

"I've got all the top clearances from Whitehall." *Had*, she corrected herself silently. "If you tell me, maybe I can help."

He raised his hands. "Okay, okay, I get it. Not here." He motioned her outside the office and down the hall. Eleanor was puzzled: the office, with its closed door, would have seemed the perfect place to talk. Who, she wondered, did Mick think might be listening?

"It's Kriegler," he said when they were outside. It was completely dark now and the air seemed to have grown even more frigid. Mick's breath rose before him in great puffs as he spoke. "The case against him isn't as strong as we'd like it to be," he admitted finally. "Kriegler hid his tracks remarkably well and the few of his underlings we've got in custody have been reluctant to testify against him." The SD were a tight-knit, disciplined bunch. They would sooner go to the grave than betray their former boss. "We've had a dickens of a time getting anything from him. We've turned all the screws. Applied pressure. He won't break." Kriegler was a master interrogator himself, knew better than anyone how to hold out. Eleanor, in point of fact, had never broken anyone. But she had spent enough time at SOE to know how to tear apart a witness.

Mick continued, "The War Crimes Tribunal thinks the case is too big for us to handle here. They want to transfer it to Nuremberg. But we're getting a lot of pressure from Third Army headquarters in Munich to keep the case here and get a win for the Dachau trials."

"I can help," Eleanor offered, without considering whether she actually could. She leaned in close. She pictured Kriegler's dossier back in London, the recounting of his cruelty. "You need the background on Kriegler, the lines of questioning, the details for cross-examination. I've got it." Eleanor had watched the moves of Kriegler and the SD bastards unfold from London like a game of chess. While she still didn't have the answers she was seeking as to how the girls had been betrayed, she knew the crimes of Kriegler and the others all too well. "I can get you documents." Another bluff; the proof she could offer had all burned along with Norgeby House. And she couldn't have gotten it for him in a trial not two days away. "I'll testify for you, sign an affidavit. And you need to get inside his head, figure out what matters most, where his dark places are."

"Then tell me how."

She shook her head. "Not until you give me what I need. Ten minutes alone with him."

"What makes you think he will speak to you?"

"Because I know him," she said, hearing how ridiculous it sounded.

"You've never met him."

"And the Nazis you've hunted across Europe? You never met them either, right? But you knew them, their family histories, their backgrounds, their crimes." Mick nodded. "That's Kriegler for me."

"He's different. He won't break."

"It can't hurt to try."

"This is nuts!"

"Most unorthodox," she agreed. "Do you want the trial or not?" He didn't answer. "Look, I don't have time for this. If you aren't going to give me access, then I'll be on my way to my next lead." It was a calculated bluff. Dachau was her last shot. She only prayed he didn't know this.

"Anyway, it's impossible to give you access. He's being transferred to Nuremberg at first light."

She had made it here just in time, Eleanor realized. She never would have gotten access to Kriegler at Nuremberg. "Then let me talk to him now."

"Ten minutes," he relented. "And I get to be present."

"Fifteen," she countered. "And you can listen outside the door."

"Are you always this difficult?"

She ignored the comment. She'd spent the better part of her life being called difficult just for doing what the men did. "He won't talk if you're there," she explained.

He stared at her for one beat and then another. "I don't see how you can do it," he said. She held her breath, waiting to be told no, to be turned away as she had been so many times these past months and years. "But I'm out of other options. Not now," he said slowly. "Turning up in the middle of the night will attract too much attention. We'll leave at five in the morning. We need to be there before the transport comes to take him to Nuremberg." She wanted to see Kriegler now. But she nodded, knowing it was better not to push.

Mick led her into another building and down a hall. It had been freshly painted since the war, she could tell, cleaned to make it suitable for the Allied officers to stay, to erase the awful things that had happened here. He opened a door to a narrow room with a bed and washstand. "I'll see you in the morning," he said before closing the door.

Eleanor did not sleep in the cold, sterile barracks, but waited for the hours to pass. She lay awake, imagining her girls arriving at the camp as the laborer's testimony had described. She took small comfort in the fact that several of them had come together. How had they found one another? It seemed unlikely they had been arrested in the same place. Eleanor wondered over and over: What would have happened if they had received word sooner that the radio had been compromised and it was a trap? They might have split up and gone to ground. Instead, they were arrested and, in most cases, killed. It was her fault. She could have pursued her doubts, forced the Director or someone above him to listen sooner. But she hadn't—and her girls had paid the price.

When at last the sky began to pinken over the pine-capped Bavarian hills, Eleanor washed as well as she could and changed her dress. She started outside. The air was crisp with a hint of dampness, as though it might snow again, but not right away.

Mick was waiting for her in the predawn stillness, the smoke from his cigarette curling upward as he opened the door to a jeep. Eleanor fought the urge to ask him for one. They climbed into the jeep, letting him drive again, and he navigated to the gate where she'd arrived the previous day. Neither spoke as they passed through.

He parked the jeep and stepped out. She followed, the edges of her skirt pulling from her boots where she had tucked them. They were inside the camp now. He led her wordlessly through the arch in the guard house, only the crunching of their boots against the snow breaking the silence. She looked for the infamous *Arbeit Macht Frei* sign over the entranceway, but it was gone. Inside the gate, there were rows and rows of barracks. She stared as though one of the girls might walk from one of the buildings at any moment. *Where are you?*

"Show me," she said to Mick. Though it would tell her nothing, she needed to see where the girls had died. "Show me everything."

He traced a line in front of them from left to right. "Arrivals came down this road, through the entrance with the railway station by the SS barracks." Eleanor imagined her girls, exhausted and dazed, being forced to march down the path. The girls would have walked with heads high as they had been trained, showing no fear.

Mick led her down the semicircle of barracks, stopping at the final one. "This is the interrogation block where they would have been questioned and killed." His voice was factual, emotionless. "There's a crematorium out the back where the bodies were taken." Eleanor had asked for everything and he would spare her none. She touched the bricks in horror.

"Is that it?" She gestured to a low building with a telltale chimney stack.

"The crematorium. Yes. The prisoners referred to it as 'the shortest escape.'"

"I want to see." She walked around to see the twisted, charred metal then knelt in the earth, sifting the gravel through her fingers.

"Come," he said finally, helping her to her feet. "We only have a little time before they will take Kriegler for questioning. No one can know that I've let you in."

He led her to the right, where a section of barracks had been cordoned off with barbed wire. "This is where we keep him and the other prisoners awaiting trial."

"Not in the interrogation cell then?" she asked. It would have seemed fitting.

"If only. We need to preserve that for evidence."

The soldier guarding the barracks eyed them uneasily. "It's all right," Mick said, flashing credentials at him. The guard stepped aside. Mick turned to her. "Are you sure you want to do this?"

She crossed her arms. "Whatever do you mean?"

"I've been at this a long time and it's been one heartbreak after another. The truth," he added darkly, "is sometimes the very opposite from what you expect it to be."

And once out, Eleanor thought silently, *you can't put it back any more than returning a mist of perfume to a bottle once it has been sprayed.* She could walk away now. But she thought about Marie, who with her endless questions had always wanted to know the truth, about where the agents would be going, what they would be doing. About *why*. "I'm ready."

"Come then." Eleanor squared her shoulders. Inside the barracks, the floor was dirt and a rotten smell came off the stone walls. He led her from the room and down the hall, stopping in front of a closed door. "This is it." It was different from the others, reinforced with steel and a peephole in the middle.

Eleanor peered through. At the sight of Hans Kriegler, she gasped with recognition, recoiling. The face she had seen so many times in reports and photographs was now just a few meters away. He looked the same, perhaps a little thinner, wearing khaki prison garb. She'd heard stories about Allied troops exacting their revenge on prisoners. But, except for a pinkish scar across his left cheek, Kriegler looked no worse for the wear. And he was so ordinary, like a bookseller or merchant one might see on the streets of Paris or Berlin before the war. Hardly the monster she'd imagined in her mind.

Mick gestured with his head. "You can go in."

Eleanor stopped, unexpectedly frozen in her tracks. She stared at the one man who might have all of the answers she had been searching for. For the first time, there was some part of her that didn't want to know the truth. She could go back, tell some of the families at least that she had found where and how the girls died. That much was true and for most of them it would be enough. But then she saw the girls' parents, the agony in their eyes when they asked why. She had sworn to herself that she would find out what had happened and why. Nothing less would do.

The cell was a barracks room, small and rectangular. There was a bed with a blanket, a small lamp. A coffeepot sat on the corner. "This is how we house prisoners?"

"It's the Geneva Convention, Ellie. These are high-ranking officers. We're trying to keep it clean, no allegations of mistreatment."

She shook her head. "Surely my girls received no such consideration."

"You'd best go in," Mick urged her. He looked uneasily over his shoulder. "We don't have long."

Eleanor took a deep breath and started through the door. "Herr Kriegler," she said, addressing him as a civilian, refusing to use the title he did not deserve. He turned to her, his expression neutral. "I'm Eleanor Trigg."

"I know who you are." He stood politely, as though they were in a café and had arranged to meet for coffee. "So nice to finally meet you." His tone was familiar, unafraid and almost cordial.

"You know who I am?" She could not help but sound off guard.

"Of course. We know everything." She noticed his use of the present tense. He gestured toward the coffeepot. "If you would like some, I can ask for another cup."

I'd sooner drink poison than have coffee with you, she wanted to say. Instead, she shook her head. He took a sip, then grimaced. "Nothing like the coffee back home in Vienna. My daughter and I loved to go to this little café off Stefansplatz and have Sacher torte and coffee," he remarked.

"How old is your daughter?"

"She's eleven now. I haven't seen her in four years. But you didn't come to talk about children or coffee. You want to ask me about the girls."

It was as if he had been expecting her, and it made her uneasy. "The female agents," she corrected. "The ones who never came home. I know that they are dead," she added, not wanting to hear him say the words. "I want to know how they died—and how they were captured."

"Gas or gunshot, here or another camp, does it matter?" She blanched at his dispassionate tone. "They were spies."

"They weren't spies." She bristled.

"Well, what would you call them?" he shot back. "They were dressed in civilian clothes, operating in occupied territory. They were captured and killed."

"I know that," she said, recovering. "But how were they captured?" He looked away, still recalcitrant. "You know those women had children themselves, daughters like yours. Those children will never see their mothers again."

She saw it then—something shifted in his eyes, a flicker of fear breaking through. "I won't see mine again either. I'm going to hang for what I've done," he said.

If there is a just God. "You don't know that for sure. If you cooperate, perhaps you might get a life sentence. So why not tell me the truth?" she pressed. "The things I want to know have nothing to do with the prosecution," she added, forgetting for a moment her promise to Mick that she would help him. "You've got nothing to fear from your own side anymore. All of the others are arrested or dead."

"Because there are some secrets one must carry to the grave."

Which secrets? she wondered. And why would a man who was at the end of his days choose to remain silent?

She decided to take another tack. She reached into her bag and pulled out the photos. She handed them to Kriegler and he flipped through them one by one. Then he paused and held up one of the photos.

"Marie," the man said with a glint of recognition in his eye. He pointed to his face, a poorly healed scar. "She fought with her nails, here and here." Leaving him a mark he could never erase. "But ultimately she did what we asked. Not to save her own life, but his."

"Vesper?"

He nodded. "I shot him anyway." Kriegler seemed emboldened now. "It wasn't personal," he added, his voice dispassionate. "I had no more use for him…or her either."

"And Marie?" she asked, dreading the answer.

"She was put on a transport from Fresnes with other women."

"When?"

"Late May." Right after Julian had returned from London. So much sooner than Eleanor had imagined.

"So you had the radio by then?" He nodded. "But we were still receiving messages." And transmitting them, she added silently. Every fear she'd had during the war was true.

"Messages from us. We got the first radio from Marseille, you see. But since London already knew that circuit was blown, there was no point in transmitting from it. So we played around with the frequencies until we found one that the Vesper circuit used. We were able to impersonate the operator to get London to transmit information to us."

The radio game, just as Henri had said in Paris. Eleanor recalled her suspicions, the ways in which some of Marie's transmissions had sounded just fine, others not at all like her. The latter, as she suspected, were actually being broadcasted by German intelligence. Eleanor had kept her concerns silent at first, and later when she had spoken they'd been brushed aside by the Director. But here they were now laid out in front of her as plainly as a winning hand of cards splayed on a table. If only she had acted on her suspicions and pushed harder with the Director to find out what was happening.

There was no time for guilt, though; her precious moments to question Kriegler were rapidly ticking by. "But how? I learned in Paris that you had the radios and were able to play them back to London. You didn't have the security checks. How did you manage?"

"We didn't think it would work." A smile crossed his face and she held her hands down so as not to reach across and slap him. "There were so many ways the British would have seen through it. At first we thought they were just careless, preoccupied. Only later did we realize that someone in London actually wanted us to get the messages."

"Excuse me? How can you say that?"

"In mid-May 1944, I had occasion to be away from headquarters. One of my deputies, a real *dummkopf*, got cocky. He sent a message to London acknowledging that we were on the other end of the line. When I found out, I had him court-martialed for treason."

"Who in London, exactly?" Eleanor had sent many messages herself. But she surely didn't know about the radio game.

"I have no idea. Someone knew and kept transmitting anyway."

Eleanor's mind reeled back over the people who had access to broadcast to Vesper circuit. Herself, Jane, the Director. It was a very small group, none of whom, she felt certain, would have done it.

Before Eleanor could ask further, Mick knocked at the door, gesturing for her to come out. "Time's up," he said when she stepped into the hall reluctantly. "Did you get what you were looking for?"

"I suppose." Eleanor's mind reeled at Kriegler's assertion that the Germans had *told* London they had the radio. That London knew. She was aghast—and puzzled. She had been there at headquarters for every single day of the operation, and she had never imagined—much less heard—of such a thing.

Mick was watching her expectantly, waiting for the information he needed. She had forgotten, in her distress about the girls, to ask Kriegler the questions she had promised for Mick. But it didn't matter. She'd had the answers he needed all along. "He confessed to the murder of Julian Brookhouse. Said that he shot him personally at SD headquarters in Paris in May 1944."

Mick's eyes widened. "You got all that in ten minutes?"

She nodded. "If he denies it tell him that I was secretly recording the conversation. And that I am prepared to testify against him at trial." The first part was a lie; the latter was not.

Mick turned toward the cell. "I need to go in there and speak with him now, before the transport comes. If you don't want to wait for me, I'll have one of the orderlies drive you back to base."

"I'll wait," she said. She had nothing but time now.

A few minutes later, Mick came out of the cell. "Kriegler asked to see you once more." Surprised, she walked in to once again face the most evil man she had ever encountered.

"I'm going to cooperate with the Americans." His expression was somber now, and she knew Mick had confronted him with the evidence about killing Julian. "But before I do, I want to help you." It was a lie, she knew. He wanted the truth about the girls to go with him to his grave. Only there was fear in his eyes now. "If I do, will you put in a good word for leniency for me?"

"Yes." She would never forgive Kriegler or let him walk free again. But a long life alone with his crimes seemed more punishing.

The German's eyes glinted. He slid something across the table. It fell to the ground and he kicked it toward her. It was a small key. How he had managed to hang on to it through his arrest and interrogation was beyond her. "Credit Suisse in Zurich," he said. "Box 9127."

"What is it?" she asked.

"An insurance policy, so to speak," he said cryptically. "Documents that hold the answers you've been looking for." Eleanor's heartbeat quickened. "I'll never walk free again, but I will give you the answers for Marie and the other four I sent—and their daughters." It was, perhaps, the smallest act of contrition.

Then something about his words stuck. "Did you say that there were five girls?" He nodded. "Are you certain?"

"They all left Paris together. I signed the order myself. One died when the train car exploded."

Four should have arrived. "But the witness's report only spoke of three girls. What happened to the other?"

"Never accounted for. There were a dozen ways she could have died. But for all I know she might be alive."

Eleanor leaped up and burst from the jail cell, starting past Mick in a run.

CHAPTER TWENTY-EIGHT

ELEANOR

Zurich, 1946

A light snow had begun to fall as Eleanor crossed the Paradeplatz and started toward the massive stone headquarters of the Credit Suisse. As bells of Fraumünster Church pealed nine thirty in the distance, she wove between the suited bankers making their way to work.

Eleanor had left Germany in a haze, traveling south by train. They crossed the snow-covered Swiss Alps, which just a year ago had formed a natural barrier to escape for so many, without incident. She clutched the key Kriegler had given her during the entire trip.

Mick had run after her as she fled Kriegler's cell. "Do you think it's true?" she'd demanded of him. "Do you think one of my girls could still be alive?"

"That's tough." Mick hesitated. "I want to say yes. But you know the odds. The man is a liar. Even if he is telling the truth about putting a fifth girl on the train in Paris, that doesn't mean she's alive. If she was, she would have turned up by now. There are a dozen reasons she might not have made it to the camp, none good. I just don't want to see you get hurt."

"There's probably nothing in the safe-deposit box either." She waited for him to disagree, but he did not.

"So don't go," he said instead. "Stay here. Help us with the trial."

"If Kriegler had given you a lead about one of your men, would you leave it alone?"

"No, I suppose I couldn't." He understood that it was impossible to walk away from even the slightest sliver of hope of finding those who had been lost. "Then go see what's there and come back quick. You're a damn fine woman, Eleanor Trigg. We could use someone like you here permanently. We could use *you*," Mick had pressed. "Your experience would make a great addition to our team."

Was he really trying to recruit her? Flattered, Eleanor considered the offer. She had no job now that she'd been dismissed from SOE, nothing waiting for her anymore back at home. The work would suit her.

Then she shook her head. "I'm honored," she said. "But I hope you'll forgive me if I say no, or at least not now. Your work is so important, but I've got mine and I'm not done yet."

"'Miles to go before you sleep,'" he offered with understanding. His words were reminiscent of the American poet Robert Frost.

"Exactly," she replied, warming to him. They were kindred spirits, each alone and searching. Though she had only just met Mick, he seemed to understand what she was feeling better than anyone. She was sorry to leave him.

Leaving Dachau, she'd desperately wanted to search for the missing girl Kriegler said might be alive. But she didn't have a single lead, not a document or witness to go on, other than his word. And the safe-deposit box in Zurich, which he'd suggested might contain the answers she was seeking about the radio, had beckoned.

She entered the bank now, the sound of her sturdy heels clicking against the floor and echoing off the high ceiling. Dark, gold-framed oil paintings of somber men adorned the walls. She passed through two enormous columns and entered a room marked *Tresorraum*. Vault.

Behind the marble-topped counter, a man in a striped ascot looked down over his spectacles. Without speaking, he passed her a slip of white paper. She wrote the number of the safe-deposit box down on it and returned it to him. As he read the information, Eleanor braced for questions about who she was, whether she owned the box. But the man simply turned and disappeared through a doorway behind him. That was how it worked, she mused. No names, no questions. The beauty and the evil of the Swiss bank. Through the doorway behind the counter, she could see a wall of metal boxes stacked high and wide, like tiny crypts in a mausoleum. What other secrets might they hide? she wondered, stashed there by people who had not lived to see the end of the war.

A few minutes later the bank man returned with a sealed oblong box bearing two locks on the top. Eleanor took out the key Kriegler had given her. How had he possibly been able to keep it hidden in captivity?

The bank man produced a second key. He inserted it in one of the locks, then gestured for Eleanor to do the same with hers. She tried to insert the key, but it did not seem to fit in the lock. Her heart seized. Mick was right; Kriegler had duped her. But looking closer she could see that the key was worn and a bit rusty as well. She brushed it off and tried to straighten it, then maneuvered it into the lock.

Eleanor and the bank man turned the keys in unison. The box opened with a pop and the man lifted a second smaller box from inside. The bank man took his key and disappeared, leaving her alone.

Eleanor opened the safe-deposit box with trembling hands. There was a stack of Reichsmarks, worthless now, and a separate stack of dollars. Eleanor took the latter and tucked it in her pocket. It was blood money, but she did not care. She would see that it went to the families of the girls who had left behind children, now motherless.

Beneath the money, there was a single envelope. Eleanor opened it carefully. There was a piece of paper inside, so thin and tissue-like that it threatened to tear as she lifted it. She unfolded the paper carefully and scanned it. Her eyes filled. Before her, in black-and-white, were the answers she had been seeking. It was, as Kriegler had promised, everything.

It was a radio transmission from Paris to London, dated May 8, 1944: "Thank you for your collaboration and for the weapons that you sent us. SD."

This was the transmission that Kriegler had mentioned, sent by one of the underlings, overtly signaling to London that the radio had been compromised. The transmission was stamped "Empfangen London." Received in London. Somehow she had never seen it. But someone in London had allowed the transmissions to continue even knowing the Germans had the radio.

Why had Kriegler given it to her? Surely not a change of heart, a sudden altruism. Nor did his fear of prosecution fully explain a revelation so bold. No, it was the truth about the crimes the British government had committed, the blood that was on their hands. Releasing it was his final act of war. What would he have done with it if Eleanor had not come to Dachau? she wondered. He might have found another way of getting the word out. Or he might have taken the secret to the grave.

But what to do with it? She had to find a way to bring the truth to light. To reach those to whom it mattered most. The truth, once out, would spell the end, for the Director and herself, for all of them.

Still, Eleanor had made a promise to her girls. There was no choice. She had to set the record straight.

Wiping the tears from her eyes, she started from the vault.

CHAPTER TWENTY-NINE

GRACE

New York, 1946

Grace poured sugar into her coffee, watching it disappear into the blackness below. She looked up, taking comfort in the sight of Frankie hunched over a file across the office and the uneven hum of the radiator.

It had been a full week since she'd left the photos at the British consulate. She'd wondered if it would be hard to go back to normal, as if the whole business with the girls had never happened. But she had slipped back into her old life like a comfortable pair of shoes. The room at the boardinghouse, now graced by her mother's plastic hydrangeas, felt more like home than ever.

Still, she often thought about Mark and how puzzled he must have been to wake up and find her gone. She'd half expected him to call, but there had been silence. She thought about the girls, too, and about Eleanor and why she had betrayed them.

Pushing aside the questions that had sent her on the crazy quest in the first place, Grace resumed typing a letter to the housing board. Frankie crossed the room and handed her a file. "I was hoping you could fill this out for me." She opened the file. There were papers from the Children's Aid Society for the placement of a child with a family. Grace was surprised; usually they referred these types of matters to Simon Wise, over on Ludlow, who specialized in family law. But then Grace saw the names on the form and she understood why Frankie was handling this one. The child to be fostered was Samuel Altshuler. And he was being placed with none other than Frankie himself.

"You're taking Sammy in?" she asked, almost not believing.

"The kid deserves a solid home, you know? And what you said about it being hard to get involved, that really stuck." Grace's mind reeled back to their conversation over the phone when she was in Washington. She had said it as a caution. But he had taken it the other way and jumped in with both feet. "So I'm going to take him. At least if they'll let an old bachelor have a kid."

She reached out and squeezed his arm, her admiration soaring. "They will, Frankie. They definitely will. He's the luckiest kid to have you. I'll get these typed right away and I'll deliver them to the agency myself."

It was nearly two o'clock that afternoon when Grace returned from the courthouse. The office was empty, but Frankie had scribbled a note: "Gone to get some things for the kid's new room. Back soon." His words seemed to crackle off the page with excitement and purpose.

Her stomach rumbled, reminding her that she had missed lunch. She picked up the bag containing her egg salad sandwich and started for the door. Time for a quick bite on the roof before Frankie returned.

She opened the door to the office, then stopped short. There, in the corridor, stood Mark.

"Hello..." she said uncertainly. Their encounter on the street last time had been a coincidence. Now he had come here purposefully, looking for her. Surprise and happiness and anger seemed to rush through her all at once. How had he found her? Her mother, or her landlady perhaps; it would not have been that hard.

"You left," he said, his voice more wounded than accusing.

"I'm sorry."

"Was it something I said? Or did?"

"Not at all." She could see how confused he must have been. "Things between us just felt, well, complicated. And then I found this." She reached in her bag and pulled out the wireless transmission that proved Eleanor's guilt. She had almost destroyed it after returning to New York. But she hadn't, and despite trying to put the whole matter behind her, she kept the paper with her. "Finding out the truth about Eleanor, plus everything between us, it was just more than I could take. I was overwhelmed."

"So you left."

"I left." But running away had changed nothing. Eleanor's guilt was still there, plain on the page. And so were her feelings for Mark. "I'm sorry I didn't say anything."

"It's okay. All of us have things that we keep hidden. There's a lot you don't know about me." He paused. "When we were in Washington you asked about my time with the War Crimes Tribunal. I wasn't ready to talk about it then, but I am now. You see, I was finishing up law school when the war broke out. I wanted to enlist, but my father insisted I take a deferment and finish school before going abroad. He'd banked everything on my school and my being a lawyer was needed to keep us afloat. So I doubled my classes to finish early. I enlisted the day after graduation and they put me in the JAG corps and deployed me. But by then it was all over, just the cleanup.

"One of the first cases I faced in Frankfurt was the Obens trial. Have you heard of it?" Grace shook her head. "I didn't think so. They worked hard to keep it out of the papers. Obens was an American GI in one of the companies that liberated

Ravensbrück. He and the others were sick with what they had seen, not right in the head. When they captured a German who had been a guard at the camp, Obens shot him, in cold blood, and in violation of the rules of war." Grace blanched, imagining good men just like Tom, only too far gone. "I wanted to prosecute the matter. It wasn't combat—it was murder, pure and simple. But my superiors would hear none of it. They were only focused on trying Germans and they didn't want to dilute the story of the Allied victory.

"I wouldn't leave it alone. So they came up with a story about how I was doing it because my family was German." She recalled his surname: Dorff. Some part of her had known he was of German descent, but she hadn't wanted to ask. "They called it treason."

"So you resigned?"

"Before they could court-martial me, yes. You must think I'm a coward. I'm sorry for not telling you sooner."

"No, I think what you did was brave. But why are you telling me now?"

"Because I think you blame yourself for Tom's death and that's why you keep running. But none of it is black-and-white. Not your choices, not my choices and not Eleanor's either. I'm sure there were reasons for what she did."

"Maybe."

"You don't believe me?"

"I don't know what to believe anymore. But I'm awfully glad you're here." The words came out before she realized she was saying them. She could feel her cheeks flush.

"Really?" He took a step closer. "Me, too."

"Even if it's complicated?"

"Especially then. I'm not here for easy."

He wrapped her in his arms then and they stood motionless for several seconds. She looked up and their eyes met. He looked as though he might kiss her and this time she really, truly wanted him to. She closed her eyes as his head lowered. Their lips met.

There was a noise behind them. "Grace, would you believe I got Sammy a bike and..." Frankie's voice trailed off as Mark and Grace broke apart, too late.

Grace cleared her throat. "Frankie, this is Mark Dorff. He was a friend of my husband's." The explanation just seemed to make things worse.

She watched as Frankie looked from her to Mark, then back again, braced for what he was going to say. She could not tell from his expression if he was angry or amused.

"I wasn't expecting you back so soon," she offered.

"Yeah, well, remember that woman you asked me to check on?" Frankie looked uneasily at Mark, as if unsure he should speak in front of him.

"It's okay. Mark knows everything."

"I was over at immigration earlier, checking on some things for Sammy's adoption papers. I saw my buddy at customs. He found her entry file."

"Eleanor's?"

"There wasn't much to it. She came to America a day or two before she died, arrived by plane."

Grace nodded, her heart sinking again. She knew that much from the passport she'd seen at the consulate. What had she expected, really? A customs form could hardly tell what had gone on inside Eleanor's mind, what she was doing in New York and whether it related to her betrayal of the girls. "Thank you," she said to Frankie, still grateful for his efforts to help her.

"The only other thing in the file was this." He pulled a small tablet from his jacket and opened it, pointing at the notation he had made. "This was the address she listed as her destination in America." Grace scanned the entry. Her spine began to tingle. An apartment in Brooklyn. And below it, in Frankie's chicken-scratch writing, the entry from the log: "Person(s) receiving." As she read the name he'd scribbled below it, her blood ran cold.

"I have to go," Grace said, reaching for her bag. "Thank you!" She kissed Frankie so hard on the cheek that he fell back in his chair.

"Do you want me to come with you?" Mark called after her.

But Grace was already out the door. There were some things a woman had to do alone.

CHAPTER THIRTY

ELEANOR

London, 1946

"Eleanor." The Director looked up from his desk. It had been four days since she'd left Zurich. She stood unannounced in the door to his office now, paper in hand. "I wasn't expecting you back so soon. How was your trip to France?"

"In France, I found nothing."

He leaned back in his chair and reached for his pipe. "Well, that's too bad. I'm grateful to you for trying, but we always knew it might be a wild goose chase with nothing to come of it after so much time. Hopefully it has at least put some of your questions to rest."

"I didn't say nothing came of it," she interjected. "I said I found nothing in France. But then I had the opportunity to go to Germany and interview Hans Kriegler."

"Germany." The Director paused, unlit pipe dangling in midair. "Kriegler's being tried at Nuremberg, isn't he? How did you ever manage that?"

"I managed. I was able to speak with him at Dachau, where he was being held, before he was transported. He led me to this." She held out the document from the vault. "You knew that the Germans had the radio set. And yet you kept broadcasting classified information."

He took the paper from her. "Eleanor, that's preposterous!" he blustered, a beat too quickly before reading it. "I've never seen this document before in my life."

She held out her hand. But it wasn't the return of the paper she was seeking. "The transmission log. Let me see it. And don't tell me it was lost in the fire," she added, before he could respond. "I know you kept a copy of your own." The Director regarded her unflinchingly. Then his expression changed to one of resignation. He turned to the file cabinet behind him, dialed the combination of the safe lock and twisted the handle. The drawer popped open and he handed the thick file to her.

Eleanor thumbed through the pages and pages of transmissions between London and F Section, organized by date. Then she came to it, a copy of the transmission she'd gotten from Kriegler. London had received it after all. It was identical to the paper Kriegler had given her, except for the received stamp—and the second sheet of paper stapled behind it. "Message not authenticated," the second sheet said, a warning flag from the operator who had received the message. And then a separate notion: "Continue transmissions." Someone had issued a directive to keep transmitting despite the warning that the message was a fraud. And though she had never seen it in her life, the memorandum had been printed on Eleanor's own letterhead.

"You kept this from me."

"I didn't include you," he corrected. As if that made a difference. She had kept transmitting, unaware that the concerns she had raised over and over to the Director had in fact been substantiated to SOE by the Germans themselves. But her superiors, the Director and God knew who else, had kept the information from her so that they could keep transmitting. And it had gotten the girls arrested, cost them their lives. She had long suspected something was wrong, that the broadcasts were not authentic. But the notion that her own agency would willingly sacrifice its own people was staggering.

"You knew that if I saw this, I would stop the transmissions altogether. *You* should have stopped the transmissions. You were broadcasting to the Germans, sensitive information that put all of our agents at risk."

He stood up. "I had no choice. I was acting on orders." How many times had she read that in the reports of captured German war criminals, who said they were powerless, that they had no choice but to commit the atrocities by their own hands? Then the Director sat up straighter. "But even if that were not the case, I still would have done it. When we realized that the Germans had the radio, it was an opportunity to feed them information about operations—false information that would redirect their defenses elsewhere ahead of D-Day. And it worked—surely if the Germans hadn't thought we were amassing forces elsewhere, Allied casualties would have been much worse. If that blasted radio operator hadn't flagged the message that was supposed to be from Tompkins, it would have kept working. It worked," he repeated, as if to convince himself.

"Not for my girls," Eleanor replied sharply. "Not for the twelve who never came home, or for the other agents like Julian who were killed." The information London had fed to the Germans over the radio had revealed their locations and activities, led directly to their capture.

"Sometimes a few must be sacrificed for the greater good," he said coldly.

Eleanor was dumbfounded. She had worked for the Director; supported him. The strategic way he approached the difficult work they'd had to do, deploying agents like chess pieces on a board, was one of the things she respected most about him. She had never imagined him to be like this, though: cold, cynical. "This is outrageous. I'm going to Whitehall."

"And tell them what? It was a covert program, wholly sanctioned. Where do you think authorization came from in the first place?" It had not just been the Director, but the highest levels of government that had approved the plan. She saw then the full extent of the betrayal.

"I'll go to the newspapers." Something had to be done.

"Eleanor, have you stopped to think of your own role in the affair? You knew that the transmissions were suspicious. Yet you continued to transmit the information over the same frequencies to the same operator."

Eleanor was stunned. "You can't be suggesting..."

"You even sent the message signaling that Julian would be returning to the field. And when the operator said to switch landing fields, you okayed that as well. You sent Julian to his death, Eleanor. You didn't press harder because you knew on many levels that no matter what, the mission had to go forward."

"How dare you?" Eleanor felt her cheeks go red with anger. "I never would have done anything to jeopardize Julian—or my girls."

But the Director continued, "And make no mistake about it. Your name is on all of the outgoing transmissions. If that gets out, the world will know that you are to blame.

"I never wanted it to come to this." The Director's voice softened. "I thought it was all in the past when you left SOE. But you couldn't leave well enough alone. And then that business with Violet's father. He brought his questions to his MP and they said there was to be a parliamentary inquiry. I sent off the files I could to Washington."

"And burned the rest," she said. He did not reply. The truth was almost too awful to believe—the Director had destroyed Norgeby House, the very place they had worked so hard to build, to bury the truth forever. "You sent me off, too," she added slowly as the realization came to her.

"I kept receiving reports of you asking questions," he admitted. "You wouldn't leave it alone. I thought getting you out of

London, sending you to look into things in France, would buy time." He hadn't counted on her getting to Germany and speaking with Kriegler. But she had, and the things she learned had changed everything.

"So what are we going to do about it?" she asked.

"There is nothing to be done. Parliament will conduct its investigation and find nothing and it will all go away."

"What do you mean? We have to let the truth be known, tell Parliament."

"For what, so they can further denigrate the work we did at SOE? They've always said we were inconsequential, even damaging, and we are to give them proof to support it? SOE is my legacy and yours, too." He would do anything to keep that intact. "The truth changes nothing, Eleanor. The girls are gone."

But to her, the truth had to prevail.

"Then I'll go myself." The words were an echo of the threat she had made when she suspected the radios. If she had made good on it then and followed through, some of the girls might be alive today. But she hadn't. The threat this time was not a hollow one. She had nothing left to lose. "I'll go to the commission myself."

"You can't. It's your word against mine. Who do you think they'll believe—a disgruntled former secretary, or the decorated colonel who headed the agency with distinction?" He was right. She just as easily might have betrayed the girls. There was simply no truth to contradict him.

Unless there was a witness. "Kriegler said one of the girls never made it to the concentration camp where the others perished. That she might still be alive. Do you know anything about that?"

An uneasy look crossed the Director's face. "I received a visit from one of the girls not long after the war. She wanted help expediting a visa to the States. I helped her because it seemed like the right thing to do."

More likely he was happy to send her as far away as possible. "Which one was it?" Eleanor asked.

"The one you never thought could do the job, oddly enough. And ironically, the one whose transmissions were being faked by the Germans—Marie Roux."

She brought her hand to her mouth. What Kriegler had told her was true.

"She survived SD interrogation and Fresnes prison. Tough as nails, in the end, and damn lucky."

Joy surged within Eleanor, but it was quickly replaced by anger. The Director had known and had not told her. "What did you tell her? About the arrests, I mean."

A look flickered across the Director's face. "I told her nothing."

She couldn't believe anything he said anymore. "Where is she?"

"Leave her alone. Let her move on with her life."

But Marie was the one person who knew that Eleanor had nothing to do with betraying the girls. She was the only one who could corroborate the truth about what happened to the Vesper circuit. "The address." She could tell from his expression that he was going to refuse. "Or I will leave here and go directly to Parliament." She held out her hand.

He started to argue, then turned wearily to the file cabinet behind him. He pulled out a sheet of paper and handed it to her. "Eleanor, I'm sorry." She took it from him, not responding.

Then she tucked the paper in her bag and began the last leg of her journey.

It was almost eight thirty on a Tuesday morning when Eleanor stood in the center of Grand Central, waiting anxiously. Before leaving England, she had wired Marie: "Coming to America and I need your help. Please meet me at the information kiosk in Grand Central on February 12 at 8:30 a.m."

Eleanor stood uncertainly in the center of the station now, suitcase in hand. The flight had been a hot, noisy affair, making stops in Shannon, Gander and Boston before finally reaching New York. She'd arrived by plane the previous night and taken a room by the airport. As the hands on the clock reached half past eight, she looked around anxiously. She had arranged the neutral meeting point rather than going to the address the Director had given her, fearing it would be too much.

Five minutes passed, then ten. Why hadn't Marie shown? Had she not received the message? The message the Director had given her might have been outdated or wrong. Or perhaps she was angry at Eleanor for what she thought Eleanor had done, and was refusing to meet her at all.

Eleanor set down her suitcase, which had grown heavy, beneath a bench. She looked around the station, contemplating her options. There was a message board at the side of the round information kiosk, little bits of paper stuck to it. She walked closer. There were pictures of missing soldiers and refugees from families seeking information. There were notes, too, about meetings or missed meetings. She scanned the board, but did not see anything addressed to her.

She stepped away from the message board, her heart sinking. It was nearly nine, well past the time she had asked Marie to meet her. There could be only one conclusion: Marie was not coming.

She had to get to Marie. Eleanor reached into her purse and pulled out the slip of paper the Director had given her with Marie's address, an apartment in Brooklyn. She could go there and ring the bell. But what if Marie didn't want to see her? When she had learned Marie was alive, it was hope against everything she had known. To Eleanor, the notion that Marie was alive and unwilling to see or forgive her was unbearable.

For a minute she looked around the station, wanting to give up. If Marie wouldn't even see her, what point was there in going on?

Then she squared her shoulders, steeling herself. She had to see Marie and explain what really happened. This was about more than Marie's feelings or forgiveness; she needed Marie to help prove what had really happened during the war. With Marie's help, they could bring the truth to light about the betrayal that had killed so many of her girls.

She would go to Marie's flat, Eleanor decided, and insist that she listen. She started across the station.

Outside the station, she paused to get her bearings. She looked at the passersby, wanting to ask someone for directions. She approached a group of commuters waiting near a bus stop. "Excuse me," she said to a man who was reading the paper. But he did not seem to hear. As she turned to find someone else, she spied a phone booth at the corner. Perhaps the operator might have a number for Marie.

Eleanor crossed the street to the phone booth. Then she faltered; perhaps it was best just to go find Marie, rather than calling and giving her a chance to say no. She stood indecisively, caught between the phone booth and the bus station. As she turned back toward the bus station, something across the street caught her eye. A flash of blond hair above a burgundy print scarf, like the one Marie had worn the first day she came to Norgeby House.

She had come after all! Eleanor's heart began to pound. "Marie!" Eleanor called, starting back across the street. The woman started to turn around and Eleanor stepped hopefully toward her. There was a loud honking of a car's horn, which seemed to grow to a roar, and Eleanor turned, too late, to see the vehicle barreling toward her. She raised her hands in a protective gesture. She heard a deafening screech of the brakes, felt an explosion of white pain.

And then she knew no more.

CHAPTER THIRTY-ONE

GRACE

New York, 1946

Grace gasped as the door to the apartment opened. "Marie Roux?"

The woman's eyes flickered. Her eyes bore a bit of fear, but something more…resignation. "Yes."

For a moment, Grace was frozen with disbelief. She had spent so much of the last few weeks seeing Marie's image, first in the weathered photograph and later, after she had returned it, in her mind's eye. Now the woman was standing before her, come to life. There were little changes since the photo had been taken, faint lines around the mouth and eyes. Her cheeks were a bit more sunken and the hair around her temples bore strains of premature gray, as if she had aged lifetimes in a few short years.

"Who are you?" the woman asked. Her English accent, refined but not overly posh, was exactly as Grace had imagined.

Grace faltered, unsure how to explain her role in the affair.

"I'm Grace Healey. I found some photographs and I thought…" She stopped and pulled out the lone photo she'd kept.

"Oh!" Marie brought her hand to her mouth. "That was Josie."

"May I come in?" Grace interjected gently.

Marie looked up. "Please do." She ushered Grace inside and led her to a small sofa. The apartment, no larger than Grace's own room at the boardinghouse, was clean and bright, but the furnishings were spare and there were no photographs or other mementos adorning it. There was a door at the rear and through the opening she could see a tiny bedroom. Grace wondered if Marie hadn't been here long or, like herself with her own flat, simply hadn't made the place into her home.

Marie held up the photograph. "Is this the only one?"

"There were others, including yours, but I left them at the British consulate. I've been trying to get these photos returned to the right person," Grace explained. "Is that you?"

"I don't know." Marie looked genuinely uncertain. "I suppose I'm the only one left."

How? Grace wanted to ask. Marie had been listed among those killed as part of Nacht und Nebel. But the question seemed too intrusive. "Can you tell me what happened during the war?" she asked instead.

"You know that I was an agent for SOE?" Marie asked. Grace nodded. "I was recruited by a woman called Eleanor Trigg, because I spoke French well." Grace considered interrupting Marie to tell her about Eleanor, then decided against it. "After training, I was dropped into northern France to work as a radio operator for a part of F Section called the Vesper circuit." Marie had a lyrical, looping style of speech and it was not hard to imagine her speaking fluently in French. "Our leader was a man called Julian. We blew up a bridge before D-Day in order to make things harder for the Germans.

"But somehow our cell was compromised and we were all

arrested, or at least Julian and I were. They shot Julian." Marie's face crumbled at this last part, and she almost seemed to relive it as she remembered. Grace's heart ached for this poor woman, who had been through so much. "I was interrogated in Paris, then sent to prison. I found Josie again there, but she was too far gone to make it." The grief in her words poured forth, as though she had never shared it before with anyone.

"Josie was another agent?"

Marie dabbed at her eyes. "And my dearest friend. We were put on a train, bound for one of the camps. Josie managed to detonate a grenade and blow up the railcar. After the explosion, I lost consciousness. I awoke weeks later in a barn. The Germans had missed me, or left me for dead. A German farmer found me under the railcar rubble and hid me. I stayed there until I was strong enough. By then, the invasion had come so I found a British unit and told them who I was."

"And then?"

"Then I went home. My train arrived at King's Cross. There was no one to meet me. I wasn't expecting a parade; no one knew that I was coming. So I went and collected my daughter, Tess. We boarded a boat for America straightaway."

"So you never went back to SOE?"

"Only once. I asked the Director for help expediting our papers to get to America. There was no one left. Eleanor had been dismissed. The others were all gone."

There was a sudden clattering at the door to the apartment and a girl of not more than eight walked in. "Mummy!" she said with just a hint of an English accent, throwing herself into her mother's outstretched arms.

Then she pulled back to look questioningly at Grace. "You must be Tess," Grace offered. The child looked so much like her mother that Grace had to smile. "And I'm..." She faltered, not sure how to explain her presence here to the girl.

"A friend," Marie finished for her.

Tess seemed satisfied with the explanation. "Mum, my friend Esther in apartment 5J invited me over to play and stay for dinner. May I go?"

"Be home by seven," Marie replied. "And give me one more hug first." Tess folded herself into her mother's outstretched arms for a fleeting second, then bolted for the door. "I'll never take for granted getting to see her every day," Marie said to Grace when Tess had gone.

Marie stood up. "I have more photos," she added, shifting topics abruptly. She walked to an armoire and pulled out a yellowed album. She handed it over hesitantly. Unlike the staid photographs that Eleanor had possessed, these were candid shots and they played out like a movie of the time the circuit had spent together. There was a snapshot of young men playing rugby in a field, another of a group around a table drinking wine. They might have been at Oxford or Cambridge, not on a mission in France. "The boys, they took photos on the tiny little camera we'd been given during training. I pulled the film off Julian that last day. And I kept it in places they would never think to look. Only when I reached America did I have it developed."

"Wasn't it dangerous to take these?"

She shrugged. "Certainly. But it's so very hard to explain what those months in the field were like. It was worth the risk. Someone needed to know."

In case none of them made it, Grace thought. She imagined the loneliness and terror, how much these bits of camaraderie must have meant. "That's Julian?" Grace asked.

"Yes. And Will beside him, always. You would not have known they were cousins," Marie said. Two young men not more than twenty or so. One was fair, with a smattering of freckles and a quick smile. The other was tall with sharp cheekbones and dark, piercing eyes. In another picture, he looked down lovingly at Marie. "He seemed fond of you," Grace observed.

"Yes," Marie said quickly, seeming almost embarrassed. "He loved me," Marie said, her voice full with emotion. "And I, him. I suppose it seems strange that our feelings developed so quickly in such a short time," she added.

"Not at all," Grace replied.

"I watched him die," Marie added. "Held him in my arms. It was all I could do."

"That must have been terrible." Grace reflected on how awful it had been, losing Tom. But to have witnessed it, as Marie had, would have been unbearable. "And his cousin, Will?"

"I honestly don't know. He was supposed to fly back to France and pick me up, but I was arrested. I tried to find out what became of him before I left London. But he had disappeared." Her face was grave, and Grace could tell the mystery of what had become of Will haunted her as much as losing Julian and Josie.

"When was all of this?"

"May of 1944."

"Just weeks before D-Day."

"We did not last to see it." The work that Vesper circuit had done blowing up rail lines and arming *maquisards* had surely stopped many German troops from reaching Normandy and the other beaches faster. They saved the lives of hundreds if not thousands of Allied troops who might have had the Germans there waiting for them. But most never knew the difference they had made.

"We were betrayed," Marie said bluntly. "When I was arrested and taken to Avenue Foch, they had one of our radios and they forced me to broadcast back to London. I tried to omit my true check, the code I was supposed to give to verify my identity, in order to signal to London that something was amiss. But they ignored my signal—in fact, they broadcast back that I had left it out, which was what ultimately caused the Germans to shoot Julian. It was as if the British knew the radio was compromised but wanted to keep transmitting anyway."

"Do you have any idea who might have betrayed you?" Grace

asked. She dreaded telling Marie that it had been Eleanor, and half hoped she might already know or have guessed.

"Before leaving London, I asked Colonel Winslow—he was the Director of SOE, Eleanor's boss. At first he tried to deny that there was any betrayal at headquarters at all. But when I confronted him with everything I knew from the field, he suggested that it was Eleanor. He showed me a memo from Eleanor's desk that ordered the radio transmissions to keep going even after London knew the broadcasts had been intercepted." Marie's eyes filled with tears. "I could hardly imagine it. It didn't make sense."

"So you didn't believe it was Eleanor?"

Marie shook her head emphatically. "No, never. Not in a million years." Grace was puzzled. Marie herself had seen the document, which seemed to implicate Eleanor. Was Marie so blinded by loyalty? "Why not?"

"When I saw Julian for the last time at SD headquarters, he had just returned from London, where he'd seen Eleanor. He told me before he died that Eleanor had been worried about the radios. She specifically worried that there was something wrong with the transmissions and warned me to be careful. Of course, by then it was too late. But she tried to warn me. That's how I know she wasn't behind it."

"But if not her, then who?"

"I don't know. Colonel Winslow told me to go to America and find a fresh start, to not look back. So I did. I sent him my address as he asked and he sends a stipend check monthly. I thought I had put it all behind me. At least until the message from Eleanor came." Marie walked to a closet and opened it to reveal the suitcase Grace had last seen in Grand Central.

Grace was stunned. "You had it all along."

"Eleanor had wired me that she was coming to New York."

"How did she find you?"

"The Director, I'd imagine. He knew I was coming to New York and had arranged the paperwork. It wouldn't be so very hard to find me. And Eleanor was very good." Grace nodded. Finally she understood why Eleanor had come to New York. "In her telegram, Eleanor asked me to meet her at Grand Central. Part of me didn't want to see her," Marie added. "It was a very painful chapter of my life and I had put it away forever—or so I thought."

"So you didn't go to meet her?"

"No, I went. I couldn't stay away. The telegram asked me to meet her at eight thirty. But my daughter, Tess, got sick and was home from school. It was after nine o'clock by the time I could get someone to watch her so I could make it to the station, and by then Eleanor wasn't there. I figured she would try to contact me again. Eleanor was very persistent that way. But I couldn't find her, so I left. Later that day, when I learned what had happened, I went back."

"That's when you took the suitcase."

"Yes. I had seen it there that morning, but didn't get close enough to notice that it belonged to Eleanor. Only later, after I heard the news, did I put two plus two together and realized it was hers. After what happened, I couldn't just leave it there."

"Do you mind if I look inside her suitcase?"

Marie shook her head. "I haven't opened it yet. I couldn't bear to."

Grace laid the suitcase down on its side and undid the clasp. Inside, Eleanor's belongings remained neat, untouched. Grace scanned the contents, taking care not to disturb them. At the back, nearly buried, was a pair of white baby shoes.

"Those are mine," Marie said suddenly, reaching for them. "That is, they belonged to my daughter. Eleanor had no children. But she had these for my safekeeping."

"So she brought them with her for sentimental value?"

Marie smiled. "Eleanor had no sentiment. She did everything with purpose." She turned the shoes upside down and as she did, a metal chain fell out of one of them. Marie retrieved it from the floor. "My necklace." She held up a chain with a butterfly locket. "Eleanor kept it safe for me after all." She batted back tears as she secured the necklace around her neck. Then she studied the baby shoes again, a look of realization spreading across her face. She started working at the bottom of one of the soles with practiced fingers. "Shoes are some of the best hiding places."

Inside the heel was a tiny piece of paper. Marie unfolded it carefully and showed it to Grace. It was a mimeograph of the order Grace had found in the file. Grace reached into the suitcase to see what else Eleanor might have brought. She pulled out a small notebook. "She always had a notebook," Marie remarked, smiling at the memory.

Grace flipped through the pages. "There's to be a parliamentary hearing on what happened to the girls. And look..." She pointed to one of Eleanor's notations: "Need Marie to substantiate the Director's role."

"So she wasn't coming to tell me what happened. She needed my help to prove that she had nothing to do with the radio game."

"Do you believe her?"

Marie brushed the hair from her eyes. "Absolutely. The Director's story never made sense. Julian told me before he died that Eleanor was worried about the radios and they wouldn't let her cease transmissions. Whoever did this, it wasn't her." Marie's face fell. "Eleanor needed me and I failed her. And now it's too late."

"Maybe not," Grace said suddenly, an idea forming. In the end, Eleanor had died fighting for her girls, just as she had in life.

"But of course it is. Eleanor's dead."

"Yes. But what did she want more than anything?"

"To learn the truth."

"No, to make sure the world knew. She died too soon to tell them. But we can do it for her." Grace stood, holding her hand out to Marie. "Come with me."

CHAPTER THIRTY-TWO

GRACE

New York, 1946

One month later, Grace walked out of Bleeker & Sons at the end of the day and took the subway north to Forty-Second and Lexington. She reached the street and found Mark, waiting for her at the corner. "You do have a way of turning up," she teased. It was a joke, of course; this time she was expecting him. After abandoning him at Frankie's office to find Marie and then figuring out how to help her, Grace had returned to work to find him gone. He was needed back in DC on business, he'd told Frankie. She phoned him to apologize. She didn't want him to think the kiss they had shared had put her off (very much to the contrary). He had been understanding, and though he was expected back in DC that night for work, he promised to let her know the next time he was in New York.

Mark was as good as his word: he'd phoned the previous night to say he would be in town for work and could she meet him for a drink? Grace had said yes straightaway, had taken care through the seemingly forever day at work not to mess her curls or smudge her makeup. She was genuinely excited to see him. She could get used to these fun meet-ups every few weeks, without obligation or surprise.

"So the British government itself betrayed the girls?" Mark asked.

Grace nodded. "They wanted the Germans to think that everything was fine and that the circuit was still active. So they kept broadcasting, as if everything was normal. They kept broadcasting and deploying agents and weapons. They wanted the radios in place so they could plant false information about the time and date of the invasion."

"But that would mean that they sent the agents into a trap."

"Yes." Even confronted with absolute proof, it was still impossible to believe. Grace shuddered. The girls had been arrested and SOE had let them disappear, just as surely as the Nacht und Nebel program had intended. "That governments could do such things to their own people..." But of course that was the lesson of the war. People had scarcely believed the things the Germans had done to their own people. In the other countries, too, Austria and Hungary and such, people had turned on their Jewish neighbors who had lived beside them for centuries.

"Who's to say that it stopped with the British?" Mark said. "The Americans had great stakes in misleading the Germans right before D-Day, too. They might have been in on the radio game as well somehow. We'll probably never know."

Or would they? Grace mused. If Raquel could get them back into the archive at the Pentagon... She pushed the thought from her mind. "Why didn't the truth come out after the war?"

"No one wanted to think about the past. It all changed, you see, the players and the sides. The Russians were suddenly the Soviets. German scientists, who had helped kill people by the millions, were being brought to the US instead of prosecuted in order to work on the atomic bomb. The British government was happy to leave the whole thing buried."

"Except Eleanor. She wouldn't leave it alone. They had kept up the radio game intentionally, undermining everything she had built—Eleanor wanted the world to know."

"What happened after you saw Marie?"

"When we realized the truth about what had happened and Eleanor's innocence in the matter, I knew we needed to finish the job she'd set out to do—getting the real story into the proper hands. I helped Marie prepare a testimonial about what had happened during the war. Frankie used a contact of his to reach out to the British ambassador in Washington and get Marie's statement to Parliament." Grace had wondered if Marie would need to return to London to testify. She didn't know if the poor woman would have what it took to return to the country she'd left behind. Fortunately, they'd received word that the statement would suffice. They had not known if it would do any good.

But just a few days earlier, Frankie received word. "The girls' dispositions have been changed, too. From 'missing, presumed dead' to 'killed in action.'" Three words that could mean so much. "Josie is going to be nominated for the George Cross."

"And Eleanor?" he asked. Grace shook her head. She would remain a footnote in history, unknown but to a few. But of course that was what she had always wanted.

So much of the truth had died with Eleanor and would never be known. Of course, there was much they would never know. Who knew among the British? Was it MI6 that had made the calculated decision to sacrifice the agents or had SOE betrayed its very own?

But it was a reckoning, a start.

"Two champagnes, please," Mark said to the waiter when they were seated in Stiles' Tavern, a simple, unpretentious spot not far from Grand Central. "We have to celebrate."

"Are you back in New York for a case?" she asked after their drinks had come. She lifted her glass.

"Not exactly. I've been offered a position with the War Crimes Tribunal. Not Nuremberg, but one of the satellites."

"Oh, Mark, that's wonderful!"

"I should thank you. Working with you on finding out the truth about Eleanor and the girls made me realize how much I missed that sort of work. I decided to try again."

Grace raised her glass. "To your new position," she offered.

"To second chances," he said, a deeper note to his words. They clinked glasses. "I wanted to see you."

To see her, Grace realized, before he left. Her hand hovered in midair. He was going back to Europe for good. She took a sip, the bubbles tickling her nose. She had no right to mind. They'd shared a few fleeting moments together and she couldn't expect more. Still, she had gotten used to the idea of him, and the thought of him leaving made her sadder than she expected.

"I was wondering..." He faltered. "I was wondering if you would like to come with me."

"I'm sorry?" She thought she had heard him wrong. To go to Washington was one thing, but to upend her life and move to Europe...with him.

"I could arrange a position with the tribunal for you. With your investigative skills, you'd be a real asset." She considered it for a moment.

"You could even follow up more on SOE and the other girls." He held the chance to continue Eleanor's journey out in front of her like a promise. Part of her wanted to take it, to follow him to Europe, to pursue the work she had started. But it would still just be running.

"Gracie, there's something special between you and me." Her breath caught. He was acknowledging aloud what they both felt, but had not dared to admit to one another until now. "I've felt it since the moment I ran into you a few weeks ago. Don't you?"

"Yes." She felt it, too, and couldn't have denied it, even if she wanted to.

"Life is too short to let something like this pass us by," he pressed. "Why not take a chance on that?"

He was offering her not just a job, but a life together. The idea of picking up and moving to Europe with Mark was outlandish, even crazy. Yet a not-small part of her wanted to say yes. She had finished with the story of Eleanor and the girls. There was really nothing holding her back.

Except that it was time to write her own story now. "Mark, I'm honored, and there's nothing I want to do more." His face rose with hope and she cringed, bracing herself for what she had to say next. "But there are things I have to take care of here." The office was teeming with more clients every day. And Frankie, caught up in getting Sammy adjusted to school, needed her more than ever. "I'm not saying no, just not right now. Maybe in a few months when things are more settled."

But the future, they both knew, was promised to no one. He pushed back from the table, accepting.

"One last thing," she said, when they walked outside of the bar. "I'd like to pay for Eleanor's funeral. That is, if it's still possible." She deserved a real gravesite with her name for someone to remember—the girls had been denied that. Grace took the check from Tom's attorney out of her purse and signed it over to him.

He looked at it and whistled low. "That would be one hell of a funeral."

"If you could send the rest to Marie to use to care for her daughter, I'd be grateful." Though Marie had been grateful for all Grace had done to help set the record straight for Eleanor and the girls, there had been a part of her, Grace could see, that wanted to be free of the past. Grace had decided not to bother her further and let her get on with her life.

"I'll see that it's done."

"Goodbye, Grace," he said, his hazel eyes holding hers. He kissed her once, sweetly, and just long enough.

She fought the urge to lean in once more, knowing if she didn't leave him now, she might never go. "Good luck, Mark."

She crossed the avenue toward Grand Central, unencumbered and unafraid, and started through the doors of the station, headed for the life that awaited her.

★★★★★

Author's Note

A few years ago, I was researching topics for my next book when I discovered the amazing true story of Vera Atkins and the women who had served as agents for Special Operations Executive (SOE) under her leadership in Britain during World War II. I was immediately captivated by the heroic endeavors of these brave women, who went unheralded for many years after the war. I was struck, too, by the fact that many of the women never came home.

As an author of historical fiction, I must constantly navigate the delicate balance between the needs of the story and the obligation of historical integrity. While some of the characters and events in *The Lost Girls of Paris* are based on fact, the novel is first and foremost a work of fiction. There was no way I could adequately capture the heroics of the many women who served at SOE, and so I have created composites in Marie and the other female agents in the book inspired by them. Eleanor Trigg, Colonel Winslow and all other characters in my book are fictitious.

I have taken great liberties with the ways the women trained and deployed. The places in which they operate and the missions they undertake were created for purposes of the story. And without saying too much and spoiling it for those who read the Author's Note first, the ultimate explanation as to what happened to the girls, while inspired by the many articulated theories, is also a product of fiction.

For those who are interested in reading more about the real women of SOE, I recommend *A Life in Secrets: Vera Atkins and the Missing Agents of World War Two* by Sarah Helm and *Spymistress: The True Story of the Greatest Female Secret Agent of World War Two* by William Stevenson.

Acknowledgments

In creating *The Lost Girls of Paris*, I needed to research and write the individual stories of three women across three different time frames and five countries. This was both the most rewarding and most difficult endeavor I have ever undertaken as a writer and it would not have been possible without my editor, Erika Imranyi. Working with Erika is a novel-writing master class every single day (usually by email at 5:00 a.m.) and I count her time, talent and patience among the great blessings of my life. Erika is the captain of my dream team at Park Row/Harlequin/HarperCollins, which after a decade just keeps getting better. I am especially indebted to my publicist, Emer Flounders, for his tireless work. Deepest thanks also to Craig, Loriana, Brent, Margaret, Dianne, Susan, Shara, Amy, Heather, Randy, Mary, Merjane and Natalie.

I am forever grateful to the true powerhouse of my publishing world, my agent, Susan Ginsburg. Susan, her assistant, Stacey, and their team at Writers House bring energy, foresight and zealous advocacy to my writing career every single day. Susan's vision and faith have made my deepest dreams come true, and I don't know where I would be without her.

Writing a book can be a lonely endeavor. I feel so fortunate to be part of a community that values and sustains books. This includes my local booksellers, Julie at Inkwood Books in Haddonfield, New Jersey, and Rita at BookTowne in Manasquan, New Jersey (representative of the many wonderful independent bookstores across the country), and the many librarians at the Cherry Hill and Camden County libraries. And the book world has been buoyed as never before by the internet and social media. I am profoundly grateful for my author pals, reader friends and generous book bloggers and reading websites. I fear if I start mentioning them by name, I will leave someone out. Special love to my sounding board, Andrea Katz at Great Thoughts.

I am also deeply appreciative for the entire community in which I live. After spending a decade all over the world, I feel so blessed to live a mile from where I grew up and to see people I've known my whole life on a daily basis. I am particularly thankful for my colleagues at Rutgers School of Law for their constant support, to the teachers, administrators and families at our elementary school, and to the folks at the JCC who come up and ask about my new book while I am half-naked in the locker room.

I have in the past said that it takes a village to write a book. With the passage of time, I have decided that it is more like an army. I am so thankful for my husband, Phillip, who shares the front lines with me; for my mom, Marsha, and brother, Jay, who are our active duty, and make our lives better every day; for my in-laws, Ann and Wayne, who are the precious ready reserve; and to my forever friends in the trenches, Steph and Joanne (thank goodness my memory is longer than yours!).

And finally to the three little muses who share me so begrudgingly with the writing world, perhaps not always understanding why they have to, but trusting me that it is for the best. Without them, none of this would be possible, or worthwhile.

QUESTIONS FOR DISCUSSION

1. The title *The Lost Girls of Paris* refers to twelve female intelligence agents who disappeared while on their missions overseas. But the title has greater significance as well. In what ways are the three lead characters—Grace, Marie and Eleanor—lost, and how are they ultimately found?

2. The women in the novel defied common conventions about gender during the 1940s. How do you think the characters' experiences might have been different if they lived in today's world? In what ways might their experiences be similar?

3. Grace, Marie and Eleanor have very different backgrounds and come from very different worlds. But what are some commonalities between them and their stories? Which of the three women did you relate to most closely, and why?

4. Bravery and sacrifice are important themes throughout the book. In what ways did you see these themes playing out in each of the story lines?

5. Why do you think the mystery of the suitcase and its contents resonated so powerfully with Grace? If you found a mysterious suitcase abandoned in a train station, like Grace does, what would you do?

6. War makes ordinary people do extraordinary things—whether it's going to great lengths to survive, or sacrificing one's own life to save others. What impacts does the war have on the characters in the book? How might the characters' lives have unfolded differently had the war not happened?

7. Each of the women in the book are put in a position of having to make a choice. Were there things you wished the women had done differently throughout the book, or did you agree with their decisions?

Read on for a spellbinding excerpt from Pam Jenoff's runaway New York Times *bestseller,* The Orphan's Tale, *available now.*

1

Noa

Germany, 1944

The sound comes low like the buzzing of the bees that once chased Papa across the farm and caused him to spend a week swathed in bandages.

I set down the brush I'd been using to scrub the floor, once-elegant marble now cracked beneath boot heels and set with fine lines of mud and ash that will never lift. Listening for the direction of the sound, I cross the station beneath the sign announcing in bold black: Bahnhof Bensheim. A big name for nothing more than a waiting room with two toilets, a ticket window and a wurst stand that operates when there is meat to be had and the weather is not awful. I bend to pick up a coin at the base of one of the benches, pocket it. It amazes me the things that people forget or leave behind.

Outside, my breath rises in puffs in the February night air. The sky is a collage of ivory and gray, more snow threatening. The station sits low in a valley, surrounded by lush hills of pine trees on three sides, their pointed green tips poking out above snow-covered branches. The air has a slightly burnt smell. Before the war, Bensheim had been just another tiny stop that most travelers passed through without noticing. But the Germans make use of everything it seems, and the location is good for parking trains and switching out engines during the night.

I've been here almost four months. It hadn't been so bad in the autumn and I was happy to find shelter after I'd been sent packing with two days' worth of food, three if I stretched it. The girls' home where I lived after my parents found out I was expecting and kicked me out had been located far from anywhere in the name of discretion and they could have dropped me off in Mainz, or at least the nearest town. They simply opened the door, though, dismissing me on foot. I'd headed to the train station before realizing that I had nowhere to go. More than once during my months away, I had thought of returning home, begging forgiveness. It was not that I was too proud. I would have gotten down on my knees if I thought it would do any good. But I knew from the fury in my father's eyes the day he forced me out that his heart was closed. I could not stand rejection twice.

In a moment of luck, though, the station had needed a cleaner. I peer around the back of the building now toward the tiny closet where I sleep on a mattress on the floor. The maternity dress is the same one I wore the day I left the home, except that the full front now hangs limply. It will not always be this way, of course. I will find a real job—one that pays in more than not-quite-moldy bread—and a proper home.

I see myself in the train station window. I have the kind of looks that just fit in, dishwater hair that whitens with the summer sun, pale blue eyes. Once my plainness bothered me; here it is a benefit. The two other station workers, the ticket girl and the man at the kiosk, come and then go home each night, hardly speaking to me. The travelers pass through the station with the daily edition of *Der Stürmer* tucked under their arms, grinding cigarettes into the floor, not caring who I am or where I came from. Though lonely, I need it that way. I cannot answer questions about the past.

No, they do not notice me. I see them, though, the soldiers

on leave and the mothers and wives who come each day to scan the platform hopefully for a son or husband before leaving alone. You can always tell the ones who are trying to flee. They try to look normal, as if just going on vacation. But their clothes are too tight from the layers padded underneath and bags so full they threaten to burst at any second. They do not make eye contact, but hustle their children along with pale, strained faces.

The buzzing noise grows louder and more high-pitched. It is coming from the train I'd heard screech in earlier, now parked on the far track. I start toward it, past the nearly empty coal bins, most of their stores long taken for troops fighting in the east. Perhaps someone has left on an engine or other machinery. I do not want to be blamed, and risk losing my job. Despite the grimness of my situation, I know it could be worse—and that I am lucky to be here.

Lucky. I'd heard it first from an elderly German woman who shared some herring with me on the bus to Den Hague after leaving my parents. "You are the Aryan ideal," she told me between fishy lip smacks, as we wound through detours and cratered roads.

I thought she was joking; I had plain blond hair and a little stump of a nose. My body was sturdy—athletic, until it had begun to soften out and grow curvy. Other than when the German had whispered soft words into my ear at night, I had always considered myself unremarkable. But now I'd been told I was just right. I found myself confiding in the woman about my pregnancy and how I had been thrown out. She told me to go to Wiesbaden, and scribbled a note saying I was carrying a child of the Reich. I took it and went. It did not occur to me whether it was dangerous to go to Germany or that I should refuse. Somebody wanted children like mine. My parents would have sooner died than accepted help from the Germans. But the woman said they would give me shelter; how bad could they be? I had nowhere else to go.

I was lucky, they said again when I reached the girls' home. Though Dutch, I was considered of Aryan race and my child—otherwise shamed as an *uneheliches Kind*, conceived out of wedlock—might just be accepted into the Lebensborn program and raised by a good German family. I'd spent nearly six months there, reading and helping with the housework until my stomach became too bulky. The facility, if not grand, was modern and clean, designed to deliver babies in good health to the Reich. I'd gotten to know a sturdy girl called Eva who was a few months further along than me, but one night she awoke in blood and they took her to the hospital and I did not see her again. After that, I kept to myself. None of us would be there for long.

My time came on a cold October morning when I stood up from the breakfast table at the girls' home and my water broke. The next eighteen hours were a blur of awful pain, punctuated by words of command, without encouragement or a soothing touch. At last, the baby had emerged with a wail and my entire body shuddered with emptiness, a machine shutting down. A strange look crossed the nurse's face.

"What is it?" I demanded. I was not supposed to see the child. But I struggled against pain to sit upright. "What's wrong?"

"Everything is fine," the doctor assured. "The child is healthy." His voice was perturbed, though, face stormy through thick glasses above the draped cream sheet. I leaned forward and a set of piercing coal eyes met mine.

Those eyes that were not Aryan.

I understood then the doctor's distress. The child looked nothing like the perfect race. Some hidden gene, on my side or the German's, had given him dark eyes and olive skin. He would not be accepted into the Lebensborn program.

My baby cried out, shrill and high-pitched, as though he had heard his fate and was protesting. I had reached for him through the pain. "I want to hold him."

The doctor and the nurse, who had been recording details

about the child on some sort of form, exchanged uneasy looks. "We don't, that is, the Lebensborn program does not allow that."

I struggled to sit up. "Then I'll take him and leave." It had been a bluff; I had nowhere to go. I had signed papers giving up my rights when I arrived in exchange for letting me stay, there were hospital guards… I could barely even walk. "Please let me have him for a second."

"Nein." The nurse shook her head emphatically, slipping from the room as I continued to plead.

Once she was out of sight, something in my voice forced the doctor to relent. "Just for a moment," he said, reluctantly handing me the child. I stared at the red face, inhaled the delicious scent of his head that was pointed from so many hours of struggling to be born and I focused on his eyes. Those beautiful eyes. How could something so perfect not be their ideal?

He was mine, though. A wave of love crested and broke over me. I had not wanted this child, but in that moment, all the regret washed away, replaced by longing. Panic and relief swept me under. They would not want him now. I'd have to take him home because there was no other choice. I would keep him, find a way…

Then the nurse returned and ripped him from my arms.

"No, wait," I protested. As I struggled to reach for my baby, something sharp pierced my arm. My head swam. Hands pressed me back on the bed. I faded, still seeing those dark eyes.

I awoke alone in that cold, sterile delivery room, without my child, or a husband or mother or even a nurse, an empty vessel that no one wanted anymore. They said afterward that he went to a good home. I had no way of knowing if they were telling the truth.

I swallow against the dryness of my throat, forcing the memory away. Then I step from the station into the biting cold air, relieved that the *Schutzpolizei des Reiches*, the leering state police who patrol the station, are nowhere to be seen. Most likely they are fighting the cold in their truck with a flask. I scan the train, trying to pinpoint the buzzing sound. It comes from the last boxcar, adjacent to the caboose—not from the engine. No, the noise comes from something inside the train. Something alive.

I stop. I have made it a point to never go near the trains, to look away when they pass by—because they are carrying Jews.

I was still living at home in our village the first time I had seen the sorry roundup of men, women and children in the market square. I had run to my father, crying. He was a patriot and stood up for everything else—why not this? "It's awful," he conceded through his graying beard, stained yellow from pipe smoke. He had wiped my tear-stained cheeks and given me some vague explanation about how there were ways to handle things. But those ways had not stopped my classmate Steffi Klein from being marched to the train station with her younger brother and parents in the same dress she'd worn to my birthday a month earlier.

The sound continues to grow, almost a keening now, like a wounded animal in the brush. I scan the empty platform and peer around the edge of the station. Can the police hear the noise, too? I stand uncertainly at the platform's edge, peering down the barren railway tracks that separate me from the boxcar. I should just walk away. Keep your eyes down, that has been the lesson of the years of war. No good ever came from noticing the business of others. If I am caught nosing into parts of the station where I do not belong, I will be let go from my job, left without a place to live, or perhaps even arrested. But I have never been any good at not looking. Too curious, my mother said when I was little. I have always needed to know. I step forward, unable to ignore the sound that, as I draw closer now, sounds like cries.

Or the tiny foot that is visible through the open door of the railcar.

I pull back the door. "Oh!" My voice echoes dangerously

through the darkness, inviting detection. There are babies, tiny bodies too many to count, lying on the hay-covered floor of the railcar, packed close and atop one another. Most do not move and I can't tell whether they are dead or sleeping. From amid the stillness, piteous cries mix with gasps and moans like the bleating of lambs.

I grasp the side of the railcar, struggling to breathe over the wall of urine and feces and vomit that assaults me. Since coming here, I have dulled myself to the images, like a bad dream or a film that couldn't possibly be real. This is different, though. So many infants, all alone, ripped from the arms of their mothers. My lower stomach begins to burn.

I stand helplessly in front of the boxcar, frozen in shock. Where had these babies come from? They must have just arrived, for surely they could not last long in the icy temperatures.

I have seen the trains going east for months, people where the cattle and sacks of grain should have been. Despite the awfulness of the transport, I had told myself they were going somewhere like a camp or a village, just being kept in one place. The notion was fuzzy in my mind, but I imagined somewhere maybe with cabins or tents like the seaside campsite south of our village in Holland for those who couldn't afford a real holiday or preferred something more rustic. Resettlement. In these dead and dying babies, though, I see the wholeness of the lie.

I glance over my shoulder. The trains of people are always guarded. But here there is no one—because there is simply no chance of the infants getting away.

Closest to me lies a baby with gray skin, its lips blue. I try to brush the thin layer of frost from its eyelashes but the child is already stiff and gone. I yank my hand back, scanning the others. Most of the infants are naked or just wrapped in a blanket or cloth, stripped of anything that would have protected them from the harsh cold. But in the center of the car, two perfect pale pink booties stick stiffly up in the air, attached to a baby who is otherwise naked. Someone had cared enough to knit those, stitch by stitch. A sob escapes through my lips.

A head peeks out among the others. Straw and feces cover its heart-shaped face. The child does not look pained or distressed, but wears a puzzled expression, as if to say, "Now what am I doing here?" There is something familiar about it: coal-dark eyes, piercing through me, just as they had the day I had given birth. My heart swells.

The baby's face crumples suddenly and it squalls. My hands shoot out, and I strain to reach it over the others before anyone else hears. My grasp falls short of the infant, who wails louder. I try to climb into the car, but the children are packed so tightly, I can't manage for fear of stepping on one. Desperately, I strain my arms once more, just reaching. I pick up the crying child, needing to silence it. Its skin is icy as I pluck it from the car, naked save for a soiled cloth diaper.

The baby in my arms now, only the second I'd ever held, seems to calm in the crook of my elbow. Could this possibly be my child, brought back to me by fate or chance? The child's eyes close and its head bows forward. Whether it is sleeping or dying, I cannot say. Clutching it, I start away from the train. Then I turn back: if any of those other children are still alive, I am their only chance. I should take more.

But the baby I am holding cries again, the shrill sound cutting through the silence. I cover its mouth and run back into the station.

I walk toward the closet where I sleep. Stopping at the door, I look around desperately. I have nothing. Instead I walk into the women's toilet, the usually dank smell hardly noticeable after the boxcar. At the sink, I wipe the filth from the infant's face with one of the rags I use for cleaning. The baby is warmer now, but two of its toes are blue and I wonder if it might lose them. Where did it come from?

I open the filthy diaper. The child is a boy like my own had been. Closer now I can see that his tiny penis looks different from the German's, or that of the boy at school who had shown me his when I was seven. Circumcised. Steffi had told me the word once, explaining what they had done to her little brother. The child is Jewish. Not mine.

I step back as the reality I had known all along sinks in: I cannot keep a Jewish baby, or a baby at all, by myself and cleaning the station twelve hours a day. What had I been thinking?

The baby begins to roll sideways from the ledge by the sink where I had left him. I leap forward, catching him before he falls to the hard tile floor. I am unfamiliar with infants and I hold him at arm's length now, like a dangerous animal. But he moves closer, nuzzling against my neck. I clumsily make a diaper out of the other rag, then carry the child from the toilet and out of the station, heading back toward the railcar. I have to put him back on the train, as if none of this ever happened.

At the edge of the platform, I freeze. One of the guards is now walking along the tracks, blocking my way back to the train. I search desperately in all directions. Close to the side of the station sits a milk delivery truck, the rear stacked high with large cans. Impulsively I start toward it. I slide the baby into one of the empty jugs, trying not to think about how icy the metal must be against his bare skin. He does not make a sound but just stares at me helplessly.

I duck behind a bench as the truck door slams. In a second, it will leave, taking the infant with it.

And no one will know what I have done.

Copyright © 2017 by Pam Jenoff